"You liked the dance, didn't you?"

"I think it's you that I like," Trey admitted, reaching for the bottom of her mask and gliding a finger along the top of her cheek where it rested. "May I?"

He edged the barrier upward slightly, waiting for approval.

"No." She stepped back quickly. Unsteadily. "I'll meet you later, but the mask stays on."

He must have looked confused, because she added, "Can you be at the back entrance in fifteen minutes?" Then her gaze skittered up toward the clock on the wall. His time was up.

He nodded. Without another word, his mystery woman turned on her heel and walked out of the room, her hips swinging in a walk that took his breath away.

He was having the damnedest time reading this woman. But she was the hottest, most diverting female he'd ever laid eyes on.

Fifteen minutes couldn't come soon enough....

Dear Reader,

Every now and then a character steps onto the page who takes the story right out of my hands. This was the case with Courtney Masterson, my unassuming financial researcher with a sexy secret life! She knew what she wanted from this story long before I did, and she guided me in such fun and interesting directions, I couldn't help but follow to see where she led.

As for my hero, Trey Fraser, the filmmaker turned Hollywood agent, he's the kind of guy we'd love to meet. It seemed romantic to me that what attracted him to Courtney wasn't another pretty face so much as the fact that she was "different." But she can't hide her smart side or her sexy side, and Trey is fascinated by her. Don't we all hope the right guy can see beyond the superficial?

I hope you like Courtney's sensual awakening in *My Double Life!* I sure had a blast dreaming up this one. Look for me with my brand-new Twitter ID @JoanneRock6 and don't forget to watch for upcoming releases at www.joannerock.com.

Until next time, happy reading!

Joanne Rock

My Double Life
&
Wild and Wicked

—

Joanne Rock

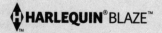

HARLEQUIN® BLAZE™

ISBN-13: 978-0-373-79753-0

MY DOUBLE LIFE

Recycling programs
for this product may
not exist in your area.

The publisher acknowledges the copyright holder
of the individual works as follows:

MY DOUBLE LIFE
Copyright © 2013 by Joanne Rock

WILD AND WICKED
Copyright © 2003 by Joanne Rock

For questions and comments about the quality of this book,
please contact us at CustomerService@Harlequin.com.

H HARLEQUIN®
www.Harlequin.com

Printed in U.S.A.

CONTENTS

ABOUT THE AUTHOR

Joanne Rock is a three-time RITA® Award nominee and veteran of the Harlequin Blaze series. *My Double Life* is her twenty-ninth full-length title for Blaze! When she's not writing for Blaze or Harlequin Historical, Joanne is dreaming up YA books with her sister-in-law writing partner and fellow Harlequin author, Karen Rock. Joanne's books have been reprinted in twenty-seven countries and translated into twenty languages. She has a master's degree from the University of Louisville and is still coming to terms with sending her oldest son off to college this year. As the mother of three teenage boys, Joanne has perfected the arts of baking chocolate chip cookies, removing grass stains from football pants and giving opinionated advice on writing brilliant essays for English class. Look for Joanne online at www.joannerock.com or at www.facebook.com/JoanneRockAuthor.

Books by Joanne Rock

JOANNE ROCK

MY DOUBLE LIFE

For anyone battling chronic disease,
this book is for you. May you find depths of
strength you never knew you had, and friends
who will support you on your path.
I salute your ability to keep moving forward
and find inspiration in your journey.

1

"COURTNEY, I HAVE two words. *Washboard. Abs,*" My colleague Fawn hissed in my ear as we walked down the hall toward the private entrance to the company conference room. "This talent agent is hotter than most of the A-list actors he represents."

I worked as a financial researcher at one of the most prestigious private wealth management firms in Los Angeles, but the chat around the watercooler was probably the same as in any other office. We drooled over hot guys as much as the girls working the counter at the local In-N-Out Burger. We just saved the ogling for behind closed doors. Like now.

"Really? Did you want to brief *me* on the prospective client then?" I asked, pausing outside the conference space to wave a file folder under her nose. I had worked hard to compile the background details on this potential client's financial picture so Fawn could go into her meeting prepared. "I forgot to include the latest report from TMZ in my research notes, so maybe you know more about this guy than me."

Frowning, the fastest-rising account executive at

Sphere Asset Management poked me in the arm with the cap of her pen.

"Wise ass." Fawn shook her hair for the third time in the last two minutes, a needless habit she had for making sure every golden tress was in place. But she was the head of the team that had put together Trey Fraser's financial profile, giving a face to the anonymous underlings who actually did more of the grunt work in financial analysis. With her taupe pantsuit elegantly draping her slim, toned physique, she turned heads everywhere she went—no easy feat in Hollywood, land of the beautiful. "I know the basics about his assets. I can close this deal with my eyes shut. But if there's a chance Trey Fraser is not seeing anyone, I'm going to make my move."

I liked Fawn. Really, I did. She was a brilliant market analyst and down-to-earth enough to hang out with the support staffers like me, a behind-the-scenes researcher for the big shots in the company. But since she was a great example of the universe blessing some people with way too much, she made the more insecure women of the world feel a bit…lacking.

For example, I would never dream of making a play for Trey Fraser, Hollywood royalty and son of the most famous independent producer of the last decade. All of our clients were high-net-worth individuals, but Trey was in a different class with a healthy dose of fame and personal magnetism in the mix. So I couldn't help but be a little contrary as I heard our receptionist show the client into the meeting room on the other side of the sleek cherry door.

"You can't flirt with clients," I warned Fawn. "Let alone date them." The rules were strict at Sphere.

"Are you kidding me?" Fawn smoothed the front of her suit jacket and pinched some color into her cheeks in a trick I'd seen Scarlett O'Hara perform once on-screen. "Scoring with a guy like Trey is worth leaving the company. Wealth management firms are a dime a dozen in L.A. Men like that, on the other hand, are rare."

It took an effort not to roll my eyes. "Easy for you to say when you've got headhunters calling you every week."

And even though I'd always been great at my job, I'd never had those kinds of opportunities. Face-to-face interviews were a unique brand of torture for me. I would be researching investment portfolio options and computing potential stock returns for our clients for the rest of my career.

Fawn winked before she opened the door, totally unruffled. Normally, I would have scurried right back to my office since speaking with clients was definitely *not* my thing, even though, technically, I could have sat in on the meeting. I usually took a behind-the-scenes approach, even if I had made some strides toward greater self-confidence after discovering some aptitude for dancing this year. But I was curious about our visitor.

Besides, who would notice me standing in the shadows when our star asset advisor walked in to take her seat at the head of that polished mahogany table? I probably wouldn't have any chance to glimpse Trey Fraser's touted washboard abs. But sometimes even those of us who had grown up surrounded by celebrities had our moments of rubbernecking with the really big names.

And frankly, as someone interested in business and finance, I was more curious about a mogul-in-the-making like Trey than I would have been about a flavor-of-the-week movie star. Even though he *had* taken some serious flack in the media for the lawsuit he was rumored to have in the works against his famous father, who'd been Trey's former employer before Trey had opened the talent agency.

So, walking through the open door, I helped myself to a tiny peek from under bangs so long the tips touched my lashes.

I expected a big group would be accompanying him, but there was only one man waiting for Fawn as she walked in. Tall and slim-hipped, he wore a black suit with a black dress shirt open at the collar. He would have appeared vaguely dangerous with high cheekbones, angular features and dark eyes. But when he smiled, his whole face changed, his eyes crinkling into familiar lines at the corners. He looked a bit Mediterranean, and I remembered some old scuttlebutt that his mother was an Italian actress whom his famous father seduced when she was barely legal.

Trey Fraser was only thirty-ish, but he was handsome in that George Clooney, gorgeous-even-when-he'd-be-eighty way. No wonder Fawn had been fluffing her hair and pinching her cheeks.

"Hi," he said suddenly, turning toward me. "I'm Trey Fraser."

I'd been spotted.

He stalked toward me, hand extended as if to draw me into the room. Heart pounding and feet sticking to the floor, I froze in disbelief that he'd seen through the camouflage my long bangs usually provided. Along with my poorly fitting suit, which I wore with running shoes since I never met with clients.

Who noticed Courtney Masterson when Fawn was around?

"H-h-hi," I managed, though my stuttered greeting was so quiet he might not have heard.

Damn it. Hadn't I conquered the speech impediment?

His hand enveloped mine with a warm squeeze while I sought any excuse to leave. *Out of your league!* my brain shouted at me. *Retreat!*

The moment in which our hands clasped probably only lasted a fraction of a second. But since I'd never been that close to a certified hunk, let alone touched one, I took in every last detail from the clean scent of his faint aftershave to the way his hair swooped in a wave over his forehead.

"Courtney?" Fawn said from behind him, sounding puzzled. "Would you like to join us?"

Of course not. I didn't make a habit of sitting in on client meetings, even though as a financial researcher I had more knowledge about the person's assets than anyone on staff. But saying as much meant risking another mortifying stutter-fest.

Why had I decided to play Peeping Tom today?

"Come on in," Trey said, stepping out of the doorway to gesture me inside.

It'd be impolite to utter something like "No freaking way" in front of a customer. So I did the next-best thing.

I spun around and fled the scene, my tennis shoes making quick work of the hallway as I dashed into my office and shut the door behind me.

Was I a little shy? Duh. It had started with the childhood stutter, continued with a mom who was embarrassed by me and snowballed into an insecurity with a life of its own. Going near a Hollywood hottie was—for a girl like me—just plain stupid. Moth to a flame and all that. I think my wings were already singed.

But I was working hard to overcome the shyness.

I'd never get close to the Trey Frasers of the world, though he was seriously hot and would probably fuel my private fantasies for a long time. Instead, I was working on another approach to my issues and making baby steps toward conquering those self-doubting demons in my head.

In fact, I needed a dose of that heady medicine right now before my heart pounded out of my chest. So I grabbed my gym bag from under the desk, and checking to be sure the hallway was clear, headed out the back door. I would indulge in the latest fitness craze, which had slowly turned into my one source of real physical confidence in the past year.

I'd learned that there was nothing like a little pole dancing to bring out the tigress in any woman.

NICE GIRLS RAN from him.

As he sat through his meeting at Sphere Asset Management, Trey Fraser couldn't stop thinking about the brunette who'd fled from his presence earlier.

He tried to listen to her colleague as she walked him through the nuances of interest allocation, but he kept seeing a pair of darting gray eyes that looked anywhere but at him. He told himself it didn't matter, since he had no time for women in his life right now, anyway. His father had thwarted him professionally last winter, and Trey would have his hands full for the next few years just trying to prove to the world that he was a different kind of man—a man of his word. Tough to do when they were both in the film industry and his father—Thomas Fraser II—had a hell of a lot of clout.

Still, it frustrated Trey that his ongoing and very public rift with his dad had made the kind of head-lines that sent Pretty Gray Eyes running. Courtney, he recalled. He'd been deemed the most ungrateful son in Hollywood history for even considering a lawsuit against his father for breach of contract. He'd been dubbed "Mr. Entitled" in industry papers and the main-stream press hadn't painted him much better. Didn't they realize that the only reason his father threw up one roadblock after another in Trey's career was to make sure success never came too easily? As a self-made man, Thomas insisted that obstacles made a person stronger. Tougher.

So he considered it his parental duty to be sure Trey encountered plenty, even when they bordered on ille-gal. But while Trey was trying to salvage a career, his charismatic father ate up the media attention.

"How does that sound, Mr. Fraser?" A flirtatious feminine voice intruded on his thoughts, calling him back to the meeting.

Crap. He'd completely zoned out of the interest al-location discussion. The financial adviser—Fawn Bar-rows—stared at him like she was sizing him up for her next meal. Clearly, his bad press hadn't scared her off, but then again, she had a cutthroat business vibe that Trey's dad would admire. Trey, for his part, was still mortified over the bad press that had followed his most recent altercation with Thomas at a high-end restaurant. Stupid of him to think his pops would respect basic so-cial conventions and not confront him in public.

"Fine." He stacked up the paperwork for Sphere

Asset Management's proposal. "I'll think it over and get back to you."

He had to lock down some financial advice to be sure his start-up company was protected from his former business dealings with his dad. Too bad he couldn't have discussed his needs with Courtney instead. She'd had an honest face at a time in his life when he seemed to have a target painted on his back. Something about her had reached past the laser-focus he'd brought to his work over the last six months.

"Are you sure?" Fawn's lips pulled together in a way that looked dangerously close to a pout for a professional businesswoman. But she turned her attention to the file folder in front of her. "If you move forward with the lawsuit to sue your father's company for breach of contract—"

"I have not filed a lawsuit." He couldn't help the rumors, though. He'd allowed himself to get too comfortable working under his father's banner, thinking he could simply make movies. He hadn't anticipated how many ways he and his father would butt heads. "Those rumors are pure media speculation."

Although the gossip certainly gave him reason to think he would have a case. Thomas Fraser had not been an easy man to work for, but Trey had been willing to put up with his old man's constant lecturing and life lessons as long as he could make a film his way. But Trey's emotionally complex, low-budget movie had turned into one long product placement shot, complete with corporate sponsors. Actors were axed without consulting him, replaced with bankable stars. When Trey balked, the whole project was shut down and he was left without a job—a fact he'd discovered when the locks on his office were changed.

Worse, he'd let his temper get the better of him in a recent showdown with his dad, which only contributed to Trey's reputation as someone tough to work with. Guess there had been a life lesson in there, after all. Don't mix work and family.

"But if he comes after you, shouldn't we ensure your assets are protected?"

Trey hoped it wouldn't come to that. "Precisely why I've set up this meeting, Ms. Barrows, but I'm not ready to commit at this time."

"Perhaps if I understood your business goals better, I could make some specific recommendations for investments." This woman wasn't giving up. She stuck her nose in the file folder on the table once more. "I'm unclear about this second start-up company mentioned in my notes. Won't you need all your liquid assets available to support another business?"

He tensed.

"Who told you I have a second company in the works?" He'd kept that information secure for months in a town that loved to sniff out a secret.

Fawn smiled as she folded manicured fingers together. "Our client research is excellent here."

"You misunderstand." Anger tightened his jaw. How many other people knew about his intentions to expand his small talent agency and start up his own film production company to go head-to-head with his father? "No one is supposed to have access to that information."

Her smile slipped. "I'm just reading what's in the file."

"Who did the research?"

"One of our financial researchers. Courtney." She stood, apparently beginning to understand that he was not a happy customer. "I'll go ask her about this."

Trey got up to follow, surprised the reticent brunette had dug up the pay dirt that could damage his plans. "I'd like to speak to her directly."

"Of course." Fawn indicated the door she'd shut earlier, the same one that Courtney had stood in half an hour ago. "Her desk is back here."

They walked past lavish offices full of mahogany bookshelves and sleek bronze awards on the walls, then turned down a hallway toward more simple workspaces. Here, computers and stacks of papers balanced on smaller, functional desks. Fawn Barrows paused in front of an open door with a brass nameplate beside it.

Courtney Masterson.

"I'm afraid we missed her," Fawn announced after peeking behind the door at an empty chair. "It looks like she took her bag, so I'm guessing she's gone for the day."

On the verge of demanding the woman be contacted via cell phone or text, Trey thought better of it.

"Fine," he said tightly. "But I want to speak to her at her earliest convenience."

Shoving an extra business card into the woman's hand, he turned to leave.

"Certainly—"

"Thank you for your time, Ms. Barrows." Trey couldn't afford to waste another minute at Sphere.

He had a client who needed some hand-holding tonight—an actor whose nice-guy image would benefit from some tarnishing to get him the kind of multilayered parts his skills warranted. And at Trey's agency, that meant Trey himself would be out on the town to make sure the deed was done.

After all, he wanted every one of his current clients working by the time Phase Two of his business plan got underway. A phase that might very well have been compromised by the research skills of one gray-eyed female he'd obviously underestimated.

2

DANCE CLASS. The lights, the music, the people from all walks of life blowing off steam, just like me.

Simply walking into the studio lowered my blood pressure and made me feel at home. Here, no one judged me. You'd think this place would be full of twenty-somethings learning how to pole dance for their hot boyfriends. But it wasn't like that at all. The women who came here were often older, some had just had a baby, and all were looking for a way to feel good about themselves. It wasn't just pole dancing that attracted these clients. It was our awesome instructor, Natalie Night, who had a way of making the disenfranchised feel welcome here. She was the reason I came back, week after week.

"Are we ready, ladies?" she asked now, striding across the red mats in the back studio for the advanced class. Wearing a simple black leotard beneath a tiny pink T-shirt with the name of a local band silk-screened on it, she cranked up the music and stepped up to the pole.

I stepped up to mine, too, grateful that I'd finally

be able to put Trey Fraser out of my head. What was it about that man that had thrown me for such a loop?

"We'll do our routines in a minute," Natalie assured us, wrapping one leg around the pole to pull herself up. "But first, I'd like to go over that move we all had trouble with last time. Those lifts are killing us."

She scaled the pole quickly to demonstrate the proper technique and we knew to wait and watch her while she explained what to do. And then, all of a sudden, she slid down.

Crash.

The fall happened so fast, I barely had time to process it. Heart in my throat, I ran over to her.

"Natalie?" I stood looking down at her, totally panicked. "Are you okay?"

I was freaking out to see the most agile, gorgeous, talented dance teacher lying with her leg cocked at a scary angle on the mat beneath her pole. Two students stood behind me, their multiple images eerily reflected in the mirrors surrounding us. A hardcore rap tune still blared from the speakers, and the music that normally pumped me up now felt horribly out of place.

"I think we should call an ambulance," one of the other women suggested. She was new to the advanced class, and I forgot her name, but she sported a different nose ring every time I saw her. Today's was a purple daisy.

"No." Natalie finally answered, her only movement the flutter of her glittery eyelids. "I think it's just a sprained ankle, but let me… Just give me a minute, okay?"

"A sprain? Your ankle looks like it's dislocated," I murmured, as someone turned down the music. "I was scared it was your neck or your head. You fell so fast I couldn't tell what happened."

Then again, I'd been distracted by thoughts of Trey and my awkward exit after meeting him. But Natalie had never fallen before. She was like a goddess in the studio, her body so strong and pliable she could do anything. She'd been my first teacher, back when I'd been scared to death to try this crazy sport at a bachelorette party for one of the women I worked with. I hadn't even wanted to go to the party and was dragged to the studio against my will by well-meaning colleagues.

While the other women in the office had gotten into the spirit of sexy dancing, I had hung back. But Natalie made me feel welcome, giving me a private tutorial so I wouldn't be self-conscious. She'd encouraged me so much that I came back again because—wonder of all wonders—I'd been kind of good at dancing. And I liked it because it required no speaking skills whatsoever.

Lo and behold, I still danced. Privately. Secretly. No one from work knew. But Natalie had been instrumental in giving me this arena where I felt talented. She was still my favorite teacher even now that I was an advanced student.

"Freaking baby oil," Natalie muttered darkly, opening her eyes to meet my gaze. "The beginners' class was in here before us and someone must have been wearing body lotion or something."

"Yikes." I'd learned quickly when I started pole dancing that any kind of cream was a no-no. You wanted to stick to the pole, not slide off it. "I can drive you to the hospital whenever you're ready."

"Absolutely not." She gripped my hand with perfectly polished leopard-print nails, an artistic manicure that must have taken some time. "Courtney, my first show is tonight at Backstage."

The urgent look in her light green eyes reminded me how important this was to her. She'd been trying to break into the club scene for months, but in a city full of gorgeous, out-of-work actresses, it wasn't easy to land a good dancing gig. Talented women like Natalie were up against model-beautiful eighteen-year-olds who lied about their ages and would bare all between dance sets to rake in tips at the gentlemen's clubs.

Natalie had an idea for a burlesque show, something classy that required serious dancing chops. But she needed someone to give her an "in" at a good club to get the act off the ground. Backstage had given her a trial run to do an abbreviated version of the show, which highlighted the pole. I'd seen her practice the number, and it was sexy as hell without being...graphic.

"I'll call them," I offered, looking around for my gym bag where I'd stashed my phone. I was only too happy to help.

It was thanks to this woman that I'd developed some long overdue personal confidence this year. I owed her.

"Courtney, listen to me." She moved to sit up and all three of her students—me included—rushed to support her. She shooed us back with an impatient hand, because she was one stubborn, strong chick.

"I'm listening," I assured her, pointing wordlessly to the vending machine on the far wall until one of the other students jogged toward it to get Natalie a drink. "Just don't overdo it until you're sure you're not going to put any stress on that ankle. It's swollen already."

"I'll get some ice," Purple Nose Ring murmured before disappearing.

"Courtney. Sweetie." Natalie leaned forward to cup my face in her hands like I was five years old. Her bracelets jingled as she tipped my chin up to meet her eyes. "You're a great dancer."

I preened a little inside, my heart warming to hear high praise from someone I admired on every level.

"It's because you've been so patient with me," I reminded her, remembering the nights she'd stayed long after the other students left so that I could tackle the pole without as many onlookers.

"It's because you're an excellent hard worker and you've got discipline like no one else I've ever taught."

I prepared to dissemble some more, because *wow*. I had no coping skills for that much praise. Ask me about my defense mechanisms for criticism, though, and I could give detailed notes complete with dates that chronicled my experience. My mother—a famous interior decorator with her own television show—had explained to me at an early age that I was never to speak in front of her clients, her camera crew or anyone else in her professional life because I was an embarrassment to her. That kind of criticism from your own mom was…damaging, to say the least.

But before I could get any words out, the other dancers returned with water for Natalie and ice for her ankle, which we propped on a folded towel.

"Ladies…" Natalie turned expectantly to the three of us when we finished our first aid efforts. "I need someone to take that trial dance set for me tonight at Backstage."

Was she serious? No one could fill her shoes.

I remembered I had to get my cell phone and call the club on her behalf.

"Courtney should do it."

"Courtney, you have to take her place."

The other dancers spoke at the same time, which must have been why my ears deceived me.

"Excuse me?" I was already pawing through my gym bag for my phone. "I'll call Backstage—"

"You'll do no such thing." Natalie reached for my phone, apparently spotting it inside the duffel before I did. She tucked it behind her back as she eyed me in the mirror-lined studio. Huge overhead fans whirred softly, stirring the stale, vaguely sweaty air.

My heartbeat was even louder than when Trey Fraser shook my hand. And that was saying something.

"Are you insane?" I protested. "You have to cancel."

"I worked too hard for this live audience audition." She stared at me with that patient, steady gaze that had once given me the courage to try my first extended butterfly move on the pole. "Cort, I need that job."

I knew that was true. Natalie's scumball ex-husband had managed to drag their divorce through the courts just long enough to clean out her savings. Her work as a dance instructor probably paid some bills, but L.A. was an expensive city. Natalie had been over the moon when she landed this performance for the club owner.

A ball of fear twisted in my stomach.

"I'll mess it up for you," I whispered as cold sweat started to bead on my forehead.

My fellow students disagreed with me, chiming in to back Natalie up, but I couldn't really make out their words. My whole focus remained on my friend and that look in her eyes that foolishly seemed to suggest I could do this.

"I'd rather lose it that way than simply call and cancel. At least if you dance the routine for me, I'll have a chance. By the time the gig starts in the fall, my ankle will be better." Natalie brushed the bangs out of my eyes. "I have a blonde wig you can wear. It'll be like acting. Without any speaking lines."

The difficult thing about my dear friend was that she knew all the right buttons to push. And Natalie was perfectly aware that one of the ways I'd convinced myself to stick with pole dancing was to assume a new personality whenever I stepped into the studio. When I came here, I wasn't Courtney Masterson, CPA.

I became someone else entirely. Someone who could lose herself in rap music and pole dancing moves.

Right then, I could almost have imagined that a wig would help me get through this if I stepped into Natalie's shoes for the audition. And let's face it, no matter how insecure I was, I couldn't say no to the person who gave me the gift of dancing in the first place. My performance would suck, and I would definitely make an ass of myself.

But for Natalie, I would at least give it a try.

"I want the wig," I said finally. "And everyone in here is sworn to secrecy, okay? I'll get fired if anyone—"

Anything else I might have added—other conditions and a laundry list of worries—were lost in a crushing hug while the women around me squealed and promised to take my secret to the grave.

Crap.

"I'd just like to know one thing." I knew I would probably be sick to my stomach before I drove over to Backstage, which was halfway across town. "What time do I go on?"

"THE FIRST SHOW is at eleven." Trey checked his watch while he waited for his client to finish feeding his dog, his fish and two snakes coiled in a cage that rested on the dining room table of the guy's Malibu beach house.

He'd known damn well that Eric Reims would bail on this outing unless he showed up to drag him out by the ear. Trey had been telling the actor for three months that he needed to get out in the public eye more, to stay out late and cause a few scenes, but the guy had never delivered. The dude was too young to be such a home-body, yet Eric was one of those performers whose personality only came out in front of the camera. The rest of the time, he was more of a quiet observer of life.

But like so many other actors, Eric had gotten screwed when Thomas pulled the plug on the dark emotional drama that Trey had planned, wreaking havoc on Trey's industry credibility and severing their professional ties. To make amends, and in an effort to save face, Trey had gone into the talent management business six months ago solely to put all those actors back to work. Half of the affected talent already had management, but Trey had sworn he'd find work for every last one of the new, young faces that he had roped into the project. So his talent agency was new, but Trey was dedicated as hell, and one by one he'd find roles for his clients. Of course, his famous last name helped.

He didn't care what the media thought of him nearly as much as he cared about his debt to the cast of the movie he never got to make. Once that was done, he'd close the talent management shop and move on to the next phase—opening his own independent film company within the next few months. He still owned the rights to the film he'd optioned back when he was a producer with his dad's studio, and Trey had every intention of making that picture himself. With the kind of artistic integrity he'd envisioned from the start.

"I'm almost ready," Eric called from the aquarium that divided the billiard room from the dining area. "I'd like to make the first show so I can be home early."

Trey poured himself a drink at the bar next to the pool table, trying to focus on his client's revamped bungalow instead of the potential professional trouble that a certain Sphere Asset Management's financial researcher had created for him. He should be ticked off about her digging into his private affairs, and to a certain extent, he was. But another part of him simply wanted to see her again.

It didn't take a genius to figure out *which* part.

"You're twenty-six years old." Trey forced himself to concentrate on his client. He poured Eric a drink, too, realizing the guy needed to loosen up. "Why do you need to be home early? The fish aren't going to be throwing any wild parties while you're out."

Eric's father was an A-list actor, but the old man hadn't given his kid any help in the business. Trey had related immediately. Besides, he liked Eric for his talent and his work ethic, even though he had zero sense of the film business.

"Strip clubs are…not my usual scene."

Trey guessed that was an understatement judging by the shelves and shelves of books that lined the billiard room. If Eric had read even a fraction of them, he must spend a lot of time with a book in his hand.

"Backstage isn't a strip club—more of an exotic dance place. A lot of successful dancers got their start there." Splitting hairs, maybe. "Although, in all honesty, the acts get grittier as the night wears on."

Or so he'd heard.

Taking his drink, Eric grinned. "You wouldn't be dragging me there unless it had a sketchy reputation."

"Hey, I've given you opportunities to go out on the town and get wild on your own, dude." Trey clinked his glass against his friend's before downing the rest of the chilled top-shelf chilled vodka he'd found in the freezer of a mini-fridge. "Now you're stuck with me because I need to get you on the radar of a few more casting agents and this outing will help."

"You don't need to go with me, man. This time, I'll get out there. Seriously." Eric grimaced as he drank his shot.

"Not that I don't trust you, but I'm going with you." He was sending Eric out for an audition next week and he wanted to get the guy's face in the celebrity gossip pages. Timing was critical. "I need you to land that lead role next week."

"When you put it that way…" Eric straightened his tie. "We'd better get going."

"Now you're talking." Trey set his glass on the bar and picked up his phone. "The car is waiting, so let's roll."

Forty minutes and a lot of weekend traffic later, they arrived at Backstage, where the bass pumped so loud the sound vibrated up Trey's shoes. He stood a few feet behind Eric as they strode up to the velvet ropes outside the VIP entrance. A sizable line had formed at the main doors, but there was no one in front of the VIP curtain except for the bouncer with a guest list.

There were no paparazzi here, but that didn't matter.

Eric had been in a few highly recognizable teen flicks. All it took were a few people to recognize him and start snapping pics or video with a camera phone. Hell, even the dancers did stuff like that when they were between breaks, so it was a common enough practice. Trey just had to keep his client here for a couple of hours to be sure the guy would show up on the gossip blogs tomorrow. After the first few times, the story wrote itself for the bigger tabloid magazines, and two weeks from now, Eric would suddenly be seen as a Hollywood playboy.

Casting directors would fall in love with a whole new image. Trey just hoped he didn't get painted with the "bad boy" brush, too. Not only was that kind of thing a distraction, but he didn't need any more press these days.

"Come right in, Mr. Fraser." The bouncer was already unhooking the velvet barrier. He wore a headset and adjusted the mouthpiece as he spoke quietly into it, no doubt calling ahead for front row seats.

As usual, Trey battled old guilt at the way his road in life was so often paved by his father. The bouncer would have recognized him as a Fraser, not because of his fledgling talent agency and definitely not because of the films he'd helped make with zero production credit. His dad insisted Trey would do better forging his own way in the world, so he'd been careful not to give him any professional recognition.

"Thanks." He tipped the security guy well as they weaved through the club toward the front, gritty rap music taking the place of the slow number that had been on a moment before.

Trey noted with satisfaction that a number of heads turned as they walked through the main aisle toward seats that were so close to the action they could touch the center stage. Eric had already been recognized, it seemed. The bulk of his work done for the night, Trey settled in for the first show. He could discreetly do some research on Courtney Masterson from his cell phone, since he needed to confront her first thing tomorrow morning.

But one look at the blonde high-stepping her way to center stage made him shove his phone back in his pocket.

Hot. Damn.

And he was not a "hot damn" kind of guy. Especially not about women in places like Backstage, where legitimate dancers were mixed in with women who'd let you pay for just about anything in the VIP room if you had a fat bankroll. His tastes were a little more refined since he preferred to propel a woman to sexual frenzy because they were both into the moment—not because he'd paid for a lap dance.

Yet something about the performer who pranced her way toward the strobe-lit pole made him sit up straighter. She wore a tissue-thin body suit with silver feathers strategically placed over her breasts and in a V around her hips. Straight, platinum hair grazed her shoulders, the sleek shine and perfect bangs making him think it was a wig. A black-and-silver domino mask covered the top half of her face, but he could see her wink at the audience through the eyeholes.

He didn't even blink as she caressed the silver pole with one hand and twirled around it on a pair of do-me stilettos. What was there about her that captivated the hell out of him?

"Nice." Eric's voice next to him set his teeth on edge,

partly because, in his concentration on the dancer, he'd forgotten his client was there. But even more because he'd forgotten he wasn't the only one drooling over the woman.

What had gotten into him today? First the rogue attraction to a shy accountant, and now this? Trey had clearly put sex so far on the back burner that his libido was having some kind of joke at his expense.

"I thought gentlemen's clubs weren't your kind of place," Trey shot back, suddenly tense.

"I definitely pictured something a lot more sweaty and tacky." Eric slid a hundred-dollar bill onto the stage, just a few feet from where the blonde now scaled the pole with the agile grace of a jungle cat. "But dancing like that takes training. She's good."

Trey ground his teeth together. He should be happy that Eric was settling in. Even better, a young woman on the arm of her distracted boyfriend had a videophone trained on Eric, so Trey's nice-guy client had just been recorded slipping a tip to an exotic dancer. That was exactly what he'd wanted when he'd planned this night out.

Before he'd seen the dancer in question.

Unaccountably ticked off, Trey forced himself to pull his phone from his pocket and research some basic information on Courtney Masterson. Maybe it was just because the blonde arching around the pole had a passing resemblance to the accountant that he kept watching her out of one eye. Even with her mask on, the bone structure of her face looked similar, from what he remembered.

Not that he was checking her out or anything.

That little slice of denial ended when the dancer

hung upside down from the pole with one leg, her face almost eye level with his. Their gazes locked for a long, heated moment.

Right before she blew him a kiss.

CLEARLY, I'D lost my mind.

As soon as that air-kiss left my lips, I wanted to take it back. I was courting disaster in every way possible, flirting with a hot client while hanging upside down by one leg. Count 'em. One.

It was a wonder I hadn't broken an arm yet. And I knew with certainty that I'd get fired from my con-servative risk-management firm if anyone recognized me. But I had entered the Dance Zone. A place where nothing could touch me, and I was a sexy, desirable dance goddess. It was a necessary fiction to spin for my subconscious to get me through the nerve-racking, scary-as-hell night.

I needed it to win Natalie the job she deserved. And it had the added benefit of making me feel—for a few moments at least—as though Trey Fraser had noticed me in a way he never would have back at the Sphere offices.

"Yeah, baby," some random man shouted from the back of the room, making me lose focus during my superhero lift.

Another guy whistled.

My gut knotted as I recalled what an imposter I was. Could that person have whistled in a sarcastic way? While I obsessed over that possibility, I missed my next flip and slipped on the pole.

No!

In a panic, my eyes went back to Trey. Sexy, mas-

culine, gorgeous Trey. And he still looked at me like…
Wow. I got all hot and bothered again.

I totally nailed the next move—an inverted cater-
pillar thing that took me a whole month to master. I
felt like a show-off, flexing slender muscles for Trey's
benefit, openly preening and arching. But seeing his
expression reminded me why women learned provocative dances in the first place.

To seduce men.

Watching him watch me was a turn-on like nothing
I'd ever experienced. Natalie's routine didn't involve
any stripping—the costume was skimpy enough to start
with—but I felt so turned-on by him, I could absolutely
see myself peeling off clothes for this man's benefit.

I wanted his eyes on me all the time. I wanted to
make his mouth water, his body ache.

The hoots and hollers from the crowd encouraged me
as I dismounted from the pole, landing in a sleek pose
before I crawled on all fours to the edge of the stage.

Right in front of Trey.

His nostrils flared. His jaw flexed. I could see his
chest rise and fall with the force of his breath.

I made a slow show of getting to my feet, tossing my
hair and rotating my hips in a protracted roll. Hardly
knowing what I was doing, I operated on instinct.
Doing what felt good.

Now I turned so my back was to Trey. Hands on
hips, I arched my spine to give him an eyeful of high-
cut silver sequins that showed off my…cheeky side.

I flipped my hair one last time and glanced over my
shoulder. This time I didn't just blow a kiss. I slapped my
ass with the flat of my palm and the crowd went wild.

The sound brought me to my senses. What was I doing?

Embarrassed now that the music had stopped, I felt my inner showgirl desert me. It was suddenly just me—Courtney Masterson—alone on stage in a blond wig and a goofy mask.

Casting one last look at Trey, I saw the spell was broken for him, too. He still looked at me, but he wasn't on the edge of his seat anymore. He talked to the guy next to him—some actor I probably should have recognized.

What made me think Trey Fraser had been attracted to me?

Hurrying off the stage, I nearly turned my ankle coming down the two stairs that led into the dressing area. Only to find Trey had beaten me there.

My fantasy man was standing between me and my return to my boring, normal life. Had he recognized me? I couldn't even ask him, because if I did, my tongue would seize up, just like back at the office, and I'd give myself away for sure. Now, more than ever, I couldn't let my stutter get the best of me. I'd use some of the speech techniques I'd learned—talk fast, talk slow, talk soft, anything to talk my way around that damn hitch in my words.

Unfortunately, as I stared at the chiseled features and mega-masculine bod of Trey Fraser, I was more nervous than I'd ever been in my life.

3

"HAVE WE MET?" Trey blurted with all the finesse of a kid in junior high asking a girl out for the first time.

Suave, dude. Really classy.

The dance diva in silver sequins shook her head, the black and silver on her mask flashing as she moved. Up close, she wasn't as tall as she'd appeared onstage. She still moved with athletic grace, but there was a subtle difference in the way she carried herself, as if some of her confidence leaked away once she stepped out of the spotlight.

He wished he could see behind the mask.

"No?" Trey felt like an idiot for following her after the dance, but he'd been so mesmerized he hadn't even thought about what he was doing. Besides, something about her seemed familiar. "I'm Trey Fraser," he offered, hoping that would help her remember him. "I know it sounds like a pickup line, but I honestly thought we might have met before."

Extending his hand, he waited for her to return the greeting, but club security was by her side in an instant. Belatedly, Trey realized a couple of other guys who'd seen the show had the same idea as he did and now stood behind him, waiting for a word with the sexy blonde.

Crap.

"Mr. Fraser," one of the security guards addressed him politely while the other beefy bouncer chased away the rest of the salivating throng, "I'm sure Ms. Night would be happy to speak with you backstage where the dancers have a lounge."

"I didn't mean to bother you," Trey said around the muscle-bound bulk between him and the woman. "Great job up there."

Before he could turn away, the bouncer put an arm around the dancer's shoulders and shuffled her a few steps closer to Trey.

"It's no bother, Mr. Fraser," the club employee assured him, straightening a dark blue tie and flashing an ingratiating smile. "I'm sure it's Ms. Night's pleasure."

Meaning it was part of her job.

And didn't that just put things in perspective for him? What the hell was he thinking, following a pole dancer around like some champagne-swilling VIP who thought anything in the place was his for the taking. He hated the idea that this was exactly the kind of crap his father pulled all the time. Thomas Fraser II went through life assuming the world was his for the taking.

"Of course," the dancer said very softly. She'd stepped forward to take Trey's arm. "Th-this way, please."

He went with her only to make sure they were out of earshot of the bouncer. She led him behind a black curtain into a small reception area with a door she left open. A compact couch and a couple of ottomans were situated around a coffee table with a large arrangement of orchids and greenery. A waitress popped through the doorway almost as soon as they entered, but when the dancer shook her head to refuse service, Trey gave the server a tip and sent her on her way.

"Ms. Night, is it?"

"Natalie." She spoke quickly, in a breathless rush. "Stage name."

He vaguely recalled seeing "Natalie Night" on a program posted at the entrance of the club. Back onstage, another performer already entertained the crowds, the breathy music and pounding bass punctuated by a few male shouts of approval.

"Well, Natalie, I won't keep you. I only came back here because I didn't want to get you in trouble with the club management." He took in the gilt framed mirror behind the sofa and on the ceiling, guessing this room was designated for private dances and more. Not once in his life had he paid for "extra" even though he had been inside clubs like this in the past. What more might Natalie offer if he was so inclined?

"I'll be fine," she assured him, tugging on the strap of her costume to move the material toward the edge of her shoulder. "Tonight was just a trial run for—" She paused. Smiled tightly. "For me."

She seemed to speak with deliberate patience, articulating slowly as if she might be annoyed at having to converse with a fan. Not that he blamed her. But he was too curious about that comment to walk away yet.

"This is your first night on the job?"

"A public audition for a role in the—" she drew a hand through her hair, the medium-length platinum strands settling right back into place "—fall lineup."

The movement distracted him from her words, his

eye going to all the bare skin her costume exposed. With sudden fierceness, he realized he did not want her in the fall lineup. Not one damn bit.

"You don't want to work here." He pictured the club bouncers shoving her into VIP rooms with high-paying guests who would be only too glad to dole out money for a private show. "I know you'd be a featured performer with your talent, but some clubgoers don't always respect the dancers' boundaries. You wouldn't want to have to…you know…entertain clients back here."

Then again, she must know what the job involved. And he was probably way out of line to tell her how to live her life, but damn. She was too talented to deal with rich jerks.

"I'll worry about that when the time comes." She spoke so softly he had to lean closer to hear her.

Close enough to catch her scent—some light, barely-there fragrance.

"I have no business telling you what to do." He tried to back away and get out of there but found himself still standing way too close to her.

He wanted a look behind the mask and settled for trying to discern her eye color under the black domino mask. Blue, maybe.

"Didn't you like the dance?" she asked, shifting from one sky-high heel to the other, her precisely painted lips moving with slow precision as she spoke.

Seized with the urge to lick all that glossy pink away until he could see the real color beneath, he felt his blood surge. He wanted this woman, even though he didn't know one damn thing about her.

"I liked the dance a whole hell of a lot." That didn't

explain what made him follow her. Or what made him stick around when he had no plans to pay for a private performance. "Too much. Maybe that's why I don't think you should perform it in a place like this where the dancers are encouraged to work overtime."

It was difficult to gauge her reaction under the barrier of the mask. But her mouth curved in a sly, sexy grin that raised his temp a few degrees.

"You were a great audience," she confided in that soft tone that made him feel as if they'd already been intimate. "I couldn't have done it without you."

He was close enough to kiss her. And the way she spoke to him made him think she might welcome it. But the clock on the wall chimed the hour just then, dragging her attention away.

"I've got to go," she announced, straightening her shoulders.

Was his time up already? He wondered if he was supposed to tip her even though all they'd done was talk.

"Wait." He was so distracted tonight he didn't know what he was doing. But he didn't think he'd be able to focus on his work or his plan to one-up his dad if he didn't find some stress relief soon. And this woman had definitely flirted with him. "Can we meet later? No strings?"

He could send Eric home with the driver and take a cab to his own place.

"I'm sure that's against club policy." Her rebuff seemed carefully worded.

Because she was cautious, or because she was trying to let him down easy?

"But you don't officially start work here until the fall."

"I won't work overtime—now or then," she reminded him, throwing his words back in his face.

"So meet me for the hell of it." Suddenly, that sounded like the best reason ever. He'd planned, plotted and thought through his every move so carefully over the last six months, shutting down his personal life completely to focus on resurrecting his career and his name.

Why not do this one thing just because he wanted to? Just because Natalie Night was sexy and intriguing?

"You really did like the dance, didn't you?" From another woman, he might have guessed she was fishing for compliments. But she sounded genuinely surprised.

And that didn't make sense. Pole dancers worked the stage because they craved the spotlight and they were confident about their bodies.

"I think it's you that I like," he admitted, reaching for the bottom of her mask and gliding a finger along the top of her cheek where it rested. "May I?"

He edged the barrier upward slightly, waiting for approval.

"No." She stepped back quickly. Unsteadily. "I'll meet you later, but the mask stays on."

"Seriously?" He didn't know what surprised him more. That she would agree to meet him or that she would want to remain anonymous when she did.

Although a vision of her draped all over him, her lean thighs straddling him while she wore nothing but sheer fabric and feathers, packed a punch so powerful it took his breath away.

"Can you be at the back entrance in fifteen minutes?" Her gaze skittered up toward the clock on the wall again.

"Yes, but won't there be a crowd congregating there to see you?"

"Really?"

Again, that seemingly innocent surprise made no sense. Was she playing him?

"Security will walk you to your car, but I think they'll discourage you from meeting anyone from the club once you're off the clock."

She frowned.

"I'll handle that," she said finally, taking a step backward. "And Trey?"

"Yes?" He heard the music change and knew another act was taking the stage.

"I'm really glad you were here tonight."

She turned on her heel and walked out of the room, her hips swinging in a walk that was gently feminine and not purposely seductive. Or so it appeared to him.

He was having the damnedest time reading this woman.

Would she really meet him, or was she already planning to send security after him as soon as he showed up in the parking lot? Trey had no idea. But she was the hottest, most diverting woman he'd ever laid eyes on.

And he planned to enjoy every possible moment he had with Natalie Night. There would be time enough tomorrow to quiz the Sphere Asset Management researcher and get the answers he wanted.

Maybe after indulging his overheated sensual imagination with Natalie, he'd be able to look into Courtney

Masterson's gray eyes and see the calculating woman she really was and not the sexy accountant his brain had conjured.

THIS WAS BAD. Really bad.

I stumbled into the dressing room and scooped up my duffel bag, desperate to get out of the club before Trey realized I'd left. Because even though my heart was beating like a hummingbird's—a jillion beats per second—I knew taking things further with a client would be out of the question. Unlike Fawn, no head-hunters were heaping job offers at my feet.

It stood to reason that I shouldn't have made a plan to meet him. But I'd felt tongue-tied and blurted the first thing that came to mind to get past him and into the dressing room. I figured I'd bought myself fifteen minutes without having to make excuses or explain myself.

"Nice job on the pole, New Girl." Another dancer smiled at me as I swept my tubes of mascara and body glitter into the bag.

Six feet tall, at least, the woman was an ethnic blend à la JLo and flat-out gorgeous. The fact that she was mostly naked and applying pink body paint around her left breast only added to her stunning appearance. She looked like she was wearing a body suit of tattoos.

"Oh. Um." Tough to make eye contact with a half-naked woman, but I tried. "Thank you. I'm Court—that is, I'm Natalie."

As much as I needed to get going, I didn't want to alienate Natalie's future colleagues.

The pink-painted beauty laughed. "You're not the only one hiding an identity, *Natalie*. We do love our stage names in this business. I'm Kim, but everyone here knows me as Kendra."

"Nice to meet you." Bag packed, I took an extra minute to admire the butterfly she'd somehow painted upside down on her chest. "Your artwork is amazing."

"Yeah?" She straightened and eyed herself critically in a mirror banked by fluorescent lights. "Everything looks sort of green in these mirrors."

"It's really good." I dug in my bag for a shapeless beach dress to cover my costume.

"Did you see Eric Reims in the crowd?" she asked, dipping her thin artist's brush into a palette with black paint.

"Who?" Tugging the collar closed, I felt more like my old self again.

"The actor in the front row. He's been in some teen movies, but last summer he did a low-budget romantic comedy." She shaded the background of a flower with light strokes. "You couldn't miss him. He was the hottest guy next to the stage."

Personally, I begged to differ, but I had a vague impression of a youngish, polished blond man seated next to Trey. And yeah, he'd be fine if you went in for the baby-faced types. I'd only had eyes for Trey.

"I think I know who you mean." Shuffling back a step, I wanted to call Natalie and tell her the good news. The club owner had already told me my spot was secure for the fall lineup.

That meant Natalie had a job. It felt good to think I'd erased a small part of my debt to my dance instructor. I could never have experienced a night like this—a thrill on so many levels—without her.

"He sat next to Trey Fraser, the hot-headed son of

Thomas Fraser, the big producer." Kendra picked up a small tin of rhinestones and carefully applied them to the butterfly's antennae. "I think I read that the son is Eric Reims's agent now."

At the mention of Trey's name, I got all worked up again. I'd never been the boy-crazy kind, not even when I was a preteen and everyone else salivated over the most popular guys in school. Maybe it was knowing I couldn't compete, or that I'd only embarrass myself. But even through college and my years in the workforce so far, I just hadn't dated much. A couple of fumbling relationships with guy-friends. Nothing like the breathless, Tilt-A-Whirl feelings that Trey inspired.

The thought of walking away from the chance to be with him tonight hurt anew. How often did opportunities like that come around?

Before I could answer Kendra, the guy who seemed to be the head bouncer stuck his head in the dressing room, knocking belatedly on the open door.

"Ms. Night?"

Nerves tensed, I straightened. The longer I hung around there, the more worried I became that I'd mess something up for Natalie. I felt like Cinderella at midnight and the chimes were already ringing.

"Yes?" I responded, my mask still in place.

"Mr. Fraser is waiting for you by the back door. May I escort you out?"

Panic exploded in my chest while Kendra let out a deep, throaty laugh.

"Looks like the New Girl was working the room better than I realized." She set down her tin of rhinestones and lifted a palm in the air.

It took me a minute to realize she was waiting for a

high five. Heaven knows, it didn't feel like a moment to celebrate for me.

Finally, I gave her the necessary hand smack and tried to smile.

"G-guess I'd better get going." I stumbled through the words a bit because I was super nervous. I couldn't go out the back door if Trey was waiting for me there. He was at least five minutes earlier than we'd agreed.

Praying for an escape plan to come to me, I hitched the strap to my duffel higher on my shoulder and moved toward my bouncer escort.

"Don't do anything I wouldn't do," called Kendra, a teasing note in her voice suggesting I should do whatever the hell I wanted.

I wish.

"Can I carry that for you?" the huge man asked. He looked like he'd been at the gym every day of his life and I was amazed he'd found a suit coat to span those shoulders.

"No, thank you," I squeaked in a rush, darting forward before he could insist on taking it.

"This way." He gestured left and I nodded meekly, hoping he didn't try to make conversation.

I needed to hang back and find a way out.

The music coming from the dance floor had turned into a screechy female vocal over heavy bass drums. The result sounded like someone having sex and I pictured myself going out into the parking lot with Trey and getting sweaty and naked. Forcing myself back to reality, I noticed there weren't many doors around, let alone any labeled with a big red Exit sign.

But as soon as I saw a glimpse of flashing purple strobe lights, I knew I must be near the front of the club and the main stage. So, without a word to Mr. Big and Beefy, I turned a sharp left and zipped down the hall toward the music.

Was it my imagination, or did I hear a male voice calling after me a couple of seconds later?

I didn't look back as I pushed past half-dressed waitresses and men with glazed and drunken eyes. A couple of guys materialized before me, but I ducked around them with ease. I was a woman on a mission. Seeing a crowd around the front entrance, I edged through the throng and shoved the heavy steel door open.

Hitting the pavement at a run, I left Backstage behind and headed for my SUV. When the engine turned over and I reversed out of the parking spot, I knew I should feel relieved. I had secured a job for Natalie and escaped Trey Fraser. He would never know that the mystery dancer on stage was one of the wealth management experts who would be servicing his account.

Yet the only thing I felt as I pulled onto the highway was a deep sense of loss that I'd had to deceive the only man who'd looked at me twice. The only man who'd propositioned me for a one-night stand.

Even worse, going back to my regular life would feel like a huge letdown after all this. But at least my behind-the-scenes role at Sphere would keep me away from Trey. After tonight, there wasn't any reason in the world I'd ever see him again.

4

"CAN I HELP you?" the redhead behind the desk at Sphere Management asked, an old-fashioned teacup steaming beside her.

Almost as much as Trey steamed right now.

He couldn't be sure if he was more frustrated about being stood up the night before or about the leak in his small organization that made his professional plans public knowledge.

"Courtney Masterson." At least he knew where to find her.

Natalie Night would have to wait.

"Certainly." The receptionist lifted the handset on her phone. "May I give her your name?"

"Trey Fraser." Not for the first time, he wished he had a name that wasn't so well recognized in this town.

His photo hadn't shown up on the gossip blogs this morning, but it was early yet. Eric's face had been all over the internet long before dawn. It would be a minor miracle if none of those same photographers had Trey in a shot.

"Thank you." The woman's expression remained a

polite mask, but he see could her lips tighten almost imperceptibly.

While she put the call through, Trey planned his approach. He would be professional. To the point. But he wasn't leaving without some answers.

"I'm sorry, Mr. Fraser." The receptionist rose from her seat behind the massive desk. "Ms. Masterson isn't answering her phone. Did you have an appointment with her this morning?"

"I made it clear to Fawn Barrows yesterday that I wanted to meet her researcher as soon as possible. I assumed she would convey as much to Ms. Masterson." Irritation furrowed his brow. "Is Fawn in the office?"

"I'll check." The woman pressed a button and spoke to someone. Moments later Fawn appeared.

"Good to see you, Trey." She wore a gray suit and had a file folder tucked under one arm. She shook his hand and seemed less flirtatious than the day before. "I heard you were looking for Courtney?"

He nodded. Waited.

"I saw her earlier this morning. She must be away from her desk." Gesturing him toward the doorway she'd emerged from, she left her folder on the reception desk. "Why don't you come on back and I'll see if I can locate her?"

Following her into the private corridors of Sphere Asset Management, Trey followed her along the same passage they'd navigated yesterday.

"I saw your father optioned the rights on a new book in today's *Variety*." Fawn peeked into the same office that Courtney hadn't been in yesterday.

Trey looked through the open door at the researcher's desk. A navy blue jacket was neatly folded over the high-backed leather chair. A good sign she was nearby?

"I'm not sure why he wants to make that into a film." He didn't want to talk about his father. But inevitably, people asked about him.

"I know, right?" Fawn turned on her heel and crossed her arms, as if she was ready to launch into a full-blown conversation around the water cooler. "He usually makes the big commercial pictures. Action adventures. Bankable stars. I was really surprised he picked up such a quiet, thoughtful book."

Trey had known why the moment he saw the deal. His dad had an insatiable need for competition to prove he was the best. Therefore, he'd make a film to go head-to-head with the movie Trey had planned while he was still in charge of his own division at his father's company. Trey had vowed to make the picture one day. Now his father was lining up a project with a similar tone and audience so he could do it better.

Could they have a more messed-up relationship?

"Go figure." Trey shrugged and then straightened as he saw a woman appear from a nearby office.

A brunette with her head down, deep in thought as she studied a page in a thick open ledger.

"Ms. Masterson?" He snagged her attention moments before she would have collided with him.

Her head snapped up.

"Oh!" She was so startled she lost her grip on the ledger. Wide gray eyes met his gaze. "Sorry!"

The book hit his toe before tipping onto the floor. In a flash, she was kneeling at his feet to scoop it up, her body so close he could swear he felt her warm breath on his thigh.

Or was that wishful thinking?

He ground his teeth together and reminded himself why he wanted to find this woman in the first place. Maybe his missed opportunity with Natalie had made him see sexual scenarios everywhere he looked.

"No problem." He reached down to help her to her feet, cupping her elbow in one hand.

She looked different than she had the day before. Without a suit jacket on, she seemed less rumpled and more…curvaceous. A simple white silk tank flattered her breasts even though the high-cut neckline revealed nothing. Her chestnut-brown hair was twisted into a messy knot and tendrils sprang from the front and back, some framing her face and some twining around her neck.

Still, it was her dove-gray eyes that drew him in. That, and the fact that her breath hitched when he touched her. He released her now, his fingers slow to relinquish the warmth of her bare arm.

"Courtney, you remember Trey Fraser?" Fawn prodded when neither of them spoke for a long moment.

"Yes." She said the word with slow deliberation while Trey breathed in her scent. It was something green and fresh, so subtle he was tempted to lean closer to identify it.

"I'd like to speak to you privately," Trey informed her, needing to put the barrier of a desk between them if he was going to have a useful conversation.

And that had to be the priority, even though something about her put his senses on full alert. Perhaps because her body reminded him of Natalie's. Same basic proportions. Maybe even the same height, if Natalie hadn't been wearing the sky-high heels she'd sported for her dance.

"O-kay." Again, her speech seemed slowed down, the way one might speak to a child. Something about that oddly lilting pattern reminded him of Natalie, as well. "Come with me."

She hustled past him without another word. Fawn had disappeared, probably returning to her office to pore over the pages of *Variety*. Although, in this town, maybe that made good business sense even if you weren't in the film industry.

Trey followed her progress down the hall, indulging in the back view without shame. Courtney Masterson did not showcase her assets with the same abandon that Natalie had—the brazen ass slap came tantalizingly to mind—but her figure was every bit as enticing.

Inside her office, she gestured to the seats near an open window before closing the door behind them. He appreciated her taking his request for a private talk seriously. Still, he didn't sit until she joined him near the matching wingbacks on either side of a small cherry table. When she lowered herself into one, he did the same.

"How can I help you?" She had put her jacket on.

He wondered why she hid behind the shapeless clothes and sensible shoes. With her lack of makeup, the effort to play down her natural attractiveness seemed purposeful.

"You included some information in your background report on me that shouldn't be public knowledge." In an effort to keep his eyes off her legs, he took in the details of her office. Degree from UCLA. A corkboard with a photo of her holding a margarita among a bunch of other women doing the same. She looked different. Relaxed and happy.

What interested him about the picture, however, was that the women knelt on red mats in front of a shiny silver pole. Given his recent jaw-dropping introduction to the finer points of pole dancing, he couldn't help but think about Natalie.

Damn it.

"I didn't think I included anything private." She frowned and the movement shifted a trio of light freckles near her mouth.

He wondered absently what her skin tasted like right there.

"You referenced a possible business expansion beyond the talent management," he reminded her, trying hard to rein himself in.

She must not have needed the file to know what he referred to because she nodded immediately. "Yes. I remember."

"No one knows about that." Tension tightened his shoulders. Hell, maybe his father was already aware about Trey's professional plans. That would account for the sudden interest in more artistic films.

"No? I do." A smile curled her lips now, and no matter that she flashed him a mildly triumphant look, he had to admire the obvious pride she took in her work.

"I need to learn your source for that information."

"I'm not at liberty to say." Her chin jutted as she laced her fingers into a tight knot.

He noticed she wore no rings. Was she seeing anyone?

Not that he was in the market himself. After he'd had a ring handed back to him by his only attempt at a serious relationship, he was in no hurry to head down that road again. Heather had left him during one of his many disagreements with his father, the up-and-coming actress siding with his dad. Leaving Trey to wonder if she'd ever dated him for *himself,* or if she was wooed by the family name and the access to a famous producer. But two years after that breakup, Trey now found himself curious about someone new.

"You're hardly a journalist. Your sources aren't protected."

"If you become a client, you will appreciate our commitment to discretion at Sphere."

"I won't if it violates my privacy."

"Mr. Fraser—"

"Trey," he corrected.

"Trey," she relented. "Anything we discover in our research goes no further than the agent who makes a pitch for your business. In this case, Fawn."

He leaned forward in his seat, determined to impress upon her how much he had riding on this business plan remaining confidential.

"Based on a professional move my father made yesterday, I have to question if the information has already spread further than that." He stared into her eyes and willed her to understand. "If there is a leak among the few people who still work for me, I need to know."

She peered down at the floor, her lips twisted in indecision. He pounced on that moment of hesitation.

"Courtney— Can I call you Courtney?"

At her brief nod, he continued.

"My father is as ruthless a businessman as you'll ever meet. Sure, he puts on a charming public facade in this town, but he's got a shark mentality when he sees blood in the water, and right now, he sees mine."

"Wow." She gave a lopsided smile, their knees so close they were almost touching. "I guess I'm not the only one with a parent who doesn't believe in coddling."

"You could say that." He returned her smile and felt strangely honored to know something personal about her. She didn't strike him as the kind of woman who would be easy to get to know. "I would have been wise to choose a profession far outside of Hollywood, but I ended up really enjoying the movie business."

She watched him with cool gray eyes, but a small tic started at the blue vein in her temple. He could see her heart beat in a quick rhythm that matched his own.

"You make a convincing case, Trey." Her voice hit a throaty note that made him think of long nights rolling around in bed.

His bed. Her bed. Didn't matter.

Maybe he would only be wasting his time to try and find out the whereabouts of Natalie Night. Maybe he should be seeking out Courtney Masterson's adventurous side instead.

"I'm willing to put all my persuasive skills to work." He wanted to drag her closer, lift her out of the wingback and into his lap. "It's that important to me."

I NEEDED TO take deep breaths.

Really, really deep breaths.

Because if I didn't get some air soon, I would melt at Trey Fraser's feet for the second time in twenty-four hours. And while it was one thing for dancer Natalie Night to flirt brazenly with this well-known Hollywood insider, it wouldn't be a possibility for me. At. All.

"That's not necessary," I informed Trey. "No more persuasion needed."

Although I might require mouth-to-mouth resuscitation if Trey got any closer in his Italian silk suit with his tanned, oh-so-capable-looking hands resting on his knees. I definitely felt a fainting spell coming on.

Trey equaled too much of a good thing for a girl with the most modest of romantic aspirations. Right then, I would have settled for getting him out of my office before he discovered my real identity. From my seat by the window I saw a few pieces of damning evidence that could betray me if he noticed them. One was a VIP pass from Backstage that I'd kept like a freaking trophy to remember my triumph last night. It wasn't super visible, but stuck out of my purse near my chair.

I'd also kept a white feather that was currently draped over my desk blotter—front and center. Yes, I was truly an idiot.

"Really? You'll tell me where you found the information?" He straightened and I wondered if he employed seduction as a coercive technique very often. Just the mere thought of it was enough to make me concede whatever he wanted.

Besides, the sooner he left Sphere, the better.

"Well." I licked my lips because my mouth had turned dry. Amazingly, I hadn't stuttered, though. Somehow, I'd maintained my composure and my words flowed with only little halts in between. "I actually farm out the most rudimentary of research, so I didn't personally unearth the news that you may expand your talents into your own film company."

His hands tightened and his mouth drew into a flat line.

"So I need to convince someone else to talk."

"No." I wouldn't part with the person's name or she'd never help me with my profiles again. "I'm familiar with her methods and I can guarantee that news like this came from unsecured cyber data online."

Trey sprang out of his chair. "You paid someone to hack my computer?"

"Of course not." I couldn't help a sigh. Sadly, most people were unaware how vulnerable their data was when they stored it online. "You probably have outdated internet storage. I happen to know she saw your business plan in a visual presentation piece that came up in a routine search."

"Routine?" He started pacing around my office, running a hand through his hair. "You call invasion of privacy *routine?*"

"Our searches are aggressive, but never unethical." I firmly believed this or I wouldn't have patronized the research company. "You can't expect us *not* to look for clues to a client's business online. It's like you're posting information on a public bulletin board and then asking people not to look."

Sort of like me putting a stupid white feather on my desk and hoping against hope that Trey wouldn't see it. But who would have thought he'd show up at Sphere today, asking for *me* of all people?

He stopped beside my desk, so close to the feather, he could almost touch it. I tried to maintain eye contact and not give away the clue to Natalie Night's real identity. But it was impossible not to look at the elephant in the room.

Nervous sweat broke out along my forehead, and although my hair covered it, I wondered if my cheeks were also bright red. Just thinking about it made me flush more.

"I see." His fingers grazed my desk, resting lightly beside a photo of my home after I fixed it up. "Perhaps you could tell me how to secure the information better in the future? I'd like to get rid of all traces of any business plans."

His beautiful, dark eyes met mine, and I got lost for a minute. Trey was unbelievably handsome. He had shades of the whole Latin-lover thing going on, but he also had a warm attentiveness about him that would flatter any woman. Geesh, to him I was just a random research accountant who had come in contact with his world and he was making me feel like the center of his undivided attention. It was a heady thing.

"Courtney?" he prompted.

"Um." I tried to stop thinking about the washboard abs Fawn promised he had, but I'd been secretly eyeing his midsection, looking for traces of those muscles in the gap of his unbuttoned jacket. "I'm not really the best person to advise someone on digital security."

"I'm sure you know enough that you wouldn't make the same mistakes I have." He didn't seem dissuaded in the least.

And then it happened.

Trey looked down at my desk. His eyes landed on the feather.

I'm pretty sure an audible gasp escaped my lips because he looked over to me abruptly.

"I-in that case—" I stammered at first, so I rushed my speech to put the words out there before I could bungle them more. "I'd be happy to give you some tips on safeguarding your information online. I'll send you my notes at the end of the day."

He still stared at the feather. Oh, crap.

I stood, hoping it would signal the end of the meeting so we could go our own ways. Instead, he picked up the sleek white quill and gave me a long look.

My heart raced. I was dead if he recognized me. Memories of twining myself around the pole last night came roaring back in vivid detail. I'd danced for him. No one else. How on earth could I expect him *not* to know it was me?

"Courtney." His attention returned to the feather. He smoothed the soft fibers between his thumb and forefinger, a slow, deliberate touch.

Intended to taunt me with a dangerous knowledge he could now hang over my head?

Or was that careful masculine attention designed to remind me how seductively persuasive he could be? I didn't know whether to be scared or...excited. Right then, I was caught in a frenzied place somewhere in the middle. I couldn't catch my breath. My mouth went so dry that speaking was no longer an option.

"Mmm?" I stuffed my hands in my blazer pockets before I made a mad grab for him.

"Would you consider meeting with me privately?"

I looked around my office, all too aware of the closed door.

"I mean," he clarified, "would you be able to meet with me outside of Sphere?"

"I'm not a client rep. Actually, I don't usually meet with clients." The suspense was killing me. If he knew my secret alias, why didn't he just say so? Why not simply run to my boss and put me out of my misery?

"Then I appreciate you seeing *me* outside of work."
He waved the feather, almost like it was a teeter-totter,
between two fingers. Then he set it down. "Thank you."

Was he thanking me for seeing him last night at the
club? Or was he assuming I would agree to the meeting he'd just requested?

His expression gave away nothing.

But no matter that there was a fifty percent chance
he'd recognized me and could blackmail me forever,
he was still the most compelling man I'd ever laid eyes
on. Furthermore, he'd noticed me yesterday, even before I dressed up in showgirl clothes to take Natalie's
place at Backstage. I couldn't forget the way he'd invited me into the conference room, his eyes gazing
into mine as if I was an attractive woman and not just
a Sphere employee.

"I suppose I could find time during a lunch break."
I would keep this professional. Expense the company.
There was nothing in my contract that said I couldn't
bring in new business. If anything, there were financial incentives to do just that.

"Today?" he prompted. "I've got several things I'd
like to discuss with you."

Such as? I wanted to shout, my nerves stretched to
the breaking point. But if what he wanted to say was in
any way related to last night's moonlighting, it would
be better to meet outside the office. Maybe I could convince him to keep my secret.

If nothing else, I could indulge in the heated attraction I missed out on the night before when I gave him
the slip. It only seemed fair to have that chance back if
I was going to lose my job for the sake of one mistake.

"I've got a lunch meeting in-house today." I had to

step closer to him in order to peer down at the weekly calendar open on my desktop. "How about tomorrow?"

I felt incredibly aware of him standing next to me, a little closer than was strictly professional. My thighs shifted beneath my skirt in an effort to quell the sudden heat, but that only intensified the feeling.

"How about tonight?" he pressed, lowering his voice so that he spoke in close proximity to my ear.

A sweet shiver swept through me. It was all I could do not to close my eyes and tilt my head back to grant him full domain over my neck. Shoulder. Anything else he wanted.

"A lunch meeting would probably be more appropriate." I sounded like a prude, but I clung to the hope that he didn't recognize me. That my guilty conscience played tricks on me and saw danger where there wasn't any.

He nodded but still didn't step back. The feather remained on the desk in the narrow space between us.

"If you insist. Can I pick you up at noon tomorrow?"

Bad idea. This would only lead to trouble. Yet just like the previous night, I found I couldn't refuse him.

"S-sure." I swallowed hard. "I hope I have enough to offer to make it worth your while."

It was the sentiment of an insecure woman and one that I shouldn't have spoken aloud. I knew better than to undercut myself.

"More than enough." He smiled like the big, bad wolf might have done after polishing off grandma. "See you then, Courtney."

He turned on the heel of one polished leather loafer and I thought I might be able to take a deep breath again. But he paused by my bookshelves to pick up the silver-framed photo that I'd noticed him eyeing from across the room earlier.

It was that picture taken at our receptionist's bachelorette party last year—the party that had first introduced me to pole dancing. I wondered why he wanted a closer look.

He set it down and departed before I could ask. When I took another peek at it, however, I got a damned good idea.

The dancing pole wasn't all that obvious in the background since it could be mistaken for a ceiling support or the base of a tall floor lamp. Yet there could be no mistaking the logo on the back wall of the dance studio. If you looked close enough, you could see the name Naughty by Night painted on the brick.

My heart lodged in my throat as I wondered what he thought when he'd looked at that.

Did he know my secret?

5

THE NEXT MORNING, Trey wandered across the grounds of the Spanish-style villa where he'd spent his childhood whenever one of his parents wasn't carting him around Europe or New York for their careers. He had a question for his father, so he'd come to the source. Not that he was looking forward to their meeting.

"What the hell are you doing here?" Trey's father greeted him outside the converted art studio on the back lot of the elder Fraser's expansive Malibu beach property.

A big, robust man in his seventies, Thomas Fraser II had a grizzled beard and a shock of thick white hair that currently stood up in all directions. Behind him, sculptures in clay and marble in various stages of creation crowded the tile floor. In addition to being a famous producer, the older man was a sculptor in his spare time. Personally, Trey had always thought his father might have ADD, since he could never sit still for more than a minute at a time and he always needed something new to hold his attention. He was a creative genius in a lot of ways, but his follow-through sucked. Trey had hoped when they first went into business together that their opposing styles could balance each other out. He had overlooked the fact that his father also liked to have his own way at all times.

"Hello to you, too." Trey stepped past his father into the open-air ground floor of the studio, where a long panel of windows slid aside to allow in breezes off the Pacific. When he was a kid, the art studio had been the pool house. "And believe me, I wouldn't be here if I thought you'd give me a straight answer over the phone."

Better to see his father's face in person. That way he could distinguish fact from fiction when he questioned him about his latest deal. Trey wouldn't have risked a confrontation if he didn't need the truth. Courtney's research had given him a lot to think about.

"Bah," his father grumbled, turning his back on Trey to wash his hands in a utility sink against one wall. "As if you're entitled to straight answers. What right do you have to question me about my business anyway?"

"Who said it was a business concern, Pop?"

Trey ran his hand along the graceful lines of an unfinished marble horse. The piece was a favorite of Trey's, originally intended as a tribute to his mother, but that romantic notion was quashed when his dad took up with someone else. Trey's actress mom hadn't spent much time with her three sons when they were young, but she had taken them to the Tuscan countryside every summer to stay with their maternal grandparents, a welcome respite from their self-involved father. Damien and Lucien, his younger brothers, had moved out of the L.A. area as soon as they turned eighteen, ready to put some space between themselves and their over-bearing dad.

"Since when do you have any concerns but work-related ones?" His dad yanked a linen towel off a rack and gave him a sharp look as he dried his hands.

Trey wandered over to a sculpture of a woman's torso, the high, taut breasts directly at the viewer's eye level, thanks to a raised pedestal. The arched spine and flared hips made him think of Courtney.

And Natalie. "Since I learned I need to watch my back twice as much when I do business with family."

"Nonsense." His father made a dismissive gesture. "Your problem is that you haven't had a personal life since Heather. That's why you're too intense. A man needs a woman."

Trey refused to discuss his romantic entanglement with the only woman he'd ever fallen hard for. A woman who been more romanced by the idea of being married to a Fraser than the reality of loving Trey.

His dad might be a pain in the ass, but he had personal magnetism to spare. The old man's shoes were damn big to fill and Trey sometimes wished he hadn't put himself in the same arena as his father.

"You certainly haven't deprived yourself of women," Trey observed lightly, anxious to get off the subject.

Ignoring the comment, Thomas walked to a bar off to one side of the room and took out a heavy crystal decanter.

"Drink?" he asked, filling a glass with amber liquid.

With his father, there was no telling if it was the best Scotch or a new dandelion wine recipe he'd whipped up in the same damn utility sink where he washed his stone-cutting tools. His father liked to think of himself as a Renaissance man, but his skills as a vintner were sketchy at best.

"No." Trey moved toward a tall chair near a pub table in the middle of the room and took a seat. "This isn't a social call."

He needed to see his father's expression when he asked him about the film rights he'd obtained to a story suspiciously similar to the one Trey had tried to make while working for his dad's company. He needed to understand the guy's intentions. Sure, his dad had always been ridiculously competitive, especially with Trey. But would he really make a film just to spite his son? Trey felt as if he was missing something and he hoped that this face-to-face time would help him figure out why his father had moved to a new level of aggression in the ongoing family war for Hollywood fame.

Couldn't his father see it was Trey's turn for recognition? Trey's time to shine?

"I've noticed you haven't been social since I shut down your last film." Thomas strolled around the studio, drink in hand, eyes roving over his creations. He stopped now and again to brush stone dust off one or trace a groove along a clay model.

Fighting to hang on to his patience, Trey reminded himself he was here to get answers, and that he couldn't let his father distract him with their twisted personal relationship. That was how Trey had gotten talked into joining his dad's film company in the first place—misplaced sentimentality and the hope that they could work together as adults even if they'd had a contentious relationship in his youth.

Bad idea.

"With good reason." Trey took out his cell phone and

scrolled through the entertainment news items. "But I think you owe me a heads-up if you're going to try to muscle out the picture you wouldn't let me make." He read aloud, "'Fraser Films options *Quiet Places,* a Vietnam war book about an unlikely friendship between American POWs.'"

"So?" His dad took a long drink, not even looking at him.

"I've got a fantastic, gut-wrenching screenplay about POWs during the Korean war. You know that."

"Yours has an Aussie POW. My project is more firmly American."

"Right. Good point." Trey switched off his phone and stood. He'd gotten as much of an answer as he needed. His father wasn't committed to the film as much as he was committed to pissing off Trey. That didn't mean he wouldn't make the movie. But so far the story hadn't excited him on an artistic level. "I'll let you get back to work."

His father said nothing. Trey was almost to the door when he heard him clear his throat. Shake the ice cubes in his glass.

"I heard you've been keeping late hours on the town." He said it casually, as if it was a simple observation.

Trey turned around. He needed to get the hell out of his old man's house, but he waited for the other shoe to drop. No doubt his father had a reason for bringing up the only late night Trey had enjoyed in a long time.

"Disappointed I didn't invite you?" He kept his tone light, but tension knotted the muscles across his shoulders.

"I'm concerned, Trey." He set his empty glass on the

pub table before picking up a small pick and approaching a clay figure of a lion's face. "You've got some underage clients in that new talent agency of yours. I'm not sure it sends a good message to the parents of young actresses when their manager is patronizing dance clubs with his clients."

"I'd be surprised if anyone thought anything of it." Los Angeles wasn't some Heartland small town where an agent might be viewed as a seedy character.

"Trust me. All it takes is one well-placed article to turn that into a scandal." He took the pick to the lines of clay fur around the noble creature's face. "You'd hate to lose your young clients. They're the future of any good agency."

"End scene." Trey used his hands to pantomime snapping shut a slate. "Great take, Dad. Too bad the cameras weren't rolling."

"I try to help you, Trey," his father argued. "I only push you so you achieve more success. Don't you see? It's a father's role."

Trey couldn't think of many fathers who took the role so seriously, but he wouldn't go down that road again. He'd found out what he needed to know.

"Okay, Dad. Thanks." Shaking his head, he walked out of the studio and across the lawn to his car, ticked off that he'd made the drive all the way out Pacific Coast Highway just to be treated to more games.

At least he had figured out his father's next move. Thomas was still trying to maneuver Trey like a chess piece in a game that he'd never wanted to play.

Good thing the next item on his appointment list was lunch with Courtney Masterson. The seemingly shy research accountant had been full of all kinds of interesting surprises the last time they met.

For the last twenty-four hours, he'd been thinking about her a lot. That white feather on her desk had sparked his imagination and made him wonder about how she spent her time when she left the office. It was a crazy idea that Courtney would have anything to do with Natalie Night. But the picture of her inside the dance studio had definitely spurred the thought.

Chances were that Courtney had only gone to the studio for a bachelorette party. Naughty by Night advertised events like that often enough in local media outlets. Yet Courtney shared a few key traits with Natalie, including the rare ability to turn him inside out with just a look. So, even though a connection between the women was highly unlikely, Trey's fantasies were having a field day with the idea.

Besides, returning to Backstage would be dangerous for him if there was any chance his father would sink so low as to go gunning for his reputation. To be safe, Trey would keep his fantasies to himself.

Or better yet, he'd keep them between him and Courtney.

TEN TIMES I'D PICKED up the phone to cancel the date. Er, lunch meeting. Ten times.

But when I heard the receptionist, Star, clicking down the hall in her heels, I still hadn't made the call that would end this madness. Now there was no turning back.

"Courtney?" Star tapped lightly on the open door, her red hair piled high like a school teacher from another era.

There was something very proper about Star with her retro hairdo and her china teacup, which she carried around the office from nine to five. But appearances were deceiving because she was the same colleague who chose to have her bachelorette party at Naughty by Night. I had her to thank—or blame—for turning me into a featured attraction at the local gentlemen's club.

"Yes?" I stood, ready to bolt from my office for this lunch appointment even though I had removed any incriminating evidence of my Backstage adventure. Or even my dancing.

"Pendleton wanted me to give you this." She handed me a fat folder from the boss. The file had the name of a well-known Silicon Valley company typed on the tab.

"A new account for me to research?" I took the folder from her and laid it on my desk, all the while realizing I was extremely let down that she wasn't here to announce Trey's arrival.

"Not only that." Star smiled and wiggled her eyebrows. "He asked me to tell you that he'd really like you to consider taking the lead on this one."

"Me?" My heartbeat faltered a little. "He knows I'm a behind-the-scenes person."

Pendleton had been there for my interview with the company. He knew better than most how awful my public speaking skills could be. Still, having client contact could increase my paycheck if I ever felt ready to tackle it.

"Maybe he's noticed you're not as shy as you used to be." Star straightened the chain of the vintage looking cameo necklace that she wore. "And, by the way, Trey Fraser is waiting for you out front."

An undignified yelp of alarm escaped me.

"Why didn't you say so?" I hissed at her, grabbing my purse and checking my teeth in a mirror tucked inside a bookshelf.

"You're fun to surprise," she admitted, walking with me as I hurried down the hall.

"So you can see me trip and maybe even stutter?" Everyone in my office had heard the glitch in my speech at one time or another. But I had to admit, they'd all been very cool about it. And, except for the occasional clueless summer intern, everyone was very patient with me if I got into trouble with my words.

It was mortifying to have people try to finish my sentences for me.

"No." From behind me, Star tucked a tag back into the neckline of my shirt. "Because you're way more animated than most people on staff here."

"That's a new way to put it," I grumbled, even though I realized what she meant. There were some people in accounting who you'd swear didn't even have a pulse.

"Go get him, Courtney," Star whispered in my ear as I opened the door into the reception area. "And don't worry if you don't come back after lunch. I can always cover for you."

The words rang in my ears as I snagged my first view of Trey. A gorgeous, breathtaking view. I still couldn't believe I'd had a chance with him the other night. And I really, really couldn't believe that I'd ignored it and gone home.

I had to stop letting old insecurities run my life.

"Hi," I said lamely, halting in the middle of the foyer.

Animated? I couldn't think of a single word to say to the man. He wore jeans and a faded red T-shirt, but his shoes were killer. Distressed leather loafers—sort of Italian gigolo meets American cowboy. He looked delicious.

"You ready?" He grinned and I wondered what he had in mind for lunch.

Probably not nearly as much fun as what I was imagining right now. Besides, I had dressed in a boring khaki skirt that hung to my knees and a white T-shirt that I'd bought in the men's department. I've always figured that with the right jewelry, a man's shirt could make a fashion statement. Although the statement I was making now was probably something like—*I've given up!* I guess I was trying hard *not* to dress for seduction since that's all I had on my mind.

And no matter what fantasies I might have had about Trey, relationships with clients were off-limits.

"I hope so." I had my digital tablet tucked in my bag and a few notes prepared to help him with cyber security. "That is, yes."

Belatedly, I remembered to be more firm. Direct. If I was going to succeed as a public speaker, I had to articulate better.

"Great." He glanced down at my feet and I remembered I wore canvas tennis shoes. "Those are perfect for what I have in mind."

I was relieved, since I'd had every intention of bringing a pair of high heels to work today specifically for this lunch. But my mom had called right before I went out the door, rattling me with her monthly barrage of questions about what I planned to do with my life. She still didn't acknowledge me in public since I continued to embarrass her in her perfect world, but she hadn't given up on her quest to mold me into a better human being. She still signed me up for elocution classes I didn't attend, and design workshops intended to help me learn how to dress with more flair.

Um. No thanks, Mom.

"Really?" I stepped through the office doors and out into the noontime heat. A few threatening clouds were rolling by, but for now the day was just humid and hot. "Are we doing a vending truck? There's a Greek guy the next block up who sells gyros that are…" I was too enraptured with my culinary memories to describe the taste "…amazing."

"No." Trey guided me through a handful of suit-wearing businessmen who walked elbow to elbow, all talking on their cell phones. "My car's this way."

Trey's hand on the small of my back was fleeting but sexy. My skin tingled in that spot even after he ended the contact.

"Now I'm curious." About Trey, I realized. Immediately I felt flustered. "I mean, about where we're going."

"Do you like surprises?"

"Actually, yes." I spotted a low-slung black Jag down the street and guessed it belonged to him. "You might not think that a shy, quiet girl like me would go for surprises, but my parents were both older when I came along and they never did anything without major planning."

Trey's hand moved to my back again and he guided me around a corner onto a side street. Turned out the Jag wasn't his. I caught the tiniest hint of his scent and wished I could move closer.

"Shy?" he asked, tilting his head at an angle to peer into my face. "I would have never taken you for shy."

Oh, my God. Something about his tone of voice made me think he knew my secret. He knew I was the dancer at Backstage. My heart pounded wildly and my feet got a little tangled.

Trey took my arm, an amused smile on his face.

"Here's my car." He pointed to a big white sport utility vehicle.

"I would have never taken you for an SUV kind of guy." I was happy to redirect the conversation since I had no idea what to say to his assertion that I wasn't shy. Everyone thought I was shy—at least, people who didn't know me.

"Then I guess we're already surprising each other," he observed lightly, opening the passenger door for me and helping me up into the cab.

He came around to the driver's side and hopped in. We buckled up and he pulled smoothly out into lunch-hour traffic even though it was crazy busy.

"So you like driving a tank?" I used the side mirror to make sure he wasn't crushing the smaller cars in the next lane when he moved to the right. "I would be a nervous wreck in this thing."

I was a nervous wreck anyway, being alone with Trey in an enclosed space. A lifetime of my mom's scathing comments came back to haunt me as I wondered if my outfit matched and if I could get through lunch without stumbling over my words. To distract myself from negative thoughts, I tried to focus instead on his vehicle and wondered if he'd been driving the SUV the other night at Backstage. It seemed plenty roomy. We could have really…had fun.

I had to fan myself to keep from overheating as I pictured his hands all over me.

"It's a work vehicle," he assured me, heading west on Sunset Boulevard. "Being in business for myself means I do my own sweat labor. Sometimes I need to haul stuff around."

Or invite exotic dancers into his backseat? I sneaked a glance at his thighs and pictured me straddling them.

"You're a talent agent." I rolled the window down and let in a little breeze to help cool me off. It was fun being up this high. And I never got tired of the ocean. I lived close to it, but I didn't see it enough. "How could you possibly get sweaty while talking to casting agents and mailing out headshots?"

That got a laugh out of him, and I enjoyed the sound as we left downtown L.A. behind. He seemed way too serious for a guy born into Hollywood royalty. I knew money didn't equal happiness, but more often than not, it helped.

"You, of all people, should understand that I have bigger aspirations than managing my client list." He passed a tourist rubbernecking at a couple of reality stars who stood in a crosswalk with their arms full of shopping bags. "So I work a lot more hours in a day than my primary business demands. But this vehicle has proven helpful even for the talent agency. I have a big-name actor who signed with me and he won't go anywhere without his St. Bernard. I'd never fit Buddy in a sports car."

"I'm very curious about your film company development." I studied his profile to see if I'd ventured into a forbidden topic. "I'd love to know more about that if you don't mind discussing it."

"Depends. Are you asking for yourself or as a representative of Sphere?"

"Definitely for myself. But I didn't mean to—"

"It's fine." He opened the sunroof and I peered up

at the palm trees and cloud-filled sky. "I've learned to be cautious, but what's the harm in talking to someone who already knows the plan?"

The miles flew by as he filled me in on a few basics of the industry. I knew a thing or two about start-up businesses, but nothing about the birth of a film company, so I learned a lot. It quickly became obvious that Trey knew what he was doing. It also occurred to me that his father was foolish to let a sharp industry insider like Trey get away.

By the time he turned the SUV up a steep, winding road in the Pacific Palisades, I'd almost forgotten about our lunch date. Er, meeting.

"Where are we?" I looked more closely at my surroundings and felt certain I'd never been here. It seemed an unlikely place for a restaurant.

"Our picnic destination."

"W-we're having a picnic?" I hesitated on the words because a picnic felt much more like a date than a meeting. And suddenly I felt more pressured. Wary.

"I realized yesterday that I've been busting my ass for months to recover some professional credibility, yet no matter how much I do, my dad is still going to be waiting for me to make a mistake." He pulled into a parking lot near a grassy field with a sign that read Will Rogers State Park. "I figured I'd better take time to enjoy the journey because I'm sure as hell nowhere near the point in my life where I can escape the old man's shadow."

He shut off the SUV and came around to open my door. I began to get nervous now, the relaxed atmosphere of the ride dissipating under the pressure of... helping Trey Fraser enjoy the journey. But he seemed unaware of a shift in mood as he headed around to the back of the vehicle and popped open the rear door.

"Ready?" he asked, handing me a blue blanket while he grabbed a huge, insulated bag. "I hope the rain holds off."

"Wow." I couldn't think of anything else to say because my brain was busy calculating how much time and effort he must have put into planning this. Packing a picnic struck me as incredibly romantic, even though I knew he couldn't mean it that way.

And yet…what if he did?

I was back to worrying he knew it was me on the stage at Backstage. After all, I could believe that Natalie Night might have gotten under his skin. But me? Courtney? Hell, I was an accountant, and even *I* couldn't make that one add up.

"What?" He looked my way as we walked past an empty polo field toward some deserted picnic tables. "Are you anti-picnic? An ant phobia, maybe?"

"No." I followed him past the picnic table to the shade of a big tree, where we stopped. "I'm just surprised that we're picnicking for a business meeting."

"First of all, you said you liked surprises." He took the blanket from me and spread it out in the shade, careful to avoid any tree roots. "Second, I only threw in the part about business to make sure you came."

His eyes met mine, and his voice dropped down into that range of quiet intimacy.

"Oh." Apparently he'd had a plan all along. My heart pounded so fast that I felt a little lightheaded. I told myself to speak slowly. Really slowly. Because I was so far off-kilter I was sideways. "Why? That is, why is it important for me to be here?"

This was his chance to call me out on my double identity. He could end the tension right now and confront me on the duplicity. Part of me thought I'd feel better to just acknowledge it. I could always throw myself at his mercy and beg him not to tell my boss.

In fact, being at his mercy didn't sound bad at all.

"I want to know more about you, Courtney Masterson." His expression revealed nothing.

Still, my skin hummed everywhere as if he'd just touched me.

"On a personal level?" I wrapped my arms around myself despite the heat of the day because I'd developed goose bumps everywhere.

"I think you know the answer to that." He pointed to the blanket. "Have a seat."

I claimed a corner closest to the tree trunk and tried not to hyperventilate. For a few minutes, I watched him unpack the picnic satchel in silence. He pulled out a bottle of excellent champagne and two cut-crystal flutes. I was put in charge of pouring the champagne while he produced cheeses, fruits and a couple of mini baguettes. He had cold salmon on ice and a few chocolates in there, too.

While I fumbled with the foil wrapper and placed a linen napkin over the cork to extricate it, I watched Trey work on the meal presentation. I appreciated him letting me process the whole "I want to know you personally" news at my own speed.

"You're putting Wolfgang Puck to shame," I observed as he cut strawberry slices to fan around the center of the fruit plate.

"I figured I would pull out all the stops to seduce

the senses." He held out a strawberry slice toward me. "Would you like a bite?"

My heart stopped. I wondered vaguely how long I could still breathe without that vital organ in motion, but then it kicked into gear again. Now it hip-hopped at a pace that felt like triple-time. This was really happening. I could lose my job for this.

But I was very far from the office right now.

Self-consciously, I parted my lips and leaned forward. Trey's eyes dipped toward my mouth as he fed me, his knuckle grazing my chin then falling away.

"Delicious." He hadn't even tried a berry. He simply focused on my lips.

I was completely flustered. Totally turned-on, but disconcerted too.

"You didn't need t-to go to all this trouble," I told him, unused to such intense male attention.

"Didn't I?" He took the champagne bottle from my hands and finished the job I'd forgotten about. The cork made a light pop when it came free. "I think you're wrong there. The last time I invited you out, I was stood up."

He poured my champagne so calmly, no one watching us would have guessed he'd just lobbed a live grenade into my world.

6

TREY DIDN'T FEEL the slightest bit of guilt for shocking Courtney's socks off.

She was pale and speechless as he handed her a champagne glass and picked up a flute for himself. He hadn't planned on outing her over lunch, hadn't even known for sure that she was the dancer he'd propositioned earlier in the week. But he'd had a strong hunch and it seemed like something that needed to be addressed before they moved any further.

Her reaction put his doubts to rest.

"How d-did you know?"

"I wasn't sure until just now." He shifted slightly closer to her on the blanket. "But it was bugging the hell out of me that I could be so damn attracted to that dancer *and* you at the same time. I'm a one-woman kind of guy."

He tipped his glass lightly to hers, the clink making a soft chime in the quiet heat of midday.

"What did you think when you saw the feather?" she asked between small sips.

"I thought it was a coincidence...a cruel trick of the

universe…to toss a white feather in my path the night after I let a feather-clad bombshell slip away." He fixed her a plate and passed it to her since she seemed preoccupied and worried.

Not exactly the mood he'd been going for.

"But then, when you saw the photo of me at the dance studio, you knew?" Absently, she took a grape and he was relieved to see her relax just a little.

He'd bet Courtney needed a hell of a lot more relaxation in her life. And he had a good idea that she found it on stage. He was fascinated by how open she'd been when she was dancing. How confident.

"No. Like I said, I didn't know for sure that it was you until just now. But when I saw that picture in your office, it made me want to know more about a place called Naughty by Night."

"Oh, no." She set down her plate. "You didn't."

"I called and asked to speak to Natalie." He'd guessed the "Night" in the name of the studio was no accident. "They said she'd dislocated an ankle two nights ago and was recovering at home. By the time I did the math, I knew she couldn't have been the one at Backstage."

"My company will fire me." Courtney shook her head, her long dark hair falling in her eyes but doing little to hide her distress. "If they find out—"

She made a helpless gesture and he caught her hand in his.

"They won't find out from me."

"Really?" Her narrowed gaze told him she didn't count on it.

"It won't do my reputation any favors to hang out with exotic dancers when I'm still representing a few underage clients." Awkward, to say the least.

Moreover, he wouldn't give his father the satisfaction of besting him in the credibility department. Not after all the questionable tricks his dad had used to cheat and manipulate his way through the industry.

"So you'll keep this secret." She seemed to weigh his sincerity, her gray eyes searching his.

There was something about her tentativeness that made her irresistible. Maybe it was because so many women he'd known were unflinchingly confident and bold in their decisions. They had to be to make it in the film business. Courtney, on the other hand, seemed to think things over carefully.

Yet he had the feeling that anyone who made it past her scrutiny would be a lucky, lucky man.

"I'd like to keep a whole lot of secrets for you." He set aside his glass and slid their plates to the far side of the blanket.

She peered through her bangs at the nearest tree line and then turned to look back across the polo field toward the parking lot. He already knew it was empty.

"I'd like an example." She hooked a finger in the long gold chain around her neck and slid a simple leaf charm back and forth.

"An example?" He'd be hypnotized if he kept watching the motion of that charm as it drew his attention from one shapely breast to the other beneath her plain white T-shirt.

"What kind of secret can you keep?" she prompted, unaware the blood flow had slowed to his brain.

He clasped her hand in one of his, halting her nervous jewelry play. Gray eyes widened at his touch. He breathed in the moment and the woman, inhaling the faintest scent of her light perfume.

"This kind." He covered her lips before she could come up with any other delaying tactics.

He didn't kiss her. Not yet. Right now, he simply brushed his mouth over hers. Softly. Beneath his hand, the pulse in her wrist went wild, and the knowledge that he'd excited her so easily pumped up his own heart rate.

Only then did he increase the pressure and take a measured taste. Her lips were plump and warm and mobile, parting lightly to accommodate him. Before he went further, he tugged the fullness of her lower lip between his teeth, sucking gently. She tasted like strawberries.

Even better, she purred with pleasure at that small contact, her whole body relaxing under his touch.

Heat blasted through him and it didn't have a damn thing to do with the midday humidity. Courtney had a strong, distinct effect on him, like a thirty-year-old whiskey he'd never tried before. And a triple shot wouldn't be enough.

He told himself to go slow. Seduction, right? That was his focus. Yet that soft, pitchy sigh she'd made had gotten right under his skin, and he found himself reaching for her, drawing her closer by the small of her back.

"Wait." She laid a hand on his chest, her cool, slender fingers sliding over his T-shirt with the gentlest pressure. "What are we doing?"

Relaxing his hold on her, he flattened his hand against her spine but couldn't quite let go.

"What I've wanted to do since I first saw you outside the conference room at Sphere." He remembered the hair falling over her eyes, the long bangs hiding too much of her. "Taking a taste."

"You're a Fraser." She frowned at this but—thankfully—did not pull away.

He could almost see her nimble mind working through the implications.

"Not a damn thing I can do about that." He slowed down his breathing, kept his voice level. No easy feat.

Hell, the memory of her in sheer fabric and feathers, crawling toward him on all fours, seared through his brain like a laser. As much as he had revisited that moment in his fantasies at night, he was in no position to deal with it here. Now.

"Why w-would—" She stopped herself and he felt her tense. "You. Are. Famous." Her words became clipped. Impatient, almost. "We move in very different circles."

He was fascinated with her lips and the way she formed her words. Deliberate. Thoughtful. A far cry from the way most people in this town spoke. His father, for one, could spew one lie after another without a second thought.

"That doesn't matter to me." He took a page out of her book and revised that statement after giving his words some more thought. "No. That's not true. I think it's a bonus that you have no ties to the film industry. I'm so sick of the gossip and fishbowl existence."

She nodded. "And you can keep secrets?"

"Like nobody's business."

He braced himself for more questions as a few storm clouds moved in overhead. Instead of quizzing him, however, she twisted her fingers in his T-shirt and drew him closer, arching toward him.

"In that case, how about another kiss?"

POSSIBLY I WAS channeling my inner dancing girl. Because I had entered another realm when Trey kissed me. Inhibitions fell. The insecurity I'd wrestled with my whole life was banished into the next century. I felt beautiful. Empowered.

And so very hot.

I burned from the inside out as Trey's hand moved up my spine. My head spun like I'd had way more champagne than the three sips I took earlier. Thank heavens this was a public park. Even though it looked like No Man's Land right now, a park ranger could come along anytime. That should help me keep my clothes on.

At least, I thought it would. There was no telling what spontaneous combustion might do.

I wished I could record this moment forever and replay it like a film. I'd break it down frame by frame and go over and over each one. Sometimes I'd focus on his touch and where his hands heated my body. Other times, I'd concentrate on his kiss and how the play of his lips felt on mine.

As it stood, I only had Right Now, and my senses were so overwhelmed I felt like one mass of tingling nerves. Even my hands buzzed with an almost electric charge. And yet it was only my mouth he focused on, treating it with the most exquisite care.

He kissed like a god. Not too hard. Not too soft. Just awesomely right. I sank backward from this kiss, melting down onto the blanket, boneless from this erotic tasting.

Gently, he cradled the back of my head before it hit the quilted cotton. Better yet, his body followed mine down, so that I had the subtle pressure of his chest against my breasts, the warm weight of one thigh pinning mine. A cooling breeze floated through the trees and rattled the leaves, the rest of the world silent except for a slow rumble of thunder in the distance and the rasp of our breathing. I would never forget this moment and the magic Trey wove for me. Had I said I wouldn't be getting naked? I was already rethinking this as he bent one knee, his thigh falling deeper between my legs.

Yessss.

I hadn't said the word aloud, but I was pretty sure I expressed it with my whole body. My legs inched wider. My arms crept around his neck.

Sex loomed in the air, and we hadn't even taken any clothes off yet.

"Come home with me." Trey's words whispered in my ear, the idea implanting itself in my consciousness so subtly it was like I'd thought of it myself.

Go home with Trey.

The idea was insane, and yet the thought was captivating. If he could really keep this secret…would I take the risk? New risks had become more appealing ever since my dance at Backstage. What if I was on some kind of lucky streak where things worked out for me? Then again, maybe I would just lose my heart to him and end up hurt. The more I knew him, the more I liked him. And that made being with him a whole lot riskier than an anonymous sexual encounter, such as the one I might have had with him at Backstage that first night.

More thunder rumbled and the breeze turned suddenly cool as he rolled off me.

"We'd better pack up," Trey said, glancing at the sky, which was growing darker by the second.

I grabbed the champagne and flutes just as the first fat raindrops hit. Squealing at how cold it felt, I helped him with the blanket and we took off running for the SUV while the skies opened up.

It turned into a deluge in seconds. Trey had the satchel with the food over one shoulder and held the quilt above our heads, but it was already too late. Our shirts were soaked. My hair was plastered to my head. I probably had mascara lines dripping down my cheeks like some kind of Goth clown.

When a loud thunderclap sounded, I almost jumped out of my shoes and grabbed his shoulder. Trey tucked me under his arm and tugged the blanket forward. I felt the heat of his chest right through his soaked shirt and wished I could stay out in the rain forever.

How did I get so lucky as to have this man notice me?

When he hit the remote button to unlock the SUV, I made up my mind. A chance like this might never come my way again and I would regret it forever if I didn't savor the moment. I would worry about my heart later. And in the meantime, I'd just guard it extra carefully.

"Let's go to your place," I said while the blanket still covered us. Even with the noisy downpour above our heads, my softly spoken words bounced around the enclosed space.

No missing my request.

He paused outside his vehicle, standing silently beside me in the rain for a moment before he turned to look at me. His brown eyes were even darker than normal, a heated intensity shining there that I hadn't seen before. Not even when I'd slid around the dance pole half naked for his entertainment.

"Thank you." He kissed me—a quick, hard meeting of the mouths that seemed to seal the deal. "You won't regret it."

That last part was a whisper in my ear before he pulled away. Shivers chased up my spine and my nipples beaded beneath my shirt. And it had nothing to do with the rain.

Right now, I just wondered how fast his vehicle could go.

WE LAUGHED A LOT on the ride to Trey's place. That was a fun surprise since I still felt a little jittery about going with him, but we finished our picnic in the SUV and I fed him while he drove. There were sexy moments when he nipped my finger or sucked on it a little longer than necessary. But I also enjoyed myself on a whole other, non-sexual level and wondered how that was even possible.

Somehow, Trey made me more comfortable than I'd ever been with a guy.

"You live in Brentwood?" I had suddenly noticed our whereabouts even though the rain limited visibility.

"In the Mandeville Canyon area." He slowed down as we turned onto a residential street. "It's not as elaborate as my dad's spread, but I like it over here."

I tucked the leftover food back into the satchel and double-checked the cork in the champagne bottle. Yes, technically we were carrying around an illegal open container. But it'd been closed since we returned to the vehicle and how could we toss expensive champagne after just a few sips? Maybe Trey could afford that kind of decadence, but I hated the thought of wasting.

"I've seen pictures of the house you grew up in." There had been a feature on it in the office copy of *Ar-*

chitectural Digest. I was struck anew by the vast differences in our backgrounds. Even our current lifestyles. "Out on Malibu Beach, right?"

"Yes." Brow furrowed, he drummed the steering wheel and his shoulders tensed. His good mood seemed to disappear at the mention of his dad.

I promptly redirected the conversation.

"I'm in Mar Vista." And lucky to be there, even if my place was ancient. "It's my dad's house, but I'm in the process of buying it from him at a ridiculously low price. I think he wants the house to make up for the fact that he checked out on my childhood."

Leaving me alone with my hypercritical, perfectionist mom. I often wondered how he'd envisioned me dealing with her as a kid when he'd been scared of her as a grown man.

Trey slanted a sideways glance at me as he turned into the driveway of a private estate that sat far back from the road. Ivy covered the gray stone walls of a home that looked like something out of an English gardening book. Shrubs and landscaping partially hid a facade that was both romantic and charming, not at all what I'd expected from the hyper-masculine man in the driver's seat.

"My mom did the same." Trey hit a button on the dashboard and the polished wood garage door tilted upward. "I think she was so tired of battling with my old man about their marriage that she had no fight left in her when it came time to settle custody of the kids. So we got stuck with my dad."

"She was young, right?" I remembered pictures of his mother, the actress his father allegedly seduced when she was still a teen. "Maybe she thought your dad would provide better for you."

We pulled into the dark garage and the door lowered silently behind us. I suddenly became very aware of Trey and what I had signed on for by asking to go home with him. My heartbeat quickened.

"It's tough to forgive a parent who ditches you though, isn't it?" He switched off the ignition and turned toward me, giving me his full attention.

It was a heady thing.

I shrugged. "Having dealt with my mom, I can't completely blame my dad."

"That's really..." He looked off into space for a minute as if searching for the right word. "...kind. A very kind way to look at it."

The warmth in his dark gaze was almost a caress and I was tempted to lean toward him. Into him. I knew things were moving way too fast, but I didn't care. No one had ever paid attention to me the way Trey did. No one had ever looked at me with that predatory heat that made my toes curl.

"I d-d-don't know about that." Oh, God. Who knew I would stutter from being turned on? I took a deep breath and tried to stay calm. "I tried being bitter about the whole situation at first." I felt like I should own up to the truth. "But it was too exhausting and nonproductive."

"Courtney." He covered my hand with his. "I don't want you to be nervous."

He referred to my stutter. He'd heard me trip over my words and interpreted it as nervousness. I wasn't sure what to say.

"If you have any doubts—"

"I don't." I was emphatic about this much. I squeezed his hand where it covered mind. "I'm not nervous."

He didn't make a move to go inside. Or ask me about my speech issues. In the short, awkward silence that followed, I bit my lip. Then blurted out the truth.

"I have speech issues. A disorder." I was never sure how to label my condition in a way that made people understand. I hated the word "stutter." "It's dysphemia. A kind of speech disfluency," I clarified. Then, even as I realized I was babbling, I added, "A problem with my coarticulators."

"Oh." He nodded, trying to take it all in. "I didn't mean to pry—"

"No." I shook my head. "You've been very nice about it. It can intensify when I'm nervous or emotional, but right now, I'm honestly not nervous."

"Okay." He reached across his body to cup my chin in his hand. "That's good."

"Actually, it causes no end of problems for me even now, long after extensive speech therapy."

A smile hitched one side of his lips. "I'm glad you aren't nervous."

"Oh." I felt a little light-headed now that he actually touched me. My skin buzzed with new sensitivity. "I am a bit…twitchy. Anxious, I guess."

The wolf's grin he unfurled showed a row of perfect white teeth. I liked making him smile like that. It made my temperature spike and my breath quicken.

"Me too." He leaned closer, his breath warm on my lips as his nose brushed mine. "How about we go inside?"

I looked around the front seat, remembering how I'd pictured us together in it. I'd concocted elaborate fantasies after I'd left Backstage, imagining what might have happened if I'd met him in the parking lot that night. My legs straddling his thighs. The seat reclining to accommodate us.

Was it silly of me to still be thinking about that?

"How about a kiss first?" I became a different woman with Trey. Bolder. Sexier.

And very turned-on.

He shook his head slowly, his thumb brushing over my jaw in a gentle swipe. "Once I start kissing you, Courtney, I don't think I'll be able to stop."

7

HE WAS A GROWN MAN. That meant he should be able to make it into the house before he touched her. He would *not* undress her in the garage.

At least, that was the mantra he kept repeating as they stared at each other in the dim light of the enclosed space. But watching the way her T-shirt rose and fell with each breath she took, he wondered if he could deliver on those good intentions. There was something irresistible about her complete lack of awareness of her own appeal. The more he got to know her, the more amazed he was that she'd ever set foot in front of the crowd at Backstage.

"Let's go inside," she whispered, her words mesmerizing him no matter how unconventionally she spoke them—fast, slow, soft. "Lead the way."

Trey levered open the driver's side door and moved around the hood to help Courtney out. He took her hand, not trusting himself to touch any other part of her. He was doomed to be forever turned-on by the scent of motor oil since it would always remind him of this moment.

"I can't believe I invited myself here," she murmured behind him while he disarmed the security alarm on the door into the kitchen.

"Are you kidding me?" He turned to gauge her expression, needing to reassure her. "I've been sending you mental telepathy messages to come home with me ever since we first met." When she smiled, he ushered her inside and locked the door behind her, sealing them in the kitchen together. "Seriously. You're probably brainwashed from the force of all that mental manipulation."

She shook her head and laughed, her gray eyes sparkling with humor through those long bangs.

"Is that right?" She set her purse on a chair with shaky hands, her eyes darting around nervously.

"Absolutely." He pitched his keys on the black granite countertop and then forced himself to rein himself in. Take his time. He carefully placed his fingertips to her temples. "I'm sending a new message now."

"Well you're not very good at this," she teased. "I can't hear a damn thing."

"That's why it took you so long to come home with me." He tapped his forehead. "Not enough brainpower behind my coercion."

"So what's the new message?" She shifted from foot to foot, possibly uneasy.

Possibly feeling the same heat he did.

"You want me to just tell you?" He stepped out of his shoes and kicked them aside. Her smile faded as she tilted her head up to look at him.

"Yeah. Just...say what you want."

His heart rapped out a heavy beat, his whole body attuned to her. Her breath. Her heat.

"I'd like that kiss now. The one you suggested in the garage."

He saw a flash of awareness in her eyes, a darkening maybe, right before her hands landed softly on his chest.

"You can't be real," she said, shaking her head. A furrow creased her forehead. "I don't have this kind of luck."

He wondered vaguely who had stolen this sexy, smart woman's confidence and he had an urge to pummel the party responsible. But for right now, he covered her hands with his and lifted them higher, onto his shoulders, before twining them around his neck.

She stumbled into him, her body flush against his, and she let out a soft gasp at the contact.

"We're both getting lucky, Courtney. It goes both ways." He ran his hands down her arms, down her sides, the heels of his palms grazing the fullness of her breasts before they caressed her ribs through her T-shirt.

Beneath half-lowered lashes, she studied him. He was keenly aware of her body against his, from the taut peaks of her breasts to the slight shift of her hips.

"In that case..." She stretched up on her toes, her clean scent teasing his nose until he inhaled deeply. "Here you go."

Her lips brushed his, cushiony plump and slightly sweet. A spark jumped somewhere inside him, igniting a current that went through his bloodstream at lightning speed. His body responded instantly. Fully.

He wrapped his arms around her back and held her close, pinning her tight, creating delicious friction that made his pulse pound. He backed her against the kitchen island, his hand protecting her spine from the granite. Deepening the kiss, he took her mouth, claiming it for himself. Her tongue played over his, and he wanted to savor every sensual gift she was willing to give him. But right now he needed more. Much, much more.

Using all his willpower, he pulled back and stared down into her passion-filled eyes. They were blue-gray now. Her cheeks glowed pink and her lips glistened, even more bee-stung than normal. All that from his kiss.

"I don't want to rush you." Yet he really, really needed to rush her.

A wicked, knowing grin curled her lips. "Trust me, you're not."

She leaned in to finish the kiss, misunderstanding him. He gripped her shoulders, holding her steady for three long heartbeats while he battled for control of himself.

"Good. But I don't know how much finesse I've got to offer right now." Which ticked him off, because he'd like nothing better than to take his time with her. To seduce her, mind and body, so she'd come back to him for more. "Ever since that dance you did…" He shook his head, knowing it made no sense. "It's like I've been hypnotized. You're all I've thought about."

He lifted a hand to brush aside her bangs, to see her fully without a domino mask or the barrier of brunette fringe.

"I'm not Natalie," she clarified. Straightforward. Honest.

And dead wrong.

"You are the only Natalie I know." Yeah, he understood the owner of Naughty by Night went by that name. That didn't mean a damn thing to him. "It's you that's been driving me crazy night and day."

A new understanding lit her gaze. She nodded.

"I've been thinking a lot about that night, too." Her hand went for the snap on her khaki skirt. "I think I know what you need."

His brain seemed to flatline as he stared at her shimmying out of the twill cloth. She wore pale cotton panties trimmed in lace underneath it.

"What—" His mouth went dry when he tried to croak out a word. He licked his lips and made another attempt. "What are you doing?"

"A command performance. I think the resurrection of my Natalie side will help us both." She stepped out of her skirt and took him by the hand. "Come with me."

"You don't have to." His gait was as stiff as the rest of him but he followed her into the living area, a room visible from the kitchen. "But then again, if you really want to…"

She put her hands on his shoulders and gently urged him to sit on the dark leather sofa.

"I can't promise you the same level of performance without a stage," she admitted, her hands twisting the hem of her T-shirt. "But I never got around to trying out my lap dance skills, so maybe I can give you a different kind of show."

Trey couldn't hold back another second.

"I don't think I have the stamina to wait any longer." He reached for her, one hand on each of her knees to draw her down onto his thighs. Spreading her legs wide, he cupped the curve of her butt, tucking the heat of her sex against the straining erection that tested the strength of his fly. "Maybe you can dance for me some other time?"

"Mmm." Her soft gasp echoed the hiss of air between his teeth at the feel of her. Since she seemed to agree, he wasted no time hiking up her T-shirt and tossing it aside. Her full, high breasts were even more impressive in simple cotton than they'd been encased in formfitting white sequins. He raked down her bra strap with his teeth, inhaling the scent of her skin. When the delicate fabric of the cup fell away from the soft fullness of one peak, he fastened his mouth around the crest and suckled hard. His joints damn near turned to water at the taste of her combined with her delicate moan of approval.

Courtney's fingers slid under his shirt, tracing his abs and smoothing over his pecs. She was so soft and feminine, her whole body curving into him. Heat ratcheted up in the living room, the air turning sultry. His skin had a light sheen of sweat from the effort to hold back.

As she tugged his shirt higher, he broke the kiss long enough for her to pull the fabric over his head. Her gray eyes ate him up, and his muscles twitched under that hungry gaze. Something had shifted in her since that first time they'd met. It was as if that dance at Backstage had lit her up from the inside.

"Washboard abs." She smiled and traced the ridges on his stomach. "Fawn wasn't kidding."

He had no idea what she was talking about, but having her hand so close to the waistband of his jeans was practically making him delirious so maybe he hadn't heard her right.

"I need us naked," he muttered, past the point where

he could filter his thoughts. Heat throbbed through him so hard he couldn't do anything but touch her. Give her pleasure.

She was right there with him though, her hands already going to work on the buttons of his fly. He saved her the trouble, lifting her up and settling her on the sofa next to him. Her dark hair spilled around her shoulders, her finger twisting idly around one lock as she stared up at him like his personal sex goddess. He was about to shed his clothes when he remembered the only condoms in the house were upstairs.

Damn it.

"Come on." He urged her to her feet, careful not to look at her directly. The sight of her mostly undressed would only slow him down when he needed to move fast. "We have to get to my bedroom."

"That's okay—" she began.

"Condoms," he shot back, knowing that explained everything.

"Right." She was on his heels as he reached the top of the stairs, her bare breasts brushing his back until he had no choice but to stop and pin her to the nearest wall. Fill his hands with those gorgeous breasts and trace circles around the taut crests with his tongue. He teased one and then the other until she gasped for air. Only then did he let her go, leading her into the master suite.

He crossed the bedroom floor and released her hand as they neared the bed. He dug in the nightstand drawer. Finally, he had the box in his hand and then a foil packet ready. He laid it on the pillow before he turned back to her.

Gave in to the temptation to look at her.

She had her arms crossed over her breasts, a halfhearted effort to cover herself. Instead, the gesture framed the creamy lushness, making his mouth water.

"You were about to get naked, remember?" she prompted, her eyes wandering over him. Lingering at hip-level.

"Right." He slid off his jeans and boxers, freeing himself from the strangle of denim.

Not a second too soon. He pulled Courtney into his arms, slanting a kiss over her lips that quickly turned carnal. She flexed her fingers into his back, nails lightly scoring his skin as she met each thrust of his tongue. Soft mewls in the back of her throat were his undoing, the needy sound echoing everything he felt. Everything he wanted.

He unfastened the front clasp of her bra and let the material fall away completely. In the rays of late-afternoon sunlight slanting through wooden blinds, she looked like a film noir heroine, her curvy body pale and perfect.

"Please," she gasped with a quiet desperation he hadn't expected. "I don't want time to think. I just want to feel."

She sealed her soft curves against him and kissed him with an abandon he recognized from her dancing. For a split second, he wondered if he should wait. Explore that comment. But he was so far beyond waiting that the thought evaporated under the play of her mouth on his.

He hooked a finger in the lace trim of her underwear and tugged it down long, lean legs. She stepped out of the panties and quickly returned to his arms, her forehead bowed into his shoulder.

"Are you okay?" He tipped her chin up, scanning her face for clues to her mood.

She was a dizzying mix of that spunky dancer he'd seen on stage and the hesitant financial researcher with smoldering eyes. Which woman was real?

"Today is like a dream," she whispered. "I don't want it to end."

He cupped her cheek, her delicate jaw fitting in his hand. Suddenly he wanted to wrap her up and take care of her. She'd gotten under his skin so fast it scared him, but he wasn't quitting this now.

"So we'll keep on dreaming," he whispered back to her, brushing his thumb over her cheek and back down to her full lower lip. "This is just the beginning."

A half smile kicked up one side of her lips.

Lifting her off her feet, he laid her on his bed, her dark hair spilling across the white pillow. He kissed his way down from her mouth to the soft hollow of her throat, the elegant arch of her neck and shoulder.

When he reached the valley between her breasts, he licked a path south. Stalled around her navel so he could trace the indent with his tongue. She smelled so clean. Like soap and lemons, maybe.

And then the condom passed from her hand to his. But she tasted too good to stop what he was doing, her hips rocking into the bed, her head tossing from side to side the closer he got to her sex. Setting aside the condom packet, he kept on kissing her. The tops of her thighs. The slick folds between them.

Her ragged cry filled his ears as he tasted her, his tongue flicking deeper and deeper.

She orgasmed in seconds, a surprised gasp his only warning before she twisted beneath him, her whole body undulating with the force of her response. He kept on going, absorbing every shudder, her thighs shifting restlessly over his shoulders until his whole body screamed with the need to take her.

By the time he found the condom and rolled it on, her eyes were wide and unfocused.

"Wow," she murmured, her hands running over his chest as he stretched over her. "Just…wow."

"I could say the same about you. Seeing you this way?" He shook his head, at a loss for words. "You blow my mind."

Stretching over her, he nudged her thighs wider with his knee, stroked back her hair from her damp forehead, and eased inside her. Fully. Deeply.

The hot clamp of her around him was perfect, with the aftershocks of her release gently pulsing around him. She locked her arms around his neck, her gaze focused on him while her body let him know how much he pleasured her. That soft squeeze had to be the most incredible aphrodisiac ever. She was so ready for him he thought he'd lose it then and there. He had to close his eyes and wait a second.

When he'd steeled himself for the feel of her, he wrapped her in his arms and started to move, wishing he had more to give her this time. But he'd been too focused on work to date anyone, let alone have great sex.

And who the hell was he kidding? He couldn't last for her because she'd become his fantasy woman. Smart and savvy, sexy and seductive. He ground his teeth against the feelings, but then another climax hit her and he was powerless to hold back. The rocking of her hips against him, combined with the sexy moan that tore from her lips, totally undid him.

He shouted. Gripped the headboard. Lost himself in her.

Sex had never been like this. Not with anyone. Courtney was his hottest fantasy come to life. Utterly uninhibited. So totally *his*. He wasn't quite sure what had happened between them, but together they'd unleashed a kind of sexual chemistry most guys only dreamed of.

When he recovered enough to remember his own name and roll off her, he wondered if he could talk her into spending the night. He wanted her—again and again—but didn't want to be presumptuous. What if she didn't feel that same connection that he did? He didn't have much of anything to offer her except a good time. His feud with his father was an ugly mess and he refused to involve anyone else in it.

Besides, recovering his position in Hollywood was going to take all his focus over the next couple of years. Dating—and all the guesswork that came with figuring out what women wanted—was not something he had time for.

He didn't want to give her false hope for a future. When he cracked open an eye to face her, though, she had a wry smile on her face. A wicked gleam in her eyes.

"Guess you didn't need a lap dance, did you?"

"COURTNEY?"

I was just leaving dance class three days later when Natalie followed me out of the studio, the *thunk, thunk* of her crutches making it tough for her to sneak up on anyone. I paused near the juice bar at the main entrance, glad to see her. She hadn't been teaching classes since her injury—the ankle had been dislocated, not just sprained—but she still came into work to oversee things.

Today, she wore a pink sarong over her black dance leotard, her blond hair tucked into such a neat bun that she looked like the ballerina she used to be. Well, aside from the henna tattoo of a thorny vine around her neck.

"Hi!" I felt like throwing my arms around her because I was happy. Absurdly happy. I hadn't seen Trey since we'd spent the night at his place, but we'd texted and called even though we had both been busy with work. I planned to see him tonight.

Finally. His most recent text had told me to bring my domino mask. But I had an even better surprise in store for him than that.

"You look great," Natalie observed. I was still wearing my sheer costume from the Dance of the Seven Veils, which we'd practiced tonight. "Do you have a minute for a Pomegranate Power-Up?" She pointed to the juice bar. "On the house."

I resisted the urge to glance at my watch. I didn't have many close friends and my dance instructor ranked as one of the best. So I made time even though I knew Trey would be expecting me soon. He'd said he was "sending a car" for me.

As if I was one of his star clients. Ha!

"Sure." I dropped my gym bag on the floor and had a seat on one of the polished red stools in front of the hammered steel bar. "Do you need help? It must be really tough getting around—"

"I'm fine," she assured me, setting the crutches against the bar. "Have a seat."

We exchanged a few words about her injury while

Natalie fixed the vitamin-packed drinks. She sold teas and other health foods here, and there was a small gift shop across the foyer. I'd been so intimidated the first time I set foot in here. Hard to believe the dance studio was almost a second home to me now.

"So, care to share what's given you the new bounce in your step?" she asked as she passed my drink toward me in a martini glass, complete with a toothpick full of raspberries. "Everyone has commented on it. Half the girls believe it's because you nailed the job for me at Backstage. But personally, I think it must be a man."

I knew I needed to keep a lid on my relationship with Trey. I mean, if he was going to keep it secret from my employer, then I shouldn't be blabbing about it either. But I could tell Natalie a few things, right? The news was practically bursting out of me.

Ever since I'd slept with Trey my life felt...fuller, better, happier. It was like a switch flipped inside me that night and I just didn't feel the weight of my old insecurities any longer. Dancing at Backstage was part of it, too, but most of the change in me was because of Trey. I felt like I'd been living a fantasy ever since we met.

"Maybe it's a little of both," I admitted, launching into an abbreviated tale of meeting Trey, deleting the part about him being a client and omitting his famous name. I called him "Tom" just because it got awkward telling a story about someone without using a name. And technically, he was Thomas the Third in his family. I hadn't found out much about his two younger brothers, but I knew they lived up in Sonoma Valley and that one of them ran a thoroughbred farm.

"Doesn't it worry you that you met him at Backstage?" Natalie asked, coming around to my side of the bar and settling next to me on one of the stools. "Men can be really…weird about women in sexy professions. I mean, they love to head to the dance clubs, but how many of them will take an exotic dancer as a girlfriend?"

"It's not like I was stripping," I was quick to point out. "You know Backstage isn't that kind of place. Besides, Tom and I have agreed not to take this seriously."

"Right. Just be careful, okay?"

Didn't she see how happy I was? I felt compelled to elaborate.

"Natalie, my whole life turned around after you made me go on stage for you." Some hidden part of me had stepped into the spotlight and really liked it. "I'm seeing someone. I'm more confident. I'm stuttering less." Sort of. Trey didn't seem to notice my speech issues, which made me not notice them either. "I was even asked to take a face-to-face role with a new client at Sphere, so I'll be coming out of the back offices for the first time to give a small part of a roundtable presentation."

I'd also emailed Trey a few investment ideas—no big trade secrets, just some general advice geared toward his situation. I knew he'd need start-up cash for the next phase of his plan to launch an independent film studio and I'd already studied his financial profile. I would have done the same for any friend. But he'd seemed really impressed and I can't deny…that felt good.

Natalie drummed her black and silver painted nails on the bar for a moment.

"It's just such a big change, you know?" She picked up her toothpick full of berries and tugged one off with her teeth. "Call me jaded, but I always worry when I see someone do an about-face in their personality when a man is the cause."

"He's not," I said firmly, readjusting the gossamer-thin blue veil that was slipping off my shoulder. "I owe it to you for pushing me. Not just that night at Backstage, but all year." When Natalie tried to deflect the praise with a wave, I wouldn't let her. "I mean it, Nat. Dancing really helped me see that I could be good at something besides numbers. Something fun."

Part of the reason I'd chosen a finance major back in college was that it sounded like something I could do on my own. I could stay in a back room with a calculator and not have to make conversation with anyone. The plan had worked to perfection, but I guess I was getting tired of always remaining behind the scenes. Time had taught me that my decorator mother had a skewed vision of perfection, and just because I failed to meet her standards didn't mean I didn't have valuable things to say.

I was just about ready to finish my drink when the bell on the front door rang. It was too late for any more dance classes, but when Natalie started to tell the tall, strikingly lovely newcomer this, I realized I knew the woman.

"Hi, Kendra." I slid off my stool at the sight of the gorgeous dancer from Backstage, the one who'd covered herself in the awesome body art.

Too late, I remembered she wouldn't recognize me without my wig and mask. Plus, I was supposed to be Natalie that night.

"Hi." She cocked her head to one side to study me. "Do I know you?"

Awkward.

"Er. Um. I've s-seen your act," I said. "You do beautiful body paint."

"Thanks." She smiled, her long, dark hair floating around her like some goddess in a Renaissance painting. "I was looking for Natalie?"

"Yes?" Natalie stood with the help of her crutches and shook the other woman's hand. "I'm Natalie."

"Right." Kendra nodded, frowning. "Nice to see you again. I live around the corner and the owner at Backstage asked me to drop by one night and find out if you'd like a spot sooner than the fall lineup. Even if it's just a single appearance. Kind of a 'back by demand' thing." Her eyes went to Natalie's ankle and the cast around it. "But maybe you're not in dancing form with that injury?"

"I'm afraid not," she demurred, shaking her head. "But tell him I can't wait to get started in September."

"Wait," I intervened, seeing an opportunity to relive one of the most exciting nights of my life. Plus, there had been such a fantasy element to it. What would Trey think of watching me again? "Natalie, why don't you wait to decide until after you see your doctor tomorrow? She did say the cast was just precautionary."

Thankfully, my dance mentor stood a little behind me, so when I turned to look at her, I gave her a wink to let her know I had an angle.

"Um." Natalie frowned. "I don't know."

"Can she get back to you?" I asked Kendra. "Do you have a card or should she call the club directly?"

Kendra's gaze passed back and forth between us and I wondered what she thought of my forceful intervention. But I was so wound up about the possibility of dancing for Trey again in public, I wasn't thinking about any consequences.

"She can call the club." Kendra backed toward the glass door. "I'm just a messenger girl. Plus…" She hesitated, her palm on the handle. "I was curious how things went with Trey Fraser that night at the club."

"Trey." Natalie stared at me. Hard. "Fraser."

"Yeah. He asked for you after your number—" Kendra shook her head. "I get it. None of my business." She smiled, apparently not taking offense. "See you soon, Natalie."

She pushed through the door and headed off into the night. The hint of smoggy air curling through the air-conditioned studio wasn't half as oppressive as Natalie's dark glare.

"What?" I draped a light sweater over my veils to help deflect attention once I left the studio. But honestly, I was excited to dance for Trey in this costume.

"Trey Fraser. Hollywood royalty."

I didn't want to know what was so wrong with that. She'd warned me, after all. But right now, I didn't care to hear any more cautious advice.

"I didn't meet him after the show." That much was true. "My new guy's name is Tom, remember?"

"Sure." Natalie wasn't born yesterday. She folded her arms across her chest and crossed her legs. I could see where all her young dance students had signed her cast with pink magic markers.

"But thanks for the warning." I gave her a smile and headed for the door, already thinking about my private dance engagement with Trey tonight. "And I would love to do that show for you if you want me to. We could split the pay. Think about it, okay?"

I felt guilty for referencing the payout for the dance, but it was the only tool I could think of that might get her to say yes. For now, she settled for a nod.

"Maybe. Be careful, Courtney."

Her words reached me when I was halfway out the door, all my thoughts devoted to how fast I could take my veils off tonight and still give Trey the most sizzling performance ever.

8

MY PHONE CHIMED with a text as I headed through the door into the night. Pulling it out of my purse, I read the note from Trey:

The limo is parked behind the dance studio.

Although I was tempted to run down the street, I was fully aware of the costume I wore. Seven silk veils tied in a myriad of strategic places required elegance. Grace. They made me feel beautiful.

As I navigated my way through the smoggy night past a doughnut shop and an Asian food market, I still couldn't believe I was having a secret affair with the sexiest and most controversial talent agent in Los Angeles. Or that he seemed perfectly content to keep my secret from my company. Of course, I knew that alone didn't protect my job. I'd have to make sure no one saw us together. And that could be tough because Trey was a favorite of photographers. He appeared in *Variety* and on *TMZ*. His name came up in the gossip blogs, not just because he happened to be one of the city's most eligible bachelors but also because of his famous family.

He figured hiring a car for us tonight would be less

obvious than taking the SUV, which a few persistent members of the paparazzi would recognize. I had told Trey that I didn't mind driving to his place, but I'd discovered he was sort of old-fashioned about wanting to chauffeur me around.

When I turned the corner behind the Asian specialty place, I saw a pair of headlights switch on across the street. That had to be him. Fighting the urge to walk faster, I carried myself with all the dignity I could muster so that my outer veil—a floor-length red number that made me look like an elegant Indian woman—wouldn't flap up and reveal the secrets beneath it.

That was for later.

In the quiet of a street bordered by a warehouse that was closed for the night, I heard the soft electric swoosh of a car window being lowered.

"Excuse me, miss?" Trey's face was suddenly visible in the back of the black stretch limousine. His gaze ran lazily over my outfit. "I'm looking for a hot brunette who just finished a dance class around here. Have you seen her?"

My veil covered my head, but Trey knew exactly who I was. I looked around to be sure no one else was nearby as I crossed the street.

"No." I rolled my hips suggestively as I closed the distance to the car. "But if it's a dance you're looking for, I might have just the thing."

A vehicle turned the corner toward us, catching me in the headlights for a moment. Trey came out of the car in a flash, drawing me inside before he followed and closed the door behind us.

"There's not much room for dancing in here," he admitted, his eyes roving the red veil. I could tell he was searching for a way in.

He looked fantastic in a dark suit and a white shirt with no tie. His hair stood up in front a little, like he'd dragged his hand through it a few too many times during the day. I could smell a hint of his aftershave now that I sat close to him, and I thought about how nice it would be to kiss his throat down to where the top button of his shirt collar was undone.

A surge of delicious anticipation ran through me and I was already getting hot for him.

"Maybe not the kind of dancing your girlfriend does," I teased, glancing at him out of the corner of my eye. "But I know other, *erotic* dances that they don't teach in any studio."

Perhaps it was all the veils I was wearing, but I felt kind of like a genie set free from its bottle. I didn't think there was any way I'd go back to the confines of my former existence. I'd turned shameless.

"Is that so?" He tried to appear dubious, but I could see the flash of undisguised male interest in his eyes. His pupils widened. Nostrils flared.

My heartbeat sped in response. I thought about the things he'd done to me the last time we were together. The way he made me feel. My God. I'd never had orgasms like that. Ever. Just thinking about his mouth all over me made my skin tingle.

We hadn't left the curb yet, but with the tinted windows up and the partition closed between us and the driver, it hardly mattered.

"Absolutely." I slipped a hand beneath his jacket to feel the warm strength of his pecs through the thin cotton poplin of his shirt. "It's all in the movement of the hips. Would you like a demonstration?"

"I've missed you," he said, suddenly serious.

I was surprised and a little caught off guard. Maybe it was easier for me to handle a bigwig Hollywood insider if I played a role—borrowed a little of my "Natalie" attitude. My secret shadow side. My double life.

"It doesn't matter to me if we have dinner." The things I was hungry for could only be provided by this man. In private. "We can go straight back to my place and get reacquainted." I breathed the words against his neck, kissing his jaw and savoring the rough stubble of his five o'clock shadow.

I wanted to feel that abrasion over my entire body.

"No." He shook his head, all intense determination as he banged on the roof of the limo and the car shifted into gear. "I need to feed you first."

There he went, going all caveman again. But I'd be lying if I said I didn't enjoy it. The last time he'd fed me at our picnic, I didn't eat much, but I'd had a great time.

"Sure." It was late, but I'd been too excited about this date to have anything earlier so I felt a little hungry now. I traced a teasing circle on his skin around one flat male nipple. "I'll have whatever you're serving."

"Don't worry," he growled in my ear, nuzzling my neck until the veil fell aside. I shivered a little from the tingle on my skin. "We're eating somewhere private. You can dance all you want."

"Really?" I couldn't imagine myself dancing in a restaurant, but I knew there were VIP rooms for special customers.

"Really. I had something catered but I told the wait staff we'd serve ourselves."

"Oh." I tried to picture this. Did he mean at his house?

"Besides," he paused to nip my earlobe and then licked the place where his teeth had grazed. "You're going to need to fortify yourself for what I have in mind."

Pleasure tripped over my skin in a warm rush. I debated stripping off the veils right there and climbing onto his lap, but I couldn't let him talk me out of my clothes every time I saw him. He deserved the show I had in mind.

"Good thing I took my vitamin this morning." My mind went on a little journey just thinking about what might happen between us tonight.

As we headed out of downtown and toward the Pacific Palisades, I languished against the leather seat while Trey skimmed a hand beneath the first layer of my veils. Exploring.

My skin tightened at his touch, my body so ready for his.

Beneath the layers I wore the scantiest undergarments imaginable. The scrap of lace masquerading as a bra was already abrading my skin where my breasts had perked up with interest at his touch.

"How's your stamina?" He lifted his head, all business sounding even though his eyelids were heavy with arousal. His voice rough with desire.

"Pretty good since I started dancing regularly." I couldn't resist touching him. Car rides in Los Angeles could be long. "How about you?"

"I'll be honest with you. I'm on a mission." He gripped my wrist in a light hold, preventing me from traveling too far up his thigh.

"And what might that be?" I didn't mind being restrained by this man. Not even one little bit. In fact, I could picture some scenarios where being pinned beneath his powerful body would turn me inside out.

It's scary how much I trusted him, but I really liked how he treated me.

"I'm not sure if I should reveal my ultimate plan." He arched an eyebrow, teasing me.

"Does it involve lots of sex?" I asked, unable to help myself.

"It does."

I squirmed in my seat.

"Tell me," I urged him, my thigh brushing his. "Please."

He rubbed his thumb lightly over my wrist where he still held me. Was it my imagination or did my pulse beat faster just because he stroked that vein with a slow, deliberate touch?

"I'm going to make you sexually dependent," he finally revealed. "On me."

I knew he was joking, but it still sent a thrill straight to my toes. Actually, it went straight to other places first.

"I had no idea such a thing was possible." My throat went dry from this conversation.

My thighs…that was another story.

I shifted positions, wanting contact with Trey.

He released my wrist to wrap his arms around me. One around my waist and the other under my knees. He pulled me up on his lap and I lounged crossways there, one breast nestled against the hard plane of his chest. He felt hard everywhere, in fact. My breath was in short supply.

"I assure you, it's very possible." He skimmed one hand up my waist to cup my breast. There, he repeated the same idle stroke with his thumb that he'd done on my wrist a minute ago.

It felt even more potent.

A moan escaped, but before I had the chance to think about it, Trey kissed me. He was slow, methodical, thorough. By the time he stopped, I realized the car had stopped too. I could hardly see straight and wondered how I'd ever get out of the car to have dinner.

"So while you're making me sexually dependent on you, how do you make sure you don't…" How to word this? "How do you make sure you don't become sexually dependent *on me* in the process?"

It was a ridiculous question, even for the wildly flirtatious conversation we'd been having, but I had to ask. Just to see what he said.

"That's a problem I'm still working on," he admitted as he set me back on my seat so he could open the door for us.

Even through my sensual haze, I felt a happy warmth in my stomach that was completely separate from sex. This was the feeling of a teenager. That warm, silly joy that filled you up and made you want to dance.

He liked me.

TREY COULDN'T HAVE scripted a more perfect night to bring Courtney here.

They sat on the stone patio behind his mother's vacant house, an ultramodern setting overlooking a bluff high up in the Palisades. His mother rarely visited the place but maintained the property to use as a base when she travelled to the States. Trey and his brothers all had keys, but they let one another know when they needed the place. Trey had blocked out tonight to be with Courtney.

The fog had lifted enough that they could see down to the canyon below and the view didn't disappoint. The catering company had lit the outdoor fireplace, and its warmth kept the evening chill at bay. Candles had been lit under hurricane chimneys on the table. More candles hung in sconces from the pergola overhead. The steaks and side dishes had been placed in the warming drawer when they arrived. All Trey needed to do was take their plates outside and pour the drinks.

Now, as they finished a Canadian ice wine his brother Damian had recommended for their chocolate torte and strawberries, Trey watched Courtney across the built-in stone table.

"This is amazing." She lifted her glass to gesture toward the view and the house.

"My dad gave the house to mom as a parting gift when she divorced him." One of his father's classier moves.

"Don't most couples try to take things from each other in the divorce settlement?"

"I think Dad was just glad that she didn't try to take custody of the kids. He'd cheated on her and she knew it—the whole town knew it—so I think he wanted to maintain her goodwill." That wasn't the whole truth though. "Actually, I think my mom was the love of my dad's life. He just wasn't ready to settle down."

"He seems like an interesting man," Courtney noted, taking her napkin from her lap to wipe the corners of her mouth. Her manners were elegant and neat.

"Interesting?" He nodded. "I'll grant him that much, I guess."

"Does he get along with your brothers?" She unclipped some gold baubles from one of the veils around her shoulders and attached them to her fingers.

"No." He stacked their empty plates and slid them aside. "Damian and Luke don't even speak to the old man. They moved up north to follow business interests. Damian started breeding horses and Luke opened a craft beer venture with a local farmer along the Sonoma Coast."

"Sounds great. If they need any advice about diversifying and maintaining profitability—" She stopped herself midsentence. "Whoops. Sometimes it's hard not to think like a financial advisor."

Trey grinned. "I will pass along your name."

She shrugged, the flames behind her outlining her body in a warm glow. "I don't work on commission. I just happen to believe in what we do."

"What advice do you have for me on profitable diversification?" He wondered how much expertise she was hiding in the back offices of Sphere Asset Management. He hadn't learned much about her work yet, but in the texts and emails they'd exchanged during their days apart, he'd discovered she often stayed late at the office. She'd been at her desk the night before until ten.

"We probably shouldn't mix business and pleasure, right?" She toyed with the silk around her shoulders, its short fringe blowing in the evening breeze.

He wanted to hear her say "pleasure" again. And again. Almost as much as he wanted to provide her with that particular commodity.

"Now that you mention it, my thoughts are starting

to turn carnal." He'd had a bedroom suite cleaned for their arrival. He happened to know the fireplace inside was already lit, the balcony doors open to the night air on the second floor.

"It's the chocolate torte," she teased. "There's something very sexy about it. I think it's an aphrodisiac."

"I'm pretty sure it's you." He skimmed aside one of the layers of fabric that covered her upper arm.

"Wait!" She tugged the scarf back into place. "I need that."

"I think clothes are going to get in the way of what I have in mind."

"Then you must have forgotten that I wanted to give you a private show." She pushed back the cast-iron seat, the legs making a metallic scrape along the stone floor of the patio. "Do you have a sound system out here?"

She passed him her MP3 player. The screen was lit and a song cued up.

"Of course." Standing, he strode to a small panel that controlled the outdoor lights, fountains, and entertainment systems. "I could bring down a full-size movie screen if you care to watch a film out here."

He connected her device to the speakers and pressed Play.

"You Hollywood types," she scoffed, taking her place in the center of a small courtyard surrounded by flowering bushes. "So over-the-top."

The music began then, a slow, seductive flute that made him think of those cartoons where a snake charmer made a cobra dance. Or maybe it was Courtney's moves that brought that image to mind. She undulated in a smooth wave, her body as sinuous as a gymnast's.

He stalked closer. Even though he could see in the firelight—especially with all the candles burning—he wanted a front row seat for this. He'd almost forgotten how different she was when she danced. She seemed to become someone else as she spun and leaped, pulling off a veil and tossing it into the bushes.

Someone utterly confident. Outgoing.

Smoldering.

He held her gaze while she twirled out of another layer. A yellow veil drifted to the floor as her music swelled with horns and strings. She picked up her pace, high kicking in a circle. Shimmying out of a yellow piece of silk that acted as a skirt. There was another skirt beneath this one. Maybe even two. He squinted to see through the remaining veils but couldn't.

She rang the little bells she'd put on her fingers earlier, the sound blending seamlessly with the music coming through the speakers all around them. She arched into a partial backbend and plucked off a gold-colored veil that had been tied around her neck like a cape. He never would have guessed she wore so many layers. The fine silk clung to her body but didn't hide her curves.

She approached one of the posts of the pergola and spun around it like she would a dancer's pole. It was too thick for her to climb, but the gesture reminded him of her moves that first night he'd seen her. She met his eyes for a moment and he guessed she was thinking about that electrifying experience too.

His body hungered for hers.

Another layer of skirt came off in a swoosh of emerald material that ended up around his neck as she danced past him. Her skirt must have brushed a patch of primrose flowers near the edge of the patio because

the scent wafted toward him. He could see through the
veils that remained on her body. A sheer pink number
was knotted above her breasts, the fabric parting to
reveal her midriff and a gold chain around her waist.

A cream-colored swath of silk hugged her hips, a
slit on either side of her lean, toned thighs. The candle-
light made her skin glow, the sconces swaying slightly
in the breeze.

The music slowed, returning to a lone flute.

Courtney's chest rose and fell quickly as she looked
up at him through dark lashes. It took all his willpower
not to reach for her. Wrap his hands around her hips and
draw her closer. His fingers itched to remove those last
two veils himself. To free the loose knots and worship
her beautiful body with his mouth and hands.

She lifted her chin, tossing her bangs out of her eyes.
And in one quick movement she yanked off the top
veil. Then the bottom. The music faded to silence as
she stood before him in the tiniest bra and panty set
imaginable. Three triangles of cream colored lace that
had been hidden beneath her costume.

"No applause?" she asked finally, not moving as they
stared at one another through a fog of heat and longing.

At least, that's what was happening for him. Steam
rolled off him in waves.

But she deserved more than just his caveman lust.
Trey tried to make his brain synch up with his mouth
to give her the praise her dance warranted.

"I've studied film my whole life. Color, movement,
sound." He clutched at the veil that still rested over his
shoulder, the green silk a poor substitute for her soft
skin. "But I've never witnessed a scene that engaged

all my senses the way you just did, Courtney. I'm completely…captivated."

Even as he said it, he realized he may have revealed more than he'd intended. But hell. She stood there all but naked after sharing something really special with him. She'd revealed something too.

"W-wow." She tilted her head, almost as if she was trying to deflect the praise. "I would have been happy with a…" She took a deep breath that he recognized was an effort to control her speech. "With a kiss."

"Don't accept anything less than you deserve," he bit out with a fierceness he felt to his toes. "Ever."

9

I WAS SHAKING, and not from the temperature outside.

Cool air off the Pacific brushed past my exposed flesh, the touch of moisture turning to steam as it neared my heated skin. So I definitely wasn't cold. The shaking was a direct result of Trey's words. And the look in his eyes.

Holy. Cow. The look in his eyes.

Could I be falling for him? I realized for the first time what an apt metaphor that was—falling. Because this feeling was exactly like being at that gut-sucking precipice of a big roller coaster and knowing it'd be a scary trip down. Still, I couldn't get off the ride now. I'd signed on for this, hadn't I?

Then his hands were on me and I hit the downward slide. Sensations roared through me until my nerve endings ran the show. Trey's mouth warm on mine, his tongue sliding along the seam of my lips in an erotic plea. My fingers clutching his jacket lapels in an effort to hold myself up since my knees had turned liquid beneath me.

I knew I'd be mostly naked at the end of my dance,

but I hadn't known I'd feel *this* naked. Being up close to him while he remained dressed and I was unclothed gave me a hot, sexy feeling. I rocked my hips from one side to the other, liking the slight friction of his wool gabardine against my bare skin. And, of course, I was rewarded by the hard strain of what lay beneath his fly.

"We're going inside," he growled in a tone that implied I should not argue.

As if.

He whipped off his suit jacket before I could blink and wrapped it around my shoulders. Confused, I realized that he looked behind him as he nudged me out from under the sheltered pergola. There were no houses across the bluffs and no neighbors to speak of, since we were on a cliff that jutted way out over the canyon. But with lights visible down below us, maybe he was worried someone would see me as we hurried toward the house.

How considerate was that?

As soon as I thought it, I had a flash of worry. *What if he just doesn't want to be seen with me?* But I knew that was the old, insecure Courtney. That kind of thinking remained my go-to reflex—had been all my life— so it was tough to ignore. Yet I *would* ignore it. Nothing was going to rob me of this night with Trey. He did more than *want* me.

He cared about me.

I could feel it in his touch. See it in his eyes.

When we neared the boxy, modern home built on four different levels, some of the windows were lit from within and I could see lots of light wood and chrome. Heavy pendant lamps looked like they came straight out of a manufacturing plant. They were sleek and industrial-looking, as were the rubberized staircases and stainless-steel countertops in the kitchen. But we didn't head toward the main section of the house.

Trey guided us around a corner to another patio surrounded by gardenia trees. He slid aside the screen so we could enter an open French door into a large bedroom suite. A fire blazed behind a black cage screen, open on both sides. A sleek stone hearth wrapped around it where it jutted into the room. A gray spread covered the low king-size bed, and there was a painting of a red poppy on one wall, but that was the only color against the neutral walls and light bamboo floor.

It felt as if I'd walked into a dream. This empty, gorgeous home perched high on top of a bluff was a place apart from reality, a place I didn't belong. But then, all my time with Trey felt that way. He was my alternate reality. Being with him brought out some latent sensual animal in me and I loved the feeling. That was probably why I'd tried dancing again tonight, to recreate the magic of that first time.

Trey flicked the suit jacket off my shoulders with the barest nudge of his hand. His greedy gaze roamed all over me and I forgot to feel anything but the joy of being with him. I wouldn't back down from this magical chemistry. I wouldn't cheat myself of Trey Fraser.

So I wound my arms around his neck and kissed him like there was no tomorrow.

I lost myself in that kiss. In him. I melted into him, burrowing between shirt buttons and tunneling into his sleeves to touch his hot skin. He couldn't undress fast enough for me. Maybe I'd used up all my patience in my own striptease.

His shirt and jacket hit the bamboo floor in a flash.

His belt slid free and so did the zipper of his pants. I backed him over to the bed, toeing off his socks even as I tugged down his boxers. Then his mouth fastened on my breast and I couldn't focus on anything else. I felt the light teasing of his tongue around the crest and then he drew me between his lips and flicked at the taut nipple.

It was almost as if he'd touched me between my thighs, because a warm heat vibrated there, too. Urgent now, I reached between my breasts to unfasten the bra already sliding down my rib cage.

I heard a low growl in Trey's throat, a predatory rumble at odds with his usual urbane demeanor. I knew he must be seriously on edge too and that was a heady turn-on by itself. I felt privileged to see him like this— stripped of the famous public persona. With me, he was simply Trey. My extraordinary lover.

He lifted me off my feet and carried me to the bed, eyeing me with a dark, hungry look. My toes curled as I gazed up at him in the firelight, his gorgeous body unveiled. The bed beneath me was so soft, the man hovering over me so rock hard. I couldn't wait to feel him on top of me, his strength against my curves. With Trey, there was no awkwardness. I felt feminine. Womanly. Sexual.

And oh, God, did I want him.

He took his time touching every part of me with a thorough attention I never dreamed any man would have the patience for. His hands smoothed and circled, massaging any lingering tension away. Warm kisses to my breasts mingled with the skillful kneading of his fingers along my shoulders, down my arms until we clasped hands. Passionate and tender at the same time.

Maybe it was selfish, but I lost myself in the bliss of his undivided devotion to me, to my pleasure.

He found erogenous zones in places I would have never guessed anyone would look, stroking with deft fingers until I hung on the brink of orgasm. Who would have thought the arch of the foot could be so incredibly sensitive? But when he pressed his thumb there, all the while kissing his way up the inside of my calf, I melted. Just totally melted.

By the time he covered me and slid deep inside, I flew apart in seconds.

I saw stars behind my closed eyes—tiny pinpricks of light that burst into bright flashes as I came over and over again. I think I'd been holding back so long that it was impossible to wait another second when I felt him move thick and sure inside me. I clutched his shoulders, my fingers flexing deep in his skin to hold him tight to me.

My hips rolled against his, wringing every last bit of pleasure from the aftershocks, and yes, I enjoyed the hell out of the way my body moving against his made him growl with approval. The way his hot breaths grew faster against my neck as I—yes, stuttering, quiet Courtney—drove this magnificent man absolutely crazy with desire.

God, yes.

"Courtney." He whispered my name in my ear right before he found his own release, the word filled with a tenderness I hadn't expected after the way we'd teased and tempted each other all evening.

He anchored my body to his, sealing us together for long moments where we shared the same breath. The same heartbeat.

In the aftermath, I couldn't move. Languid pleasure made my limbs heavy and I sprawled beneath him, gasping. I breathed in the scent of him, of us, and absorbed the feel of the warm, gorgeous man beside me.

I told myself not to think about the fact that I was falling for him. That I'd started that downward spiral even before this incredible encounter. I cautioned myself not to attach too much meaning to decadent, heady sex. Just because I had rocked his world on a physical level didn't mean he had deep feelings for me or long term plans, right? I vowed not to obsess about what this night together meant.

I was here to enjoy this time with him for however long it lasted. I could not lose my heart to a man from such a vastly different world, a man whose life was lived in the public eye. Still, even as I tried not to think about the future, a small part of me was already envisioning lazy Sunday mornings spent in his arms. Scintillating nights where we drove each other to frenzied highs…

To squelch the fierce want rising up inside of me, I gathered up my pride and independence and boldly inched away from him. Not enough to be a rebuff, just enough to cool the still-heated air between us. I turned on my side to stare at him, his profile as compelling as the rest of him. I tucked both my hands beneath the folded pillow so I wouldn't be tempted to reach out and touch him.

"Can you stay?" he asked, turning on his side, too. "I didn't think to ask you before, I was just so glad to finally see you again." He stroked a hand over my hair, making me wonder what I looked like.

A train wreck, probably.

But his words suggested he didn't find me unappealing. At all. Had I mentioned that I felt like a sex goddess with those good endorphins flowing through me? This sensation could become addictive.

"I hitched a ride here," I reminded him, grateful to put the ball in his court on the sticky question of whether or not to spend the night. "So it's up to you when you want to send me packing."

The way his brow furrowed made me think I'd been too flip about it.

But then, his expression eased.

"Guess I'll hold you hostage a while longer, then." He smoothed a strand of my hair between his thumb and forefinger. "It took too long for me to see you this week as it was. Your work must keep you busy."

We'd gone three days without seeing each other. I was glad to know I wasn't the only one who'd been eager after that initial date.

"I've been given new responsibilities." Given the way I wanted to curl up against his chest and forget about the world, I figured it would be a good idea to talk about my work. Better than admitting how crazy I was about him.

"Is that a good thing?" Still holding that lock of hair captive, he used the ends like a paintbrush, twirling them around my shoulder.

I had to consider his question for a moment. Partly because what he was doing felt really good. And partly because I wasn't sure how I felt about new work without an increase in my paycheck.

"It's exciting. I've been at Sphere for almost three years, doing the same job. Thinking about a new facet of the company will be interesting." I explained to him about my previous behind-the-scenes role and my impending presentation to a client. "It's all the more flattering for me because of my speech issues."

"That doesn't make you nervous?"

"A little. But after dancing at Backstage, I figure I can handle a few new risks." My eyes had been opened that night. I wasn't going back to my passive, take-what-I-can-get approach to life.

"Good for you." He released my hair, and I shivered at the way it slithered down my arm and slid across my back to rest on the pillow behind me. "Have you ever considered acting lessons?"

This surprised a laugh out of me.

"Excuse me? I'm a numbers person, not a Hollywood wannabe."

"Sometimes acting classes can help people who are nervous in front of an audience. They can lessen your nerves and help you relax."

"Really?" I tried to picture myself in the Actor's Studio and failed. "Tough enough standing up in front of ten people in my own office. I don't think I could handle a big class in front of strangers."

"Just a thought." He shrugged before turning over to grab a remote that turned the gas fireplace down to a lower setting. The room grew darker.

"How about you? You've been pretty busy this week yourself. How's your work going?"

Trey tugged the sheet over us, reaching behind me to be sure I was fully tucked in. My heart squeezed inside my chest at his sweetness. He drew me closer so that he cradled my head on his biceps.

"I've got almost all of my clients working now. That guy I dragged to the show at Backstage—Eric Reims?

He's going to snag a big part next week. I can feel it in my gut."

"Really?" I tried to recall the actor's face, but my memories of that night centered around the man in bed next to me.

"Yeah. The casting department on the film is nuts for him and the director just got back to me that he wants another meeting." Trey nodded with satisfaction, as if that was all the proof he needed. "Once Eric snags this, I just have two teenagers that I need to find work for."

"So your entire talent agency represents the actors you originally hired for that film your father axed?" I'd read extensively about Trey's business dealings when I'd prepared Sphere's reports for Fawn. I knew the basics about the blowup with his dad.

"Plus a few others I've met since then. But they're all working now except for those last two kids. Once I find them solid jobs I can move on."

A cool breeze blew through the open French doors, making the flames in the fireplace waver and pop.

"And open the film company you don't want anyone to know about." I couldn't resist brushing my cheek along the warm skin of his inner arm. Amazing that hard muscle could make such an enticing pillow.

"Yes." He tensed and I peered up at him to see his expression. "Although now I'm having second thoughts about what my first project should be, since my father purchased the rights to a story similar to the one I wanted to make—"

He stopped himself from whatever he'd been about to say, his jaw clenched tight.

I tried another approach. "Why do you think he does stuff like that? I told you that my mom has al-

ways been tough on me too. But she's never actively…
thwarted me."

A perfectionist by nature, my mother had always
been disappointed in what she perceived as my perpetual flaws. The stuttering was only one example. My
lack of ambition, my wardrobe, my long bangs…there
were plenty of things she found not to like. But while
she complained about those faults, she didn't want to
see me fail.

Odd that anyone's parent would.

TREY TOOK HIS time answering. He wasn't sure how
much to share, for one thing. He was also surprised
that she'd asked him such a question.

Most people wanted to know more about his father,
the wealthy independent filmmaker who'd made his
mark on the industry after being raised by foster parents
in a humble part of Oakland. Thomas Fraser was an
American legend—a real-life embodiment of the American dream. It was a theme he'd revisited plenty of times
in his films, too. His dad was charismatic and loved
by the media, no matter that he'd been a hard parent.

"It has to do with him being a self-made man." He'd
heard plenty about that growing up. "He's afraid that
if he doesn't challenge his kids, we'll be soft. He never
believed in allowances when we were young, and he
doesn't believe in giving us anything now that we're
grown."

Not even a credit on a film Trey worked hard on. Not
even an acknowledgement of a job well done.

He shifted on the bed to lie on his back, drawing
Courtney with him. She propped her elbow on his chest
and rested her head in her hand. Her dark hair pooled

on his skin, spilling onto his hip and arousing awareness in spite of the fact he should be sated. For now, at
least. But even talk of his dad couldn't dim the after-
buzz of the greatest damn sex of his life.

"Maybe he thinks he's helping. Or maybe he's followed that behavior pattern so long that he doesn't
know how to relate to you any other way." She gave
him a sheepish grin. "Then again, that could be my
own years of therapy talking."

He hated the idea that Courtney's mother had driven
her to those lengths, but she seemed comfortable with
that part of her past. Far more comfortable than he felt
about his dad.

"I'd be surprised if there was any way my father
could view his actions as helpful."

"People can rationalize a whole lot of things. You're
a filmmaker of sorts. You ought to know we are each
the hero in our own dramas, right?"

He nodded, intrigued by this woman. What had
started out as strong physical attraction became more
interesting by the moment.

"So your dad probably thinks you need him to succeed."

Trey found that hard to believe, and yet…it sure as
hell was a kinder explanation for his father's actions
than he'd ever credited the old man with.

"Maybe. But I tend to think he's just obsessively
competitive." Trey sighed and folded the pillow under
his head so he could see her better. "I know he believes
our mom spoiled us—which was impossible since we
didn't see her more than a few weeks a year—and that
it's a father's job to be tough on his sons."

"Wonder how he would have been with a daughter."

She traced idle circles on his skin and he thought about halting this conversation with a kiss.

And more.

"Difficult to say." Although he guessed it would have been more of the same. Refusal to praise any accomplishment. Continually pushing her to strive harder in life.

"Your brothers aren't married?"

He stroked her hair. The warm skin of her shoulder.

"No." He couldn't picture either of his siblings settling down. They enjoyed the bachelor thing too much.

And after this night with Courtney, Trey was strongly reminded why he needed to make some time in his life for women too. More specifically, time for Courtney. She was…amazing. Memories of her dancing for him, spinning around the patio in sheer veils, would be etched into his brain forever.

"Did you ever come close?" Her throaty whisper was another kind of touch altogether, the sound revving him up again. Already.

"What?" He'd lost the thread of the conversation in vivid images of how they could spend the rest of this night together.

"M-marriage," she clarified, clearing her throat as she stumbled over the word just a little. "Has anyone ever tempted you?"

He wished like hell he'd kissed her before the talk turned in this direction. He was pretty sure he couldn't get the "M" word smoothly out of his mouth, either.

"Once." He definitely didn't want to discuss this. Crossing his fingers, he tried flipping the question around. "How about you?"

She frowned, lowering her lashes to hide her pretty

eyes from him. Was she hurt that he hadn't shared anything about Heather? He was already regretting the abrupt conversational turnabout. No matter that he'd wanted to keep things uncomplicated between them, he owed her more than a terse one-word answer after what they'd shared.

But then Courtney met his gaze and smiled.

"Me? Are you kidding?" She flopped back onto the bed beside him and wrapped an arm around his waist. "Definitely not the marrying kind."

10

LIES. LIES. ALL LIES.

I crept through the house the next morning in search of coffee, wondering how I could have concocted such a bald-face fabrication about not being the marrying kind. What had happened to me since I met Trey that I was behaving like a completely different person?

The early morning sun spilled into the kitchen from a panel of high windows with eastern exposure. A sleek sideboard near the breakfast nook contained all the coffee essentials in plain sight, from a state-of-the-art java maker to a sugar container.

I'd already showered and dressed in the T-shirt and shorts Trey had given me in the middle of the night when we'd raided the kitchen for a snack. We'd fed each other Lucky Charms and tried to turn the shapes into a hieroglyphic-style language. I'd had fun spelling out naughty things on his naked abs right before I… Well, suffice it to say, I'd tried to pay him back for the immense amount of pleasure he'd given me in bed.

Judging by his reaction, I think I accomplished the task fairly well.

Now, waiting for the coffee to brew, I padded bare-foot around the huge kitchen. Trey had chosen this place for us last night because of the private patio and the views.

I had to admit, the other half lived well.

"Sneaking out on me already?" Trey's voice startled me as he entered the kitchen.

Whirling around from where I'd been daydreaming at the picturesque window, I took in his shirtless appearance. He did have washboard abs. Fawn had been one hundred percent correct.

"I might have if you didn't have any coffee," I teased, pointing to the pot, where a curlicue of steam drifted out the top. "But I'm a prisoner of caffeine. Now you won't get me out of here until that cup is ready."

"Excellent news." Trey stalked closer, a pair of old jeans riding low on lean hips.

It was all I could do not to lick my lips.

"Mmm." Distracted, I tried to remember the Lucky Charms code for, "Let's get naked."

"Can I make an observation?" He pulled two mugs out of a cupboard overhead and set them on the counter.

Something in his tone triggered a bit of wariness. He sounded more serious this morning. That put me on edge because I wasn't ready for this to end. Hadn't we enjoyed an amazing time together?

Hadn't I worked hard to keep things uncomplicated?

"Umm, sure." I smiled until my cheeks hurt.

"You don't stutter around me. Especially not lately."

"Oh. Right." I hadn't been expecting that. I relaxed a little, taking a seat on the bench at a built-in breakfast nook. I drummed my fingers on the French country table.

"Have you noticed?" He pulled out the carafe and filled the mugs.

"Actually, I don't stutter much around people I'm comfortable with these days." Although, just thinking about my stutter made my tongue feel a little sticky, like it was going to trip over itself any second. I forced myself to speak slower. "It has more to do with new situations or new people—if I feel any pressure or worry."

He frowned. "So back when we first met…I was making you nervous?"

I remembered sort of fibbing about that to him, saying I hadn't been nervous. But what did it matter now?

"I…" I took a deep breath as he put the sugar bowl and a spoon in front of me. "I liked you."

My cheeks heated and I felt ridiculous. As if it was big news that I'd been crushing on him.

"You say that in the past tense." He sat across from me and stirred sugar into his coffee. "What's changed?"

I felt as if I was missing something in this conversation. What was he driving at?

"I guess I feel more comfortable around you now that—" How did I put this? "I mean, it seems you kinda like me, too, if last night is any indication."

He put down his spoon with a laugh.

"No secret there." He studied me with his golden brown eyes as if I was a puzzle to solve. "What I guess I'm getting at is this—if you can find ways to make yourself more comfortable in your job, why can't you take over the role that Fawn has at Sphere?"

I nearly choked on my first sip.

Coughing, I had to put the cup down. Yes, this feminine grace of mine was one of many reasons why I didn't have Fawn's job.

"Trey, I'm not an account rep. I barely got through my interview at Sphere, I was tripping over my words so much." It was mortifying to remember. "I could never meet with new people all the time and sell them our services."

"So leave the sales to someone else." He covered my hand with his, his olive skin a contrast with my pale fingers. "But your financial advice is genius. That email you sent me outlining ways to ensure I have start-up cash for the next phase of my business model was brilliant. You should be a highly valued member of that staff."

He spoke with such sincerity that I almost bought into it. But then I remembered that the "me" Trey knew was a hybrid Courtney/Natalie mix. A bolder version of myself. An illusion I'd cooked up on a stage. I didn't bring that same confidence into the rest of my life.

I took a slow sip of coffee as I thought about how to frame my reply.

"I'm content with my job," I said finally. "Although I'm flattered you thought my advice was useful, I didn't really go into the depth necessary—"

"But you could have," he pressed. "If I wanted to explore those options for diversifying my investments, you could have pointed me toward exactly what I need, couldn't you?"

"Maybe." Actually, I had a hard time being modest about this one area of my life. I was excellent at my job. I studied financial news closer than most people in this town read *Variety*. It made sense to me.

"I want you in charge of my account at Sphere."

"Oh, no." I rose from the table and paced in front of the sideboard. "That's a bad idea."

"Why? I want my money working for me, and you know how to make that happen."

"So does Fawn," I reminded him. Plus, Fawn would pass along my recommendations anyhow. It would be just the same as working with me, only she was a more articulate, elegant face for the business.

"I like you better," he insisted stubbornly.

Nervousness set off every one of my panic buttons as I thought about how badly this could go. Why had I sent him that email? If I'd just let him figure out his finances on his own, none of this would have happened and we'd be taking a long, luxurious shower together right now. Or maybe chasing each other around the huge hot tub I'd spotted in a corner of the yard last night.

"What happens when we—that is, what if things don't work out between us personally?" I didn't want to think about that, but I had to be realistic.

Trey Fraser was a fantasy man.

He rose from the table, capturing my shoulders between broad hands.

"We're grown-ups," he assured me. "I'm not going to become some petty jerk if you decide you don't want to see me anymore."

Me? Not want to see *him?*

Clearly, he was just being polite.

"Even if I wanted to take over your account," I shook my head, approaching the problem from another angle, "I couldn't. It's not my job."

"If a client specifically requests you, Courtney, it will be your job." He kissed my cheek and some of my worries melted a little. "All I want to know is this—do you have any objections to working with me?"

Now was my chance to shut down this crazy line of

thinking. It would only stir problems at work. But selfishly, I liked the idea that I might still see him, even after we weren't involved romantically.

And the pride in my professional abilities that I usually stifled was definitely making noise now. I knew I could put his money to work more effectively for him.

"Of course I won't object," I conceded. "I'll do whatever I can to help you get that film studio off the ground."

A WEEK LATER, Trey had to admit that Courtney had more than lived up to her word.

He waited for her in the conference room at Sphere, reading over the thick packet of proposed investments she'd generated for him. He'd made the call requesting her to personally oversee his accounts the same day she'd agreed to it, and by the next day, she'd been knee-deep in research for him.

So much so, in fact, he hadn't seen her in person since they'd spent the night together. Guilt nipped at him now for putting her in a position where she felt she had to prove something to him, her boss and her coworkers. Still, as he read through her comprehensive suggestions for everything from selling his European property to renting out a yacht he rarely used, he knew that he'd made a smart business decision by insisting on her as his account rep.

Yet what had he done to their fledgling personal relationship? He'd put them on an uneven footing by becoming her personal client. He'd practically ensured she'd be too busy to go out with him. For all he knew, maybe he'd sabotaged something really special between them for the sake of one-upping his father. But he'd put together a profile of her short-term returns on investment based on some examples she'd outlined in her suggestions for his business, and he'd been floored to think how well she'd done for Sphere clients.

All while the account reps took the majority of the credit.

"I'm sorry to keep you waiting, Trey." Courtney breezed into the conference room a moment later, her white tennis shoes at odds with a deep rose-colored suit that flattered her dark hair. "I took my lunch hour at the dance studio and traffic was crazy getting back here."

He'd be willing to bet she had no idea she still wore her sneakers. The quirky clothes that would have made him smile a week ago made him feel like crap now, since she'd had to rush on his account.

That wasn't the only thing he noticed. Her hair was pulled back in a low ponytail that rested on one shoulder, her bangs swept to one side. One eye was still partially covered in the long fringe, but the other met his gaze directly.

"It's okay." He got to his feet to greet her, fighting the urge to pull her into his arms. He looked over his shoulder at the open conference room door and lowered his voice. "I'd kiss you, but I'm guessing you'd prefer I don't."

Her cheeks flushed a pink that matched her jacket.

"Ah. Yes. But a rain check would be welcome."

"Is anyone else joining us?" He eyed the door again. "If it's just us, I could take you out for a meal since you skipped your lunch."

"I'd better not, but thank you." She strode back to the door and closed it, sealing them in the privacy of mahogany wainscoting and heavy bookshelves full of imposing tomes. "Piles of work to do at the office."

"I'm sorry if this was too much, Courtney—"

"No!" She rushed to reassure him, taking the seat beside him so he caught a whiff of her fresh, green scent. "Not at all. This new responsibility has been an eye-opening experience for me. It's been busy, but great."

"Honestly?"

"Yes." She smiled, her hand dropping onto his arm as she shifted closer. "I was worried at first about how everyone at the office would react, but they seem happy for me. You sort of forced me to live up to my potential around here, and that's been a good thing."

"Good, except that I haven't gotten to see you alone all week." He didn't want to pressure her more, but damn it, she was in his head all the time lately. "Let me take you out tomorrow night."

"I can't." Her fingers slid away from his arm.

The knot of disappointment in his chest surprised him. He hadn't planned on getting so close to her so fast. Especially when his professional life had to come first until he got out of his father's shadow for good.

"Some other time then," he started.

"Unless you want to come to Backstage for my show," she blurted.

"What?" He hoped he'd misheard.

"After the success of my first show, they want me to return for a repeat performance." Her gray eyes sparkled with mischief.

"I thought that first night was a fluke." He tried to recall what she'd told him about dancing at the club. "You said you were filling in for your friend because she was hurt."

Just thinking about her half naked on that stage, with a room full of greedy male eyes on her, made him tense all over.

"I was." She leaned closer as if she was afraid someone in the hall could hear her already quiet voice. "But the show was such a hit they offered Natalie Night a one-time slot before her regular appearances begin this fall."

"And you took it?" He hadn't realized he'd spoken the thought aloud until she answered.

"I haven't accepted yet, but I plan to." Maybe his relief showed on his face because she rushed to continue. "You have no idea how that first show turned my life around. I braved an audience when I've always been incredibly insecure. I met you. I got a job for my friend." She ticked off the points on her fingers, her simple gold bangles tinkling softly with the movement. "I'm being trusted with more work responsibilities when I never would have guessed I'd operate on this level."

"But the risks are greater for your job now, right? I thought you needed to be careful no one recognizes you or you could have problems at work." He figured reminding her of the stakes was better than sounding like an autocratic, possessive jerk and telling her flat-out not to perform.

Because, damn, he did not want her anywhere near that stage again.

Her lips flattened into a hard line. "I suppose you're right. I just thought it would help Natalie. And, of course, let me relive an exciting moment."

Trey shoved aside the investment proposal on the conference table and took her hands in his.

"At the risk of sounding arrogant, I'd like to think

it wouldn't be half as exciting without me." His heart slugged a heavy rhythm in his chest while he waited, hoping like hell she'd agree.

She slanted him a smoky look. "That's not arrogance. That's a fact."

"Well, then." His hands itched to touch her. To skim over her curves and slide under the hem of her jacket to feel what she wore beneath. "I don't think you can make your engagement because I don't plan to be at Backstage tomorrow night."

"No?" She arched a brow, undressing him with her eyes. "Where will you be?"

"I'm going to be tied up with a brainy brunette—"

"Tied up, you say?" She leaned closer, breathing him in.

"A figure of speech." He skimmed a finger along her knee under the table.

"Not if I make it a reality."

The conference door swung wide without warning. Trey settled back in his chair slowly, but he noticed Courtney sprang from him like she'd been burned. Her cheeks were an even brighter pink than before.

The receptionist backed into the room, her attention focused on a silver tray with a teapot, teacups and bottles of water.

"Th-thank you, Star." Courtney shuffled some papers on the table.

"Sure." Star peered their way as she set the tray on a credenza against the far wall. "Sorry I didn't get the refreshments here earlier."

"No problem. Thanks," Courtney repeated. Her hands shook slightly, the papers she held quivering with the motion.

Seized with the urge to cover her fingers with his, Trey was reminded of the awkward woman he'd first met in this room. Courtney's confidence really had come a long way in a short time. What if he was depriving her of a chance to solidify that self-esteem by discouraging her from dancing at Backstage?

When her coworker departed, Courtney's elbows hit the table, her shoulders slumping forward.

"Who am I kidding?" she asked herself more than him as she covered her eyes with her hands. "This is insane."

"What is?" He leaned forward, too, gently tugging away one arm so he could see her better. "I'd say it's insane that you've waited so long to claim your rightful place here. You have too much to offer to take a backseat."

She pried open one eye, still hiding the other.

"I never stutter in front of Star. She must have known something was up."

"She probably thought you were nervous during one of your first client meetings, which would only be natural."

After a long moment, she nodded. "Maybe."

"Would it really help you to dance again?" He didn't want to deny her something that had been…therapeutic. Her pole-dancing half dressed in front of salivating guys might give him nightmares, but if it helped Courtney work out some of her anxieties, he could grit his teeth through one more performance.

He hoped.

"I don't know." Her voice was thin. Her face pale. "I definitely can't afford to lose this job. You're right about that much."

"But you *want* to dance," he clarified, trying to get to the heart of the matter.

She dropped her other arm and folded her hands on the table. Looking at him full-on, she said, "Only if you're there."

A bolt of heat shot through him at the thought. He might hate the idea of anyone else seeing her. But he couldn't deny the appeal of Courtney performing for him alone.

"I wouldn't miss it."

11

BEING LESS NERVOUS apparently made me *more* nervous.

I realized this fundamental truth as I compulsively adjusted and readjusted the strap on the back of my domino mask while I sat at the mirrored makeup table in the Backstage dressing room.

Not many of the other dancers had arrived yet since I would be on stage first, but wigs, headdresses, hot rollers and hair dryers were strewn from one end of the room-length counter to the other. The bass line from a sultry soul song thumped through the floor and vibrated in my feet while one of the white lights surrounding my mirror flickered on and off with an electric buzz. The two girls that went on after me were circulating in the crowd, leaving me alone for now.

And somehow, feeling more confident earlier that evening had caused a weird mood tailspin. I began wondering why I wasn't nervous, ultimately deciding I couldn't do a good show unless I was completely overwrought, since that was how I'd gone out onto the stage the first time I'd performed in public.

So I went about the business of getting completely

spun-up. Never a tough assignment for me. I just hoped Trey was out there in the crowd. Maybe seeing him would distract me from this mental muddle, the way it had last time.

Inside my makeup bag, I heard my cell phone buzz. I still had ten or fifteen minutes before my entrance, so I retrieved the incoming text. An update on some activity in the Asian markets, but nothing earth-shattering. To calm my nerves, I scrolled through the rest of my messages from the last couple of hours. An unidentified number caught my eye.

It was from Star. Strange, since she rarely texted me.

"The woman who taught dance moves at my bachelorette party is performing at Backstage tonight! I'm going with Lisa from HR to cheer her on if anyone wants to join us..."

Oh. Crap.

The message had been sent to...I scrolled back to the top...six other women besides me. Three of them worked at Sphere. Star must have gotten some kind of update that Natalie Night had a show this evening and decided to make it a girls' night out. That message had been sent over an hour ago.

While I contended with a new wave of panic, my phone buzzed again.

"I'm by the bar! Where R U?"

It must be a text to the group. The kicker on this one? It had been sent by Fawn Barrows.

Natalie had told me this was a bad idea. Trey had discouraged me from doing this, too. Yet I had persisted and ultimately prevailed. And now I was going to go down in flames in spectacular fashion. That is, if my sweating palms didn't cause me to slide off the pole and break my neck first. Actually, that would be preferable to being unmasked by Fawn Barrows, Ms. Perfect.

"Ms. Night?" The head bouncer stuck his head in the door without knocking, his usual M.O., I recalled. "Are you ready?"

My heart rate sped. Hyperventilation loomed as a distinct possibility. I nodded, since there was no way I'd be able to utter a coherent sentence.

What the hell had I been thinking to schedule this stupid dance appearance? I should have just been happy with the strides I'd made in my life instead of getting greedy. And let's face it. Possibly I'd done this in some lame effort to make sure Trey remained interested in me. I didn't want to examine that possibility. Maybe I'd never really believed that I deserved a guy like him.

"Ms. Night?" The bouncer frowned, stepping fully into the dressing area.

Shoving my cell phone back into my bag, I tucked my purse into a bin beneath the dressing table and headed toward the door. I wasn't ready. But I couldn't just sprint out of the club the way I wanted to. Natalie wouldn't be invited to return as a performer in the fall if I did. And I had no one to blame for this but myself, so the least I could do was see it through to its natural—disastrous—conclusion.

"TREY FRASER?" THE FEMININE voice sounded vaguely familiar and Trey's gut sank before he turned around to see who'd recognized him.

Courtney would be making her appearance any moment, and the last thing he wanted was to be engaged in a conversation that took his focus off her. He wanted to watch her for one thing. And he suspected she might need to see him—make eye contact—as soon as she came out here. Possibly he was overestimating his importance in all this. Yet his gut told him she might be more nervous about this appearance than she'd originally thought.

"Yes?" He turned as the lights dimmed and the music changed to a tune more appropriate for a burlesque show.

"It's great to see you!" the slim blonde in a red sheath dress said. "Remember me? Fawn Barrows from Sphere Asset?"

Shit.

Trey hoped his face didn't convey his feelings. His gut sank to his toes as Courtney was introduced as Natalie Night. He applauded automatically, his eyes still on Fawn.

"These are some friends from work." She gestured vaguely to three women beside her. "We know the dancer and wanted to cheer her on."

His mind raced. They knew the dancer? Who the hell did they think it was? Then he recalled the photo in Courtney's office and put the pieces together. Courtney must have met her dance instructor the same time as these other women from her workplace. But while she'd kept up the dance lessons, the rest of them had forgotten all about Natalie Night. Until now.

Courtney was screwed if he couldn't think of a way out of this.

A collective cry of alarm went up from the audience and he spun around in his seat to see what was going on.

Courtney wavered on unsteady feet, her hand awkwardly clenching the pole for a moment before she straightened. Had she slipped? Just then her eyes met his through the mask and she leaped gracefully up on the stage, winding sinuously around the steel support.

"What happened?" he asked a guy to his right holding a longneck and watching Courtney like a hawk.

"She stumbled before she got all the way up." The guy rolled his eyes. "Although she seems to know how to handle a pole." He gave a crude laugh.

Trey's knuckles itched to connect with the dude's jaw.

"So what are you doing here?" Fawn piped up from over his shoulder, her hand coming to rest on his elbow to get his attention.

"Watching the show." He shifted away from her, although he did give a polite nod in her direction.

He wouldn't be taking his eyes off Courtney again.

She'd attracted him the first time he'd watched her, commanding his attention with a mature sensuality that was rare in clubs like this, where most of the dancers lied about their ages. And tonight? Courtney mesmerized him. Now he understood what it cost her to give this performance. Understood the consequences if she failed. Dancing had given her something her speech issue—and possibly her mother—had robbed her of early in life. Seeing her fight for that new level of confidence was way sexier than her high-cut costume, which showed a whole lot of thigh, or the transparent sequins that revealed the small of her back.

He was so damn fascinated, in fact, he didn't take much note of a fracas developing to his left. His brain registered the sound of squealing women and people shoving, but that was all until a petite redhead stumbled against him. "Careful," he warned the woman automatically.

He had only a vague impression of her, his focus on Courtney, until the redhead stuck a camera in his face and plastered her cheek against his.

"Smile for the camera, Trey!" she urged, a flash blinding him as she snapped a picture.

A bouncer arrived an instant later with hushed apologies to Trey. He steered the staggering, laughing female away, along with a couple of her friends, but not before Trey saw them high-fiving each other as they congratulated themselves on snagging a "money shot" of a Hollywood insider.

He wanted to haul Courtney off the platform and shuttle her to his SUV so they could ditch this place. Together. It sounded like her music was winding down.

"Wow." Fawn leaned forward to speak into his ear, her shoulder brushing his. "It must be tough to be photographed everywhere you go."

Her fluttering eyelashes and touchy-feely body language might not have been a big deal on another day. But right now, he didn't have the patience for it. He wanted to get the hell out of Backstage now.

"Yeah, I'm probably going to take off." Except how could he walk away while Courtney had one leg wrapped around the pole, her back arched seductively.

And when the guy next to him gave a wolf whistle and waved a hundred dollar bill at the stage, Trey knew for certain he couldn't leave Courtney alone.

"Are you sure?" Fawn tucked her hand around his forearm. "Why don't you stay and have a drink with us? I'll introduce you to the dancer."

The dancer who wasn't Natalie Night. How the hell was he going to get Courtney away from here without her friends and colleagues discovering a secret that could potentially cost her her job?

Courtney slid down to the floor, her performance at an end. As silver confetti rained from the ceiling, Trey knew he didn't have much time to make a plan.

I HAD TWENTY different problems to deal with as the audience broke into wild applause. But the only one that mattered right now was removing Fawn Barrows's manicured nails from Trey's arm. I stared daggers at that possessive feminine claw, willing it off my man.

And he *was* mine.

It might only be temporary. For this week, this month or—please God—even longer. But right now, Trey Fraser counted as the man in my life, and I feared for my actions if my gorgeous coworker didn't rethink the way she was coming on to him. She slid herself around Trey more fluidly than I'd moved around the steel pole during my dance. The woman was good. She was also smart, successful and untouched by insecurity. If I could grow fangs, they'd be showing already.

I ran my tongue over my incisors, curious.

A peripheral movement caught my eye and I realized that Trey was gesturing for me to come off the stage. Belatedly, I remembered that I hadn't taken a bow and the applause was quickly dying. The music had changed. The silver confetti no longer fell from the ceiling, signifying the end of my act. Behind Trey and Fawn, Star beckoned me to join her. She knew both Natalie and me fairly well and wouldn't be fooled by a mask for long.

As I scurried off the stage, my stomach churned and I wondered how to avoid all my colleagues from

Sphere. I couldn't believe I'd ignored Natalie and Trey and booked this appearance in the first place.

"Great show, Natalie!" someone shouted as I descended the steps, shaky and off my game.

Paper money in varying denominations fluttered in my face, but a bouncer arrived in time to make the guys waving it back off. I gladly took his sizable arm and allowed him to lead me toward the dressing area. Darting waitresses rushed past with trays of mixed drinks while a few Nordic-looking models passed out samples of some new brand of Russian vodka.

"Natalie!" a familiar feminine voice called behind me while strobe lights flashed all around. "Wait for us!"

I knew that had to be Star. I gauged the distance to the changing rooms and realized I'd never make it. Even if I ignored her and somehow did get to those doors before she did, she would follow and knock until I answered. And it wasn't like she was alone. If she had been, I would have risked sharing my secret. But the other women with her had no reason to keep my risqué hobby under wraps.

Turning slowly, I kept a hold on the bouncer's arm.

"I n-need a m-m-minute," I told him, my tongue like a cold engine failing to turn over in the winter. I'd learned that analogy from time spent with my New Yorker father.

Thanks, Dad.

"Hi, Natalie!" A chorus of greetings arose. And suddenly the women from my office were descending on me, along with others who'd attended Star's bachelorette party once upon a time. Worse, in the middle of that sea of smiling faces stood Trey.

My colleagues would ruin me, and Trey would be

there to witness it. Right now, I wished more than anything that he wasn't here to see my disgrace. Star hugged my shoulders.

Was she close enough to see behind my mask?

"H-hi," I mumbled, fingers running over my mask, tugging slightly to ensure it covered as much of my face as possible. "Th-thanks for—"

"Ms. Night." Trey stepped forward, wrapping a protective arm around me, his hand landing in the middle of my back. "My car is outside if you still have time for our meeting."

Confused, I nodded mutely, hoping against hope he had thought of a way out of this. Besides, even if I'd known what to say at that moment, I wouldn't have been able to get it past my lips without a lot of fits and starts. It was just that kind of situation.

"Meeting?" Fawn frowned, insinuating herself on Trey's other side. "We're going to buy our friend a drink, Trey. Come with us."

She looped her arm through his free one and I had a quick vision of us engaged in a tug of war.

"Sorry." Trey shook his head, all business. "Ms. Night is one of my agency's new clients. We've been trying to work out our schedules for this consultation for the last two weeks."

He was already drawing me back. The head bouncer with the very thick neck and a walkie-talkie on his hip took Trey's cue and used his big arm to separate me from Star and the rest of the women.

"I'll have your car brought around, Mr. Fraser," the guy assured him, using lightning fast skills with the walkie-talkie so that he already had a valet in motion outside.

Oh, my God. This was going to work.

"Thank you for coming," I articulated very slowly, purposely trying to make my voice a little deeper so they wouldn't recognize it.

Still, Fawn frowned, and I wondered if I'd tipped her off about my identity with the slow speech.

But Star was assuring me I had put on a wonderful show while Trey and the bouncer hustled me out of the club.

"My bag. In the d-dressing room," I said to Trey, feeling awkward about walking through the main bar in my costume. Luckily, no one paid much attention to me while I was sandwiched between two guys, one big enough to block a tank.

"Can you take care of getting her things?" Trey asked the bouncer, who nodded as he continued to fire off directions into the two-way radio.

Amazingly, the distance between me and my colleagues widened. Fawn wasn't chasing after us to unmask me. Maybe I'd made it through tonight's debacle without being recognized. Without losing my job.

We neared the exit as another bouncer in a skin-tight muscle shirt approached me with my duffel.

"Kendra said this one is yours." He thrust the black canvas bag into my arms.

"Thanks," Trey answered, tipping the guy generously. He also had a bill ready for the head bouncer when the behemoth with no neck opened the back door for us.

The night smog rolled over me, a moist and welcome embrace. Leaving the noise and the throbbing music behind us, we stepped out into the dark. I'd taken a cab here, knowing Trey would meet me. A valet in a white jacket appeared and gave Trey a vehicle, his head briefly bowed.

"I'm so sorry, sir." He gestured toward the back parking lot, which was smaller than the front. There wasn't even a valet stand back here, so the guy must have run around from the front to meet us.

"Where's my SUV?" Trey asked, passing the guy a bill even though he hadn't done his job.

In L.A., it was wisest to tip all the time—as much money as possible—if you were any kind of celebrity. The last thing you wanted in this town, where image meant everything, was to be denied a favored table.

"It's just over there, sir." He pointed again, but a white Escalade rolling to the curb blocked my view. "Your father asked me if I'd wait to bring the car so he could speak to you."

Beside me, Trey stiffened. I froze. The tinted window on the Escalade came down in a soft swish, and a distinguished-looking older man leaned out to wave at us, his gray cashmere sleeves pushed up to his elbows to reveal strong forearms.

"Hello, Trey." He smiled with what might be interpreted as warm affection, but I could feel the tension in Trey's every muscle as he tried to shelter me with his arm.

He passed me the key to his SUV and took off his jacket with one smooth move. "You don't have to wait for me," he murmured as he settled his jacket on my shoulders. Then he took a step toward the Escalade.

"Hello, Dad."

12

So...I'd been dismissed.

I lingered behind Trey in the heavy night smog, his Italian silk blazer a sorry excuse for the shelter of his arm, even if it did smell delicious—like him. He said I didn't have to wait, and judging by the way he stood beside the Escalade without introducing me, he was excluding me from the most significant parts of his life.

Two weeks ago, I would probably have skipped happily over to Trey's SUV to wait for him, grateful for any fraction of his world he wanted to share. Now? I had a new sense of my own worth and I didn't feel like standing in the shadows around a guy I really cared about. Especially not once their conversation started to get heated. Trey gestured with his hands and shook his head. Their voices rose, but not enough for me to make out what they were saying.

Through the windshield of the Escalade, I met the elder Fraser's gaze, his face illuminated an unearthly blue by the dashboard lights. I was a little surprised the well-known producer didn't have a driver to shuttle him through city traffic, but then Thomas Fraser II had a reputation for being a hardworking man's man, a self-made multimillionaire. The press loved his rags-to-riches story, a young boy abandoned by his drug-addict mother rising to fame and wealth. It was pure Hollywood.

He must have pointed me out to Trey, because just then Trey turned and noticed me still standing there in the dark. Was it me, or did he look impatient? I willed away the thought and refused to be self-conscious. Was I a part of Trey's life or not?

Even if the answer was no, I wanted to learn the truth. I couldn't call myself a strong, independent woman unless I had the courage to know where I stood with the man I'd been spending some very memorable nights with. I would consider this part of my personal transformation. Even if it broke my heart.

Taking a deep breath, I strode closer.

"Hi." I spoke the word perfectly. Clearly. And with conviction. But I did sort of hope I wouldn't have to say much more. I thrust my hand through the window of the Escalade even though it proved an awkward angle. "I'm C-Courtney."

I shivered in an attempt to hide my stutter. People naturally stuttered a bit when they were chilly. Relief disintegrated, however, as I realized that I'd given my real name to someone who'd seen me exit Backstage in a dancing costume. And a domino mask.

Oh. Crap. What had I been thinking to give this man—a man Trey butted heads with constantly—the power to wreck my life? Worse, I'd provided him with the ammunition to hurt Trey through his association with me.

Trey steadied me with an arm around my waist as I rose on my toes to shake hands with his father.

"A pleasure to meet you, Courtney. I'm Thomas." He said it with the slightest emphasis on the second syllable, a hint of Spanish in his speech. I was pretty sure one of his parents had been Spanish but I couldn't recall which. His grip was strong and sure as he took my hand, and if he thought it weird that I wore a mask, he said nothing.

He smiled at me, nodding slightly. I would have thought him charming if not for Trey's brittle stance beside me. I could feel his quiet fury in the tension of his muscles.

"My father was just leaving," Trey explained, keeping his gaze leveled at his dad. "We're done here."

"Consider what I said," Thomas told him, his jaw set. His expression was the opposite of the warmth he'd shown me. The metamorphosis happened again—in reverse—as the older man turned my way once more. "Perhaps I'll see you tomorrow night, Courtney. Trey will be at a black-tie gala. I'm sure you'd enjoy it."

I didn't have time to reply. He gave me a jaunty wave before he leaned back in his seat and edged the car forward. Thankfully, Trey read his dad's intentions and drew me far enough away that the Escalade didn't risk running over my toes.

"He seems as interesting as he's portrayed in the press," I said diplomatically, not quite sure what else to say with Trey silent beside me.

My initial guess was that he was angry.

Angry his father had invited me to an event that Trey hadn't plan to include me in? Or was he feeling simple frustration with an overbearing parent? I tried not to take it personally that I'd had to hear about the black-tie gala from his father.

But once again, I had the impression of Trey trying to keep me removed from his public life.

"He's interesting," Trey muttered, guiding me toward his SUV. "I'll grant him that."

A valet jogged past so he could have the door of the vehicle open for me when I arrived. I put a foot on the running board and propelled myself into the passenger seat, my heart full of mixed emotions. I was still glad that Trey had come to Backstage tonight. So grateful he'd talked our way out of the awkward meeting with my Sphere colleagues. Yet now, I wondered if he was trying purposely to hide me away from the people who mattered in his life. His father was his rival and yet Thomas Fraser knew more about Trey's whereabouts than I did.

A few minutes later, we were headed west on the Santa Monica Freeway, the traffic thinning as we left downtown behind. I tossed my mask and the blond wig aside, tired of trying to hide who I was behind a facade that didn't fit. The heavy fringe of my bangs slid out of the clip that had been holding them secure.

"Can I take you to your place?" Trey asked, rolling down the window to let in the damp night air.

"I'd appreciate that." I couldn't wait to change out of the dance outfit and put my double life behind me. From now on, I wouldn't use my inner Natalie Night to bolster myself. My confidence needed to come from within me.

"Sorry I didn't introduce you to my father right away." He found the passing lane and accelerated. I didn't need to turn around to see what he was running from. Obviously, his dad had provided him with some powerful demons.

"It's okay."

"It's not." He took my hand. Squeezed. "But I had the feeling our conversation was going to be confrontational. Plus, I thought you might rather make a clean getaway. I know you're concerned about people in your office finding out that you dance and I figured the fewer people you meet, the better."

"I know." I nodded, recognizing the wisdom of that caution. "But I was so caught off guard I forgot I even had a mask on."

"Seriously?" He looked my way, his right eyebrow arching in surprise. The corner of his mouth lifted a fraction.

I liked thinking I could sneak through his armor.

"Seriously!" I smacked my own forehead for emphasis. "A complete space-out on my part. I stood there feeling offended when you told me I could go to the car, never considering you had a great reason for not introducing me until I was already in midsentence with your dad while covered in feathers."

He was quiet for a long moment as we passed stretch limos and convertibles, motorcycles and delivery vans.

"Is our relationship horribly awkward for you?" I blurted, now feeling tense myself.

"No." Shaking his head, he seemed to relinquish whatever worries he'd had. He let go of my hand to skim a knuckle up my arm. Even through the silk fabric of his jacket, his touch gave me a shiver. "I just hope it doesn't turn out to be uncomfortable for you. My father is very well connected. In fact, the only way he knew where I was tonight is thanks to his vast network of friends who are all eager to do him favors."

"I don't understand."

"One of the bouncers at Backstage used to do private security for my father. Apparently, the guy phoned Dad when he saw me walk in tonight." Trey put both hands back on the wheel as traffic picked up.

I missed the feel of his touch. And right now, I didn't want to think about how Trey's well-connected father might make things uncomfortable for me. I was too incensed at the way he treated his son.

"Why wouldn't he just call you if he wanted to talk to you?"

"He happened to be having dinner nearby, so it wasn't a big trip for him. But he made the effort to show up at the club because I haven't been taking his calls," Trey admitted. "I met with him last week and felt like we'd reached…an impasse."

I frowned. "Do you mind me asking what he wanted?"

Trey took his time answering as he turned down Interstate 405.

"He wants to bring me back on board with Fraser Films to oversee production of his new movie."

"After the huge public falling-out you had?" I'd read enough about their rift to understand some of the ramifications, at least from a business standpoint. I'd had to include some of my concerns in my report for Fawn. And now I had to take them into account for Trey's financial well-being.

"Tough to believe, isn't it?" Trey shook his head, a lock of dark hair falling over an eyebrow and giving him an air of disrepute that would make any woman sigh. "But that's just how he operates."

"Is it the POW film you wanted to do from the start?"

"Of course not. It's *his* POW film that he just purchased the rights for. And he wants me to develop it with bankable stars and an American sensibility..." Trey shook his head. "It could be a good film. But it's not my film. And I'm ready to start putting my own stamp on my work."

"Me too," I said with a surprising amount of vehemence. "I mean, I want that in my own professional life. To put my stamp on my work." I felt embarrassed to have jumped in with my own issues while he was talking about his for once. "Sorry to change topics like that. I just totally identify with the need to claim some recognition."

"Thanks." He sped up as we got closer to Mar Vista, and that was saying something, because he'd wasted no time leaving downtown behind us. "It means a lot that you understand where I'm coming from. I've had people in my life before who really championed my dad, always assuming my father must have my best interests at heart and thinking if I would just knuckle under I could have had the world by the tail right now."

I debated how to respond to this, because I had the sneaking suspicion the elder Thomas Fraser had his son's best interests at heart as well. "When you say 'people,' do you mean old girlfriends?"

He laughed, a warm sound that danced over my skin like a caress.

"Those too. But I've had guys that I thought were

friends really take up the old man's cause. A lot of people are drawn in by his image."

"I'm taking up your cause," I assured him. "And not just because you're paying me to." I stopped suddenly, hearing the words in my head. "That came out wrong."

"I know what you meant." His voice softened, his shoulders relaxing a little for the first time since he'd spotted the white Escalade outside Backstage. "I shouldn't have put you in such an awkward position—insisting on working with you when we already had a personal relationship."

"It's been a good nudge for me, though." I wasn't going to have a problem separating work from my personal life. I hoped. "If you hadn't insisted on working with me, I'd still be stuck in a rut." As he neared my neighborhood, I pointed out my street. "I'm on Ocean View."

"I know." He slowed down as he neared my place. "I did a Google search on you when I was trying to untangle the mystery of Natalie/Courtney."

"Really?" A thrill shot through me at the thought of him looking for me. Thinking about me.

"Yes. And I searched even more once you started working on my finances."

"Well that's just astute business," I assured him, even though I was a little nervous now. "And what exactly did you find out?"

He put on his left signal light.

"I know you live here." He correctly indicated my home. "And I know your father signed it over to you on your twenty-first birthday."

"Well. Technically he sold it to me for a bargain-basement price." With no interest. I could never have afforded the house otherwise.

"It's a great place." Trey turned off the engine before coming around to my side to open my door.

I glanced out toward the street to make sure no one was around. Trey's jacket covered most of me, but I'd rather not be seen strolling into my house in the dancing outfit and a man's suit coat.

"My dad is an antiques dealer and my mother is an interior decorator. She helped him out with this house when they were still together." For all of three years.

But I tried to tell myself the house was like me—one of their few good collaborations.

I slid down into Trey's waiting arms, my body gliding down his as he lowered me to the ground slowly. Slowly. His eyes raked over me and the hunger that had been banked back at the club flared hot again.

I tingled everywhere at the thought of being with him again.

"I might not be able to fully appreciate the aesthetics of your home tonight."

"No?" I nipped at his lower lip and he tasted so good I had to close my eyes to savor him.

His hands slid underneath his jacket to smooth down my hips. Hot. Possessive.

"Then I'll just show you one of the house's best features and save the rest for another time."

"You're the best feature." His words whispered hotly along my neck, and even though he hadn't kissed me yet, pleasure smoked through my veins.

"Come on," I urged, taking his hand to lead him around the back of the house to avoid the porch light and the small street lamp on the far corner of my front yard. "Let's go somewhere more private."

Was I still a little scared that I might be Trey's secret indulgence? The woman he wouldn't share with his friends and family? Definitely. But that wasn't going to stop me from taking this crazy, heated attraction as far as I could.

THIS WOMAN HAD him turned all around.

Sexy as hell one minute. Sweetly vulnerable the next. And underneath it all, smart and funny. Courtney appealed to him on all levels.

Trey followed her down a twisting flagstone path until he spied a blue glow from the backyard. They rounded the corner of the house, dodging crepe myrtles, to find a courtyard with a hot tub and swimming pool tucked between the building's L-shaped wings. Eight-foot hedges blocked out the neighbors, creating a private oasis. The water of the hot tub flowed over a ledge into the pool, the trickling sound as soothing as any fountain. Lotus flowers floated on the pool's surface, their flickering glow suggesting battery-operated candles. They must be on a timer or a light sensor.

"Nice." He ran a hand up a smooth wooden post supporting a balcony on the second floor that ran the length of the house.

Potted dwarf palm trees dotted the smooth stones around the pool, and a gauzy white tent concealed what he'd guess was an outdoor shower.

"It's not exactly Fraser-family luxurious, but it's home." She paused by a wide bamboo chaise longue, looping her arm through his, her fresh scent teasing his nose.

"Luxury doesn't have to be over-the-top. This is beautiful." His father had experienced so much poverty as a kid, it seemed he'd never have enough stuff to make up for it. Courtney's home, smaller than either of his parents' places, was probably built in the fifties and had the kind of charm most larger homes could never attain.

Then again, maybe the house's appeal had more to do with Courtney herself. He liked everything about her. Too much.

"You want to come inside?" she asked softly, her finger dipping just inside the sleeve of his shirt to trail along his wrist.

"Loaded question." He spun her to face him, needing to forget everything else. Forget everything but her.

"In the house?" She smiled, flirting with him as her finger found the cuff button on his sleeve and slid it through the buttonhole.

Her thumb lingered on his pulse, a simple touch made erotic because it was Courtney. She didn't need costumes and feathers to turn his head. She could bring him to his knees with just a look.

"Depends." He mulled over his options. Ready to be with her anywhere at all. Wanting it to be right for her.

She tucked a hand in his other sleeve and undid that cuff, too.

"I'm waiting…" she whispered against his neck, her lips the barest brush of softness along his throat.

Damn. She was just… Damn.

He couldn't form a thought, let alone words, so he shoved his jacket off her shoulders, tossing the silk aside. Her skimpy dance outfit glittered in the moonlight, the clear sequins making pinpricks of fire over her skin.

"Will you be too cold?" he asked, stepping back to unfasten a button on his shirt and then dragging the whole thing over his head.

Her gray eyes tracked his movements, her gaze dipping low before lifting back up to his face.

She bit her lip as she shook her head.

"Perfect." He nodded his satisfaction and reached for her, peeling the straps of her spangled bodysuit off her shoulders.

Her flesh was fragrant and supple, and she twined her arms around his neck while the rest of the costume slipped. The fabric caught around her chest, resting on the curve of her high, taut breasts.

Her skin glowed pale, a lock of dark hair twining along her collarbone to rest in the slight cleavage. Palming her spine with one hand, he plucked at the dark strands with the other, smoothing the silky softness between thumb and forefinger. Courtney sighed her pleasure, her head tipped back. Trey felt like the luckiest bastard to see her this way, uninhibited and sensual, her guard down and her fingers hooking into the waistband of his pants.

Gently, he kissed her. She tasted like cinnamon lip gloss, and he took his time licking it off, suckling the full bottom lip to savor every last bit. Her fingers flexed against his scalp, twisting in his hair before she dragged them down the back of his neck, his bare shoulders.

Her hips found his and she arched into him, rocking seductively until he crushed her to him. Her breasts flattened along his chest, their soft weight conforming to him as he peeled her outfit down to her hips. She was naked beneath the sequins, and her nipples beaded against him.

The night air felt warm here, the breeze lessened by the high hedges. Still, he edged them closer to the hot tub, wanting to make sure she wasn't cold. Besides, he was scorching both of them, his skin so damn hot he'd probably melt the rest of her outfit off in another minute.

She worked the clasp of his belt while he walked her backward to the steaming water. They stepped out of their shoes by a patio table and he ditched his belt near the screen door into the house. While he undid his pants and retrieved a condom from his wallet, she grabbed a remote from a stone bench and punched the buttons to dim the exterior lights. The spa light went off, and the pool light changed to a moody red setting beneath the surface, the floating lotus flowers still flickering above. But his eyes were well adjusted to the dark by now, and he could see her just fine.

Better than fine.

She didn't wait for him to lead her into the water. As soon as she set down the remote, she kissed his chest. Then moved lower. Trey tried to nudge her toward the pool, but she shook her head and kissed a path down his ribs, settling back on her knees.

He wanted to wait. To get her warm first and pleasure her thoroughly, but she dragged his boxers off with the crook of her finger, and he was lost. Her mouth went around him and he couldn't do anything but appreciate the feel of her soft, silky tongue gliding around the tip, down the length.

Fire blazed up his spine in answer, his hands knotting in her hair. To stop her or hold her there, he wasn't sure. He hauled in a ragged breath and looked down at the picture she made, her body twined around his while her hands glided over his hips and down his flanks.

Holy hell.

The sight of her long eyelashes resting on her cheeks, her face a picture of perfect contentment or maybe even pleasure, had him ready to go over the edge. He released her hair and gripped her shoulders, tugging her to her feet against her soft protest.

Just looking at her glistening lips had him so amped up he had to force himself to think about something— anything—else.

With unsteady hands, he tried to focus on removing the rest of her costume. Awkwardly, he slid a hand beneath the silk and sequins to free her hips. Hooking a finger on the strap of a pale G-string, he took that off too in one slow sweep.

Only when she stood there, spectacularly naked, did he lead her into the hot tub. A wide sun shelf formed the first shallow step and he pulled her down onto it. The water level was perfect for what he had in mind, but first he wanted to get her completely wet and very, very hot.

"Come on," he urged, guiding her down into deeper waters.

She reached over the edge of the tub and hit a recessed button. Bubbles rumbled beneath the surface and then broke, spraying their faces with warm water while hiding their bodies in white foam.

Her sudden smile made him want to kiss her. Taste her. Return the sensual favor she'd given him. Maybe by the time he tasted her, he'd have recovered from what she'd done to him. He still teetered on the verge of coming and he hadn't even gotten inside her yet.

"You like this?" he asked, tracing her curved lips with his finger.

"I love it," she told him, her voice steady. Sincere.

He kissed her hard, wanting to seal the moment in his memory forever. Seal her to him.

He licked and tasted, exploring every corner and nuance of her mouth until she wrapped herself around him under the water, locking his hips between her legs. He carried her that way, his hands cupping her hips, back to the sun shelf.

She didn't protest when he released her mouth to kiss down to the soft hollow at the base of her throat. To lick a circle around each breast and draw the hard tips into his mouth. She bucked toward him, but he pinned her hips with his hands, keeping her in place in the shallow water.

Then he nipped and tasted his way down her slick body, pausing to stir the tiny pool of water nestled in her navel. Pausing a whole lot longer to lick her inner thigh until he rested between her legs, right where he wanted to be. He moved to kneel on the step below the sun shelf, the perfect height to drape her thighs over his shoulders.

Her scent drove him wild, and he breathed her in, licking a path down the seam of her sex. She opened for him, wet and ready, but he took his time lapping along the plump folds of her core until she writhed and moaned. The first time she neared the edge of release, he backed off and built the tension all over again, wanting to take her as high as she'd ever been.

The second time, he couldn't hold back, and when

her spine bowed off the deck, he came at her harder, giving her everything she needed while she rode out the lush spasms.

He'd never seen anything more beautiful than Courtney right then. His head was spinning, his emotions raw as hell when he sheathed himself and entered her in one smooth stroke. He lifted her so she could straddle him, her body so pliant he could have done anything with her.

He wanted to do everything.

But for now, he anchored her waist with his arm and drove in deeper. She buried her nails in his shoulders, her cries sweet, erotic music in his ear until she came again and so did he.

His release went on forever, hot wave after hot wave pulsing through him and into her. She called out his name, collapsing against his chest, and still his body simmered with the aftermath of that release. He wrapped both arms around her, dropping kisses on her damp hair while they found their breath again.

When he could move, he shifted them into deeper water. He helped her to sit sideways on his lap while he rested with his back against the edge of the tub. The motor on the heated spa kicked off, leaving the water tranquil and steaming all around them.

She nuzzled her cheek against his shoulder, her eyes drifting closed. Trey looked up at the stars overhead, feeling lucky as hell to hold her. Too bad the ragged emotions inside him told him he couldn't afford to risk much more time in Courtney's arms.

Something had changed between them tonight. A new understanding. A deeper look inside each other. At least, he thought he understood her better, and he was damn sure she'd started to see right through him. And that gave him pause.

Courtney was one of the warmest, most genuine women he'd ever met. She didn't deserve the drama of the Fraser family, the scandal waiting to happen that was his everyday life. And already, his father knew who she was. Had to suspect something about their relationship.

Would his dad drag her name through the press? Reveal her secrets to her conservative workplace?

"My eyes are closed," Courtney told him suddenly, never looking up. "But I can hear the wheels moving in your head."

His low bark of laughter was as pained as it was amused. How the hell had she known that?

"I'm still recovering." He tipped his head to rest a cheek on the top of her head.

"Liar," she accused him softly. "I feel the tension in you." Her hand skimmed to his hip. "And not the good kind."

As spent as he was, his body responded to her suggestion. He'd trade a lot to forget about the pressures of his professional world and lose himself in her again.

"I don't like that my father saw us together. It's going to draw public attention to you."

"You can't keep hiding me." She raised her chin and lifted a hand to his cheek.

"I'm not hiding you." Although, even as he said it, he understood why she thought as much. "I'm just... trying to protect you."

"Okay." She nodded, but from her quick acceptance, he got the impression she didn't quite believe him. "What if I said I don't need protecting?"

He thought about her hasty retreat from the conference room that first day he'd met her.

"My life is a glass house." There was always someone staring in. Judging.

"If I can't handle myself, I don't belong in your life in the first place." Her thumb traced a wet circle on his cheek. "Right?"

"It shouldn't be like that—"

"But it is. You're a public figure. You'll never have a fully private personal life."

Because it galled him to admit it, he said nothing.

"You know I'm right." She dropped her hand back in the water and edged away to look him square in the eye. "So give me a make it or break it chance to prove myself."

"What?" Had he missed part of the conversation? He shook his head, unsure what she was talking about. "You don't need to prove—"

"Take me to that black-tie gala tomorrow night."

13

"STEP AWAY FROM the mirror."

Natalie pointed at me with one of her crutches, her order leaving no room for argument. I met her gaze in the wood-framed mirror of my foyer, where I'd been fussing with my hair for the last five minutes. She glared at me menacingly before thrusting a glass of white wine into my line of vision. She'd poured the drink for me an hour ago, and I had yet to touch a drop even though she insisted I needed to relax.

Knowing a command when I heard it—and respecting that she knew best because she hadn't steered me wrong yet—I finally took the wine and slumped down into a funky seventies chair that my father had sent for my last birthday. He'd never been a big part of my life, but he'd tried to make amends by sending the occasional gift from his buying ventures.

"I'm nervous," I explained, focusing on the clock now that the mirror was out of the question. We'd started off in my bedroom, but as the time ticked down to Trey's arrival I'd been too nervous to stay upstairs, peeking out the window every other minute, so we'd moved down to the foyer.

Trey would be here any moment to take me to the gala I'd wanted to attend so badly. Except ever since I'd talked him into inviting me, I'd been asking myself why I'd insisted on this crazy trial by fire when we'd only just started dating. When I'd only just started feeling more confident.

"Stop being so nervous," Natalie said, resting her ankle on the staircase. "You wanted to go to this black-tie gala. You might as well enjoy the splashy launch party and some good hors d'oeuvres."

Natalie had come over late that afternoon after I'd made an emergency phone call begging for clothes advice. She'd arrived with three dresses from her own closet, helped me choose a sleek navy blue sheath with a strapless bodice and short beaded hem, then supervised my makeup. In short, she'd been awesome. In return, I'd tried to give her the whole paycheck from my performance last night, but she'd staunchly refused. I managed to sneak half the amount into her purse when she wasn't looking.

If she tried giving it back, she'd have to deal with my stubborn side.

I sipped the wine, closing my eyes to let the crisp, chilled sauvignon blanc work some relaxation magic. "I just wish I understood why I had to rush into this."

"You're not rushing into anything. You're dating this guy, so why wouldn't you start attending events with him?" Natalie carefully lowered herself onto a polished oak step. "It's not like you're moving in with him."

"But I told him it would be a 'make or break' moment for our relationship. That we needed to know if I fit into his life or not."

Natalie frowned. "Wow. Way to pile the pressure on yourself."

I smoothed a hand over the intricately sewn blue beads just above my knee.

"I don't know what came over me. One minute, we were having a great time in the hot tub—" I'd never go in that hot tub again without thinking about what we did there "—and the next, I'm spouting things like 'if I can't handle the public eye, I don't belong in your life.'"

Along with my new confidence, I seemed to have developed a knack for self-sabotage. One step forward, two steps back.

"You really like this guy *Tom,* don't you?" She stuck her tongue out at me to remind me she hadn't forgiven me for hiding Trey's identity from her at first.

"I'm…" Oh God. I knew exactly how I felt about him, but wasn't ready to admit it. "I really like Trey."

My voice sounded funny, deep and husky, and I suspected Natalie understood what I wasn't saying. I loved Trey. Maybe it was loving him that was making me so adventurous and bold everywhere else in my life. Wise or not, love made you feel like taking risks.

"So just try to have fun tonight." Natalie set her glass of wine down on a hallway buffet table and limped over to me with the help of a crutch. "Just because you're thinking of it as a 'make or break' night doesn't mean he is."

She gave me a quick hug while I tried to pull myself together.

"Okay," I agreed, just as my doorbell rang.

Panic welled up inside me as Natalie and I exchanged a look.

Trey was right on time. Guess I couldn't put off my date with destiny any longer.

HOLLYWOOD SURE KNEW how to party.

Two hours later, I was circulating around the pool patio at Devoe House, an L.A. home procured for the launch bash of a new film called *Maybe, Baby,* which seemed to be a teen-oriented flick about rich-kid excess.

Or maybe I was blurring the lines of art and reality. Because, as I peered around the sleek pool deck of a home that had apparently once belonged to Marilyn Monroe, I saw youth, wealth and beauty everywhere I looked. This world was privilege and excess defined, right down to the tiny lobster hors d'oeuvres that I saw people take a teeny bite of and then toss.

Were their stomachs too small for two bites? Or was tossing away half-eaten delicacies some kind of status symbol?

"How are you doing?" Trey appeared with a drink for me.

I'd requested a sparkling water with lemon, since I couldn't afford to drink any alcohol when I needed to stay sharp. So far, I'd smiled a lot and spoken little. Not hard to do when Trey's friends were all more interested in him than me. Also, I don't think the waif-like starlets who only ate half a miniscule lobster hors d'oeuvre and draped themselves in Harry Winston's best really saw me as competition for one of the city's hottest bachelors.

And yes, I was feeling a bit defensive. Thank God

Natalie had loaned me a dress or I would have arrived in one of my office suits. I knew not all launch parties were this fancy, but the *Maybe, Baby* filmmakers had wanted to set the decadent tone for the movie.

Trey stroked my arm lightly. "Hey? You still with me here?"

"Uh, of course," I almost stuttered, damn it. He'd asked me something, and do you think I could remember?

"Are you okay?"

Ah, right. It wasn't like he'd asked me a mind-bender. I seriously needed to get a grip. "Great. Things are great," I answered with a shade too much enthusiasm. "I mean, thank you for bringing me here."

Trey slid an arm around me and walked us over to the railing for a drop-dead gorgeous view of downtown Los Angeles winking in the distance. Here, we had a little more privacy from the crowd and a bit of quiet away from the DJ, who had set up his mixing board on a raised patio close to the house.

Trey looked fan-freaking-tastic in a tuxedo. His classic good looks and lean muscles seemed right at home in black-tie. Silver cuff links winked in the torchlight, and he appeared as comfortable as if he wore a pair of jeans.

"Thank you for coming with me." Trey lifted my hand to his lips and kissed the backs of my knuckles, just like something you'd see Cary Grant do in an old film.

I melted inside, my enjoyment of this man chasing away my worries for now.

"But I wanted to," I reminded him, stepping closer to the rail as a waiter brushed past with a tray of drinks.

"I probably pushed too hard for an invitation. I didn't mean to pressure you into introducing me to your work world."

"I'm really glad you're with me," he said simply. "If I'd come alone, I would have made the rounds and been out the door in forty-five minutes. Having you by my side makes me stay to appreciate the view."

His eyes were on me as he spoke and my heart squeezed tight in my chest. I wondered how much longer I'd be able to keep a lock on my tender feelings for him. Even now, I wanted to blurt out that I loved him, throw my arms around his neck and hope for the best.

"So this is your world." I lifted my cut crystal glass in the direction of the Sunset Strip a mile and a half below us. "It's beautiful."

In fact, now that I knew this man's assets inside and out, I realized that he was surrounded by beauty everywhere he went on multiple continents. His life was one of luxury and sophistication. I'd seen it on paper, but I hadn't felt it in my heart until we'd come here. Maybe the diamond-clad women at this party were right not to consider me real competition for Trey. Even though we stood side by side, our lives had never felt further apart.

He clinked his glass of sparkling water against mine and turned toward me, leaning an elbow on the railing. He curved a hand around my hip to spin me around to face him.

"I'm going to borrow your line from last night," he said, leaning close to whisper in my ear. "I see the wheels turning in your head, Courtney. What are you thinking?"

Before I could answer, a tall, heavyset man in an ill-fitting suit trundled over, setting his sloshing drink on the rail between us, the scent of alcohol so strong I wondered if it might burn the varnish off the wood.

"Sorry to bother you, Trey," he began, clapping Trey on the shoulder and giving me the vaguest nod of apology. "I really need to speak to you. You have a minute?"

While I might not fit into this world, I read enough about it to recognize one of the most well-respected filmmakers of our time, Michael Diereda, a man who didn't need to wear black tie to fit into this crowd. If Trey was going to start his own studio one day, he should be talking to men like this.

"Of course," I said, even as Trey started to say that now wasn't a good time. "I was just about to refresh my drink," I insisted, giving Trey a meaningful look.

I hadn't been kidding about my commitment to his start-up business. No matter what happened between us personally, I would root for Trey professionally. Even though the thought of losing him gave my heart a painful squeeze.

Wending my way through a crowd that had started to swell since the DJ began playing, I entered the house through one of the many sets of open French doors. The caterers must not have needed to use the opulent kitchen I found myself in, since it was spick-and-span, a small bar set up near the long granite island.

"Courtney Masterson?" A booming voice cut right through the party noise and stopped me in my tracks.

Turning, I saw Thomas Fraser II with a small entourage. Trey's father wore a tuxedo jacket and white silk shirt but no tie, and his white hair was slicked back for the occasion. A stunning Bollywood starlet with inky dark hair and a tiny silver cocktail dress had one arm wrapped possessively around the producer's elbow, while several other men and women seemed to circle him like so many constellations around a bigger planet.

Self-consciously, I patted my hair. The last time this man had seen me, I'd been wearing a blond wig and a mask. How had he recognized me?

"Hello, Mr. Fraser." I offered him my hand the way I would a business acquaintance, but he kissed the back of my fingers in a gesture that perfectly mirrored his son's.

I wondered if Trey was aware how similar their mannerisms were. He possessed the same vitality and charisma that his father did. Maybe those similarities were part of the reason they butted heads so often.

"I'm glad you talked Trey into bringing you here tonight." He smiled and gave a subtle gesture to his followers to make themselves scarce. They melted into the crowd, leaving us alone by a wall of windows looking out onto the patio dotted with torches and now overflowing with guests.

"How did you recognize me, Mr. Fraser?" I cut straight to the point, wanting to make sure I understood his motives. Had he wanted me here tonight just so he could call me out as a liar?

"I keep tabs on my son," he said, tilting his chin up with pride. "He's been restless and angry with me. I worried he would make a hasty business decision that he would regret just because he was upset. So I've monitored his recent business dealings. And I've had one of my former security people quietly keeping an eye out for him."

"You mean…" I let go of his arm, not trusting him. "Are you saying you've had someone following Trey?"

"Not all the time." His chest puffed up in self-defense. "Just enough to find out he wants to open his own film studio to compete with me and that he's dating a buttoned-up financial researcher who lets her hair down by moonlighting as a...dancer."

Perhaps I should have felt threatened. He knew information I'd been trying to keep secret. He had the power to get me fired. But all I could think of was Trey and how much this would hurt him. Couldn't his father see the way his actions alienated his son? I suddenly spotted Trey, seated at a table by the pool with the famous director. As if aware I was looking at him, he turned toward the house suddenly.

The lights were all on in the kitchen, which was slightly elevated above the crowded patio, so he must be able to see me as well as I could see him. Even from this distance, I picked up on the tension in his body language as he rose from his seat.

He must have noticed his father talking to me and was probably headed straight toward us.

"Mr. Fraser," I laid a hand on the older man's arm to draw his attention. "You seem like a man who loves your son."

"He is my flesh and blood," he said with a low fierceness. "I've given him everything."

"Not your acceptance." Why should I mince words with someone who set new records for hardheadedness? Thank goodness my father and I had worked out some kind of peaceful relationship over the years. "And not your faith in his business sense. You undermine him publicly."

If there'd been any chance the elder Fraser would keep my dancing a secret from my employer, I was surely blowing it now. But someone needed to make

Thomas Fraser see he didn't always know best. Trey had helped me find my confidence—my voice. I planned to use it now to help him, even if that meant standing up to his imposing dad.

"You don't know what you're talking about." The older man's smile held an outward semblance of manners. Too bad the throbbing in his temple told me he was seconds away from blowing a gasket.

"Sir, I don't mean any disrespect, but I care enough about your son not to pull punches. I want him to be happy. If only you could—"

"I don't need advice about my son from an outsider," he hissed, stepping away from my touch. Several curious stares turned our way.

"No." I shook my head, extra quiet in the hope it would bring his voice down a notch. "I'm not an outsider, Mr. Fraser. But *you* will become an outcast in your own family if you can't see the way—"

"Utter horseshit, my dear," he said with the withering condescension that had made him a force to be feared in this town. He didn't need to shout. His anger iced the air until the almost fifty people milling around the bar went dead silent.

All staring.

At me.

Great.

He tipped his head to the side, eyes narrowed. "What do you know of a parent's love? Your own mother doesn't even speak to you."

I wasn't sure how he knew this about me—it was only partially true—but apparently he'd done a bit of digging. As a researcher, I understood the need for information, so I didn't begrudge him this. It was a low blow, yes. But I saw it for what it was—the weak, tangential argument of a man who didn't have a leg to stand on in a logical debate. Unfortunately, I didn't have the chance to swoop in for the kill in this rhetorical battle because Trey had arrived in the kitchen just in time to hear his father yell at me.

And he did not look pleased. He barreled through the curious, still painfully silent crowd to stand between us, chest-to-chest with Thomas.

"Enough, Dad," he bit out angrily. "Stay away from Courtney."

The tension in the room was so thick it was worthy of a scene in one of their films. I might have appreciated the irony if my heart hadn't been aching for Trey.

"I'm fine," I assured him, hoping my meaningful look could communicate the need for public discretion. "We were just going to step outside to talk."

I glanced back and forth from one set of dark, brooding eyes to the other. Neither man seemed inclined to follow my diplomatic nudge.

"Trey?" I appealed to the Fraser I trusted. The one who had given me the courage to jump into the fray in the first place. "Trust me. I've got this."

And I did. How crazy was that? Thomas Fraser—the bear of the movie business—had unleashed his cool wrath on me and I hadn't stuttered even once.

In fact, I wanted a chance to finish what I'd started with Trey's father. A chance to break through that blustery exterior to the deep love I suspected was suppressed underneath. Couldn't he hear the steadiness in my voice?

Trey's jaw flexed as he leaned closer to his father.

"If you come near her again, or threaten her livelihood in any way because of her dancing—"

He broke off midsentence, perhaps realizing he'd been about to publicly out me in front of a rapt crowd. Maybe he already had. I would bet I'd be the girl most often looked up on Google in Hollywood after tonight's scene.

How could he do that to me? He'd promised to keep my secret. Betrayal pinched inside me even though I knew his father brought out the worst in him. Kind of like the way my mom used to pull out the worst in me. But I was done living in the shadow of parents. His. Mine. I was done.

"Maybe we should take this discussion somewhere private," I urged. Neither of them so much as looked at me. They were locked in some kind of father-son struggle for dominance and I might as well have been invisible. And if I'd learned nothing else this past week, I totally understood I would never again allow myself to be invisible. A bit more forcefully, I said, "Or maybe I should just go."

Still, Trey didn't look away from his dad, his jaw clenched so hard he might break a crown. I knew if I pushed harder, he would back away, swoop me up and escort me out of here. But this thing with his dad would not go away. It would rule his mood for the rest of the night.

Likely much longer. Why couldn't he see that he was letting this feud with his dad take over his life?

And there wasn't a damn thing I could do about it.

Turning on my heel, I set my drink on the nearest table and didn't worry about whether or not I made a graceful exit. I finally felt comfortable in my own skin, only to realize I was more alone than ever.

14

"COURTNEY, WAIT." TREY KEPT HIS focus on the glimpses of navy blue darting and weaving through the paparazzi crowded outside the private mansion.

Courtney had taken off from the launch party without a glance back at him. But she had to wait for him to drive her home, didn't she? His chest tightened at the thought that maybe she'd had it with his messed-up family and was ready to just punch out. Call a cab and be done with him. He hastened his step.

A few cameras turned her way as she hurried past the tabloid press. A couple of flashbulbs popped—shoot first and fill in the blanks later. Little did the photographers know, that shot of her leaving the party would probably pay the most by the time gossip from this event leaked.

Damn, but his dad had screwed him over. Again.

He ground his teeth together, veering off to one side to minimize the possibility of photos cropping up of the two of them together. Not that he cared about himself. But he didn't want to jeopardize Courtney's job at Sphere any more than he already had. He was so furious with his father he couldn't see straight. How could the old man have purposely embarrassed her like that?

"Courtney?" He spotted her again near his SUV, which had been parked in a long line of expensive vehicles by the valets. Luckily he had a spare key on him.

She had her cell phone out, her fingers racing over the keypad while she studiously ignored him.

Not a good sign. Didn't she know he'd only been trying to protect her?

He picked up his pace, jogging the rest of the way down the slight incline toward her. At least they'd be shielded from the view of any partygoers. The paparazzi hadn't followed her and they hadn't seen him. That bought him a little time.

"Hey." He reached her side just as she slid her phone back into her small, beaded bag. "I'm sorry about what happened back there."

She pursed her lips, not quite a frown, definitely not a smile.

"For what happened back there?" She folded her arms, her posture rigid. "You mean for ignoring my plea to let me handle your dad? Or for announcing to the world that I moonlight as a dancer?"

Confused, he shook his head, trying to keep an eye out for anyone headed their way. He was done with being the center of attention for the night. "I came in there to prevent my father from making a big scene and embarrassing you."

"You can't be serious." She skimmed a dark lock of hair away from the eyes that had captivated him that very first day. "You realize you made the biggest scene of all, right?"

Guilt nipped as he was blasted by the possibility

she might be right. Frustration crawled up the back of his neck at the thought that he could be as bad as his father, the growing awareness that he'd blown it tightening every vertebra in his back. He wanted to get out of here, away from the party, away from the long line of cars and the valets running back and forth—away from his life.

"In an effort to protect you and deflect my father's interest in you, yes." His head pounded with the memory of seeing his dad yell at her. Damn it, he knew better than to drag someone so vulnerable into his world. "When I heard him talk to you like that—" He ground his teeth together.

"Trey, I was holding my own with him." She hugged herself against a cool gust of breeze. "I was calm. I was articulate. And I had him in a corner, which is the only reason he lashed out." She rubbed her forehead just above her temple as she turned to lean against the bumper of the SUV. "I was on the verge of making him see he was dead wrong."

Tough to imagine his father admitting that to anyone, let alone a woman he'd only just met.

"Dead wrong about what?" he asked, curious now that the high emotions had passed.

"About thinking he's such a great parent."

He leaned against the bumper beside her, close but not too close. He detected a new steeliness in her, a definite boundary between them.

"My dad won't change." He'd been around him long enough to know that. God, it had been pounded into his brain the hard way after so many years of giving the old man one opportunity after another to… Hell. Be a father instead of a dictator.

"And you know this because—?" She picked at the beads along the hem of her dress, the miniature bits of glass catching random patches of moonlight. "Has it ever occurred to you that you might be as hardheaded and stubborn as him?"

The accusation stabbed clear through him, the possibility too daunting to wrap his brain around. He'd never wanted to be compared to the old man. What would it mean if he'd inherited the things that ticked him off most about his father? He tried to shove the thought aside.

"Courtney, it was your idea to come to the gala and I brought you to make you happy." He toed a stone with his shoe. "But I've known all along that it was a risk to get involved when my father is a powder keg and you're—"

"What?" she prompted.

"Vulnerable to criticism."

She snorted. "Insecure, you mean. Well, guess what?" She got to her feet. "I'm not insecure anymore. I've changed in a lot of ways since we met, Trey. I'm surprised you haven't noticed."

"That doesn't mean you deserve to be fed to the lions on your first outing with me."

In the distance, he saw a pair of headlights turn up the street.

"I've taken risks with you, Trey, because you mean—a lot to me. I've taken off the old mask and I'm ready to show you and everyone else the new me."

She sounded steady as she said it, but the thought of her being intimidated because of him made him furious with himself. She meant a lot to him too, damn it. Too bad he hadn't shown as much when it mattered most.

The sound of an engine grew and headlights came closer. He shuffled back a step to remain in the shadows.

"I don't know what I was thinking." He shook his head, wanting her to stay but feeling he didn't deserve her. "I didn't want my dad to yell at you, but in the end," God, it sucked to admit it, "I was worse than him."

She didn't argue the point.

"I've been kept on the sidelines my whole life by people who were embarrassed by me," she said. "And then by all my own insecurities, thanks to a mother who saw me as defective." She stepped closer to the road and waved down the oncoming car. "I'm not going to be content to remain on the fringes anymore."

A taxi rolled to a stop beside her.

Real worry clogged his throat. She'd called a *cab?*

She stood there, watching his reaction or...just watching him. He didn't have a flipping clue what he was supposed to do. Ask her not to go home alone?

"I don't understand," he admitted. "I'm just not sure how to...make this right."

She touched his face in a gesture he understood all too well. He recognized the bittersweet farewell and the sadness in her eyes.

"I'm not living in the shadows again, Trey. And until you can get out from under the one looming over you, I'm not sure if it's a good idea that we keep seeing each other." She bit her lip but her voice was firm. "Talk to your father, Trey. See if you can both listen this time."

He'd never seen it coming. Pretty Gray Eyes was breaking up with him on the shoulder of a dark Los Angeles street because he was too blind to look in a mirror and see himself clearly. She waited for him to respond and he was thankful the cab driver had kept his window rolled up. Hell, he didn't know what else to do so he reached for his wallet and took out a fat bill for the cabbie. He rapped on the window and handed it to the guy along with a hoarse order to drive carefully.

Regret like a stone in his heart, he opened the door for her just as a bunch of flashbulbs went off behind him. Crap. They'd been spotted.

She shook her head as she slid inside the cab, ready to move on. "I'm sorry, Trey."

The flashbulbs kept going but he didn't care. All that mattered to him in the world was driving away in an anonymous yellow cab while he stood there like a sucker, not knowing up from down.

But Courtney had told him what he needed to do, and she was a smart woman. A woman he'd chosen as his financial advisor. Maybe it was time he started listening to her on another level, too. The time had come to make things right with his father.

A MEETING AT the party was out of the question. The paparazzi had gotten wind of the drama in the kitchen and were hot to photograph all parties involved. But Trey had tipped a valet well to find his father and bring him out of the house another way.

Now, Trey waited in his vehicle two streets over and watched as the valet approached in a golf cart. Even in the dark, Trey could tell his dad was in the passenger seat. He was relieved the old man had sense enough to be reasonable about this. Part of him had feared the guy would walk right to the paparazzi and give them the inside scoop.

As the golf cart braked to a squeaking halt, Thomas

Fraser II stepped out as easily as if he were climbing out of a limo, rolling off a few more bills for the valet, who had already made a small fortune from this mission.

Trey unlocked the passenger door so his father could get in. Once he was in the seat, he turned to his son with a dark look.

"Care to tell me why you are waiting around dark alleys for me instead of chasing after your girlfriend?" He pounded the dash with his fist for emphasis.

Would he ever understand this man?

"This isn't just about me, Dad." He needed to take ownership for his part in this mess. He owed it to Courtney to do what she asked. To listen. Putting the vehicle in gear, he tried to explain. "This is about both of us. I embarrassed her tonight and that's my fault. But the way you and I can push each other to lash out—that's our fault. Yours and mine."

He didn't expect his father to just roll over and admit his role. But maybe they could find some kind of peace. Courtney had thought it was possible, right? He flexed his fingers on the steering wheel, not sure how he'd lost so much so fast. His head throbbed.

"I try to help you," his father barked, the deep bass bouncing around the vehicle. "I got her to go to the party because I could tell you liked her. And you need a woman in your life, Trey. All you do is work."

Surprise distracted him from the throbbing in his head. His father had noticed how hard he worked? Wasn't that the pot calling the kettle black? Damn it, that was one more way he was like his dad, although he'd never fully appreciated the connection.

"You could tell I liked her because you have me followed and you check up on me all the time." He couldn't help the knee-jerk comment. It still ticked him off to have his dad's security tailing him.

"A good father looks after his sons."

That made him wonder how much his dad was watching over his brothers in the northern part of the state. And, even as he figured he should warn them, he had to admit it seemed like his father was coming at this from a point of…love.

Trey stopped at a red light and turned to look at the man who stirred up no end of trouble in his life and everyone else's. A man who interfered constantly and thought he knew best. A man who'd passed on the very traits to Trey that had made Courtney leave him.

God, he needed to understand the old dude better. Because they were way too much alike. He couldn't expect Courtney to give him a chance until he gave his father a chance.

He took a deep breath to say just that when he noticed a tear rolling down his dad's cheek.

"Ah, hell." Any other words died in his throat. How could he not have noticed how much his dad cared?

The epiphany slammed him back in his seat even harder than the knowledge that his father was genuinely upset. Sad. Maybe regretting what had happened nearly as much as Trey did.

Rattled as hell, Trey pulled over in front of a German bakery with tables out front where a late crowd had gathered for hot doughnuts.

He put the SUV in Park and shut off the engine. "What happened between you and Courtney?"

His father frowned. "She told me I undermine you publicly." He studied his nails and straightened a heavy ring on his right hand. "That I did not give you enough acceptance." Shrugging, he appealed to Trey. "What acceptance? I've fed you, clothed you and given you a start in the world. I've accepted my responsibilities."

"I don't think that's what she meant." Trey couldn't help a wry smile at the image of Courtney taking the famous producer to task for his parenting. She really had grown a lot since they'd met, finding depths of strength he'd never guessed were inside her.

Now it was time that he did his fair share of growing up as well. "Dad?" he repeated. "What exactly did Courtney say to you at the party?"

Stroking his beard, his father looked out the window at the bakery. "She said I'd be an outsider in my own family if I didn't..." He shook his head. "I don't know what she was going to say next because that's when I yelled. And right then, you came inside."

Trey's head throbbed and his chest felt vacant. That numbness again, crowding out the pain that awaited him once the events of this whole evening sank in.

"I didn't listen to her very well either," he admitted, recognizing yet another quality he'd inherited from his dad. "She told me she had things under control with you and I ignored her. She said I'm like you, and I couldn't see it."

"She said that?" His dad chuckled wryly. "I'll bet that stung."

All his life, he'd had friends side with his father when Trey got frustrated with him. They would insist the old man was well-meaning, and Trey would ignore them because no one understood what it was like to be raised by such a demanding, unyielding parent. Yet maybe they'd had a point. Yes, his dad had one hell of a backward way of showing love. But maybe Trey did too. He sure hadn't shown it to Courtney the way she deserved.

"Yes. She said that."

"You are like me." His father pounded his own chest but he was smiling. "You can see this now."

He saw it all right. He and his dad had both hurt Courtney tonight.

Trey stared at the guy who'd caused him no end of grief and told himself he was going to change. No more hardheaded pursuit of his own goals. No more film studio to rival his father's.

He and his dad were going to get on the same page. And soon.

"I want my name on the door at Fraser Films." He turned over the engine, suddenly full of new purpose. He had a whole lot to do if he was going to really get out from under the shadow of his father.

If he was going to be the man that Courtney deserved.

"What are you talking about?" His father made indignant harrumphs, but Trey now took the time to look past the smoke screen.

"I'm talking about joining forces to be bigger and better than ever instead of separating our resources and tearing each other down." Trey had thought he'd given his father his last chance when he'd worked for him the last time, but maybe he'd been just waiting for that attempt to fail. Walking away when they disagreed instead of finding a compromise. "I'm either starting a studio of my own—and you know it will be successful since I have a lot of your stubbornness in me—or we can try to come up with a way to work together and not…clash so much."

The old man didn't have much to say. But maybe that was just as well. Trey had sown the seed. Now he'd give it some time to take root.

"Where are we going?" his father asked, straightening the lapel on his tuxedo jacket.

"*We* are going make a plan to get back the girl, Dad."

His father nodded slowly. "I liked her."

"That's a good thing. Because I love her."

"I CAN'T BELIEVE you were the dancer that took Natalie's place at Backstage." Star clutched her teacup and spoke in a whisper as I sat with her at the Sphere Asset Management conference table on Monday morning.

I'd called my boss, Pendleton, on the weekend, confessed everything and assured him I was done with my double life and that I was fairly certain no one else knew about it. I'd chosen to tell Star because she'd been a good friend to both Natalie and me. As for my boss, he'd gone from shocked, to disbelieving, to vaguely amused in the course of an hour-long phone conversation. Then he'd commended my recent work and told me he hoped I'd consider taking a larger role at Sphere as long as my dancing days were behind me. So…instead of getting fired, I got an "atta girl" and the promise of a shiny new promotion if I so desired.

I didn't. At least not yet. I was still finding my footing with the increased responsibility I had, and even that didn't seem as exciting without Trey in my life. Walking away from him hadn't destroyed my newfound confidence. But I'd definitely lost the spring in my step. The lightness and joy in my heart.

My chest ached, in fact.

"Natalie dislocated her ankle that first time and she

encouraged me to take her place." I owed her for the nudge, not just because of the confidence the performance had given me, but because it had put me in Trey's path a second time.

No matter that Trey hadn't fought harder for us—for me—I wouldn't trade a minute of the incredible time we'd spent together. I saw myself differently thanks to him. I just wished he was still by my side. It wasn't as much fun being a confident, whole woman without him.

"So it was you who left with Trey after the dance." Star grinned and leaned closer, both elbows on the conference table while we ignored our work a little longer. We were supposed to be setting up the conference room for my first meeting with the new client Pendleton had given me last week. "I thought he looked awfully possessive of Natalie, and it made me worry because I was rooting for him to like you. Guess I didn't need to worry about that."

The jabbing pain in my chest must have shown on my face because she frowned.

"Did I read that whole situation wrong?" Star peered over her shoulder at the door and then glanced at her watch. The office didn't officially open its doors for another ten minutes, and my client wouldn't arrive for an hour after that. "I thought when you didn't come back to work after the lunch you shared with him…"

Remembering that lunch in the rain and the sprint back to his SUV, I had to smile. Going home with Trey had been…life-changing. I'd been crazy about him even then, because he'd seen through my Natalie disguise and still wanted to be with the real me. The sound of the coffeepot on the side table chiming that it was ready

brought me back to reality. My magical dream was over.
I was just Courtney again.

It was hard to rejoice at being a better woman when
it came with a price tag of a loneliness so heavy it felt
like it would suffocate me.

"We, uh…" I cleared my throat, emotion thick in my
voice. "He and I were just a temporary thing."

"Oh, honey." Star squeezed my wrist, comforting
and reassuring as her bracelets jangled against the wood
surface. "He sure doesn't strike me as a guy who does
'temporary.' His name hasn't been linked with anyone
in the tabloids in years."

I wasn't sure if I felt touched to think he had very
discriminating taste, or if I should be offended that I
was the only woman he'd given a short-term option for
dating. I hugged my arms around my waist and half
wished I hadn't given him that ultimatum in the aftermath of an emotional evening.

At the time, it had seemed the right thing to do.
The only thing to do. He needed to fix his relationship
with his father. And I guess I wanted to be the one to
give him that nudge. He'd done so much to help me,
after all. Maybe deep down inside I thought I'd been
helping him. But now that I was alone and miserable
without Trey?

I had to wonder if I'd made the biggest mistake of
my life.

A commotion outside the conference room doors
caught our attention and we rose to see what was going
on.

"If you want my business, you'll open your doors
now," a heavy masculine voice with a hint of an ac-

cent drifted through the door, the tone imperious and demanding.

I straightened. I knew that voice. It had argued with me in front of fifty black-tie gala attendees. Star pulled open the door to see what was going on out in reception with me close on her heels.

Our office intern, Claudia, was busy trying to placate Thomas Fraser II. He stood in the waiting area wearing an expensive suit and surrounded by an entourage of five others—three men and two women. All were dressed for business and toting briefcases, iPads or both.

Dread made my stomach sink. Was he here to reveal my secret to the whole office? Pendleton hadn't fired me, but I had told him my dancing gig would remain secret.

"C-can I help you, Mr. Fraser?" I stepped forward to intervene since our office intern looked outmatched and Star hadn't moved to greet them.

"Only if you can get top management out here to handle my concerns." He slapped a broad hand on the reception desk, the force making a decorative basket of lemons become momentarily airborne. "I've got business to transfer, but only if I can get it taken care of this morning."

Star jumped into action. "I'll see what I can do, sir."

But my boss was already on the scene, the news of a surprise High Net Worth client having traveled through the office fast. Pendleton told Star to hold his calls and to reschedule the appointment I was supposed to have in an hour since he'd need the conference room for Mr. Fraser. He then ushered the entourage into the meeting space.

Confused, suspicious and still worried I would some-how be unmasked by Trey's father, I stepped back to let the group pass.

And Thomas Fraser—that stern, cranky patriarch of the Fraser family who'd given Trey such a hard time—actually winked at me.

I might have thought I'd dreamed it, but Star glanced at me, her eyebrows raised in question. Of course, I had no clue what was going on. When the reception area was cleared of everyone but Star and me, with all the higher-ups in the meeting and Claudia tasked to make a run for more refreshments, the front door opened again.

Trey walked in.

Gorgeously rumpled, in a suit that looked like he'd slept in it, Trey paused in the middle of the reception area, his dark eyes wandering over me. Was it my imag-ination, or were there shadows under those eyes?

If this had been a Hollywood moment, the camera would have moved in for a close-up of his face the way my eyes did now. A golden glow would suddenly shine all around him through a trick of backlighting, and the audience would sigh collectively. Just like my heart sighed at the sight of him.

But this wasn't Hollywood.

I hadn't realized I said the words out loud until Trey looked around him.

"Is that a problem? Because we're only a few blocks to the southeast of Hollywood."

"Er. No." At the heat I felt rising in my face, I real-ized that all my new confidence wouldn't keep me from getting embarrassed. Especially in front of this man who still meant so much to me even if he hadn't been willing to make a break from the past and confront his father. "Your dad's party is in the conference room."

I pointed to the closed door, though I suspected he remembered where the room was. Star had been hovering near my elbow, but she used that moment to dart toward the back offices, muttering something about needing to see someone.

Leaving us alone.

"I know where Dad is." Trey stepped closer and I noticed he definitely didn't look as polished as usual. One side of his shirt collar was tucked into his jacket, while the other rested on the lapel. His hair stood at crazy angles like he'd run his hands through it too many times. But seeing him disheveled didn't do a damn thing to detract from his good looks.

I missed him so badly I hurt everywhere.

"You're welcome to join him," I assured him, my words stiff. "They only went in a minute ago."

"I know." Trey paced the reception area, checking out the artwork on the walls, in no apparent hurry. Coming closer to me all the time. "He was really proud of his mission. It was his idea for a distraction."

Mission? Distraction?

"Excuse me?" I watched him straighten a photograph of our office in London and then stop a few feet in front of me.

"I told my dad that I needed to get you back. And he plotted a scheme to empty your office of everyone but you so we could have some time to talk."

I was afraid my ears weren't working. Had he just said he needed to get me back?

"Your dad knows how to command a crowd, that's for sure." I tried to envision Trey and his father having a conversation where they weren't arguing. Where they were on the same side.

Could Trey have made some kind of family truce after all? I tingled inside, remembering that this was all I'd really asked him for. To step out of the shadow of the feud with his dad.

Could he have actually done just that? A spark of hope flared against the dark loneliness I'd been battling.

"I've realized the Fraser men are formidable when they want something." He toyed with the lemons on Star's desk, his hand close to my shoulder now. "Stubborn and hardheaded, someone once told me."

I thought about that hand touching me and couldn't take my eyes off it.

"I call it like I see it," I insisted, needing to stick to my guns even though my hunger for him welled up inside me like an endless ache. "I'm not going to sell myself short anymore, Trey. You helped me realize that I deserved more than what I was getting out of life. And now I can't settle for less. Especially not from you."

"I admire that." He stood toe-to-toe with me now, the supreme test for my willpower. "You forced me to really think about what I was doing and how I was sabotaging my future by choosing to be at odds with my father all the time."

Inhaling, I could smell his aftershave and memories of us tangled together flooded my senses.

"You…want to fix things with your dad?" Surprise and hope sparked inside me. I hadn't expected this after how fiercely he'd argued with his father. How emphatically he'd told me they'd butted heads all their lives… And given Trey was here alone with me, maybe he wanted to fix something else…

Us.

My stomach fluttered with nerves at the possibility.

"I don't know that we can ever completely repair our relationship," he admitted. "But we're going to try to find ways to join forces from a business perspective and see if we can iron out some problems that way."

"Honestly?" He'd done what I'd asked? Confronted his father after months of working against him? "You guys are…" I looked back and forth between the conference room and Trey. "…working together on this? He's really helping you so you can talk to me alone right now?"

"He set up his entrance as carefully as if he was staging a scene in a film." Trey grinned. "I never thought I would enjoy his company so much, but when we're in agreement…he's not so bad."

I was finally starting to get it. Trey hadn't just talked to his father about working together again in film. He'd had some kind of heart-to-heart that involved me. And, amazingly, the elder Fraser must have supported the decision for Trey to come talk to me today or he wouldn't have staged that big commotion this morning.

Wow.

"I think your dad is hiding a big heart under the manipulation and bluster."

"I'm starting to get that impression too." He shook his head. "I'm disappointed that it took me a lifetime to figure it out."

"I'm glad for you." I didn't want to assume anything about Trey's motives in this meeting with me. But then again, I really, really hoped that he was here to show me more than the fact he'd mended a rift with his dad.

"I'm glad for *you*." Trey caught my hand in his and

lifted it, folding my fingers down against his palm in a gesture that warmed me to my toes. "Because if it wasn't for you, I would still be hitting my head against a wall, not understanding why my dad kept pushing and testing me all the time."

The heat of his hand sent ribbons of pleasure right through my bloodstream to my heart.

"More importantly," he continued, picking up my other hand too, "you cared about me enough to give me the push I needed to see things in a new light."

Had I done that? With his dark, hypnotic gaze probing mine, I couldn't quite remember how it had all unfolded. My hip hit the edge of Star's desk and I realized my knees weren't working. Thankfully, Trey caught my waist with one arm, his other hand still holding mine.

"I was feeling awfully sure of myself that night," I said finally. "You'd helped me to face the world and see myself in a new way. I guess I figured I'd return the favor."

"So now that we know you're strong and confident while I'm hardheaded and stubborn…" His mouth neared mine, his voice lowered for my ears alone. "What do we do next?"

"Um. I'm not sure." I watched his lips, tracking their movement, wanting to feel them pressed to mine. "Make love. Fall in love. Something like that."

My heartbeat sped. Raced. Clamored.

"But not necessarily in that order," he whispered, his breath warm against my cheek. "I've already fallen for you, Courtney."

I blinked through the sensual haze to meet his eyes and found a clarity and sincerity that made me feel light as air and more hopeful for the future than I'd ever been. I started to tremble everywhere.

"Th-that's—" I slid a hand over my lips, not because I was embarrassed of my stutter but because he had the power to make me such an emotional, happy mess. "That's excellent news. Because I'm pretty crazy about you too, Trey Fraser."

He lifted my hand to his lips and kissed the fingers in that debonair way that made my heart flutter. I loved it. Loved him. But I still had a little bit of the showgirl lurking inside me, so I wrapped both arms around his neck and kissed him for all I was worth.

Right in the middle of the office foyer. Not caring who saw.

He looked a little dazed by the time I was done. I felt like the luckiest woman on earth.

"How long do you think your father is going to keep everyone distracted?" I asked, heart beating fast.

"My dad is a larger than life guy. He does every-thing to the extreme..." He glanced at his wristwatch. "I'd say we have until lunch, at least."

It wasn't even ten o'clock yet.

"How tinted are the windows on your vehicle?" I asked, a long-standing fantasy coming to mind.

He raised an eyebrow. I didn't feel the slightest bit embarrassed. I felt pretty full of myself. Full of love. And very ready to show it.

"I've always regretted that I didn't go out to your SUV with you that first night when you asked me to meet you behind Backstage," I confided. "In fact, I've been daydreaming about what might have happened between us if I had met you there."

"Never let it be said I don't fulfill your fantasies."

Trey was already halfway out the door, one strong arm steering me with him.

I tilted my head into his shoulder, contented, excited and wildly in love all at once. My double life might have come to an end, but the most thrilling part was about to begin...

* * * * *

JOANNE ROCK

WILD AND WICKED

_**1**_

"KYRA!" JESSE CHANDLER shouted to his business partner as he strode into the barn housing the offices of Crooked Branch Horse Farms. He juggled purchases from the tack shop until he reached a sawhorse table where he could set them down. "I've got all the leather you wanted. Saddles and bridles, riding gloves and a dominatrix outfit—oh, wait. That last one wasn't a business purchase."

He sorted through the new supplies in the converted old building Kyra used strictly for storage and office space. The horses Kyra bred and trained lived in much more modern quarters behind this barn.

Removing price tags and testing the leather of the new stock, Jesse waited for his best friend and colleague to appear. He'd never made her blush in over ten years of trying, but hope sprang eternal. No matter that Kyra Stafford was the one woman in Citrus County he'd never hit on, he still loved to make her laugh.

"Perfect," came a feminine purr from over his left shoulder—far closer than he'd anticipated. "I think you need an assertive woman to keep you in line, Jesse Chandler."

For about two seconds, he reacted to the sultry promise he must have imagined behind the words.

Awareness fired through him, heated his insides despite the breeze drifting in the wide-open barn doors. The Gulf of Mexico rested a mere thousand acres away to border the northwest corner of the state-of-the-art Florida horse farm and training facility. Surely the gentle wind off the water should have helped him keep cool in February.

But then Kyra stepped around him to stand by his side and look over the new tack, her long blond hair grazing his arm. Smart, sensible Kyra Stafford who had never flirted with him for so much as five seconds.

What the hell was the matter with him?

Shaking off an absurd sense of attraction he'd never felt for his best friend before, Jesse attributed the *Twilight Zone* moment to too many nights alone. He definitely needed to remedy that situation this weekend.

"Funny, I don't see any dominatrix garb here." Kyra glanced up at him with her bright blue eyes. Innocent blue eyes, damn it. And smiled. "Be careful what you wish for, Jesse."

From any other woman, Jesse would have pegged that remark for blatant enticement. But he was obviously going through major sensual deprivation if he was hearing come-ons in Kyra's speech.

Hell yeah, he'd be more careful.

Clearing his throat, he decided maybe they were just both getting too old for the game of trying to make Kyra blush. "Guess I left the spiked collar at the store." He started hanging bridles on the wall, determined to make tracks between him and this ill-advised conversation. "That's okay. I don't go for the hard-core type anyway."

"Seems like you're not going for any type lately," Kyra observed, tossing her hair over her shoulder as she leaned a blue-jean-clad hip into the sawhorse table. At twenty-four, she looked sort of like *Buffy the Vampire Slayer* meets *Bonanza*—a petite blonde in dusty cowboy boots with enough determination and drive to move mountains, or, more often, stubborn horses. "Is southern Florida's most notorious bad boy finally mellowing?"

Allowing a saddle created for one of their new ponies to slide back to the plywood with a thunk, Jesse turned to face the woman who knew him best. The woman whose question mirrored his own recent fear.

"You know I couldn't mellow if I tried." Not that he would try. He was too content with bachelorhood, even though his last girlfriend was sticking to him like glue despite his best efforts to move on. He needed to show Greta he wasn't the forever-after—or even a three-date—kind of guy.

"Why? Because there'd be ten women lined up in Victoria's Secret lingerie and armed with apple pies if they knew you were thinking about settling down?"

She tried on a pair of fawn-colored riding gloves and stared at her hand encased in suede.

Jesse grinned. "As if that would be such a hardship."

She cocked an eyebrow at him in one of Kyra's classic don't-bullshit-me looks.

He shrugged. "I don't know what's up. I've been putting in a lot of hours making final preparations around the Crooked Branch before I turn my attention to my custom homes business. Maybe I've just been working too hard lately."

He hated leaving Kyra to run the business all by herself, but that had been her stipulation from the moment they'd went in on the operation together. She'd vowed to buy back his substantial share of the farm once she'd made it a success.

And damned if she wasn't whooping butt on that promise already. As soon as she clinched one more horse sale, she'd own the controlling share of the business.

The farm had been great part-time work for Jesse in the years he'd played minor league baseball for kicks. But now that he was closing in on thirty, he was mentally ready to hang his own shingle for a custom home-building business and let Kyra go her own way with the Crooked Branch. His older brother had told Jesse last spring that he would never be able to still his wandering feet, but Jesse disagreed.

He might not be able to commit to any one woman, but he could commit to a place, damn it. Not only was he putting down roots in Citrus County, he was cementing his ties to the area by starting his own business here.

Still, he worried a little about leaving Kyra to her own devices at the training facility. Running a horse-boarding-and-breeding business wasn't exactly a cushy way of life and as the date for him to bow out approached, Jesse couldn't help thinking about all the tough jobs that Kyra would be left with to handle solo.

The physically demanding aspects of handling stubborn horses. The chauvinistic attitudes of some of the owners.

He hated the thought of anyone ever giving her a hard time.

She eyed him with quiet patience, reminding him

why she was so damn good at working with antsy horses. "Are you sure you're working, Jesse, or are you maybe overcompensating for leaving in two weeks? No offense, but this is more tack than we'll need in two lifetimes." She studied him in that open, no-holds-barred manner that had made him trust her from the moment they met. "Are you just using the excuse of work to hide out from some overeager female of the week?"

Jesse shifted his weight from one foot to the other. Caught.

Why in the hell had he thought he might be able to hide anything from this woman? Kyra's eyes might be innocent, but they were wise.

Jesse shoved the stack of too many gloves to the back of the sawhorse table. "Honestly, I'm having a little trouble with Greta lately. She looks at me and sees picket fences no matter how much I avoid her." He'd met the German model in Miami Beach last fall and they'd spent a crazy few days locked in her condo overlooking the water.

Between Greta's flashy lifestyle and jet-set friends, Jesse had assumed she wanted the same things from their time together as he did—simple, basic things like mind-blowing sex and a few hours to forget life wasn't as perfect as they pretended.

But ever since then, Greta had called him on and off, even going so far as to show up on his doorstep over the holidays to see if he wanted company.

"She thinks you're marriage material?" Kyra's skeptical tone suggested a woman could be committed for harboring those kinds of thoughts.

"Go figure. But she's damned persistent. And you know how I hate to hurt people." One of the foremost reasons he avoided relationships like the plague was to ensure he never hurt anybody. He'd learned that lesson early in life when his father had torn Jesse's whole family apart with infidelities until he walked out on his wife and kids for good.

Too bad Jesse's tact of keeping things light with Greta had bitten him in the ass this time.

"You need a different kind of woman." Kyra sidled closer.

Or was that his imagination?

"Damn straight I do." He folded his arms across his chest, unwilling to take any chances with his overactive libido today. The last thing he needed was any freaky twinge of attraction to Kyra again.

"A woman who wants the same things from a relationship you do." Her voice took on a husky quality, reminding him of what it was like to trade pillow confidences with floral-scented females in the dark.

Not females like Kyra, of course.

He cleared his throat.

"That's how I'm going to approach things from now on." Jesse turned back to the mountain of leather goods on the plywood table and mentally started dialing numbers from his address book. A night with Lolita Banker would satisfy every stray sexual urge he'd had today, and then some.

"Then why don't you let me help?" Kyra's hand snaked over to his, gently restraining him from shuffling around the new bridles. "I know exactly what you want."

Damnation. Her touch sizzled through him even as her words called to mind sensual visions. The arch of a woman's back, the pink flush of feminine skin, the sweet sighs of fulfillment as…

Jesse's gaze slid from Kyra to the mound of fresh hay that waited not ten yards away.

Holy freaking hell.

He withdrew his hand from her light touch as if burned. Then again, maybe he had been. At the very least, his brain circuits had obviously fried because there was no way in hell she'd meant anything remotely sexual.

Determined to escape that provocative vision forever, Jesse closed his eyes and clutched the new saddle in front of him like a shield. Maybe his mind was playing tricks on him because he wouldn't be seeing Kyra much once he started his new business.

"Great idea." He forced the words past dry lips, trying like hell to remember the color of Lolita's hair, the shape of her mouth, anything. "Let's grab a beer after work and you can help me figure out how to let Greta down easy. You know somebody to hook her up with?"

He backed toward the barn doors, clutching the saddle in a death grip. Perhaps it was a good thing he'd be leaving the Crooked Branch in two weeks after all. "Besides, Lolita Banker's waitressing at the bar on Indian Rocks Beach. Maybe I just need to meet someone else to help me—" *Forget all about seducing my best friend?* "Get my head on straight again."

Turning away from those vivid blue eyes and poured-into-denim body, Jesse shouted over his shoulder. "Happy hour starts at six."

HAPPY HOUR?

Why didn't they call it something more apt like frustrated-as-hell hour?

Kyra fumed as she watched Jesse's motorcycle kick up gravel on his way out of the driveway—as if he couldn't put enough distance between him and her lame attempt at seduction.

She'd had a thing for Jesse from the first time they'd met. His perpetually too-long hair, dark eyes and prominent cheekbones gave him a dangerous look that hinted of long-forgotten Seminole heritage. He wore one gold stud in his ear, which, according to high school legend, he'd had ever since his tenth-grade girlfriend convinced him they should pierce a body part together. Jesse had kept the stud long after the girl.

Kyra had met him right after the ear-piercing. She'd caught him sneaking out one of her father's horses at night to indulge in wild rides. Eventually, she'd discovered his midnight trips were more about escape than about raising hell. But that knowledge never altered her vision of Jesse Chandler as a danger-loving thrill seeker.

She'd been all of ten years old at the time and far too starry-eyed with Jesse to spill his secret to her manic-depressive dad. She'd started leaving Buster saddled for Jesse so he wouldn't break his neck riding bareback.

Every morning, Buster would be groomed and locked in his stall, his tack neatly hung on the wall.

Their friendship had cemented that summer, despite the five-year difference between them. Their paths rarely crossed in the school system, but Kyra heard all the rumors about him and collected Jesse folklore the way some girls collected scrapbooks of their favorite rock stars. She'd outgrown that infatuation with him, but the man still had the power to dazzle her. To make her wonder...

Unwilling to put her heart on the line, she'd ignored

the stray longings for her best friend over the years, even going so far as to convince herself they could operate a business together.

Crooked Branch Farms was now one of the most prestigious breeding and training facilities in southern Florida, but all of Kyra's hard work and new success still hadn't fulfilled the ache within her that had started one sultry summer night fourteen years ago. In fact, now her workplace was tainted with longing for Jesse, ensuring she could never fully escape from thoughts of him.

Ever the practical thinker, Kyra had devised a two-prong plan to solve the problem. First, she was working her way toward taking over the controlling half of the business. If she could sell one more horse this year, that goal would be attainable and she'd be able to run the Crooked Branch independently.

Part two of her plan was much more fun. She wanted to seduce Jesse and experience the mythical sexual prowess of a man who'd long inhabited her dreams.

She knew he would never settle down. Yet that didn't make her want him any less. In some ways, it made him a safe—temporary—choice for her wary heart.

If he ever noticed she wasn't sporting pigtails anymore.

Sighing, Kyra stalked back to her office and flung herself onto the futon across from her bookshelves. As she idly sifted through a stack of paperwork, she admitted to herself today's attempt to make Jesse see her as a woman had been an unmitigated flop. It's not like she wanted picket fences, either. She simply wanted a night to act out her longtime fantasy before he left their business for good.

So there wasn't a chance she'd facilitate his seduction of Lolita Banker at the Indian Rocks Beach bar. For all Kyra cared, he could just twist in the wind while Greta the German Wonder-bod made him feel guilty about not playing house with her.

And in the meantime, Kyra would turn up the heat on her own seductive plans—just as soon as she figured out what they were. Heaven knew suggestive talk wasn't the key according to her experience with him today.

How could a man be so blind?

She needed a more fast-acting approach, a surefire way to get his attention.

Just then a flyer caught her eye from her pile of paperwork. A pamphlet advertising Tampa Bay's annual Gasparilla festival. This year the mock pirate invasion of the city was sponsored by a company Jesse's older brother owned.

Her eyes scanned the paper, slowing over a phrase that suggested the festival was hiring a handful of actors to stage strictly-in-fun kidnappings of partygoers. Jesse's brother Seth had hand-scrawled a note across the paper asking Jesse to consider playing one of the buccaneers himself, in fact.

Kyra knew he had nixed the request pleading that he needed to indulge in some R & R and just enjoy the festival before his home-building gig kicked into high gear in another two weeks. She also knew that probably meant he would be searching for a flavor-of-the-week woman at Gasparilla. Especially since his usual method of telling a woman they were through was insinuating himself in a new five-day relationship.

All of which put Jesse at the festival while leaving one buccaneer slot still vacant.

She'd wanted a way to make Jesse Chandler see her

as a woman, hadn't she? She had the feeling an old-fashioned corset and fishnet stockings would do the trick. So what if pirates were usually peg-legged men dressed in rags with bad teeth?

Kyra would improvise.

And abduct the hottest man in Tampa Bay for a night he wouldn't forget.

THREE DAYS LATER, Kyra stood on the deck of the famed *Jose Gaspar* pirate boat. As the warm February breeze lifted her hair from her neck, she tugged the strings on her black leather corset a little tighter and more breasts magically appeared.

The modern day push-up bra didn't have anything on eighteenth-century technology.

Studying her reflection in the blunted steel of a costume dagger given to her by an overzealous event stylist on board the boat, Kyra thought she looked as close to a sexpot as she was possibly capable. Sure she'd never have the perfect figure of Greta the German Wonder-bod, but by a miracle of her black leather getup, she had more curves than ever before.

No matter that any spare ounce of flesh on her rib cage had been squeezed northward in order to achieve the effect. For today at least, she looked downright voluptuous.

Kyra shoved her dagger into a loop on her black cargo miniskirt. Her leather corset just reached the waist of the skirt while a gauzy, low-cut blouse skimmed her breasts underneath the leather. She hadn't bothered to wear a bra for the event given the old-fashioned lace-up garment currently holding her breathless.

She wouldn't lack for support, but if the February

226 Wild and Wicked

Gulf breeze turned cold, she'd probably be showing a little more than she'd like through the white cotton blouse. Who'd have thought the wardrobe they'd given her would be so treacherously thin?

Still, Kyra was pleased she'd taken the plunge and committed herself to today's cause. After years of near-invisibility around Jesse, she needed something dramatic to make him notice her as a woman.

How hard could it be to sway him once he noticed her in *that* way?

As the bellow of mock cannons echoed in her ears, Kyra peered across the ship deck filled to overflowing with local luminaries dressed as pirates and waved to Jesse's scowling older brother, Seth. A self-made millionaire, Seth Chandler had always enjoyed a more low-profile approach to life than Jesse. Yet Seth had been forced to don an eye patch today when the lead buccaneer had quit an hour before the *Jose Gaspar* set sail.

A role he didn't seem to be enjoying if his surly expression was any indication.

The dull roar of the crowd standing onshore near Tampa Bay's convention center jerked her thoughts from Seth back to the present. Leaning on the rail surrounding the main deck, Kyra squinted out across the water in the hope of finding her quarry.

A swirl of purple, yellow and green gleamed back at her. The Gasparilla event shared several things in common with New Orleans's Mardi Gras—its signature colors, a parade organized by Krewes that tossed beads and other souvenirs to attendees and a serious party attitude.

But the resemblance ended there. Gasparilla celebrated a distinctly Floridian heritage with its nod to a famous pirate and the events on the water. As the 165-foot boat sailed toward shore, a flotilla of over two hundred smaller watercraft followed in its wake.

And of course, Mardi Gras didn't present the opportunities for a friendly kidnapping that Gasparilla offered for the first time this year. Anticipation tingled through Kyra as her chance to open Jesse's eyes drew near.

Just as they dropped anchor, she spotted him.

All six feet two inches of rangy muscle and masculine grace talking animatedly with friends. Or maybe some new conquest. Kyra couldn't fully see who he was speaking to through the crush. Funny how her feminine radar had been able to track *him* without any problem, though.

She'd known he would be here because Seth had asked him to drop off his boat at the festival today. Jesse had mentioned that he was looking forward to spending most of the day in downtown Tampa—after the invasion of the city there was a parade, followed by a street festival into the night.

A night Kyra intended to claim for her own.

Before she could secure a solid plan for making her way through the throng to reach Jesse, Seth swung out over the mass of partygoers, signaling the start of the pirate invasion. Chaos ensued on the boat and off as buccaneers leaped, swung or ran off the *Jose Gaspar* to greet attendees and abduct a few innocent bystanders.

Born athletic and toned from days on horseback, Kyra didn't flinch at the idea of climbing a rope and flinging herself out into the mob. She was a little surprised at the substantial chorus of male appreciation as she did so, however. Apparently her fishnet stockings and brand-new cleavage invited attention because she

was seriously ogled—and groped—for the first time
in her life.

"Take me, honey!" a partygoer shouted as he stumbled into her path. Wearing a crooked three-cornered
hat emblazoned with a Jolly Roger and a Metallica
T-shirt, the guy sloshed beer over the rim of his plastic
cup onto the toe of her lace-up black boots.

Kyra righted his precarious cup and sidled past him,
her gaze scanning the crowd for Jesse. She wasn't so
desperate for attention that she'd settle for the lecher-
ous stare of a drunken stranger.

Unfortunately, her corset attracted plenty of the
wrong kind of attention.

She smacked away a hand that brushed along her
thigh, wishing she'd brought along a riding crop for
crowd control. Who'd have thought a glorified push-
up bra could turn so many heads?

Desperate to find the only man whose attention she
really cared about, Kyra caught sight of him leaning into
the shade of a palm tree planted in between the concrete
slabs of sidewalk some fifteen yards away. Focused on
her muscle-bound goal, she stepped around a strolling
hot-pretzel vendor and a mother clutching the hands of
toddler twins wearing eye patches.

Only then did she spy Jesse's companion. Greta the
German Wonder-bod giggled relentlessly at every word
out of his mouth, her perfect figure looking svelte and
toned in yellow shorts that barely covered her ridiculously tiny butt. A white T-shirt spelled out Monaco in
matching sunny yellow letters.

Kyra knew damn well Greta didn't need the aid of a
corset to give her those amazing curves. The German
model had an effortless beauty that wouldn't desert her

when the festival was over. Even if she made a living slinging hay in blue jeans.

The ache of second-guessing tightened in Kyra's chest. Would it be cruel to pull Jesse away if he would honestly rather patch things up with Greta? God knows, it looked like he was enjoying himself, his dark eyes alight with good humor and his lone dimple flashing in his left cheek.

But then again, Jesse had a way of making any woman feel like she was the center of his universe even as he plotted how to dance around any sort of commitment. His elusiveness was part of his charm.

And hadn't he just confided to Kyra three days ago that Greta wanted much more than he could provide?

Refusing to allow a little feminine insecurity to thwart her plan, Kyra charged toward the couple. No way would Jesse have invited Greta here today if he was worried that she was taking things too seriously. Greta was probably just chasing him the same way so many women did.

She pulled herself up short.

The way Kyra was chasing him for the first time in her life.

But at least Kyra knew what would come out of a relationship with her best friend. A few nights of amazing pleasure so she could get over her age-old crush on him and they would go back to being strictly friends.

Committed to her plan, Kyra withdrew a silk scarf from the pocket of her cargo skirt and wrapped one end of the filmy material around each of her hands.

She didn't have the option of carrying off Jesse over one shoulder the way a guy pirate might kidnap his wench of choice. Therefore, she had to resort to more underhanded means of abduction.

Edging up behind Jesse, she was neatly hidden from Greta's view by his broad back. A white tank shirt bearing the name of a horse show she'd competed in long ago exposed his tanned shoulders and strong arms. Low-slung black shorts hugged his hips and a very fine…back view.

A shiver of excitement jolted through her as she neared him, along with a slight tremor of nerves.

Before she could change her mind, Kyra looped her pink silk scarf over his head to cover his eyes. In a flash, she pressed herself to his warm back to whisper in his ear.

"Don't fight it, hotshot. Consider yourself a pirate prisoner." The words tripped off her tongue in a breathy rush as her body reacted to his with spontaneous heat. "For today, you're all mine."

2

JESSE RECOGNIZED the silky voice whispering into his ear. Yet he couldn't merge his image of practical Kyra Stafford with the decidedly feminine curves pressed against his back. Or the exotically scented scarf blindfolding him into a world of pure sensation.

A world where it was getting mighty damn difficult to remember why he and Kyra had always maintained a strictly platonic relationship.

For a moment, the roar of the overcrowded street faded from his hearing. The only sound penetrating his brain was the soft huff of breath in his ear as his captor demanded compliance.

Before his hormones recovered enough to reply, he could hear Greta start squawking a few feet in front of him.

"Excuse me?" Her words dripped sarcasm like a Popsicle in July. "I came here with this man. You can't just—"

"Well, it looks like you won't be leaving with him," Kyra retorted from behind him, her voice all the more familiar now that it was lifted in normal conversation.

"A Gasparilla pirate doesn't exactly need to ask your permission."

Maybe Kyra was only trying to rescue him from Greta today. A welcome intervention given that Jesse hadn't brought Greta with him and had been trying his best to avoid her. Still, she'd managed to track him down in a crowd of a hundred thousand people with unerring instincts.

She'd have him chained to her side on the first boat back to Berlin if he wasn't careful.

He held both hands up, resigned to whatever scheme Kyra had in the works. He just hoped she eased away from him soon, before his body started reacting publicly to those breasts against his spine. "Sounds like I have no choice but to surrender."

Greta's spluttered indignation took a backseat to Kyra's seductive whisper.

"Excellent decision," she breathed in his ear, steering him through the crowd and away from Greta with slow steps. "You are wise to come along quietly."

Each stride brushed her body against his, making him keenly aware she wore a blouse with no bra to speak of underneath. Those awesome C-cups couldn't belong to Kyra. Could they?

She was holding him captive wearing some kind of laced leather outfit that bit into his back even while it thrust her breasts forward in luscious offering, sort of like a—

Holy freaking hell. Maybe after all his lip about buying a dominatrix outfit, she'd decided to call his bluff.

Raw lust ripped through him with a vengeance. He stopped dead in his tracks and twisted around to face her, whipping off the scarf with an impatient hand. The sight that greeted his eyes was better than a domina-trix outfit.

No, make that worse. He wasn't supposed to be lick-ing his chops over his best friend, of all people.

She was dressed as a pirate. Not any normal pirate with a bandanna and a blackened tooth, though. More like the kind of lush X-rated lady pirate you'd expect to find in some half-baked adult film called *Blow the Man Down.*

His eyes did a slow ride over her barely there blouse partially covered by the leather corset he'd felt earlier. The garment pushed her breasts up and out and straight into any man's view, the tops of that creamy white flesh exposed while the rest was only marginally hidden be-neath thin cotton.

Where had those amazing breasts come from? Was he that blind that he'd never noticed them underneath the men's T-shirts she normally favored? And he'd def-initely never noticed her legs before. At least not like this, he hadn't. Somehow he had overlooked her lightly muscled thighs and long, lean calves in the jeans she always wore when she worked with the horses.

But her abbrieviated black skirt and fishnet stockings practically put a neon sign on those gams and screamed, Look At Me!

And was he ever looking.

Jesse was carefully scrutinizing every inch of her right down to her high-heeled lace-up boots when she cupped one hand under his chin and forced his gaze back up to her face.

Too bad he couldn't make visual contact with her. He'd obviously popped an eyeball along the way.

"What's the verdict, matey? You like what you see?"

She cocked one hand on her hip and did a little shimmy that left him gasping for a breath.

An appreciative whistle emanated from somewhere nearby. Although they'd moved out of the densest part of the crowd, they were still surrounded by enthusiastic festival attendees draped in colorful beads and drinking beer from plastic cups in the shape of old-fashioned steins.

And if Jesse found out who the hell was whistling at Kyra he'd sew the guy's lips together.

Jamming her silk scarf into the pocket of his shorts, he tucked Kyra under one arm and hauled her even farther from the masses. "Are you insane?" he hissed, wishing he could have thought of another way to get her out of there besides touching her. His hand burned where it rested on one slim but perfectly curved hip. "There are a bunch of guys halfway to drunk and slobbering in that crowd. You're a walking target for trouble in that outfit."

She shoved away from him as they rounded the corner of the Tampa Convention Center away from the water and the excitement of the pirate invasion. "The only one who seems to be targeting me for trouble is you, Chandler. Are you halfway to drunk and slobbering?"

Drunk—no. The jury was still out on the slobbering issue. There was definitely some drooling going on right now.

He took a deep breath and made a stab at sounding reasonable. "You're just a bit—" He searched for the right words as his gaze roamed her outrageous costume. Her sexy-as-hell body. "Naked to be out in public, don't you think?"

"You call this naked?" She planted one fist on her hip, the breeze from the bay blowing in to ruffle her hair and mold her blouse to her body.

Jesse swallowed—twice—but still couldn't find his voice in a throat gone dry.

"Your German plaything is showing off half her butt cheeks in those little shorts of hers today while I remain decently covered." Kyra tugged her skirt hem for emphasis.

Jesse wasn't sure he even remembered their thread of conversation anymore since the wind had conspired to show him the shadowy outline of Kyra's naked body beneath her clothes. "The skirt half of you isn't what needs covering."

He never thought he'd hear himself beg a woman to put her clothes back on. But this was Kyra, the one woman he'd always made it a point to treat honorably. The one long-term, enduring relationship he'd ever managed with any woman save his sister.

And damn it, he couldn't seem to stop staring at her breasts.

She flashed him a wicked smile as she trailed her hand along her shoulder where bare skin met the edge of her blouse. "Oh. You mean this half."

Transfixed, he watched her fingers skim over her own flesh. He couldn't have turned away if there'd been a hurricane blowing in off the bay.

Her finger paused just before she reached the top of one breast, then hooked into the loop of a single strand of gold plastic beads she wore in deference to the day. "Guess it is a bit much, isn't it? Maybe the costumer decided to go flashy because of the good media coverage Gasparilla is receiving this year. Although we're far removed from the spotlight way back here."

She looked around meaningfully at their relatively quiet position at the back of the crowd.

Not that Jesse had any intention of returning to the heart of the festival with Kyra dressed like this. She'd be fending off too many wolf whistles to have fun.

Scavenging for control, Jesse swiped a hand across his forehead. Had it ever been this hot in February before? "I think the coast is clear. I appreciate you saving me from Greta back there." That had to be the reason for Kyra's abduction scenario, right? "I don't know how she found me in a such a big crowd, but she's been glued to me all day. I appreciate you showing up when you did."

He hoped he sounded marginally normal and unaffected.

She shrugged. "Guess you lucked out then. You got what you wanted by me getting what I wanted."

"How do you figure?" Even if he hadn't been choking on his own damn arousal, he had the feeling he wouldn't have followed her thinking.

"You gave Greta the slip, which is what you wanted. I got you for the night, which is what I wanted."

Her Cheshire-cat smile fanned the flames of his already molten imagination.

Jesse refused to screw up this friendship by allowing his libido to translate for him. Surely she didn't mean what he thought she meant.

"We're friends from way back," he reminded himself as much as her. "If you need me, all you have to do is let me know."

She laid both of her palms on his chest. "But I've never needed you quite like this before."

The cool strength of her small hands permeated his shirt. No doubt she had to feel the slam of his heart, the furnace heat of his body.

"No?"

"No. Tonight isn't going to be about friendship." Her blue eyes locked on his. "Tonight is going to be about you and me, man to woman." She leaned in closer, her incredible breasts almost brushing his chest. "And since you're still technically my captive, I'm going to demand that you treat me like the woman you've never been able to see in me."

That sounded dangerous as hell. But before he could protest, her voice turned to a whisper, forcing him to listen all the more carefully.

"That means we're going to be sipping champagne instead of swilling beers. That means I expect you to feed me from your fingers. Dance with me hip to hip." She sidled closer for emphasis, her hip grazing his. "In general, Jesse, now that I've got my very own bad boy at my fingertips, I'm going to wield every trick of seduction I've ever seen you use on other women and apply them to you. Slowly."

Jesse didn't remember when his jaw hit the ground, but he definitely recalled when the heart failure started to set in. It had been right about the time the word "seduction" had rolled off of Kyra's tongue like a promise of erotic torment.

Finally, he knew exactly what she was asking.

Too bad he didn't know if he'd survive it.

KYRA WATCHED Jesse clutch his chest as if she'd just shot him in the heart with her proposition.

Did he have to be so melodramatic about this?

Finally, he raised both hands in surrender. "Okay. You win. You'd better quit right now or I'm the one who'll damn well be blushing. And I'll never make another crack about dominatrix outfits."

"I assure you this is no joke." Could she be any more obvious in her approach? "I mean it, Jess."

"No." His response was delayed, but from the stern set to his jaw, he sure looked like he meant it.

"What do you mean *no?* You can't defy a pirate." What had happened to the playful man she'd known for over a decade? Didn't he know how to indulge in a few games anymore? "I could make you walk the plank. Or I could tie you to the mast and give you fifty lashes."

In fact, the thought inspired a few other ideas....

"What are you smiling about?" He studied her through narrowed eyes.

"I was just thinking fifty lashes might be more effective if I wielded my scarf." She made a dive for the pocket of his shorts. "Where did you hide that anyway?"

He caught her wrists in a steely grip. "No. No. And hell no."

She hadn't seen such a serious expression on his face in more years than she could count. Probably not since he'd had a big blowout with his older brother about who was in charge of Jesse's finances before he left Florida to start his baseball career. Jesse had won that argument along with his financial independence from Seth.

Now, his adamant rejection stung just a little. He'd gone out with every woman in her graduating class but her at one time or another. Was she so much of a turnoff that he couldn't even conceive of one romantic evening with her?

Thankfully, her stubbornness wouldn't allow her to

be daunted. She was only asking for a night, not a happily ever after. In two more weeks he would start his own business and sever their long partnership anyway. Would it kill him to indulge this final request?

She took a calming breath, inhaling the salty scent of the bay along with the jumble of culinary aromas from food stands lining today's pirate parade route. "Hell no I can't have my scarf back?"

"Hell no you can't corral me into this misadventure with you today. Have you really thought about what you're asking me?" He loosened his grip on her wrists, lowering her hands to her sides until he finally released her.

She allowed her gaze to slide down the length of his body. "Oh, I've definitely thought about it."

Was it just her imagination or had steam started hissing from his ears?

Sure he was angry with her. But what if just a little of that overheating was rooted in sexual excitement?

"Damn it, Kyra, you usually make more sensible decisions than this. You know better than anyone how badly I suck at relationships. Which is why I don't even *have* relationships." He paced the sidewalk in front of her like a nervous father on prom night. "Did I ever tell you about that documentary I got roped into last spring in Miami Beach—*Dangerous Men and the Women Who Love Them?* They put my interview in the 'commitment phobic' section like I was some damn psychology experiment." He paused to frown. To scowl. Then he turned the full force of his glare on her. "But that ought to tell you something."

"That documentary is the very reason I picked you. Nobody's looking for a relationship here, least of all me. My life's crazy enough right now. Being with you, I can be certain there will be no risk, no commitment." She allowed her gaze to linger on his body. "And proven expertise."

"You're looking for sex?" He said it so loud pseudo-pirates from fifty yards away turned to stare.

"After food, clothes and shelter, it's a pretty basic human need." She wasn't about to feel guilty about it. She'd been saving it up for twenty-four years after all. No one would ever accuse her of being promiscuous. Or even moderately wild.

Lowering his voice, he leaned closer. "You're think-ing of love. Love is what people need after food, clothes and shelter."

"Sex seems to be serving *you* well. I'm a healthy woman with natural appetites. And since I'm not look-ing for a relationship, who better to scratch the itch than my best bud?" She leaned closer. "Especially since local legend says you're the most skilled lay in town."

"We are *not* having this conversation." Tucking her hand in his, he stalked back toward the crowd and the dozens of tents set up to temporarily house food-service stands and other vendors.

"Damn. Just when the conversation was getting really interesting." Kyra followed him, content to let him vent his outrage until he was ready to listen to her side. She had been patient for half a lifetime for this man. She could wait another hour or two if need be. "Can I at least ask where we're going?"

"We'll find champagne to sip if it kills me. And then you can never say I didn't put forth an effort today."

Score.

Kyra allowed herself a small smile of victory since

Jesse was too busy plowing through dozens of bead-clad festivalgoers to notice.

JESSE KNEW if he turned around right now Kyra would be wearing a hint of a grin—the same exact one she wore in the training arena when she'd coerced a stubborn horse into doing exactly what she wished. She'd have him leaping hurdles in no time if he wasn't careful.

Lucky for him, he had a plan.

As he guided Kyra through the mass of pirate revelers, Jesse glared at anyone who stared at his captor while he thought through his strategy. He damned well didn't want her deciding to scratch that itch with one of these leering morons.

All he needed to do was appear semiagreeable. He'd have drinks with Kyra and make polite conversation instead of talking horses. He'd spin her around the dance floor a few times—or parking lot, given their locale—in front of one of the many bands playing at the festival.

And in the meantime, he'd try not to take it too personally that she only wanted him for sex. He liked sex as much as the next guy. Probably even more.

But he'd thought Kyra was the one female in his life who saw more in him than that.

Damn.

Refusing to get sidetracked, Jesse told himself he'd fulfill her requests on his terms and then tomorrow everything could go back to normal. And if she continued to look even mildly interested in something beyond the scope of friendship, he'd flirt wildly with any woman within winking distance to remind Kyra he was an ass when it came to the fair sex.

Simple.

Assuming he could peel his eyes off Kyra's body long enough to remember how to flirt wildly with another woman. He didn't know how much more of this kind of provocation he could take. He'd never had much in the way of immunity when it came to females.

And this wasn't just any female. This was his best friend. No matter that she was tying him in knots today, he owed her more respect than to engage in a one-night stand. She might think she could handle a no-strings affair, but that was probably because she'd never engaged in a meaningless relationship before.

At least not that he knew of.

Damn.

Maybe as long as he kept their conversation on neutral terrain and his thoughts out of her corset, he'd survive this day. He wouldn't bend his personal code of honor—limited though it might be—to give Kyra what she thought she wanted. He'd end up hurting her, and she'd end up resenting him—end of story. And he wouldn't risk losing the best friend he'd ever had for sex.

No matter how heady the temptation.

He turned around to hurry her along and found her lingering around a makeshift vendor's booth consisting of a few overturned wooden boxes half-veiled with a black velvet cloth and covered in silver jewelry. No way the overgrown beach bum in a Hawaiian shirt and shades behind the melon crates had a city license to sell anything.

Worse, the guy was staring over the top of his sunglasses to get a better look at Kyra's…blouse.

Gritting his teeth, Jesse tore through a group of cigar-smoking partyers cheering in Spanish and a kid's makeshift hopscotch game to reach Kyra.

He gave the so-called jewelry clerk the evil eye and wrapped a possessive arm around Kyra's waist. It hadn't been part of his plan to touch her, but he would damn well do whatever was necessary to keep the wolves at bay while she was dressed in her pirate garb.

So what if he was being hypocritical not wanting her to be ogled by ten thousand strangers while he played the field? *He* was a player. *She'd* barely left the Crooked Branch in the past five years, and now she wanted to go manhunting in fishnets?

Over his dead body.

She smiled up at him while he tried not to notice the smooth glide of her leather corset under his hand, the wildflower scent of her that he'd scarcely ever noticed before but knew he'd never forget now.

"You ready?" He edged the words out over a throat gone dry and a tension in his body so taut he thought he'd snap with it. He needed to get this day in motion and over with.

No dawdling allowed.

"In a minute." She grinned up at him with a siren's smile, a tiny piece of jewelry in her hand. Holding it up to the light, she squinted to see a pattern on the silver loop. "I was just contemplating a nipple ring."

3

KYRA WONDERED if Jesse Chandler normally gawked at women who slid the names of erotic body parts into casual conversation.

He was definitely gawking right now as he stared at her with his perfect mouth hanging wide-open. Or at least he was until he edged out a strained "The hell you will."

Plucking the tiny ornament out of her hand, Jesse slapped it back on the velvet-covered melon crate.

"Excuse me?" Kyra stared him down, more than ready for a serious face-off with this man.

It had required major effort to edge the word "nipple" from her mouth. Kyra could discuss the particulars of animal husbandry at the drop of a hat, but somehow a nipple reference in regard to her own body struck her as rather risqué. Nevertheless, the effort had been well worth it considering she had Jesse's full attention now.

Or else the body part in question had his full attention. He stared at her blouse as if he could envision the tiny silver loop locked around the peak of her breast.

"This isn't working," he growled in one ear as he propelled her away from the jewelry vendor's display and back into the swell of the crowd. "We're getting out of here."

"Fine by me," Kyra shot back over her shoulder as they edged past a Gasparilla reveler wearing a skull mask and a cape decorated in shiny white bones. She backed up a step to avoid the man, effectively plastering herself against Jesse's chest. The hard strength of his body taunted her with sensual visions of their limbs intertwined, taut muscle to smooth skin. "That's all the sooner I can take you home and have my way with you, ye scurvy knave."

She felt his body stir behind her a split second before he nudged her forward again. "We'll see who's having their way with whom."

The strangled rasp of his voice weakened the power of his threat. Kyra smiled her satisfaction as they wound their way past a man on stilts selling eye patches and bandannas.

"Whatever would you want from me if you could have your way, Jesse Chandler?" She glanced over her shoulder to find herself eye-level with a rock-solid jaw and forbidding frown.

"Friendship of the platonic variety. And a promise never to wear leather again."

"The corset is working, isn't it?" She mentally applauded the Gasparilla costumer for hooking her up with the sex-goddess pirate outfit.

As they hit the next crossroad to Bayshore Boulevard, Jesse steered her away from the festival toward the city. In the background, Kyra could hear the marching bands in the distance as the pirate parade charged toward the convention center.

"Is it working to turn every bug-eyed male head within a five-mile radius? Yes. Is it working for the preposterous purpose of sacrificing our friendship for a few hours of great sex? Not a chance in hell." He guided her through gridlocked downtown traffic toward his motorcycle parked sideways on the street between two pickup trucks.

She'd ridden into Tampa with a neighbor, so it wasn't like she minded being given a ride home. Still, she didn't appreciate being hauled around by a man who wasn't willing to bend an inch.

Jerking to a stop by his Harley, she tried not to be discouraged as he handed her a helmet—the spare he always carried in case some brazen female talked her way into a ride. Or more.

Why couldn't *she* be that woman today?

"You think I'd forfeit our solid working relationship for amazing sex? Come on, Jesse. You know me better than that." She strapped the helmet under her chin. She didn't mind leaving Gasparilla if it meant time alone with Jesse to persuade him of her cause.

Besides, the idea of straddling his bike—and him—while clad in fishnets and a miniskirt was making her seriously hot and bothered.

Swinging one leg over the bike, Kyra gave Jesse a clear view of inner thigh, stopping just short of flashing him. A girl needed to keep some sense of mystery intact. "And you seem to be forgetting that you're not in charge here today. Leaving the festival grounds doesn't mean you stop being my prisoner, and as long as I'm calling the shots, you're going to have to please me."

She patted the leather seat in front of her. "Now why don't you give me that ride I've been wanting?"

THE SEXUAL IMPLICATION of Kyra's words echoed through Jesse's mind as he maneuvered the motorcycle around a tight turn just before the sign for Crooked Branch Farm. He was sweating bullets after the hour-long ride back to the ranch, which spread along the Crystal River in Citrus County.

Kyra's thighs hugged his hips while her sweet, sunny scent teased his nose. Her arms wrapped around his waist, pressing her breasts into his back. And he couldn't even think about that *other* part of her that grazed his jeans. Her short skirt provided intimate exposure for the pink lace panties he'd spied when she first straddled his bike.

Now all he could think about were those ultrafeminine undergarments and what it might be like to peel them from Kyra's body.

Her invitation to take her for a ride had paralyzed him for a heart-pounding five seconds. Jesse had zero experience turning down those kinds of invitations. Having realized at an early age that he was too restless to settle down, too much like his old man to tie himself to any one woman, Jesse had carefully constructed a reputation for himself as a player. With that legend-in-his-own-time aura preceding him, no woman would ever be surprised by his lack of commitment.

And in turn, he'd never disappoint anyone.

But the strategy that had worked like a charm for ten years was unraveling in a big way. First, Greta staunchly ignored all the hype about him and—according to what she'd told him earlier this afternoon—she'd sold her Miami Beach condo for an apartment in Tampa.

Now Kyra was suggesting a fling he couldn't afford to take any part in.

No matter how much his body screamed at him otherwise.

Bringing the bike to a stop a few feet from Kyra's long, low-slung ranch house, Jesse willed away all provocative thoughts as he disengaged himself from her. He needed a cool head to talk her out of the big mistake she seemed determined to make.

She slid from the bike with the fluid movements of a woman who'd ridden horses all her life. Odd that he'd never noticed the quiet grace and strength about her before.

"Come on inside and I'll get you a drink," she offered, slipping her helmet from her head to place it gently on the seat.

Jesse stared in her wake as she sauntered up the flagstone path toward the front door, her lace-up boots clicking a follow-me tempo. He'd been too caught up in her new subtle politeness to ride off into the sunset on his bike while he had the chance.

Shit.

How could he just leave without even saying goodbye? He found his feet trailing after her before his mind consciously made the decision to go inside the house.

She'd left the door open wide into the cool, sprawling home he'd helped her build on a patch of the Crooked Branch property five years ago. The mishmash of Spanish influenced stucco archways, miniature Italian courtyards and contemporary architecture had been the first house he'd ever custom-designed from scratch and he continued to be proud of it in the years since his skills had improved tenfold. The house was so uniquely suited to Kyra he couldn't picture anyone else ever living here.

He'd always felt at home here before. Today he had the impression of a fly venturing farther into a silken, sweetly scented web.

One quick goodbye and he was out of here.

"Kyra?" He didn't see her right away as his eyes adjusted to the dimmer lighting indoors. The sound of the refrigerator door thudding shut called him toward the kitchen.

She stood at the triangular island in the center of the room, tipping a longneck bottle of Mexican beer to her lips. A few damp tendrils of blond hair clung to her neck from the warmth of the day.

He'd worked side-by-side with her for years and not once had the sight of perspiration on her forehead turned him on. Was he so freaking shallow that all she had to do was slide into fishnet hose to make him start salivating?

Before he could fully form and analyze a response to that question—let alone say goodbye—Kyra set her beer on the kitchen counter with a clang.

Foam rose up in the throat of the bottle to bubble over onto the granite surface around her sink, but Jesse was too mesmerized by the sight of her strutting into the hallway to do anything about it.

Something about the take-no-shit attitude of her walk told him she meant business. He'd seen that determined stride of hers before when she was dealing with shifty horse sellers or uncooperative studs.

And he had the feeling he wasn't going to fare any better against the will of this woman than the men who'd been forced to give her a good price on her horses or the studs who procreated when and where she wanted them to.

As a matter of fact, he felt his own desire to play stud rising to the surface in a hurry.

"Kyra, I don't think—" was as much as he managed before she came toe-to-toe with him in the hall lit with flickering electric sconces intended to look like candles along both walls.

Jesse didn't realize he was backing up until his butt connected with the stucco wall behind him. Her hands materialized on his chest as if to hold him in place.

He could see the rapid rise and fall of her chest half-exposed by her low-cut white blouse. His gaze seemed stuck on that creamy white flesh no matter how desperately his brain sought to unglue his eyes.

But then his brain had a full-time job simply willing his hands to ignore the overwhelming temptation to touch Kyra.

When her lips touched his, he lost the battle.

Sensation exploded through him at the brush of her soft mouth. There was a sweet taste to her that even the beer couldn't hide, and he drank her in like water, swirling his tongue with hers in an effort to savor every nuance.

His hand moved to her shoulder, powerless to remain immobile any longer. He molded the delicate skin of her collarbone, his thumb dipping down to the gentle swell of her breast above the neckline of her blouse.

And then it was as if someone had tossed gasoline on the fire of his want for her. Heat exploded inside him in time with that touch, burning through him with a fierce desire to scoop her up and walk her into the bedroom he knew was at the back of the house.

He could only think about laying her down and unfastening the laces that held the leather garment together. About seeing the perfect breasts she'd been hiding from him her whole life.

She moaned low in her throat as she edged her way closer to him, settling those delectable breasts against the insubstantial cotton of his tank shirt. The beaded peaks rasping over his chest tantalized him to touch.

To taste.

It's just a kiss. He repeated the lie over and over again in his mind, needing to give himself permission to hold her, to indulge this fantasy come to life for just a few minutes.

Her sunny scent wrapped around him with renewed strength as their body temperatures soared. The stucco wall scraped into his back, a discomfort he barely acknowledged while in counterpoint to the lush softness of Kyra plastered to his front.

Soft blond hair tickled his arm where it wrapped around her back, teased his nose when he bent to kiss her neck and taste her warm skin.

"Jesse," she sighed as she tipped her head back, granting him free rein over her body.

He smoothed a hand down her arm and over her hip as he kissed her neck down to one shoulder. The feel of the leather corset in his hand called him back to the place where a neat bow held her outfit together.

If this was just a kiss, he wouldn't go there.

If this was just a kiss, he'd sure as hell never untie those ribbon-thin leather straps and free the breasts he wanted so damn badly.

But with the encouragement of her hips wriggling against his own, Jesse tugged one end of the bow until the laces slid free. He told himself he would be content just to look. One glimpse of those breasts and he was out of here.

Then his gaze connected with Kyra's in the moody, flickering hallway light. Perhaps his intentions were written in some small facet of his expression because she grabbed one of his hands and laid it to rest on her breast, catapulting him into major meltdown mode. The peaked nipple lined up perfectly between his thumb and forefinger as if to beg for his touch.

"Come with me," she whispered, never releasing his hand as she backed up a step.

Oh, how he wanted to.

He wanted nothing better than to come with her about ten times before morning. To make her hot, wet and mindless for him.

But to take advantage of Kyra's momentary lapse of judgment would be the equivalent of hurting her, sooner or later. Besides, he could somehow still believe himself redeemable if he didn't seduce his own best friend.

Hissing a sigh between his teeth, he had to face up to that fact. "I can't do this."

Of all the rules he'd broken in his life, Kyra Stafford was one line he had promised himself he would never, ever cross.

THE FINISH LINE loomed ten feet away in the form of her bedroom, but Kyra sensed she wouldn't be clearing that threshold soon enough.

Jesse obviously possessed powers of restraint foreign to her if he could stop himself in the midst of the conflagration that had been going on between them. Either that or those kisses hadn't affected him nearly as much as they were affecting her.

The thought daunted her in spite of the molten heat churning through her veins and the tingly alertness of every square inch of her skin. But damn it, if she didn't press her case now, she knew she'd never have another chance. Once Jesse quit helping her out around the Crooked Branch two weeks from now, she wouldn't even see him as much let alone have an excuse to indulge in sexy captive scenarios with him.

If she was ever going to live out her fantasy with him—or have an opportunity to get over his sexy self for good—Kyra needed to act now.

"You can't?" Kyra forced her breathing to some semblance of normal and scavenged for a teasing smile as she hoisted her corset back into place. "You say that as if you had some choice in the matter."

Jesse scrubbed a hand through his too-long dark hair, his gaze straying encouragingly often to Kyra's leather outfit. "It's the right choice and you know it."

"I know no such thing. I left the festival with you because I thought you understood what I expected." Had she been so wrong to think maybe they'd end up together after he'd hauled her out of Gasparilla for mentioning nipple rings? She tugged the laces tighter on her pirate garb. "You can't just quit the game now that we're out of Tampa."

"The hell I can't." He turned his back on her while she tied the leather straps into a bow. Squeezing his temples with the thumb and forefinger of one hand, he stepped out of the hallway and into the wide-open courtyard behind the living room.

"Spoilsport," she called after him, removing her boots as she followed him out into the late-afternoon sunshine spilling across the terracotta tiles. He sat on top of a teakwood table facing a simple marble bird-bath fountain in the center of the courtyard. "Maybe you ought to take me back to the festival so I can find someone more willing."

She leaned against the table he sat on, giving her a rare opportunity to be nearly eye-to-eye with a man half a foot taller than her.

"You're going nowhere today even if I have to lock you in the house to make sure of that."

She smoothed one of the leather straps to her corset between two fingers. "Why not just tie me to my bed-post instead?"

He opened his mouth to speak and snapped it shut again. He swallowed. Flexed his jaw as if grinding his teeth. Then pointed a finger in her face. "You don't know what you're asking for."

"So show me." He'd been with more women than she could count. Would it kill him to indulge her for a day? Maybe two? She edged her way closer to stand between his knees. "Especially since you robbed me of the chance to abduct a more fun captive."

Trailing a hand over his thigh, Kyra absorbed the heat of him through her fingers. The bristly hair of his leg lightly scratched over her palm.

"You've temporarily lost your mind, woman." Jesse imprisoned her wandering hand just as she reached his shorts. "What else would you have me do?"

As he held her there, immobile but far from power-less, Kyra could see the quick pulse in his neck, feel the tension in his body.

She insinuated herself farther into the vee of his thighs, their bodies a scant inch from touching. Leaning close, she whispered in his ear.

"I think I'd have you barter sexual favors for your freedom."

4

If Kyra had been any other woman, Jesse would be well on his way to making her forget her own name by now.

As he held her slender wrist with one hand, it occurred to him he'd never restrained a woman's touch before. Hell, he'd never restrained his own desire to touch for that matter.

Women had always given him the green light, and he'd always accepted it with pleasure. To hold back was an all-new experience. One which he hoped fervently he'd never have to repeat.

"Sexual favors have no place between friends. You know that." He tried not to notice the satiny texture of the skin on the inside of her wrist.

"Since when?" Her other hand slid over his chest in a provocative swirl.

Before he imprisoned that one, too. "Since always. What kind of friend would I be if I let you sleep with a low-down two-timer like me?"

She lifted a sunny blond eyebrow and met his gaze dead-on. "What kind of friend would you be if you denied me the best orgasms in Citrus County?"

So much of his blood surged south, she might as well have set up a damn IV to his Johnson. Damned if he didn't feel light-headed.

"My reputation has definitely been overstated," he managed to croak in between gulps of much-needed air.

She leaned closer, her breasts brushing his chest. "I don't think so."

Somewhere between the brush of her breasts and her whispered words, Jesse must have let go of her hands. All of the sudden, they were everywhere, on his shoulders, spilling down onto his back, drawing him closer.

Such soft, silky palms. He'd seen her riding and working with gloves on a million times over the years. Never once had he suspected she'd been protecting such smooth skin underneath that dusty leather.

He reached for her—thinking he'd insert some space between them—but instead he pulled her closer when his fingers met the cotton of her skirt. Her hips were narrow along with the rest of her body, but they curved gently from her waist, providing an inviting niche for a man's touch.

For *his* touch.

A soft moan escaped her lips, a cry both earthy and feminine. The note of hungry longing pushed him over the edge. He might have been able to resist his own sexual urges. But how could he continue to refuse hers when he'd never been able to deny her anything in over a decade of friendship?

Assuring himself he would find a way to keep things under control, Jesse slid off the table and onto his feet, never letting go of Kyra's hips. He took one look at her flushed cheeks, her half-closed eyelids, and knew he wasn't going to be able to walk away anytime soon.

She raised both palms to his chest and pressed him gently backward. Not that he moved anywhere.

"Where do you think you're going?" she whispered, sultry as Eve before the fig leaves.

"I'm going to barter for my freedom." He tugged her toward the bedroom, a room he'd built with his own two hands long before he ever suspected he'd spend any time within those four walls. "And I've got a sexual favor in mind that will curl your toes, melt your insides and make you forget all about playing pirate for the day."

OH. MY.

Kyra's footsteps followed in the wake of Jesse's as he pulled her into the bedroom. She'd dreamed about this moment more times than she could count, yet a niggling fear gave her pause. Was he acting on seductive autopilot in giving her what she wanted, or did he feel a small measure of the same sensual hunger she did?

Or what if—God forbid—he was acting out of some sense of pity?

As much as she wanted whatever toe-curling, inside-melting experience Jesse Chandler had to offer, first she needed to be certain his erotic overtures were fueled by a little passion and not some misguided sense of duty as her friend.

And she could only think of one way to find out as Jesse drew her down onto the simple white linens of her king-size four-poster bed.

She dove for his shorts.

The move wasn't exactly subtle, but until she touched him, she couldn't be entirely sure how she affected him. Granted, she would have to be blind not to notice the man wasn't turned on at the moment. But for all she knew, men automatically responded to leather corsets and a few throaty sighs.

Kyra had always been a practical, salt-of-the-earth type of girl, and she felt more comfortable getting her own handle on the situation, so to speak. She needed to see how he reacted to her touch.

"Holy—" Jesse's swallowed oath and wide eyes weren't exactly the reactions she'd hoped for.

"What?" She smoothed her fingers over the altogether pleasing shape of him beneath his clothes. She had little enough experience in this arena, but she possessed enough to be impressed.

Jesse's eyelids fell to half-mast before he caught both her hands in his. "Have you always been this much of a pistol and I just missed it?"

Their gazes connected in the dim light filtering through closed wooden blinds and sheer lace curtains. Between the setting sun and the muted colors of the room, Kyra couldn't even see where the dark brown of his eyes stopped and the black center of his pupils began.

She sat perfectly still, transfixed by the rapid beat of her heart, the steady warmth of Jesse's stare. "You ought to know I only do things all or nothing. Starting the Crooked Branch. Helping you build this house. Going for broke at the horse shows. If I want something, I am very willing to work for it."

In fact, she was quite willing to do whatever it took to make sure Jesse noticed her, to make sure he stayed tonight. But he was making it a bit of a challenge by restraining her hands at every turn.

Working on instinct, she settled for leaning back

into the Battenburg lace pillows to recline the rest of the way on the bed.

Like an indomitable force of nature, her breasts remained standing even when she lay down. Corsets rocked.

"You're a wild woman." Jesse's eyes burned a path down the leather laces holding her outfit together.

Kyra rather liked the idea of unveiling a whole new side of herself that only Jesse would see. Because she felt safe with him, she could be more adventurous than she would be with any other man. More daring.

"Wild and wicked." She ran the top of her bare foot up the inside of his calf. "That's me."

Jesse dodged the path of her marauding toes and followed her down to the mattress, pinning her hands over her head. "Not for long you're not."

His nearness cooked up a thick heat in her veins and sent a rush of liquid warmth through her body. His tanned muscles flexed on either side of her cheeks as he held her in place on the bed.

"I'm not?" She sure felt certifiably wicked at the moment.

"No." He released her hands to trail his fingers up her bare arms to her collarbone, then down her sides to rest on her hips. "In a few minutes you're going to be sated and tame."

"Promises, promises." Her limbs went heavy and liquid at the thought of what he might have in mind. "Are you sure you can deliver on such a bold pledge, Jesse Chandler?"

He surveyed her body with the slow thoroughness of a world-class artist sizing up a new project. His brown eyes flicked over her stocking-clad thighs, her short skirt and the peekaboo laces holding her corset in place. "Your pleasure is guaranteed."

Her heart jumped, skipped and pumped double time.

She walked her fingers up one sinewy bicep. "If I'm not completely satisfied, can I ask for a repeat performance until you get it just right?"

He tugged one of the laces free from its knot to loosen the corset, leaving the leather garment in place while exposing a deep vee of cleavage. The movement shifted her cotton blouse to tease over her sensitive nipples and send a rush of heat between her thighs.

"I take great pride in my work, Kyra. I would never stop until I got it just right." He skimmed his hand over the flesh he'd exposed, carefully avoiding her breasts and making her all the more urgent to be touched.

She just barely resisted the urge to fan herself. No wonder the man had captivated feminine imaginations from one end of the Sunshine State to the other. Every inch of her felt languid and restless, heavy and hungry at the same time.

Opening her mouth to speak, she was surprised to discover words failed her at the moment. She could only think about indulging her every fantasy about Jesse. Could only envision tying him to her just this once to realize the sexy dreams that had plagued her nights and prevented her from being able to appreciate any other man.

Although as Jesse stared deep into her eyes and trailed his fingers lightly down the valley between her breasts, Kyra wondered if she'd ever be able to pry this man from her fantasies.

His voice growled husky and deep in her ear. "Are we agreed then?"

She blinked, fought for a rational thought even as the magic of his hands lured her deeper into a world of pure sensation. "Agreed on what?"

"My freedom for your pleasure?" His touch hovered close to one scarcely covered nipple. So close. His breath huffed warm against her shoulder as he staked his terms for sensual negotiation.

And she couldn't have bargained for a better deal to save her life. Insistent hormones and liquid joy crept through her veins and made her amenable to anything—everything—he wanted.

"Deal."

The moment the word left her lips, her unspoken wish was granted. Jesse's fingertips smoothed over the aching tips of her breasts through the thin cotton, then plucked the sensitive crests until she shivered with wanting.

Hungry for more, she wriggled closer to him on the bed, desperate to experience the press of his chest against her bared skin. With eager, clumsy fingers, she tugged his shirt up to the middle of his chest and laid claim to his heated skin with her palms. Greedily, she absorbed the nuances of his body with her hands, mentally reconciling the muscles she'd stared at for years with the ridges and angles underneath her touch.

He felt hot and hard and better than she'd ever imagined. But if she wasn't careful, Kyra knew she'd find pleasure with him far too soon, long before she'd had a chance to tease and tantalize him.

Forcing herself to slow down, she stilled her fingers and looked up at him to find his eyes glittering with the same heat that fired through her.

But before she could celebrate that small victory,

Jesse covered her with his body, cradled her cheek in his hand and caressed her mouth with his own.

SHE TASTED LIKE honeysuckle—warm, sweet and heady. Jesse was drowning in her already and he'd only just barely touched his lips to hers.

Everything about this encounter had "mistake" written all over it, but he couldn't have stopped himself now if he tried. The hell of it was, even if he could have scavenged some last remnant of control, his sensible best friend had turned into an exotic temptress and she urged him on at every turn.

Her hands fluttered restlessly at his shoulders, delicately steering him where she wanted him. Her calf wrapped around the back of his to mold him more tightly to her, demonstrating a strength he hadn't suspected in her slight form.

He deepened the kiss, claiming her mouth for his own even as he reminded himself to be gentle. He didn't have a clue how he'd walk away from her, as if she was any other woman, tonight after he showered her with earthly delights.

But he would. He *had* to.

He'd never allowed any woman to get under his skin before and Kyra was more dangerous than most because he cared about her.

Already he was taken by surprise to realize how much her satisfaction meant to him. Maybe he hadn't wanted to be roped into this ill-advised escapade, but now that they lay so close to one another in her monstrous four-poster bed, Jesse wanted nothing so much as to make tonight one she'd never forget.

Breaking the kiss, Jesse brushed his lips across her

silky soft skin, over her cheek and down to the throbbing hollow of her neck. He'd known her for half a lifetime, yet everything about her was new and different tonight.

He'd noted in the past that Kyra was passionate about anything and everything she'd ever done—a quality he'd always admired because it was so foreign from his own love 'em and leave 'em approach. But now, having all that passion turned on him scared him to the roots of his too-long hair. Her fingers had found their way under his shirt, crawled across his chest and clutched him to her until he had no choice but to feel every square inch of her perfect breasts pressed up against him, the thin layer of cotton between proving no barrier at all. Still, he couldn't resist plunging both hands into the loosened remains of her leather corset and unbuttoning the tiny fastenings on that blouse.

Gently, he nudged the fabric aside. Exposed her all the more to his gaze.

The sensation of seeing her breasts bared to him seemed incredibly decadent, yet forbidden because Kyra was his friend. But it was all so damned awesome he wanted to kneel before her gorgeous body and worship her in ways no other man had ever dreamed of.

"Kyra." Whispering her name in the darkness, Jesse wondered if he'd ever be able to speak it again without getting turned on. "Lay still for me so I can look at you."

Her blue eyes glittered back at him in the near darkness that had settled over her bedroom. Her restless hands slid away from his chest to fist at her sides. "I'm not good at being still."

She wriggled against the simple lace bedspread as if to prove the point. Fleetingly, Jesse remembered how difficult it had been for her growing up with her father when he was in a depressive state. A high-energy teenager and a tired old man who only wanted to retreat from life had been a challenging combination on both sides.

"But I've never gotten to see you this way before." He pinned her wrists on either side of her head, levering himself above her in a half-hearted push-up. "And who knows when I'll ever get another shot at seeing you naked. I plan to look my fill."

A slight breeze slid through the blinds at the window, rustling the starched curtains alongside her bed and stirring a lock of her hair to blow against his arm. She'd wrapped herself around all his senses just as thoroughly as those long blond strands conformed to his bicep.

Tonight she looked so soft and fragile. Intellectually, he knew her petite body concealed kick-butt strength and behind her delicate features lurked a sharp wit and clever mind.

Still, Jesse couldn't resist tracing her perfectly crafted cheekbones with his lips. Couldn't stop himself from skimming the smooth skin at her temple with the edge of his jaw.

"I don't think it's fair you get a sneak preview while I'm still left wondering what's in store for me." Her gaze dipped downward to linger on his...shorts. "Don't you think I ought to be entitled to a little show-and-tell here too?"

As if in a quest to be seen, his Johnson reacted of its own accord. She was killing him already and she hadn't even touched him yet.

He swallowed. Gulped. Sought for an even delivery of his words but still ended up sounding as strangled and hoarse as the Godfather in his old age. "I think you ought to behave before I have to get rough with you."

Even in the dim light he could see the answering spark in her eyes. The definite interest.

"I'd like to see you try." Her dare whispered past his better judgment and straight to his libido stuck in overdrive.

Ah, damn.

He had no business playing kinky sex games with Kyra Stafford. Why then did he find himself slipping his finger into one looped end of the loosened leather laces that had held together her corset?

"Don't bait me, woman." He tugged the slender ribbon of leather free from one eyelet after another until at last he held the long black strap in his hand. "I'm armed."

A wicked smile crossed her lips. "Do your worst, Chandler. I'm ready for you."

His mouth watered with the hunger to test the truth of that statement. Was she really ready for him right now? So soon? Before he'd even slid off her tiny skirt?

The notion teased, taunted, tempted the hell out of him. He wanted to slide his hand up under the hem of her outfit and touch every hidden nuance of her body, every intimate feminine curve that he'd never allowed himself to contemplate before.

But he didn't.

Not yet.

Instead, Jesse called upon his considerable experience in pleasing women and forced himself to choose the slower path, the one that would drive both of them more wild in the long run.

"Never say I didn't warn you." He breathed the words into her ear, grazing his body gently over hers.

Doubling up the skinny leather corset strap in his hand, Jesse pulled the end of the loop taut to make the two sides slap together with a sharp *snap*.

5

THE THIN *CRACK* of leather echoed in the sultry air, inspiring alternate waves of shivers and sizzles through Kyra. Breathless, she stared up at Jesse with his wild long hair and his broad, square shoulders and wondered what he had in mind.

He still held the long, looped strap in his hand as he grazed it lightly over her thigh. "You sure you don't want to run?"

"And lose my chance to experience Jesse Chandler's legendary prowess firsthand?" She flung the remains of her corset onto the floor and settled more deeply into the pillows. "I don't think so."

He dangled the leather tie like a pendulum over her hip, than up to her bare waist. The insubstantial little touches heightened her senses, made her crave more of his touch.

Her attention focused on the contrast of black leather against her pale skin, just in time to see him move his teasing instrument down her stocking-clad leg.

With clever hands, he walked his fingers under the edge of her skirt to tug down her thigh-high fishnets, careful never to touch her where she wanted to be touched the most. While her thighs tingled and ached, he soothed them with the soft stroke of leather and an occasional hot swipe of his tongue as he kissed her all along the hem of her skirt.

Desire trembled through her with a force she hadn't fully expected. She'd wanted Jesse forever—had fantasized about sexy interludes with him since she was barely sixteen—but in all that time, her imagination had never hinted it could be this hot between them. This wild.

She couldn't stifle the throaty whimpers, the sighs of pleasure his mouth wrought. Liquid heat seared her insides, pooled between her thighs. She ached for him in the most elemental way, and none of his skilled, seductive torments would satisfy it.

She needed *him*.

All of him.

Now.

"Jesse, please." Her hands scratched lightly across his back, tugging his shirt up and over his head.

In silent answer, he slid her skirt down her hips and pressed a kiss to her pink lace panties, just beneath the rose. Tension coiled even more tightly inside her, making her twitch restlessly beneath his touch.

But Jesse couldn't be rushed as he smoothed his hands over her hips, palmed her thighs, cupped the center of all her heat. Instead, he seemed to study every inch of her, bared completely to his gaze but for the tiny pink panties, and whispered, "How the hell did I not notice you were this gorgeous?" He licked a path from her belly button to her lacy waistband while he traced the outline of her curves with the loop of leather still wrapped about his hand. "This hot?"

Maybe because she was usually covered with dust from working with the horses. Maybe because he'd never been able to get past his early vision of her in pigtails. Or maybe because he normally had German bikini models on his arm to compare her to.

But she wasn't about to offer up her thoughts on the subject. Let him see her as steaming and sexy just for tonight.

Heaven knew, she felt pretty close to smoldering right now anyway. Especially when he slid a hand down the curve of her hip and under the scrap of pink lace.

"You can bet I won't forget now," he muttered as he inched her panties down her legs, over her knees and sent them sailing across her room to land on an antique wingback along with the leather strap from her corset. "How the hell am I ever going to look at you again Kyra, and not see…" His gaze wandered up and down the length of her naked body, sending tremors right through her. "The nip of your waist?" He kissed the curve in question. "Or the little birthmark on your hip that I never knew was there?"

His tongue smoothed the pale patch of flesh to one side of her belly button and Kyra thought she'd lose her mind.

"Maybe you shouldn't bother trying to fight it." She smoothed her hand over the tanned muscles of his chest, down to the warm heat of his belly. She followed the thin line of dark hair down the middle of his abs to the waist of his shorts. "Besides, your fascination with any woman lasts all of what—a week maybe?" She trailed her fingers along the seam of his fly until he groaned. "You can undress me all you want over the next seven days."

JESSE STRUGGLED to hang on to his control in a way he hadn't needed to since high school. The woman was pushing him to the brink with her siren's body and her erotic suggestions.

Her invitation to undress her anytime wasn't exactly going to put the lid on his lascivious thoughts down the road. Hell, knowing that enticement was out there—free for the taking—he'd be envisioning her naked twice as often.

And it didn't help that his mind was already inventing ways to justify spending the night with her. He wanted so much more from her than he could possibly take.

He needed to focus on his goal and get out of here before he lost all control.

With an effort, he leaned back out of her reach. Keeping his damn shorts on was critical to his success in this mission. If Kyra started flicking buttons free, he was a goner.

Lucky for him, she was hanging by a thread, too, despite the fact that she could talk a good game. He'd seen what she wanted, knew what she needed as soon as he'd laid that first kiss on her thigh.

And it would most definitely be his pleasure to give it to her.

Stretching out alongside her on the bed, he looked deep in her blue eyes before brushing his lips over her mouth. The honeysuckle taste of her invited him to linger, to lavish her with attention.

Her soft moan encouraged him, aroused the hell out

of him, sent his hand wandering over her sweet curves to the silky inside of her thigh.

He broke his kiss to watch her face as he dropped his touch lower to the white-hot center of her. Her cheeks flushed, her mouth opened with a silent cry.

He wanted to be inside her now, hips fused until he slaked his thirst for this woman. Normally, he was a patient man. Normally, he had endurance for every sexual trick in the book.

With Kyra, he transformed into a sixteen-year-old on a car date—pure lust and no caution.

Knowing he'd never restrain himself while their hips rested so close together, Jesse edged his way down the bed, down her body, licking every inch of her creamy skin on the way.

The scent of her body—something wild and heady, jasmine maybe—permeated his senses to implant itself in his memory. Her hips shifted, wriggled as he kissed his way past them and over the pale blond triangle that hid her from him.

He couldn't slow his progress if he tried.

The moment he touched his tongue to her sex, her back arched off the bed. Her out-of-control reaction drove him as crazy as the taste of her, the feel of her on his lips.

The knowledge that sensible Kyra Stafford was underneath him, wild and untamed as any of the fiercest horses ever sent to the Crooked Branch, nearly drove him over the edge.

He couldn't get enough of her like this, would never get enough. Dipping one finger inside her, he tried like hell not to imagine penetrating her with so much more....

But then her sex clenched all around him and he forgot about everything but enjoying every second of her pleasure. She screamed a throaty note before crying out a litany of his name, over and over and over.

And even though he knew their bargain was fulfilled and he ought to make tracks from this woman's bed, Jesse felt more connected to her than any woman he'd ever had full-blown sex with for days on end.

This was Kyra, after all. His best friend.

So despite the driving need for her he couldn't ever possibly indulge, Jesse tucked her blankets around her still-trembling body and held her in his arms. He could stay with her a little longer, couldn't he?

Just until he got his body back under control. Just until Kyra fell asleep.

Or until he let her talk him into taking this encounter a little further. He was so damn hot for her he didn't think he could move without losing it. Maybe he'd underestimated the merits of a sexual relationship.

Trailing one finger down her arm, he knew he shouldn't make decisions when he was hanging by a thread, but he couldn't resist seeing what Kyra would do next. He was dying for her touch, but she was lying utterly motionless.

He indulged a moment of pure male satisfaction to think he'd knocked her for such a loop she was still recovering from the orgasm. But then, as he listened to the long, even breaths stealing across his chest, Jesse realized he'd *really* knocked her for a loop.

She was fast asleep in his arms.

WELL, DIDN'T THAT just make a lovely picture?

Greta Ingram stared through Kyra Stafford's bedroom window at Jesse Chandler gently covering his naked *business* partner with a lace duvet. Greta couldn't remember him ever treating *her* with such tender concern.

Since when did a man turn away a European model with internationally celebrated breasts for a skinny horse trainer who probably had leather hands and dusty hair?

Sighing, Greta slipped away from the window, no longer wishing to make a scene. At least not tonight.

She'd hitchhiked from the Gasparilla festival to the Crooked Branch after Kyra had lured Jesse away with a leather corset and a lot of attitude. Confident in her own allure, Greta had hoped to entice him back with a little topless strolling around the ranch or maybe some naked moon-bathing outside his office window. But obviously the man was already engaged for the night.

Damn.

Tiptoeing across the lawn in her high heels, Greta looked longingly at Jesse's bike, wishing she could just straddle the big Harley and wait for him to join her. But after seeing the way he snuggled his partner into her linens, Greta feared he probably didn't run out of Kyra's bed the way he usually ran from Greta's after sex.

A minor obstacle.

Greta had left the hectic world of modeling and perpetual jet lag to live a more simple existence. Her home life sucked in Germany and she'd refused to look back at her verbally abusive father once she'd dug her way out of that particular hellhole.

She'd been paying her own way as a model since she'd lied about her age at fourteen. The sophisticated world of catwalks and globe-trotting that had seemed so glamorous to her then didn't glitter quite so brightly at twenty-three, however. She wanted out and Jesse Chandler had made her realize it.

What woman didn't secretly crave the kind of gallant attention and sexual bliss he lavished all over his partners? She was definitely ready to trade her stilettos for bare feet and picket fences. A man like Jesse Chandler would understand how to make her happy, how to indulge her idiosyncrasies.

He also possessed a certain charm and emotional distance that suited her wary heart. Her father had used his temper and his strength to intimidate her at every turn, making her fearful of too much in-your-face male strength.

And, truth be told, Jesse definitely made for great arm candy. A girl had to be able to hold up her head at the spring shows in Paris, after all. She'd have a lot more fun attending as a celebrity member of the audience rather than actually having to participate. This way, she could have Jesse by her side and she wouldn't have to starve herself for four days prior.

Halting at the edge of the county route that wound past the Crooked Branch and Kyra's home, Greta recalled the half-eaten fried dough she'd stuffed in her bag at the festival. Scrounging through her oversize purse while she waited for a car on the quiet road, she tugged out the napkin she'd wrapped the treat in and tore off a corner with her teeth.

After years of counting every calorie and weighing her skimpy nonfat, unsweetened, boring-as-hell portions at mealtimes, she enjoyed the taste of real food. All kinds of food.

Funny how cold fried dough still managed to bring

her so much pleasure even when the man of her dreams had just boinked another woman fifty yards away.

Maybe that was because she knew Jesse would fall in line. She hadn't met a man she couldn't manipulate since she'd left Frankfurt and her father's rages nine years ago. Surely Jesse would see the light soon and come running back to her.

But to facilitate the process, Greta realized she needed to be sure Kyra the lascivious pirate woman understood Jesse was no longer a free man.

Seeing headlights in the distance, Greta tossed the fried dough back in her bag and set one foot on the blacktop to expose one long, bare thigh. Flicking out her thumb, she brought a white Cadillac screeching to a halt beside her.

While an elderly gentleman pried open the passenger-side door for her, Greta made plans to return to the Crooked Branch for a visit with Jesse's bimbo buccaneer first thing in the morning.

Someone had to let the woman know—Greta Ingram always got her man.

6

So this is what morning-after regret felt like.

Jesse squinted at the clock next to Kyra's bed just before dawn, his eyes dry and his thoughts scrambled.

Of course, he wasn't entirely sure which he regretted more—giving into Kyra's crazy scheme last night, or having to pry himself away from the soft warmth of her sleeping form this morning.

How could any woman look so confoundedly perfect at 5:00 a.m.? Her shoulder-length blond hair swirled across the white pillow, still smooth and silky even after all their nocturnal maneuverings. Eyes closed, inky black lashes fanning her cheeks…

And her body…

Jesse didn't even dare to let his gaze wander lower or he'd never get out of her house this morning.

Limiting his visual inventory to her face, Jesse stared at her and waited for some revelation as to why the hell he'd never seen Kyra as remotely sexy over the course of their long friendship.

Had he simply refused to acknowledge what was right before his eyes all this time? Or had he been so damn shallow that he could only see the blatant external beauty in showy women like Greta Ingram?

Didn't that say a hell of a lot about his character?

All the more certain he didn't deserve to be in Kyra's bed, Jesse shoved off the crisp white linens and searched around in the dark for his shirt.

He spied it strewn across the walnut bureau, sandwiched between a simple wooden jewelry box and a framed photo of Kyra's parents on their wedding day.

Scooping up the wrinkled tank top, he couldn't help but notice a baseball card tucked into the framed mirror above the dresser. He didn't need to read the fine print to know whose card it had to be.

Jesse Chandler—rookie shortstop in the triple-A minor league.

Kyra was surely the only person on earth to have collected such a rare and simultaneously worthless item. But then, she'd always been a friend—a fan—no matter whether he was hitting the cover off the ball or falling into a major batting slump. He'd never asked her to attend any of his home games, but she'd always been there to hurl insults at any umpire who ever dared to call him out.

How could he screw up a friendship with a woman like that? Kyra could ride motorcycles, horses and— should someone happen to dare her—just about anything else that moved on wheels, wind or water. She could shoot pool, throw darts and she genuinely liked domestic beer. A guy just didn't mess with a friendship like that.

Jamming the baseball card back into the mirror frame, Jesse tugged his shirt over his head and promised himself not to let last night ruin what he had with

Kyra. It's not like they had crossed that sexual line of consummation, after all.

He'd simply pretend the heated encounter never happened and hope like hell she did, too. He'd never been the kind of guy to be plagued by morning-after regrets, and today shouldn't be any different.

No matter that—for the first time ever—he was having a hard time walking away from a woman's bed.

At least he would be checking out of his position at the Crooked Branch in less than two weeks. That meant he could avoid Kyra—avoid this attraction—and concentrate on getting his business up and running. Every house he built would prove to himself a little more that he could stay in one place, that he could commit to something.

His night with Kyra didn't do anything to change that.

And if he occasionally looked at her body and remembered the erotic-as-hell events of last night...that would just have to remain his secret.

INSISTENT RAPPING on her front door interrupted a very sexy dream Kyra had been having. She'd been envisioning a night with Jesse that had involved full-blown consummation, multiple orgasms and lots of leather.

In fact, Jesse had been just about to nudge her over that amazing sensual ledge again when the rapping at her front door pounded through her fuzzy consciousness to awaken her completely.

Blinking against the pale sunlight already streaming through her blinds, she realized it was later than she usually slept and that Jesse was no longer beside her.

He'd given her enough intense pleasure to send her

into sated slumber until nearly dawn and she hadn't given him so much as a second of satisfaction.

He'd done his friend a good deed, apparently, and then left.

She'd expected him to leave while she was sleeping, but the reality of seeing his side of the bed empty still stung. Thanks to her practically passing out in his arms, Jesse had slipped away without actually relieving her of her virginity or providing her with the complete sexual experience she craved. That stung even more. Sighing, she levered herself up on one arm and moved to investigate the loud rapping at her front door.

On the off chance that Jesse had somehow locked himself out and wanted to get back inside the house, Kyra pulled on a buff-colored cotton robe and jogged to the foyer.

"I'm coming," she shouted, half-smiling to herself as she remembered the events of last night when she really *had* been coming.

She felt the flush of arousal in her cheeks and throughout the rest of her body as she yanked open the front door and hoped she'd find the man who could fulfill the sensual longing still pulsing through her this morning.

Instead, her gaze fell upon a bonafide cowboy, a breed that had grown more rare in southern Florida over the last decade.

A tall, rangy body took up her whole door frame. Well-worn denim encased his thighs while an honest-to-God Western shirt with a snap front covered an impressive chest.

He had a craggy face worthy of any Marlboro man, complete with hat. He was the scarred, dark antithesis of Jesse Chandler's dazzling good looks and sunny charm, but Kyra would bet this man had still turned a few female heads in his day.

In fact, she was pretty sure if she weren't nursing a major crush on her best friend, her head would be turning right now. That is, if she wasn't also just a little bit nervous about what the Marlboro man wanted with her at 7:00 a.m. on a Sunday.

"Umm?" She tightened the sash on her skimpy robe and tried to rein in her scattered thoughts. Between the leftover effects of her steamy dream and the nerve-racking ability of a dangerous man on her doorstep, she felt a far cry from her normally sensible self this morning. "Can I help you?"

"I damn well hope so. I'm Clint—"

She gasped, remembering exactly who he was. "Mr. Bowman. The horse psychologist. I'm so sorry I forgot about our meeting."

She'd called his Alabama ranch last week to request some help with Sam's Pride. The horse had been raised at the Crooked Branch, and although the gelding had the sweetest disposition with Kyra, the temperamental three-year-old wanted nothing to do with anyone else. She couldn't sell a horse that balked at responding to anyone but her. Although Kyra had always been a solid horse trainer, the case of Sam's Pride stumped her.

But once Kyra had come up with the scheme to catch Jesse's attention last week, she'd forgotten all about today's appointment with the equine specialist. A horse whisperer of sorts.

Clint frowned, crossed his arms. "I waited around down by the barns, but everything is all locked up tight at the office and stable." Frank gray eyes sized up her outfit as he took a step back. "You want me to head back down there while you—dress?"

"Good idea." She appreciated a practical man. God knows she'd never run across many in her life. Between her manic-depressive father and her committed-to-pleasure best friend, however, Kyra's experience with males had probably been skewed. "I'll be five minutes if you're ready to face Sam's Pride without the benefit of coffee, ten minutes if you'd rather fuel up first."

Clint Bowman smiled and touched the brim of his hat like a character out of an old Western movie. "Coffee it is."

He turned on one booted heel and made his way across her driveway, headed for the barn.

Kyra gave herself a long moment to watch him and wonder what her life might be like if she could get over Jesse Chandler and pursue a guy like Clint.

Unfortunately, her night with Jesse hadn't come close to curing her crush. Maybe her method hadn't worked because she hadn't been able to convince him to carry out her original plan to its full extent.

She needed the complete Jesse Chandler experience, beginning to end. The whole shebang.

For years, she'd had a vision in her head of having her first time with Jesse. Perhaps she just needed to fulfill that longtime fanciful vision in order to shake her attraction to him.

Only then would she be able to pursue someone more appropriate for her.

Someone like Clint Bowman.

She turned away from the intriguing picture of a real cowboy in her driveway to make the coffee. Putting clothes on had never taken her more than sixty seconds anyway.

No sooner had she dumped the coffee grounds into the filter than she heard raised voices outside.

Or rather, a lone, raised female voice.

"...I've walked across every red carpet in Europe on these heels, I'll have you know." The tone was a mixture of feminine indignation and catty pride. A woman on a roll.

Intrigued, Kyra set down the coffee scoop to peer out her kitchen window.

Greta the German Wonder-bod stood toe-to-toe with the Great American cowboy, one French manicured finger leveled at his chest. What on earth was Greta doing at the ranch on a Sunday morning?

"For that matter," the model continued, shifting her weight from one practically nonexistent hip to the other, "ask anyone who owns the runways from Milan to Paris, sweetheart, and they'll all point to me. I earned that reputation with four-and-a-half-inch heels strapped to these very same feet." Greta tilted her chin at Clint, a gesture which only drew attention to the fact that despite the four-and-a-half-inch heels in question, the horse whisperer still had an inch or two on her.

"If I can manage all that on my own, I'm fairly certain I can negotiate a little gravel by myself."

Kyra couldn't hear Clint's reply, but she saw his mouth move, saw him apply one hand to his hat in the same courteous gesture he'd shown to Kyra and then she saw Greta's cheeks turn a huffy shade of pink before she stormed away from Clint and toward the house.

This was getting more interesting by the moment.

Kyra finished pouring water into the coffeepot, slopping a little onto the ceramic tile countertop in her haste.

A fierce rapping on her front door prevented her from cleaning up the mess.

Tempted to ignore the summons, Kyra tugged open the door again anyhow, too curious to simply go get dressed.

Greta barged inside, oblivious to common good manners. Dressed in a slinky purple silk skirt and a gold bikini top that looked like something *I Dream of Jeannie* might have worn, Greta cocked one slight hip. "Who the hell is that guy?"

"Nice to see you, too, Greta." Kyra searched her brain for a way to avoid answering the question directly. She'd never been the type to lie, but she hardly wished to discuss her horses or Clint Bowman with Greta. "If you're looking for Jesse, I'm afraid you're going to be disappointed. He's not here."

Greta smiled as she dug through a brown leather satchel she carried on one shoulder. "He rarely wakes up in the same bed he goes to sleep in. Hadn't you noticed?"

Kyra took a deep, cleansing breath and struggled not to grind her teeth. "Is there a reason you're here?"

"I came to warn you away from Jesse." Her German accent had softened to mild, clipped tones—a more Americanized Marlene Dietrich. She pulled a silver cigarette case from her bag and flicked it open to reveal a handful of long, skinny smokes with a foreign label stamped across the butts. "He's very much taken."

Kyra reached over and flipped the case closed again, unwilling to fill her house with smoke fumes. "And you think I'd be interested in this because…?"

She'd be damned if she showed Greta Ingram how much she cared about Jesse. She'd protected her friendship with him from envious girlfriend-wannabees for plenty of years. She sure as hell wouldn't get sucked into a catfight with a woman who was bound to be disappointed in the nonexistent commitment a consummate bad boy could offer.

Greta shoved the case back into her purse with a frown. "Just trying to save your heart a little wear and tear. I'd hate for you to get all hot and bothered over Jesse only to find out later that he's the unequivocal property of a woman you have no chance of displacing."

With a jaunty little shake of her perfect blond mane, Greta smiled at Kyra as if to soften the blow.

Not that Kyra was exactly reeling from the threat.

She backed into the low rock wall outlining a small fountain and miniature garden planted in the center of the foyer. Tucking her short cotton robe around her thighs, she eyed Greta as the German model paced the smooth stone floor with the restless grace of a hungry feline.

"Correct me if I'm wrong, but did you just refer to Jesse Chandler as someone's unequivocal property?"

Greta paused her pacing to fold her arms and shoot Kyra the evil eye. "Yes. Mine."

Despite the woman's hideous lack of manners, Kyra couldn't help but feel a twinge of sympathy for any female who so completely misunderstood a guy like Jesse.

"Don't you realize you're consigning yourself to an abysmal case of heartbreak if you try to tie yourself to a man who's more proud of his bachelorhood than his record-breaking minor league batting average?"

"His what?" Greta blinked, furrowing her perfectly shaped brows.

Kyra suspected it wouldn't be the last time this woman's quarry confused the hell out of her.

Sighing, she started again. "Jesse won't ever commit himself to any one woman."

Well aware of this fact, Kyra guessed that her best friend's propensity to roam was probably half the reason she'd pursued him in the first place.

Okay, rampant lust might have something to do with it, too. But beyond that, Kyra knew she would be safe trying out her long-unused feminine wiles on Jesse.

He'd never try to tie her down any more than she'd tie him. After her mom had died long ago, leaving her father in the grips of manic depression that made him emotionally off-limits, Kyra preferred not to trust other people with her heart.

But she and Jesse *both* valued their independence. She wouldn't need to worry that he'd ever get the wrong idea about potential romance between them. Yet Jesse was supremely capable of supplying her with the multiple Os she'd dreamed of, the sensual heights she'd hoped for but had never experienced until last night.

For a moment, Kyra wondered what things might have been like between her and Jesse if she hadn't been a bit wounded and Jesse hadn't been so wary. How cool would it be to hang out with her best guy friend forever and luxuriate in the great sex without worrying about getting her heart stomped?

Too bad that would never happen.

Greta hissed a long breath between pursed lips, almost as if she was exhaling the smoke Kyra had denied her. She cast Kyra a look of exaggerated patience. "The only reason Jesse hasn't committed fully yet is because I haven't made it apparent that I want exclusive rights. Once we sit down and discuss this, he'll be thrilled to be mutually monogamous."

The no-nonsense, I'm-doing-you-a-favor expression assured Kyra that Greta believed every word she was saying.

Two weeks ago, Kyra might have felt sorry for her naiveté. But now she found herself experiencing boatloads of jealousy at the thought Greta might be able to sway Jesse into a relationship Kyra would never be able to manage.

And even if he dodged Greta, what about the next slinky runway goddess who came along? Would Kyra ever be able to look at those women and not feel twinges of envy for the time they got to spend with Jesse?

But she'd be damned if she'd show any weakness to Greta. As far as the rest of the world knew, Kyra Stafford had never been—and would never be—hung up on Jesse Chandler.

"Fine." Nothing she said at this point would save Greta from believing what she wanted anyway. No sense arguing her morning away when she needed to join Clint in the barn and get down to business about Sam's Pride. "Thanks for the heads-up on your relationship with Jesse. Believe me, I'll be the first one to run in the other direction if he starts spouting the merits of monogamy."

A little voice from the deep recesses of her brain called her a liar. Kyra staunchly ignored it.

Nodding, Greta hitched her bag up higher on one shoulder. "I'll let you get back to your coffee." She stared rather pointedly at the empty mug Kyra had been flinging around throughout their conversation. "And your cowboy." She rolled her eyes at the mention of Clint and sniffed.

Before Kyra could explain that Clint wasn't "her" cowboy, Greta charged through the front door and stomped down the front walk as if her four-and-a-half-inch spikes were as durable as high-top sneakers.

Kyra couldn't imagine where the woman was headed as there wasn't a car or other mode of transportation in sight.

Obviously, Jesse was in over his head with the persistent German beauty. Not that it mattered to Kyra. He was a grown man and he could extricate himself from his own problems.

Her only concern was finding an opportunity to wrest a whole night of pleasure from him—complete with the deed that would save her from her unwanted virginity. She could be with Jesse without falling victim to his heartbreaker ways, damn it. Surely all the years she had known him—all the occasions she'd had to see the man behind the myth—would help her remain immune.

Although, after the twinges of jealousy her visit with Greta had inspired, Kyra had to admit she liked the idea of him moving to offices across town in two weeks to start his house-building business.

That left her plenty of time to enjoy Jesse Chandler on a brand-new level.

Happily ever after and monogamy be damned.

JESSE CHECKED his watch as he stood outside the private stables at the Crooked Branch. He'd been able to stay away from Kyra, for what? Three whole hours?

So maybe he hadn't done a great job of putting space between them. But he'd recalled the house-call appointment for Sam's Pride and he was more than a little curious about the horse whisperer Kyra had hired.

Besides, this was his last window of opportunity to oversee strangers' activities at the training facility. For years he'd taken it upon himself to be around when new staff members started their work or when new vendors showed up. Kyra was extremely keen about her business, but Jesse sometimes worried that her isolation on the ranch allowed her to be slightly naive about human nature.

For that matter, she often cut herself off from people on purpose, preferring equine company to the two-legged variety. Maybe it had something to do with growing up responsible for a manic-depressive father who had abdicated his authority along with his capacity to love.

Whatever the reason for Kyra's loner tendency, she hadn't developed the same abilities to read people that Jesse possessed. So he'd made it his personal mission in life to make sure no one ever cheated, deceived or swindled her.

God knows she seemed so self-sufficient in every other area of her life and work. Jesse had to contribute where he could.

Convinced he was hovering around the Crooked Branch for completely altruistic reasons and not because he simply wanted to see Kyra today, Jesse charged through the stable doors and into the high-tech horse environment Kyra had designed herself.

Wide masonry alleyways and spacious stalls lined both walls. Year-round wash stalls were housed inside the barn, providing the horses with more showerheads and better water pressure than the bathroom in Jesse's apartment.

The stables bustled with noise and activity as Crooked Branch staffers led the horses to the turnout pastures for some morning exercise. But the door to Sam's Pride's stall—the one at the very end of the long corridor—remained shut.

Picking up his pace, Jesse's boots clanked down the clean barn floor toward the closed door. He'd bet his motorcycle that there wasn't a million-dollar thoroughbred housed in a more state-of-the-art facility than the one Kyra Stafford managed. The only scent that hinted the place was a barn emanated from the pile of sweet-smelling hay tucked inside an open supply room.

Slowing his steps as he neared the closed stall door where Sam's Pride normally resided, Jesse's ear tuned to the soft throaty laughter inside the enclosure.

Soft, sexy-as-hell laughter.

Followed by a man's low whisper.

An icy-cold, clammy sort of fear trickled through his veins as he realized the feminine voice belonged to Kyra. Only it wasn't quite fear that he felt.

More like mild dread. A little anger.

Jesus-freaking-Christ, he was *jealous*.

The realization rolled over him with surprising clarity considering Jesse had never been jealous of anyone for anything before.

But he was pretty damn positive that this unhappy feeling in his gut could only be attributed to the fact that another man was making Kyra laugh right now. God forbid the guy made her blush, too, or Jesse would have to kill him.

He hadn't realized until just this second how badly he wanted to be the man to make her cheeks turn pink someday.

Gritting his teeth, Jesse burst through the stall door, determined to make sure everyone inside Sam's Pride's private retreat knew exactly how pissed he was. And the sight that greeted his eyes did zero to soothe him.

Kyra stood beside her favorite horse, stroking his nose and cooing to the beast while a way-too-touchy stranger stood beside her, his hands placed friendly-like over her hips.

In just the same spot Jesse had touched her last night.

Leveling a finger at them both, he didn't think about what to say. He merely blurted out the first thing that came into his mind.

"Care to tell me what in the hell happened to monogamy?"

7

KYRA WAS THE FIRST to move, the first to break her physical connection with the Don Juan in a Stetson.

Too bad she didn't look nearly as contrite as she should. In fact, her expression struck him as downright furious as she turned a snapping blue gaze on him.

"Care to tell me what happened to basic good manners?" she shot back.

Sam's Pride sidestepped in his stall, impatiently stomping his hooves in reaction to Kyra's displeasure. The Romeo cowboy merely crossed his arms and shuffled back to watch Kyra.

Damn the man.

Jesse had never noticed other guys ogling her before yesterday. Now, he felt male eyes on her generous breasts everywhere he went. "Good manners are low priority in the midst of my best friend being debauched."

The cowboy in the corner lifted an eyebrow. "Your best friend?"

"Damn straight." Jesse was only too happy for an

excuse to glare at the letch. His day would be complete if only this joker would take a swing at him.

But Kyra's gropey companion simply nodded and did a piss-poor job of hiding an amused smile.

Kyra shouldered her way in between them. "There was no debauchery involved here, Jesse, and I seriously resent the implication. You just interrupted an important moment between me and Sam's Pride and I won't be forgiving you anytime soon if you've set back his treatment because of this morning's melodrama."

She patted her horse on the nose before plowing out of the roomy stall.

Jesse spun on his heel to follow her and her swinging ponytail down the wide alleyway between stalls. She was back to her old self today—no leather corset in sight.

Clad in blue jeans and a man's T-shirt, Kyra wore the same clothes she always had around the ranch, but she didn't look remotely the same to Jesse. Now, instead of seeing her loose shirt that hid her phenomenal breasts, Jesse could only notice how low the V-neck dipped and how tiny her waist was where the shirttail disappeared into her jeans.

"No way are you making me out to be the bad guy, Kyra, when it was clearly *you* who was submitting to another man's touch three hours after I rolled out of your bed."

Her ponytail stilled along with her steps. Slowly, she turned to face him just inside the stable's main doors. "Submitting to another man's touch?" Her nose wrinkled. "How can you call that—" Her jaw fell open, unwrinkling her nose. "Oh my God, Jesse. Don't tell me you're jealous of the horse whisperer."

Jesse had never experienced a migraine before, but he suspected the blinding pain in the back of his head had to be sort of similar. "Of course I'm not…"

He couldn't even say the damn word. How could he possibly *be* jealous when he couldn't even edge the term out of his mouth?

"You're jealous!" Kyra squeezed her hands together in delight, drawing his attention to the incredibly soft fingers that had traveled all over his body last night.

"Jesus, Kyra, that has nothing to do with it."

"Since when have you developed a possessive streak for your one-night stands?"

That did it.

Jesse shoved open the stable doors and dragged her out into the morning sunlight, hoping they'd be able to avoid being overheard. "Last night was *not* a one-night stand."

"Does that mean I'll get a repeat performance to-night?" She blinked up at him with such a wicked gleam in her blue eyes Jesse wondered how he'd ever viewed her as an innocent.

"No." He took deep breaths to steel his body against the eager response to her suggestion of spending another night together. "That means you can't call it a one-night stand when we didn't…"

How to put this delicately?

"Go all the way?" she supplied helpfully, snagging the attention of one of the college kids Kyra hired to help exercise the horses. "Actually, I've been meaning to talk to you about that."

Sighing, he caught her by the elbow to tug her around the back of the stables. The last thing he needed was some college kid eyeing Kyra, too. He hadn't ever cared if the whole world stared at Greta in her lingerie on a Milan runway, but somehow his eyeballs felt ready to explode at the mere thought of a male eye straying too long on Kyra.

He definitely needed to get over whatever the hell was the matter with him.

"This might not be a good time with so many people around." Maybe if he just appealed to her ever-practical nature, he could extricate himself from this mess.

"It may not be a good time, but you made it the *right* time when you charged in on Sam's Pride's first session with the equine psychologist. You know how important it is to me to sell that horse, Jesse. I won't even be able to *give* him away if he keeps up the bad temper with everyone who looks at him." She propped one foot on the three-rail fence outlining the turnout pasture behind the stable and stared out at the horses who weren't being exercised at the moment.

In trainer language, the horses were enjoying "leisure time."

"And you're sure in an all-fired hurry to sell him, aren't you?" Jesse prodded, surprised to realize how much her haste annoyed him.

She flicked a curious glance in his direction before turning her attention back to the assortment of jumpers and racking horses grazing in the field before them. "He's my ticket to buying the controlling percentage of this place. If I can't unload him, I don't have any sale prospects that will be profitable enough to allow me to do that until next year."

"And I'm such a tyrant that you can't stand having me in charge here for that much longer?" They both knew Jesse was the silent partner. He'd been wandering the U.S., either as a minor league baseball player or as a student of life for most of the years they'd known one another. So it wasn't like he hung around southern Florida very often telling her how to run their business. He'd earned enough of his own money over the past ten years to never worry about how much profit the ranch turned.

"You know that's not it." She pivoted around to face him. Tucking one boot heel onto the lowest wooden bar, she propped her elbows back on the top rail.

The stance couldn't help but draw his eyes to her incredible curves. The lush body he'd been able to touch and taste just last night....

Even though he was definitely concentrating on their conversation.

"...but I really need to claim some independence," she was saying while Jesse prayed he didn't miss much.

He focused solely on her eyes.

"You're the most independent woman I've ever met and you're all of twenty-four," he countered. "How much more self-sufficient can a person be?"

"I'm unwilling to rely on other people to supply my happiness or my security."

The alive-and-well bad boy within him couldn't resist teasing her. He leaned back against the fence beside her. "Aw, come on, Kyra. You have to admit I managed to supply a little happiness for you last night."

Why did he remind her of it when he'd been so hellbent on forgetting all about it? Obviously, seeing her so close and personal with the horse shrink this morning was still screwing with his head.

"I'm not saying other people can't provide me with pleasure."

Was it his imagination or was there a tiny hint of pink in those cheeks of hers?

She cleared her throat and lifted her chin. "I just don't want to ever *rely* on someone else for…my most basic…needs."

A momentary vision of Kyra erotically taunting him with her ability to provide her own pleasure acted like a carrot dangled in front of his sex-starved body. Every inch of his flesh tightened. Hardened. Hurt for her.

Leaning into the fence, he turned away from her to look out over the horses and get himself under control.

"But it's only me helping you out here." His voice sounded strangled. "Surely you can trust me as the controlling partner for another year to give Sam's Pride time to work through his behavior issues on his own."

She stared out at some distant point on the horizon and said nothing.

"You can't trust me for another year?"

"It's not so much a matter of not trusting you, Jesse. It's more a case of me wanting to prove something to myself. I spent my whole childhood at the whim of my father's moods and I feel like I can't spend another day catering to someone else or living by anyone else's rules. I want to work for me."

"Since when do I expect to be catered to?" Where the hell was this conversation going? And how had he moved from erotic visions of Kyra to semiscary realizations about her isolated upbringing?

"You don't." She shook her head so emphatically her ponytail undulated with the backlash. "But again, this is about me. I've got a goal in my mind to be independent and self-sufficient by the time I'm twenty-five, and no bout of horse stubbornness is going to keep me from realizing that goal. I've got a buyer lined up for Sam's Pride, and with Clint's help, he'll be ready by the time the sale goes through."

The look of clear determination in her eyes reminded him of his brother's gritty resolve to support their family when Jesse's father had walked out. He'd never realized how much Kyra resembled Seth in her staunch drive to be independent, her steely will never to rely on anyone else.

Jesse, on the other hand, had never felt called to prove himself the way Kyra and his older brother did. It was enough for him to charm his way through life and without shouldering ten other people's burdens along the way.

He never ran the risk of disappointing anyone because he never offered more than what he was certain he could give.

Did it matter that what he could give was usually simple, sexual and fleeting? At least he was honest about it. No woman could ever say he'd deceived her into thinking otherwise.

He held up his hands in surrender. "Fine. Sam's Pride is your business. I just can't help but empathize with any creature who gets a shrink tossed in his direction."

A BITING ANGER lurked behind Jesse's words. So much so that Kyra couldn't help but wonder who had tried to crawl inside Jesse Chandler's head to leave him with such a wealth of resentment.

But then—almost as if she'd imagined the moment— shades of Jesse's teasing smile returned. A hint of flirtation colored his words. "Or maybe I just don't like the idea of a horse shrink who thinks he can put his hands on you."

Kyra had the distinct impression the man used his sexual charm as a replacement for deeper emotions. But she barely had time to mull over that bit of new insight before he stepped closer and made her forget all about *how* he wielded that major magnetism.

She was too busy getting caught right up in it.

"When I saw his fingers on your hips, all I could think was that I'd just touched you there." His gaze dipped down to her jeans, lingered. "And that you'd felt so damn good."

Heat coursed through her with the force of a thoroughbred in the homestretch. Yesterday she'd had to chase him down and practically hog-tie him to get him to notice her.

It was pretty heady to have Jesse Chandler pursue *her.* If not with his actions, at least with his words. Especially after he'd slipped out of her bed last night without ever reaching the pleasure pinnacle she'd found so quickly.

"Sam's Pride was sort of edgy having somebody new in there with him this morning. He gave me a nudge that was a little more forceful than usual and Clint was just helping me stay on my feet."

"Clint?" He made it sound like an infectious disease.

"The equine psychologist. His name is Clint Bowman."

"Ah." Jesse's shoulders relaxed just a little.

He looked like he belonged at the Crooked Branch today. He'd traded his shorts for jeans and a gray T-shirt with the Racking Horse Breeder's Association logo on the front. Kyra didn't need to see the back to know it read, "You're not riding unless you're racking." She had one just like it in her drawer.

Jesse stepped back from her, a clear visual cue he was retreating from any flirtation.

But Kyra wasn't about to let him off the hook that easily. After last night's encounter, she was all the more hungry for him, damn it, and no closer to getting over her ancient crush.

They needed to finish what they'd started and she planned to make some headway in the department. Pronto.

"So Clint obviously made no claims on my body." She pushed away from the fence and sidled closer. "Frankly, I'm still waiting for you to take up where we left off last night."

He was shaking his head before she even completed the thought. "I don't know—"

"Unless you're too scared?"

She could practically see the hackles rise on the back of his neck. Good. She needed to do *something* to convince him to give her another shot.

"It's hardly a matter of fear."

"Then come see me next weekend." She backed him into the fence rail, giving him no room to run. If he wanted out of this, he'd have to tell her as much.

"I've got to be in Tampa next weekend on business and then—"

She cut off whatever other excuses he might throw her way. "So stop by the week after that. The buyer for Sam's Pride is going to be here that Thursday. You can come bid your farewells to my horse and then have dinner with me."

"I want to, Kyra." A flash of heat in his brown eyes

made her believe him. "But this thing between us… it's complicated."

"I think we could figure it out if we had a little time together." She hadn't meant that to come out quite as suggestive as it sounded. Chasing Jesse had turned her into a hoyden in the course of twenty-four hours.

To her surprise, he nodded. "We definitely need to think through what this means for us down the road, anyway. I'll swing by that day and we'll…"

"Think?"

"Exactly. Besides, if you're hell-bent on selling Sam's Pride for the sake of shifting the scales of ownership this spring, I want to at least be around for his big send-off." He edged around her, and she backed up enough to let him pass.

She could afford to be gracious now that she'd won this small victory. As she watched Jesse retreat across the driveway toward the barn where he normally parked his motorcycle, Kyra was satisfied just knowing she'd see him again. In fact, it surprised her how much she looked forward to seeing him again. She would miss his recurring presence at the ranch. No matter how sporadic his appearances had been in the past when he'd been on the road, she'd always known he'd show up on her doorstep sooner or later to help her, tease her, force her not to work so hard all the time….

Refusing to worry about an uncertain future, Kyra stifled the thought. Assuming the sale of her temperamental horse went off without a hitch, she and Jesse would at least have one more evening together— alone—before he walked away from the Crooked Branch for good.

And no way in hell would they spend it thinking.

GRETA SCRAMBLED to stub out her cigarette as she spied Jesse walking toward the barn.

Finally.

She'd seen him drive in an hour ago just as she'd been leaving the training facility after her talk with Kyra. Greta had delayed hitchhiking home and headed right back to the Crooked Branch, unwilling to leave Jesse in the hands of her biggest competition for his affection.

After he'd parked his Harley in the barn and disappeared into one of the outlying buildings, Greta had staked out his bike and settled in to wait. No way would she track him down amidst a slew of smelly barnyard animals.

Draping herself over the seat of the motorcycle, she managed to strike a sultry pose just as he yanked open the door to the barn. Crossing her hands behind her head, she knew her breasts would be cranked to an appealing height.

And one of the benefits of eating all the fried dough she wanted was that the mammary twins had put on a little weight over the past few weeks.

"Going my way?" she called out across the well-lit expanse of concrete, hanging tools and small tractors. She considered flexing her legs up and over the handlebars, but she wasn't certain how well she could execute that kind of maneuver.

Besides, the disadvantage to all the fried dough was that her body wasn't always totally well balanced.

His step slowed as he neared her. "Do I even want to know what you're doing here?"

"I'm paving the way for us to be together, of course." She lowered her arms and held them out to him. "Feel free to start showing me your gratitude anytime."

And Jesse was so deliciously capable of adoring a woman. Greta hadn't fallen into all that many beds, but she'd been with enough guys to know Jesse was different. He had a way of making her feel special. Important.

Too bad he didn't seem to recognize an invitation when he heard one.

"What's the matter?" she prodded, her arms falling to her side—empty—as she sat up on his motorcycle. "Afraid your *business partner* will see us?"

She couldn't help the sarcasm that dripped from her words.

"She's my best friend," Jesse snapped, with none of his usual trademark charisma. Perhaps he realized as much because he let out a deep sigh. "Could we keep Kyra out of this?"

"My thought exactly." Greta would gladly let Kyra eat her dust as she sped off into the sunset on the back of Prince Charming's bike. "Why don't you come with me to Miami this weekend? We can go jet-skiing and I'll take you to the international swimwear show that all my friends will be in."

Most men salivated at the prospect of leggy models in bathing suits. Jesse looked like she'd just consigned him to Dante's third circle of hell.

"Sorry, Greta. I'm not on vacation anymore—can't do those spur-of-the-moment trips." He made a big production of peering at his watch. "In fact, I'm late for a meeting right now."

Greta scrambled to straddle the bike, ready to follow Jesse wherever he might be headed. She'd come to Tampa for white picket fences and happily ever after, damn it. She wasn't leaving this town without a man in tow.

"That's great." Greta smiled, batted eyelashes and tapped the most basic weaponry in the female arsenal. "Why not drop me off wherever you're going?"

"A vacant lot in the middle of nowhere?" Jesse leaned down and scooped her up in his arms. "I don't think so."

Before she could fully appreciate the titillation of being wrapped in those big, strong arms, Greta was plunked unceremoniously to her feet in between an all-terrain vehicle and a horse trailer.

"Wait!" She stormed back toward the bike, but her shout was lost in the throaty roar of the Harley kicking to life.

And much to her dismay, Jesse Chandler hauled ass out of the barn, leaving *her* in the dust.

This was her Prince Charming?

If it wasn't for the serious pleasure the man could bring a woman, Greta might have had to rethink her choice for significant other.

As it stood, she merely shouted a string of epithets in his wake as she barreled out of the barn under the power of her own two feet. She may have been living a privileged life the past few years; but Greta still remembered how to work for the things she wanted.

By the time her feet hit the smooth pavement of the winding main road, Greta had reapplied her lipstick, fluffed her hair and adjusted her attitude.

For Jesse—the perfect man for her—she was willing to put forth a little effort. Once he realized they were meant to be together, he'd come around. And then he could apply himself to the task of making up for his wretched behavior toward her today.

A blue pickup truck rolled out onto the county route from an unmarked dirt road a few hundred yards away.

Lucky for her, the vehicle was headed in her direction, back toward Tampa.

Promising herself she would learn to drive and buy herself a car very soon, Greta flicked out her thumb to hail the oncoming truck. She'd met some interesting people while hitchhiking, but she knew every time she hopped in a car with a stranger she was taking a ridiculous risk.

And jet-set, international models might take risks, but settled women who lived in houses with picket fences did not.

The truck slowed to a stop beside her. The passenger door swung out, pushed from inside. Greta stepped on the running board to pull herself up into the shiny, midnight-blue vehicle, wishing she could have had a better visual of the truck's driver before she committed to getting in.

She recognized the scratchy Southern drawl at almost the same moment she came face-to-face with the tall, weathered cowboy in the driver's seat.

"Doesn't a city girl like you know better than to take a ride with a stranger?"

8

HORSE BREEDER Clint Bowman had always been a gentleman. Treating women with courtesy and respect had been a cornerstone of his strict, Alabama backwoods upbringing and he'd implemented those teachings with every woman he'd ever met.

So it made no sense to him that he would be sitting in his truck cab stifling a chuckle at seeing Greta Ingram's million-dollar cover-girl smile morph into a red-cheeked huffy pout today.

But then, nothing about Greta Ingram made him feel much like a gentleman.

"Do you have any idea who I am?" she asked, nose tilted in the air as she settled into his passenger seat and fastened her seat belt.

Clearly, she didn't consider him a threat to an unsuspecting hitchhiker.

Reaching across her world-famous legs, he yanked her door shut. "Two *Sports Illustrated* swimsuit covers in a row sort of makes you a household name, doesn't it?"

All of America had seen her face on countless magazines over the past five years. Her perfect features, dominated by her generous, trademark lips. The woman was a walking sexual fantasy.

At the mention of her well-known status, she preened with a vengeance. Greta sat up straighter, angled her shoulders, tossed her head…Clint lost track of her flurry of movements, all no doubt designed to make a man drool.

"Good." The hair-fluff thing she did was pure diva. "Then perhaps you won't mind dropping me off downtown. Preferably near the Gasparilla events." She didn't ask. She issued orders.

"And do you find that trading on your famous face makes people more inclined to forgive the bad manners?" Shifting the truck into gear, he pulled out onto the main road.

He expected her to get all puffed-up and indignant again, but this time she only rolled her eyes and started digging through her mammoth purse. "My manners surely aren't any worse than yours. But then, the world rather expects me to be haughty. I'm rich and pampered and I find that conceit makes a damn good weapon in a cutthroat business. What's your excuse?"

He wasn't about to share his excuse. Lust—pure and simple—didn't seem like a wise thing to own up to right now.

"Nothing nearly so rational as yours, I guarantee you." He watched her wave a silver cigarette case in one hand while she excavated shiny compacts and lipstick tubes from her handbag with the other. "Need a light?"

"Would you mind?" She dropped her handful of lipsticks back in the purse. The look of gratitude she flashed his way hit him like a thunderbolt. He caught a nanosecond glimpse of what it might be like to be on the receiving end of other, more sensual gratitudes....

Scavenging through a pile of roadmaps in his truck console, Clint refused to let his mind wander impossible paths. He found a long unused lighter and flicked up a flame after two dry runs.

She leaned close to catch the fire, holding his hand steady with her own. A spark jumped from her flesh to his that had nothing do with the combustible vial of fluid he clutched.

When she glanced up at him with shock scrawled in her bright green eyes, Clint flattered himself to think maybe she felt that bit of electricity, too. Although, judging by how fast she scrambled back into the far recesses of the passenger side, it was pretty damned obvious she didn't appreciate the connection.

"You want one?" she extended the case across the cab, her hand a little unsteady.

Did he make her nervous? Hard to believe the woman who thought nothing of hitchhiking on an isolated Florida back road would be unnerved by old-fashioned sexual chemistry.

Still, he didn't see the need to say as much. At least not yet.

"No thanks. I quit." Across the spectrum of his bad habits, smoking had been the easiest to kick.

"Really?" She rolled down her window halfway and exhaled into the sultry Florida air. "I find recovered smokers to be the most sanctimonious."

She seemed to relax a little behind the weapon of her sharp tongue.

"Not this one." He tossed the lighter back in his console and half wished he hadn't discovered touching Greta was even more explosive than talking to her. "I'm a firm believer in 'to each his own.'"

She cast him a cynical look over one shoulder before staring out the truck window again. Engaged in constant, jittery movement, Greta was either nervous as hell around him or severely caffeine-addicted.

Either way, Clint couldn't help wondering if there was any way to slow her down for a few minutes.

Or for a few days. Nights.

"I'm Clint Bowman," he offered, remembering the manners she'd suggested he didn't have as they sped by local produce stands advertising oranges and boiled peanuts. "Want to have dinner with me tonight and I'll behave at my non-sanctimonious best?"

He probably shouldn't have subjected his ego to looking across the cab at her, but he'd never been a man to take the easy way out. Sure enough, her eyes widened in surprise—at least he hoped it was surprise and not mild horror—her jaw dropped open, and her cigarette fell from her hand, straight out the truck window.

Not exactly good signs for his suit.

"I don't think so." Shaking her head with more vehemence than was strictly necessary, she folded her arms across her body and shouted her refusal with every facet of her body language.

"You have better things to do with your time than hang out with an Alabama cowboy?" Normally, he wouldn't needle a woman about that sort of thing. But Clint's psychology degree and every instinct about human nature told him Greta Ingram felt more comfortable conversing under the shield of verbal sparring.

"I'll be with Jesse Chandler. I assume you know him if you're familiar with the Crooked Branch?"

He was familiar all right. "We met this morning when he was having a conniption over me getting too close to Kyra Stafford. Guess I assumed they were a couple."

Steam practically hissed from Greta's ears as they rolled through a construction site near the interstate.

"Hardly. Jesse and I have been an item for months." Her mutinous look dared him to contradict her.

"Then it strikes me as damned funny I saw him roaring away from the ranch on a Harley not ten minutes before I found you hitchhiking on the side of the road." Clint would stake his horse-breeding business on the fact that Jesse Chandler was tied up in knots over Kyra.

Which, to Clint's way of thinking, left Greta very much available to a man with a little bit of patience.

Or ingenuity.

"He must not have known I was at the ranch then, I suppose." She sniffed. Tilted her perfect nose high in the air.

"Dinner with me might make him jealous as hell." So he was ten kinds of no-good for tossing that out there to serve his own ends. But it was definitely in keeping with today's lack of manners.

The notion caught her attention.

She arched a curious brow in his direction. "You think so?"

"Nothing like a little competition for a woman to make a man get his head out of the sand."

She pursed her perfect lips. Clint stared at her mouth, so mesmerized by the sight he nearly took out a few orange construction cones on the side of the road.

"Okay," she finally agreed. "But we're only going through with it if we can find a time Jesse will be around to notice. And you need to behave like an attentive gentleman." She flashed him a narrow look as if still debating whether or not he could pull off such a thing. "If we're going to do this, we do it on *my* terms."

Yes.

"Honey, I'm all yours." Clint swallowed the smile that tickled his mouth.

He'd just talked himself into an evening with a walking, talking spitfire who also just happened to be one of the world's hottest women.

Which only proved that sometimes it didn't pay to be a gentleman.

NEARLY TWO WEEKS LATER, Jesse put the finishing touches on a custom-made strip of crown molding with his jigsaw and realized he couldn't remember the last time he'd been able to think of another woman.

God knows, he'd been trying—hard—for days now.

Switching off the saw, Jesse brushed a fine layer of sawdust from the elaborately carved piece of wood before leaving his workshop for the day. Ten days had passed since he last tore out of the private driveway that led to the Crooked Branch, kicking up gravel in his wake. Yet for long, torturous days on end, the only woman he'd been able to conjure seminaked in his mind had been Kyra Stafford.

Not good.

Out of desperation, he'd finally hightailed it out of town over the weekend. His older brother Seth had asked him to deliver his boat to the sleepy Gulf coast town of Twin Palms and Jesse had jumped at the chance for temporary escape.

Too bad the trip hadn't helped him take his mind

off Kyra. If anything, seeing his brother's newfound happiness with artist Mia Quentin had only hammered home the fact that Jesse didn't have a clue how to make a relationship work.

As he checked his watch, he realized he needed to haul ass if he wanted to make it over to the ranch in time to say goodbye to Sam's Pride.

And to Kyra.

He couldn't put off seeing her any longer. And he couldn't delay a serious conversation in which he unwound the complications of their relationship and put them back on firm "just friends" footing.

Shoving a helmet on his head, he straddled his Harley and headed north, grateful for the long ride to the Crooked Branch so he could get his head in order. For days he'd made excuses not to think about the ramifications of his night with Kyra, telling himself they hadn't really done anything anyway.

Of course, in some long-buried portion of his conscience, he knew that was a lie.

They had done something monumental that night. Had touched each other in ways that scared the hell out of him if he let himself think about it for too long.

That's why tonight had to be a quick, efficient case of get in, get out.

And *not* in a sexual way, damn his freaking libido.

He'd say goodbye to Sam's Pride because the three-year-old was a damn good horse. Jesse and Kyra had been at the ranch together the night Sam's Pride had been born. And for some reason, the horse had always followed Kyra around like a shadow, had even rescued her from the river one night when another horse had thrown her.

Jesse sort of owed it to that animal to at least be there when he got booted off the Crooked Branch so Kyra could make enough profit for her controlling partnership.

Damn, but that bothered him.

Half an hour later, as he pulled into the drive leading to the Crooked Branch, Jesse wasn't any happier with the situation, but at least he had a plan for his approach. Balancing his helmet on his bike's seat, he coached himself on the basic principles he needed to remember. As he walked toward the exercise arena, he could already see Sam's Pride trotting in circles and he ran through the mission in his mind.

Give Kyra her controlling percentage and say his own goodbyes. To the horse, to the ranch and—much as it didn't feel right—to her.

Get in. Get out.

Figuratively, damn it.

And—above all things—try not to think of Kyra naked.

Rounding the corner of the private stables, Jesse caught a better view of the exercise area and the fence surrounding it. Two figures leaned up against the rails, much as he and Kyra had earlier last week.

He didn't need to see the tall guy's face under the Stetson to know Kyra's companion was Clint Bowman—Sam's Pride's personal psychologist and Kyra's obvious admirer. The guy wasn't touching her right this second, but give him two minutes and he probably would be.

The oddly foreign sense of jealousy that he'd experienced the last time he saw them together roared back with a vengeance. All his "get in, get out" mental coaching was lost in a firestorm of "get your hands off Kyra and get the hell out of my way."

Clint noticed him then and nudged Kyra to let her know they had company. Jesse might have bristled more at the physical contact of that nudge, but then Clint took an obvious step back away from Kyra.

Smart man.

"Hey, Jesse," Kyra called, her faded jeans skimming gently curved hips and covering a pair of worn red cowboy boots she'd had since high school. Her red tank top was new, however. At least to his eyes. It bore little resemblance to the men's T-shirts she usually favored for working and it definitely showcased the amazing body he'd only just recently discovered she possessed. "Sam's Pride is in great form tonight."

Sam's Pride wasn't the only one. Kyra looked so good it hurt.

As Jesse neared, he could see the animation in her blue eyes, the restless energy of her movements. She was genuinely excited about starting a new chapter in her life. One that didn't involve him, or the horse they'd helped deliver.

Not that he intended to care all that much. She was entitled to be independent, to kick up her heels a little, right?

"He looks good," Jesse agreed, forcing his eyes to move over the sleek black three-year-old instead of the thin sliver of bared skin between Kyra's jeans and the hem of her tank top.

"Clint says he's been responding really well all week, so I'm pretty optimistic about tonight." Her gaze settled on him. Lingered. "You okay?"

He was walking away from the one steady friendship he'd managed to form in his life tonight and he hadn't been able to work up desire for any woman but her in over ten days.

Hell yeah, he was just peachy.

"Never been better."

She eyed him critically while Clint called to Sam's Pride behind her.

Thankfully, the sound of tires crunching on gravel and the squeak of a trailer in tow saved Jesse from further questioning.

"Looks like your customer has arrived." Jesse steeled himself for the easier of the two goodbyes he planned to make tonight.

A shiny black pickup truck with two cherry-red racing flames down the side slowed to a stop on the other side of the stables. Kyra strode forward to shake hands with the newcomer—a crusty rancher with a mountain-man beard and a black-and-red jacket to match his truck.

She looked utterly at ease with the horse buyer. Jesse watched her nod in response to something he said. She smiled. Laughed.

Her anticipation for the sale was palpable and not because she was a fan of a healthy profit margin. No, Kyra wanted to sell Sam's Pride to cut a few more ties with Jesse and claim the controlling partnership in the Crooked Branch as her own.

When had she developed such a thirst for independence?

Of course, maybe it had always been there and he'd just never been in town long enough to see it.

Now, Kyra waved to Clint, spurring the cowboy into action. She stared at her horse, the horse who was never far from her side while she was at the ranch, and seemed to send him a silent message with her eyes. *Behave.*

Funny that Jesse could hear it some thirty yards away.

Clint steered the horse toward the driveway and the waiting trailer. The glossy black three-year-old had been washed and brushed and adorned with his best bridle. He looked like a candidate for a horse magazine cover—until he neared the trailer ramp.

The horse danced sideways and stopped.

Jesse launched into motion, ready to help. He might not agree with Kyra's decision to sell the horse, but he knew how important this was to her and he'd do whatever he could to make sure Sam's Pride went up that trailer ramp.

He stood on the other side of the horse so he and Clint were flanking him. Sam's Pride balked, stepped backward, snorted.

"Maybe if you lead him?" Clint called out to Kyra even as the horse started tossing its head and stomping his hooves.

"I don't think so." Jesse took the reins from Clint, unwilling to let Kyra come between nine hundred pounds of willful horse and the trailer. Already, Sam's Pride was twitchy and nervous.

Kyra sidled closer anyway, reaching for the bridle as she cooed to the animal. "I can take him, Jess," she whispered, maintaining eye contact with Sam's Pride as she reached to help.

Jesse tugged the horse to one side to keep Kyra out of harm's way. "He's too unpredictable, damn it."

As if to prove his words, Sam's Pride bucked and

jumped, yanking his reins from Jesse's hands so hard
the leather burned and sliced both his palms.

While Sam's Pride pawed the air and then galloped
into the woods, Kyra's customer let a string of curses
fly and Clint whistled low under his breath.

Jesse, on the other hand, could totally identify with
the three-year-old. He couldn't help thinking the horse
didn't want a noose around his neck any more than
Jesse ever had.

"Deal's off," the bearded customer huffed, clomping
back to his fancy truck. "I don't have time to kowtow
to a temperamental horse."

"Wait!" Kyra called, hastening to catch him.

But the pickup truck's engine drowned her out as
the old guy shifted into Reverse and sped away from
the Crooked Branch.

"He's not temperamental!" Kyra shouted in the man's
wake in a rare display of anger. "He's just…"

She trailed off, shoulders sagging.

"He just wants to be near you," Clint offered, stroking his jaw as he stared out into the field.

Jesse and Kyra followed his gaze only to find Sam's
Pride quietly munching grass and swatting flies with
his tail. Almost as if he hadn't just pitched the fit of a
lifetime.

Kyra made a strangled sound that probably only reflected a tiny fraction of her exasperation. She looked
deceptively fragile and alone as she wrapped her arms
about her own shoulders and stared back at the animal
that had let her down today.

How long had she been handling all her problems
on her own?

Clueless how to comfort her given that she only

wanted to buy independence from him anyway, Jesse itched to touch her but kept his hands to himself.

Clint whistled for the horse and Sam's Pride trotted over like an eager puppy. "I think he's just really protective of Kyra." He patted the animal's neck and spoke to Jesse when Kyra didn't seem ready to talk yet. "Does he have any reason to have a special attachment to her?"

"He shouldn't, but he does. He saved her once after another horse threw her down by the river." God knows no one else had noticed her missing. Jesse had been on the road with his baseball team. Her father was too depressed to check on his daughter.

"But I've raised and trained hundreds of horses," Kyra argued, finally giving Sam's Pride a begrudging pat on the nose. "I don't understand why this one would grow so attached to me."

Clint shrugged. "I'm not sure, either, but I think he considers himself your self-appointed guardian."

Jesse couldn't help but think he didn't have so much in common with Sam's Pride after all. Instead of running from the noose the way Jesse had all these years, Sam's Pride kept running straight for it. The crazy animal wanted to be near Kyra and he wanted to take care of her.

Great. Even a horse was a more loyal friend than Jesse.

Not that Kyra didn't mean a lot to him. She always had. He'd just been so busy running in the other direction that maybe he'd never really seen it before.

He'd spent almost two weeks trying to deny the obvious. Just because he hadn't been "in and out" with Kyra didn't make what they'd done together any less intimate. And damned if he wasn't about to explode with the need to see her unravel all over again. And again.

A better man might have turned away. He wasn't a better man. Jesse already knew that about himself. And so did Kyra, yet she seemed to want him anyway.

He was through fighting what they both wanted.

As his gaze fell upon Kyra again, Jesse absorbed every nuance of the only woman he'd ever wanted to be with day after day. The only woman who'd kept his interest even after he'd seen her naked.

She laughed and jumped back as Sam's Pride nudged her bare shoulder with his nose. A twinge of longing curled through Jesse, a hunger so strong he didn't know how he'd keep himself from devouring her right then and there.

Slipping a hand around her arm, he drew her away from the horse and the Alabama cowboy who had gotten to spend more than his share of time with Kyra this week.

The ends of her long blond hair slid invitingly against his hand. Her skin felt smooth and cool beneath Jesse's touch. Vaguely he wondered how long it would take to spike her body temperature by a few degrees.

He promised himself he would find out.

Tonight.

She glanced up at him, blue eyes wide. Perhaps she was startled that he would initiate physical contact between them after how much he'd fought this. He swore he could feel the rush of adrenaline through her veins underneath the pads of his fingers.

Or was that only his own?

As they neared the side of the stables, he leaned closer, narrowing their world to just one another.

"Was it my imagination or didn't we decide that once your customer left we were going to explore this thing between us much more thoroughly?"

9

KYRA STARED into Jesse's magnetic brown eyes and knew she would get sucked in all over again. They'd left Clint far behind in the training yard, along with any other potential prying eyes. That left little distractions for her to take her mind off what she really wanted.

She'd half managed to convince herself she was insane to pursue any sort of physical relationship with him. He'd broken hearts too numerous to count, after all. And he'd been able to walk away from her for nearly two weeks after a night that had practically set her on fire inside and out. Obviously, the man was well versed in separating himself from the erotic draw of sensual experience.

Kyra, on the other hand, was not.

She'd been thinking and fantasizing about Jesse's hands on her body nonstop for days on end. As much as she wanted one more night with him—one *real* night where they saw their attraction through to its natural… climax—she had grown a tad more leery about the potential risks to her heart and their friendship.

"Did we say that?" she asked finally, wondering if

he felt the nervous pump of her heart right through her skin. "I got the impression that you weren't ready to explore things quite as…thoroughly as I'd wanted to."

"Maybe I changed my mind." His wide shoulders shielded her from any view of the exercise ring, Clint or her traitorous horse.

She had no choice but to focus solely on him.

And the words that signaled a provocative new twist to their friendship.

"Meaning you're ready to finish what we started?" An electric jolt of sexual energy fired right through her. Still, she wanted to make absolutely certain they were discussing the same thing.

She needed to sleep with him and get over her crush on him. Dispel the myth, the local legend that was Jesse Chandler.

Even as she thought as much, a little twinge of worry wondered what would happen to them afterward, but Kyra shoved it firmly aside.

He stared down at her with that dark, suggestive gaze of his. "Meaning it's taken me this long to realize we already did finish what we started, and I'm kidding myself to pretend otherwise."

"I don't follow."

He looked around the grounds for a moment, and then led her inside the stables through a back door. He didn't stop there. Guiding her through a maze of the training facility's back corridors, Jesse brought them through a side door into his old office in the converted old barn that housed the Crooked Branch's lobby and business offices.

She hadn't been in here in ages—partly because all their files were electronic and she could access any of his paperwork via computer, but also because being around his things was such a guilty pleasure.

High-gloss hardwood floors gave the office warmth and an aged appeal all the high-tech computer equipment couldn't negate. Because Jesse's office was at the back of the building ensconced in one of the two turrets of the old-fashioned structure, the walls were rounded with only a few high windows. He'd added a skylight over his desk to flood the room with natural illumination.

Now, he led her past his hammock installed between two ceiling support beams and gestured toward the curved sectional sofa that lined part of the wall. He'd bought it along with a television wall unit so he could keep tabs on the Devil Rays score while he worked. His Work Hard, Play Hard ethic would no doubt raise a few eyebrows in the corporate world, but Jesse was one of the most fiercely productive people Kyra knew.

When he wanted to be.

Sinking into the bright blue sectional, Kyra watched him pace the hardwood floor.

He scrubbed a hand through his dark hair. "It's taken me this long to realize it, but I'm not as virtuous in all this as I thought."

She blinked. Twice.

He stopped pacing. "I figured I was being so damn noble by not committing the final act that night we spent together. But the more I thought about it—and believe me, I've thought about it *a lot*—I realized that we've already committed the acts that really matter." He dropped down to sit on a sanded crate that served as a coffee table directly in front of her. "I mean, it's sort of splitting hairs to say nothing happened between us just because we didn't…finish. When it comes down to it, something big *did* happen between us and there's no sense running from that fact."

Nodding slowly, Kyra absorbed what he said but couldn't possibly fathom where he might be going with it. "So you figure now you're off the hook with me because you've already crossed the sexual line?"

"No. I figure now that I've crossed the sexual line, I'm an ass if I don't go for broke before you wise up and boot me out of your bed."

"Oh."

"The question is, are you still game?" He crowded her. Stole the air.

The ramifications washed over her with enticing sensual possibility. She became acutely aware of Jesse's knees brushing hers, two layers of denim between them not even coming close to stifling the sparks they generated.

"That depends." Her practical nature demanded they hammer this out right now, despite the rising temperature in the room. She refused to worry and wonder for another week about where things stood between them. "Let's say for a moment that I am game. I wouldn't want to be treated like a best friend once we hit the sheets."

"Who said anything about sheets? I was thinking of much more imaginative scenarios."

Her breath caught. Refused to come back for a long, pulse-pounding moment. "A figure of speech. Regardless of where we conduct our liaison, I just want to be certain there's no attack of conscience midstream."

He crossed his heart with the tip of one finger. "Luckily, I left my conscience back at my apartment. I'm morally free to have my wicked way with you."

Gulp. She was having a devil of a time staying on track here. "Which brings me to another point."

"I have to say, Kyra, I've never been with any woman who ironed out the details quite so thoroughly as you."

"If we are going to indulge one another in this way, I want the full tutorial in wickedness."

A smile hitched at his sinfully beautiful mouth. "You're not asking what I think you're asking."

Damn straight I am.

"You've got all the experience in this arena, Jesse. Teach me a few things from that seductive arsenal of yours." This way, when he left her—and he *would* leave her—she would at least have a little more confidence about physical relationships.

Not that she could currently envision using provocative wiles on any man except Jesse, but she refused to dwell on that fact. She had to believe that a night with Jesse would shatter his mystique just a little—at least enough so that she could look at other men and maybe find someone more suitable, someone more practical down the road.

"How could I unleash you on an unsuspecting male population then? Wildly beautiful *and* an expert in titillation? I think that would be giving you too much of an advantage."

"Wildly beautiful?" Kyra suspected Jesse had earned his bad-boy reputation with sweet-talking lines like that one. "We both know you're exaggerating. Wildly. I think a little more provocative advantage would be a good thing for me."

Jesse studied her. Frowned. "This is against my better judgment."

She folded her arms, growing more confident with

every moment he sat across from her that he wouldn't—couldn't—walk away from this. The attraction between them was like the force field between magnets just barely out of reach from one another. She had all she could do to stay in her seat and not give in to that pull. "It'll be a deal-breaker."

"You drive a hard bargain, woman."

"I'm thinking it's easier to deal with you in a businesslike fashion than as a pirate hussy."

He pointed a finger at her. "Don't you dare knock the pirate hussy. I'm going to have a lifelong fascination with leather corsets thanks to you."

"So do we have a deal or not?" she pressed, more than ready to put the business part of the night behind them so she could cash in on all that Jesse magnetism.

"Deal. But I have a condition of my own."

She had a good idea what sort of conditions *he* might come up with. "Forget it. I already sent the corset to a leather cleaner."

He leaned closer to plant his arms on either side of her against the couch, effectively cranking up her pulse with every inch he closed between them. "I mean it. If I'm going to be in an instructor position, I want you to agree to be a dutiful student."

She caught a hint of his scent—motorcycle exhaust, leather and male. His knees edged more firmly between hers. Licking her lips, she met his gaze. "Trust me, I'm pretty eager to learn."

"That means you'll do whatever I say?"

She couldn't wait. "Within reason."

"This could be a deal-breaker." He tossed her own words back at her, but she sensed he was bluffing when he slid one of his hands into the back of her hair to tease sensual touches down the curve of her neck.

Shivers of anticipation coursed through her. "So keep your requests reasonable and we won't have any problems."

He stroked his way over her shoulder and right down into the vee of her tank top. The palm of his hand skimmed the curve of her breast and practically made her flesh sing.

"Tonight's not going to have a damn thing to do with reason." He nudged the edge of his hand into her shirt until he reached the barely-there red bra she'd bought to go with her new top. "Or practicality." Plunging deeper, he smoothed the pad of his finger over her nipple. "It's going to be all about sensation."

Sensation poured over her in time with his words as he teased the pebbled flesh between his thumb and forefinger.

The man certainly knew how to get his point across.

"Yesss." The word hissed out on a sigh of pure pleasure.

And just like that, she found herself agreeing to anything—everything—Jesse had in store for her.

"EXCELLENT." Jesse bent to kiss a path between Kyra's breasts, mesmerized by the accelerated rise and fall of her chest. "I think we can safely say that lesson one is Jesse knows best."

Her back arched as he drew on her flesh, her hips wriggled with a delightfully restless twitch.

Most tellingly, she didn't argue.

"Ready for lesson two?" He released her long enough to murmur over her skin.

"Hopefully it's less talk, more kissing."

His hand strayed over her hip and toward the snap of her jeans. "Actually, it's less denim, more skirts. Preferably without panties. There's a good reason why men find dresses sexy, you know."

"Duly noted." She flicked open the snap herself to help him. "I can appreciate practicality."

He dragged her zipper down a few notches to discover a swath of shimmery red silk beneath the stiff fabric of her jeans. His practical business partner was full of surprises. "Although when the panties look like this, I can definitely see the appeal."

He smoothed his hand over her abdomen, teased the edge of the silk with one finger. Her skin felt so creamy perfect to his touch it was difficult to tell where the silk left off and her skin began.

Her breathing hitched as the heel of his hand nudged farther south.

"I'm ready for more," she whispered against his ear. "More lessons. More touches."

"Keep in mind lesson one."

She pried an eyelid open to stare at him with a mixture of confusion and pure lust.

"Jesse knows best," he reminded her, leveraging his position of power to the fullest.

Instead of conceding his superior sexual wisdom, however, Kyra merely reached for his belt buckle.

"Hey!" He nearly choked on the word as her fumbling struggle brushed a straining erection. God, she was going to be the death of him. "What are you doing?"

The look she gave him was pure menace. "Fighting fire with fire."

Heat flashed through him. No other woman had ever

given him so much hell in bed. Or out of it for that matter. Still, he couldn't help but admire her for not letting him get away with anything.

And truth be told, her touch felt like heaven as she slipped questing fingers beneath the denim to curve around him.

With an effort, he stopped her. Tugging those adventurous hands away, he stretched her arms up over her head as he dragged their bodies down to lie on the couch. "The most important lesson of all is patience."

She squirmed against him. "Not my forte. Especially not when I feel so...edgy."

Jesse was right there with her in the edgy department. If her hips brushed over his one more time he'd be lurching *over* the edge pathetically premature, in fact. He needed to take charge here if he wanted a fighting chance of maintaining his status as Kyra Stafford's private sex tutor.

"I can take the edge off," Jesse assured her, already sliding off the couch to help her find a release or two of her own before allowing himself the full pleasure her body had to offer him.

She grabbed his hand as he reached for jeans. "No, wait. You need to show *me* how to take the edge off for *you*. The lessons are to teach me, remember?"

Jesse felt his eyes bulge from his head like a damn cartoon character.

And that wasn't the only thing bulging.

"No." The protest croaked out a mouth gone dust-dry.

"Yes." Kyra sat upon her knees, already sizing up the situation. "And don't look so worried. I'm sure I can do this."

His blood pounded through his head so damn loud

he wasn't sure he'd heard her correctly. "Are you telling me you've never done this...I mean, *that*...before?"

He'd suspected that Kyra didn't have a huge amount of sexual experience. She'd never indicated any of the guys she dated were superserious. But then again, she'd definitely had her fair share of dates. Obviously, none of those guys had been all that adventurous in the bedroom.

"Unless you want me to ask a bunch of nosy questions about *your* sexual past, I don't think it's very polite to quiz me about mine." She whipped his leather belt from the loops, doubled it up and then slapped the sides together with a snap. "Now, get comfortable and tell me what I should be doing to drive you wild."

This had gone far enough. And if Jesse had been able to breathe past his raging lust, he might have explained as much to her.

As it stood, he settled for roping her with his arms and hauling her back down to the couch alongside him.

He muted all potential protests by clamping his mouth to hers in a kiss designed to make her forget anything and everything but him. He slid the leather belt from her hands and flung it across the office. Then he dragged her jeans down her hips, over her soft thighs and past her feet.

The patience he had touted a few minutes ago was gone, but he was determined to get it back.

Not until Kyra was naked, however.

He slid her tank top up over her arms and tugged her bra off her shoulders until both garments were somewhere in the middle of the hardwood floor. She was left clad in nothing but a scrap of shimmering red silk, a scrap which he hooked with one finger to shift and maneuver against her skin in a teasing caress.

Only when she upgraded from incoherent sighs to breathy pleas for fulfillment did he pull the panties down her legs.

"Apparently you're having a problem with the whole patience concept in all of this." He confided the words into her left ear, the one that was closest to his mouth. He nipped her earlobe for good measure, still struggling with his own desire to explore their attraction at full speed ahead.

It galled him that he, of all people, had to be the responsible one in this.

"It's never been my strong suit," she admitted, arching her neck to give him better access.

"Since it doesn't seem to impress you when I *tell* you that patience pays, I think I'd be better off proving it to you firsthand."

KYRA HEARD JESSE'S words somewhere in the back of her passion-fogged brain and knew she was headed for the equivalent of sensual torture. How could the man be so cruel to make her wait?

As for her lessons—forget it! She didn't have a chance of retaining any good provocative moves when she was so thoroughly engrossed by them. All in all, the man turned her on far too much to be of any use in her sexual education.

Then again, he turned her on far too much for her to ever consider stopping him.

Next time she'd pay closer attention. Next time she'd retain more of the nuances of his technique. For now, his fingers were finally creeping up her thigh and she thought she might come totally unglued.

She'd waited and waited for him to touch her and now—finally—he eased his hand around the wet heat of her, slid one finger deep inside of her.

And ohmigod. All the waiting had made her ready.

Her body clenched involuntarily around him, just one quick spasm she knew would be a precursor to so much more.

He must have felt it as plainly as she did because he released a stifled groan and lowered his mouth to her breast. His tongue laved her swollen flesh and nipped at the peaked center of her.

Heat radiated from the places he kissed to the most intimate places he touched as if the two were on an electric current traveling in both directions. Kyra ground her hips against his hand, but he withdrew his finger, teasing her slick folds until she thought she'd die of pleasure.

Once, she crested so high she could barely catch her breath and then he slid two fingers inside her, heavy and deep. The pressure inside her burst, exploding out in an orgasm that rocked her whole body. She dug her heels in the couch and pressed herself against him, greedy for every silken sensation Jesse could provide.

When the sensations finally slowed and then stopped, Kyra could barely scavenge a thought other than that she wanted Jesse even more than she had two hours ago and ten times more than she wanted him last week.

She experienced a twinge of fear that her plan to get over him by indulging in him completely was going to crash and burn in a big way. The man was seriously—frighteningly—addictive.

He walked his fingertips up her bare belly. "You ready to see why patience pays?"

"Very ready." Her whole body burned with the truth of the sentiment.

Unfolding himself from his place on the couch, Jesse rose to pull his T-shirt over his head. He cast a molten glance in her direction before he retrieved a condom from his pocket and shoved his way out of his jeans.

Kyra practically purred at the sight of him as he sheathed himself for her. He was all bronze skin and hard muscle—emphasis on the word *hard*. The man should have been statuary in a world-class museum. Jesse was male perfection at its most devastating.

Any lingering strains of satisfaction from the orgasm he'd given her faded in a new surge of desire. Any nervousness she might have experienced about her first time had deserted her as soon as Jesse touched her. She couldn't be in more experienced, or more talented, hands.

She glanced up at his eyes to gauge his expression. The answering heat she found there reassured her. Despite his qualms about sex complicating their friendship, he wanted this every bit as much as she did.

He lowered himself over her. Her legs inched farther apart seemingly of their own will.

The sleek male power of him gave her a secret thrill, a feminine rush of delight.

And then he was nudging his way inside her, slowly and carefully in spite of his bad-boy reputation. She was grateful for his gentleness as her body stretched to accommodate him. Muscles she'd never known she possessed protested the invasion.

A little spark of fear flared to life inside her. Not

that she didn't want this, but what if her body's resistance tipped him off about her virginal status? Or worse yet—turned him off?

But as she met his gaze in the dimming illumination from the skylight from over his desk, Jesse's eyes held no reproach, just a little concern and a lot of restraint.

Then he reached between their bodies to touch her and the rush of desire returned. Her body gave way to his, opening itself to a delight even better than all the other pleasure he had given her so far.

He continued to touch and tease until he could move inside her without hurting her. Until every move of his body added fuel to the fire that raged inside her all over again.

And once again, his patience paid off.

Kyra felt the sensual tide rising up, lifting her beyond the couch and into the realm of sublimely erotic. Only this time, when she thought she would explode with the sweet joy he gave her, Jesse found his release, too, and shouted his satisfaction to the rafters.

Afterward, as they lay quiet and still together on the curving sectional couch, Kyra wondered if he'd say anything to her about her lack of experience. Could men really tell? And if they could, would Jesse be upset with her for not telling him in advance?

She rather hoped he had no idea. Dealing with the fallout from tonight would be fraught with enough land mines without having the virgin issue thrown in the mix.

He'd touched places deep inside her on so many levels. Physically, he seemed to take over her whole body. Emotionally, she couldn't begin to contemplate the effects of this new connection with him, but she knew she'd never walk away from tonight without some kind of indelible stamp on her heart.

10

JESSE AWOKE TO a cold, empty couch and an even colder attack of conscience the next morning. Stretching the crick out of his neck, he wondered how he could have gotten such a good night's sleep while twisted pretzel-like around Kyra on his office sectional. He'd held her while she fell asleep and it bugged him he wasn't holding her now.

Somehow, she'd slipped out of his grasp early this morning before he could discuss a few things with her. He'd done a hell of a job staving off those irritating scruples last night while he'd been losing himself in Kyra. But this morning he couldn't escape the bare facts.

He'd somehow managed not only to sleep with his best friend, but a virgin to boot. Firsts for him on both counts.

The crick in his neck throbbed back to life with a vengeance as he scrubbed a hand through his hair and tried to figure out how to handle this latest development in his shifting relationship with Kyra. He'd slept with more women than he cared to admit to, yet in all those encounters he'd never been with a virgin.

The fact that Kyra had never been with anyone else scared him. The fact that she'd deliberately chosen him for her first time demonstrated a level of trust she had no business bestowing upon him.

What if he'd messed up her first time?

A guy ought to be informed of those preexisting conditions, damn it.

Scooping his jeans off a purple Tampa Devil Rays hassock, Jesse decided to tell Kyra as much. And more. Just as soon as he located her, he would demand to know what it meant that she'd squandered her first time on someone like him.

Unless of course, she *hadn't* squandered it in her mind.

What if her choice of an experienced stud had been very deliberate? A possibility which seemed all the more likely given how damn practical the woman had been her whole life.

He was surprised how much the idea stung. She wouldn't have used him like that, would she?

Jesse jammed his arms through the sleeves of his T-shirt and shoved on his boots, determined to get some answers—and, God help him, a commitment—from his wild and wicked best friend.

KYRA HAD HALF HOPED Jesse would find her and demand she come back to bed this morning. As she hung the grooming tools she'd used to brush out Sam's Pride on the stable wall, she thought about how amazing her night with Jesse had been.

So amazing, in fact, she wondered if sex could be addictive. She couldn't even ride her horse around the exercise arena without getting totally turned on by the rhythmic movement between her thighs, for crying out loud.

Obviously, she was a woman in need of a little extra sexual attention. And, in her defense, she had put off sex long enough in life where she felt like she deserved some making up for lost time anyhow.

But as she led Sam's Pride into his paddock, Kyra heard the determined clomp of Jesse's boots across the gravel driveway out front. The purposeful stride of a normally laid-back man gave her the sinking feeling *he* wasn't daydreaming about making up for lost time today.

As he rounded the corner of the stables, Kyra noticed he still wore his jeans and T-shirt from yesterday. He was a little rumpled, but if anything, the tousled dark hair and wrinkled shirt only added to his sexy, bad-boy appeal.

Of course, Kyra had always known there was a lot more to Jesse Chandler than a charismatic aura and bedroom eyes. It was just tough not to get distracted by them. Especially when she had sex on the brain.

He closed the gate to the paddock behind Kyra with a bit more clang than usual. Turning to face her, he met her gaze head-on. "Leaving in the middle of the night is *my* M.O., you know."

Unsure where he was headed with his comment, Kyra merely smiled. "Good morning to you, too."

"So if you're trying to send me a reminder that our relationship has definite boundaries, you're singing to the choir." He jerked a thumb toward his chest. "I wrote the book on boundaries."

"Trust me, I wasn't trying to send any message, I just woke up with a major cramp in my calf." Sex in

Kama Sutra positions was awesome, but falling asleep in those positions was definitely not relaxing. Kyra had been too enraptured after her second off-the-charts orgasm to move, however. "I figured I'd walk it off and check on Sam's Pride before Clint arrived to work with him this morning."

A little of the stiffness slid out of Jesse's shoulders. Had he really been worried about her?

The notion caught her off guard.

"I shouldn't be offended you fled the scene?" He reached to stroke Sam's Pride's nose as the horse moved toward the gate and involved himself in their conversation.

It surely soothed a woman's ego to have a man be so concerned about her pleasure. Kyra couldn't help the warmth unfurling in her chest as she carried a fallen bale of hay over to a neatly stacked pile that had been delivered to the ranch the day before. "Definitely not."

"Good." Giving the horse a final pat, Jesse turned the full force of his attention on her. "Then we can check that off my list and move right along to why you didn't tell me ahead of time that you were a virgin."

The bale of hay slipped from her fingers and fell to the ground with a thud.

"Excuse me?" The small voice that tripped along the morning air seemed to belong to someone else.

Jesse tossed the hay bale near the pile then maneuvered a few of the other rectangular packs into a makeshift seating area. He guided Kyra onto one stack of hay and then dropped down onto a similar heap in front of her.

"I want to know why you didn't say one word about—" he peered around the yard one more time as if scouting for potential eavesdroppers "—last night being your first experience."

Kyra sighed. Apparently men could tell about these things. "The first-time thing doesn't matter."

"It matters to me." The stubborn tilt of his chin suggested he probably wouldn't let the matter rest anytime in the foreseeable future.

Embarrassment flustered her. Made her snappish. "Is this typical morning-after protocol?"

"I've never had a morning-after with a virgin before so I guess I don't know. Honestly, Kyra, my mind is so freaking blown from last night I couldn't think straight right now if my life depended on it."

The warm swell of happiness she felt at his words unsettled her. When had it become important to her that she hold a special place in his memory? "You've never been with another first-timer? Ever?"

"Not even one."

A small sense of satisfaction chased away some of her lingering embarrassment. Besides, she was outside among her horses, sitting right in a big pile of hay with a guy who'd taught her how to drive and still changed her oil. She ought to at least feel safe enough to tell him the truth about last night. Unfortunately, sharing her first time with Jesse had tangled her emotions in ways she'd never anticipated. "I couldn't tell you because I was afraid you'd change your mind about going through with it if you knew."

"Of course I would have changed my mind. You can't just give a gift like that to a guy like me." He plucked out a single blade of straw from the bundle and tucked it behind one ear.

"Don't be ridiculous. I trusted you enough to go into

business with you. Why wouldn't I trust you with my body?"

He shook his head as he pulled another strand of hay from the bale and proceeded to tie it around her wrist. "That's the most twisted bottom line I've ever heard."

"But utterly practical." Her eyes roved over his sexy male body sprawled back against a hay bale. "And now that I've answered your question, do you want to come back to my house and see if I can improve upon last night's performance?" She fingered the collar of her white V-neck T-shirt, her wrist adorned with the bracelet made of hay. "I'd like to get a good grade from my teacher."

She watched Jesse's eyes dart to her fingertips and lower. He licked his lips…almost allowed her to divert him…and then cursed.

"Hell no, Kyra. I'm trying to have a meaningful conversation here. You can't use sexual distraction to throw me off the course."

"Don't tell me—you wrote the book on sexual distraction too?"

"You damn well bet I did." He reached for her hands, stopped them from fiddling with her neckline. "But I'm not going to lose sight of what I came here to get this morning."

She waited.

And waited.

Until finally he nudged the words past his lips. "A commitment."

She couldn't have been more surprised if he'd announced a desire to take up croquet. "You're kidding."

"I'm completely serious." His steady brown eyes attested to the truth of that statement. Too bad he also looked like he'd just taken a bite of an exotic dish he was already regretting.

"You don't have to do this, Jesse." Hurt welled up inside her that he would think he needed to offer something after last night. "Moreover, I don't want you to."

His mouth dropped wide-open. "You wanted me enough to sleep with me but not enough for anything else?"

"Of course not. But—"

"Then it's all settled." His jaw muscles flexed—a surefire sign of stress. "We are going to date. You and me. Exclusively."

And he looked about as happy about it as lancing a boil on a horse's butt. As if following up last night with a dating invitation was a necessary evil to be dispensed with as quickly as possible.

Anger, far more comforting than the hurt, broke free. "The hell we are! Jesse, it was one night. You've had a zillion and one nights with other women and you've never grilled them about dates afterward."

"Last night was different and you know it." He glared at her in the warm February sunlight, his dark eyes illuminated to three different shades of brown by the Florida sun. "Last night was special."

She felt some of her anger melting away at his words. Part of her wanted to believe him. But damn it, the man was known countywide for sweet-talking his way into just about anything. How could she really trust him on this?

"So special you're going to force yourself to endure my repeated company?" She wouldn't allow herself to get sucked in by all that charm. The hell of it was she would have been more than a little tempted by his invitation if it had been sincere. "Come on, Jesse. I'm sorry I didn't own up to being a virgin."

He shook his head as if her apology solved nothing. "If last night was special enough to you that you saved yourself for it, then it must have been special enough where you can be my girlfriend for a few weeks."

That was his idea of commitment?

Kyra couldn't believe he called a few weeks a commitment. She vowed to open her phonebook first thing this afternoon and find the man a Bad Boys Anonymous.

"Fine," she agreed, relieved to have sidestepped a bigger obstacle with Jesse but just a little stung that he had already carved out a distinct time frame for their *commitment*. "But you're being ridiculous."

He nodded. Harrumphed. "We're still doing a real date."

"Great." She stood, shuffled her bale of hay back into place, and wished she were back in bed with Jesse instead of agreeing to something he didn't want. Back in bed where things were less complicated, where she didn't have to face all the churning emotions over what should have been a simple, sensual encounter.

"You and me. Alone. Very romantic." He shoved to his feet and tossed the bales of hay back onto the pile with so much force there was dried grass flying out of the stack in every direction.

"You're terrified, aren't you?"

His jaw flexed again. "I can't wait."

Yeah, right. She struggled not to roll her eyes as he walked back toward the barn where he parked his motorcycle. She struggled even harder not to feel the hurt welling up inside her.

As he reached the barn door he shouted the final instructions in this morning's list of commitment demands. "I'll pick you up tonight at seven."

"SEVEN O'CLOCK TONIGHT?" Greta parroted back Clint Bowman's dinner request as the tall, attractive-for-no-good-reason cowboy lounged against her doorjamb. She hadn't seen him since he'd given her a ride and tried to coerce her into a date.

And although she hadn't been expecting him this afternoon, she'd known even before she opened the front door who would be on the other side. The man had major chemistry even though he wasn't classically handsome like Jesse. She could *feel* Clint Bowman even before she laid eyes on him and she didn't like it one bit.

How could she be attracted to someone so rough around the edges?

Clint smoothed the brim of his hat with one hand while he held the Stetson in the other. "That's the time I heard Jesse and Kyra agree on for dinner. I was pulling in with my truck just as Jesse jumped on his bike to leave."

"And that was at nine o'clock this morning?" she prodded, hating to think Jesse had spent another night with his too-cute business partner and that she'd somehow misunderstood Clint's story.

Then again, Greta was having more and more trouble even coming up with a mental image of Jesse lately so she had to question how much the news truly bothered her. The only man she ever seemed to see in her mind's eye these days was the rugged male wrapped in muscles who stood on her doorstep.

Nodding, he stared at her hastily tied bathing suit

cover-up as if he had a good idea what she was wearing underneath it.

Nothing.

"I get to the Crooked Branch right around nine every day to work with Kyra's horse." His knowing gray eyes fairly crackled with heat by the time he met her gaze again. "But what do you think about dinner? You still in the market to make Jesse sit up and take notice?"

Clint's hot stare made her knees weak. Her breasts tightened beneath her cotton beach robe. Her body definitely wanted this man.

Fortunately her brain knew better. She'd always avoided men she couldn't control. And she especially avoided men with whom she couldn't control herself.

Greta had the feeling Clint Bowman fell neatly into both those categories.

"I'm in." Maybe all she needed was to see Jesse again and remind herself how perfectly he fit her vision of high-class suburban lifestyle. Besides, Jesse possessed an innate chivalry toward women that assured her he would never turn into the verbally abusive sort her father had been. "But how will we know where to have dinner?"

"Why don't we meet at the ranch right about seven, too? We can always follow them to whatever restaurant they hit. Shouldn't be too much of a coincidence in a town this size." His gaze dropped south again. "Did I catch you sleeping?"

And just like that, Greta was certain Clint knew she was naked underneath the yellow knit cover-up.

Her skin tingled from her ankles to her elbows, but it downright burned in all the best places in between. "Hardly."

"Sunbathing?"

"No, I—"

"Not that a woman ever needs an excuse to run around the house naked as far as I'm concerned." He flashed her a sexy, unrepentant grin as he replaced his hat on his head and backed toward his shiny blue pickup truck. "See you at seven?"

She had a good mind to say no. In fact, the sooner she put some distance between her and the cowboy badass who made her blood simmer, the better off she'd be.

But then how would she ever make Jesse notice her or rescue her from boorish guys like Clint Bowman?

"I'll be there." She draped herself in a little extra hauteur for good measure—and to help maintain some definite boundaries with Clint. "I just hope you can control yourself because my outfit tonight will make nakedness seem positively tame."

"I'll be the epitome of restraint." He levered open his truck door. "But if lover boy doesn't take notice by the time our last course rolls around, all bets are off."

"Meaning you're only going to be able to restrain yourself for so long?" Surely she was a sick woman that his wolfish look sent a little thrill through her when she was planning to seduce…her gaze gobbled up the curve of Clint's oh-so-fine ass.

Wait. Jesse. She was planning to seduce Jesse.

"Meaning that if you're still sitting with me at eight o'clock, I'm considering you fair game for dessert."

He angled himself inside the truck cab and shifted into Reverse before she could think of a retort.

Damn the man.

But Greta had no intention of allowing Clint Bowman and his sexy-as-sin body tempt her away from her

Great American Dream. The trick would be to intercept her quarry *before* seven o'clock tonight.

She hadn't managed to survive on her own since she was fourteen without accumulating a fair amount of goal-setting skills.

And right now, she had one goal in mind to complete her mental vision of where she wanted to be in life, one man who would be the perfect counterpart to her suburban lifestyle complete with a rose garden and filled with voices raised only in laughter.

The most charming man she'd ever met.

Jesse Chandler.

A BLACK CLOUD seemed determined to follow Jesse around ever since he'd uttered the damning word *commitment* to Kyra.

That same day his jigsaw broke, spinning a piece of nearly completed crown molding into the blade sideways before it conked out completely. He'd ruined a detailed piece that would take hours to reconstruct.

Then his customer's financing had fallen through for the first custom home he was supposed to have started on Monday, leaving him scrambling all afternoon to shuffle his spring schedule and fill the void.

Now as he sped up the rural county route toward the Crooked Branch on his Harley, it started to rain.

And then pour.

By the time he reached the ranch his khakis molded to his thighs like a wetsuit. Even worse, the rain hadn't let up a bit so he wouldn't be able to take them to dinner on the motorcycle.

If they wanted to go out for his first date as part of a

couple in his entire lifetime, he'd have to ride shotgun in Kyra's pickup.

The joys of commitment.

Jesse sensed the black cloud stalking him as he parked his bike in the barn and swiped the worst of the raindrops off the seat. No, wait.

That wasn't just a dark mood stalking him.

Footsteps sounded behind him. Too close.

A black cloud in stilettos and not much else stood behind him. Greta Ingram appeared every inch the world-renowned cover model as she struck a pose in a tissue-thin scarf she'd knotted at her navel as if it was a dress.

Objectively speaking, Jesse knew she must look gorgeous, but all he could think in his current frame of mind was that she had to be damn near freezing.

He couldn't afford the complication of her tonight. He barely knew what role he was supposed to be playing in Kyra's life anyway. And he'd already spent enough time trying to send Greta a message she refused to hear. "We've got to stop meeting like this."

Her trademark full lips turned even more pouty. "Tell me about it. A barn is hardly my idea of mood-setting ambiance. What do you say we go back to my place for a few hours and I'll show you some more of my yoga moves? I've been working on limbering up my neck muscles and you'll never believe what I can reach with my tongue."

She hovered closer, almost as if she was going to start teasing him with yoga tricks right here in the equipment storage barn.

"Greta, I can't see you anymore. Ever." He hated having to spell it out in such stark terms for her but her following him around had gotten way out of control. At one time her over-the-top antics might have swayed him, but he didn't feel even remotely interested tonight.

Oddly, he could still only think of one woman naked today. Even after a night in Kyra's arms Jesse could only think about her. Despite the hellish day he'd been having and the fact that he'd gone and devoted himself to some kind of relationship with her, he had thought about being with her nonstop.

Still, Greta looked at him like he'd lost his marbles. She put her fists on her hips and stood toe-to-toe with him. "Excuse me?"

"I'm seeing Kyra now," he told her, amazed to discover the words didn't feel as awkward as he'd feared they might. In fact, the declaration felt damn good. "And I know for a fact she's not going to appreciate you following me around. Now, if you'll excuse me, I've got to go meet her for dinner."

Jesse saw the steam start to hiss from her ears, but he couldn't find it in his heart to care anymore. He was still too caught up in the revelation that it hadn't really hurt to talk about Kyra as his girlfriend.

What if he could pull through on this commitment thing after all?

He nudged around Greta, making his way toward the door. The rain had slowed, but it hadn't stopped. Clint's truck was pulling into the driveway, an odd occurrence for seven o'clock in the evening.

Or so he hoped.

The horse whisperer hadn't seriously thought he could make time with Kyra behind Jesse's back, had he? Before Jesse could think through what to do about

Kyra's admirer, Greta hustled around him to plant herself in his tracks all over again.

"What are you doing?" He held his hands up but he didn't intend to surrender to this woman.

He was a committed man, damn it.

The rain pounded down on them. Jesse didn't care much since he was already soaked. But Greta's scarf turned X-rated within seconds. Not that he noticed.

She shouted at him through the rumble of thunder, her eyes lit by a fire within. "What does it look like I'm doing? I'm putting up a fight!"

He hadn't fully processed the comment when she grabbed him by the arms, plastered her wet body to his and fused their mouths in a no-holds-barred kiss.

11

Kyra swiped a brush through her hair and peered out the window just as the thunder started. The driveway was empty but she could have sworn she'd heard Jesse's Harley rumble past a few minutes ago.

Would he be late for their first date?

Judging by how pained he'd looked as he issued the invitation earlier today, Kyra half wondered if he'd show up at all. But then, he had always kept his word to her, even while he was standing up his so-called girlfriends left and right. Would their new committed status relegate her to his "B" list of personal priorities?

She resented his attitude even while she wished he felt differently about her. He had no right to make her feel as if she'd somehow twisted his arm into a relationship. Sure she hadn't shaken her age-old crush on him as easily as she'd once hoped, but she knew better than to ever hope for him to be a one-woman man.

Didn't she?

Simmering with restless energy and more than a little frustration, Kyra marched out into the foyer and prepared to face her personal demon.

Aka her best friend-turned-lover.

She knew damn well she'd heard his motorcycle a few minutes ago. Was he dragging his feet in the barn because he couldn't face his new ball and chain?

Throwing open the front door, Kyra didn't move so much as an inch into the blistering rain before she saw him.

Or rather *them*—Greta and Jesse in a lip-lock as fierce as the storm pelting their shoulders with raindrops.

Of all the two-timing lowdown tricks…

What more proof did she need that he'd never be a one-woman man? He hadn't even bothered to be sly about his indiscretion, opting instead to practically devour Greta whole while standing no more than two feet from Kyra's front porch. And it didn't really soothe Kyra a bit that the woman stuck to him was an internationally recognized sex symbol clad in an outfit that left her as good as naked.

"It's a new commitment record for you," Kyra shouted through the rainstorm, doing her level best to keep her voice calm. Practical. "I think you lasted almost six hours this time."

So maybe sarcasm wasn't exactly practical.

She was entitled to be a little peeved, curse his two-timing hide.

Jesse pried himself loose from Greta's arms, but not without a struggle. The Wonder-bod nearly lost her outfit in the process—an outfit comprised of one artfully tied purple scarf.

But instead of appealing to Kyra by laying on the charm or spinning ridiculous tales to cover his hide,

Jesse glared at Greta. "You'd damn well better come clean about this."

Out of the corner of her eye, Kyra noticed Clint climb down out of his truck cab and stalk toward them. Impervious to the water, Clint's Stetson shielded him from the driving downpour.

Greta shot Jesse the evil eye. "You're *not* the man I met last fall. And I don't have a thing to come clean about." As Clint neared, she sniffed and straightened. "Now, if you'll excuse me, I have plans for dinner."

Jesse looked ready to argue the point, but Clint stepped in like a hero right out of an old Western. Offering Greta his arm as if she wore hoopskirts and a bustle instead of a silk scarf masquerading as a dress, Clint was every inch the gentleman.

And it was obvious from a lone protective hand around Greta's waist that Jesse didn't have a chance in hell of grilling her about the kiss that had just taken place.

Leaving him very much on his own to explain himself.

Not that Kyra needed whatever explanation he concocted for her benefit.

Determined to cut him off before he could suggest some lame reasoning for what just happened, Kyra folded her arms across her chest and stared him down. "I'd just like to point out that I thought we had enough of a solid friendship where we didn't need to play games like this."

Spinning on her heel, she ducked back onto her porch and inside the house.

"Oh, no you don't." Jesse followed her, dripping rainwater from khakis that clearly outlined his thighs. Outlined *him.* "Cowboy Clint might have spirited witchy Greta away so she didn't have to deal with this, but you don't have any choice but to talk to me."

"I most definitely have a choice," she argued, seeking refuge from those wet male thighs in the kitchen. She was not succumbing to anything charming, sexy or otherwise appealing about Jesse Chandler tonight.

The man was a first-rate cad. A cad with fire-engine-red lipstick smeared across his damned face.

He stomped his way into the kitchen, his wet socks squishing along the tiles. "On the contrary, we have a date tonight so I've already reserved this time with you. You can at least hear me out."

"Well, guess what, Romeo? Necking with another woman on my front doorstep pretty much nullifies our date." Kyra pulled a prepackaged dinner out of the freezer and attacked the shrink-wrap with a vengeance.

"That wasn't necking. That was the attack of the wicked wedding-bell woman. She was making some sort of last-ditch play for me with the kiss and the crazy outfit—"

"What outfit?" Shredding the last piece of plastic from an ancient TV-dinner box, Kyra yanked open the microwave. "And since when is a woman who values marriage some kind of villain anyway? You make her sound like a comic-book foe when maybe she's just calling you to the carpet on your fast lifestyle."

Jesse intercepted her meal before she could chuck it into the microwave. "How can you defend her after she practically suffocated me? In front of you, no less? She's been following me around for months, Kyra. And you know I've told her the deal more than once."

Kyra hesitated. Considering. She was being unreasonable and she knew it. But damn it, seeing Jesse kissing another woman had hurt her more than she could admit.

"I don't think you can call it suffocation when you were standing there with your arms at your sides making no attempt to push her away."

"She surprised me!"

Kyra tugged the Chicken Kiev with both hands, tossed it in the microwave and stabbed the keys to start heating her meal.

She needed to insert some space between them and move on. Even if the kiss wasn't his fault, she was quickly realizing how much it was going to hurt when she had to let him go. Something she'd never really considered before. "Fine. I believe you. But please excuse me if I don't feel like having dinner with you or being any part of a bogus committed relationship."

"You *are* having dinner with me." Jesse stopped the microwave, and inserted himself between Kyra and her chicken. "It's not going to be out of a box from the freezer. And the commitment I made to you is hardly bogus."

Kyra forced herself to quit grinding her teeth. But how could he say that to her when he'd already tangled himself up with another woman? Jesse's whole life had been one entanglement after another. He probably didn't know how to live any other way.

"It was a commitment based on sex." Surely that wasn't the premise for most healthy relationships.

"First of all, let's not knock sex." He stared at her with steady brown eyes that had a way of making her heart beat faster even though she was definitely still angry at him. "And second, there was more to it than sex and we both know it."

Admitting there was more than sex at stake here would be like admitting…too much. And damn it, she wasn't foolish enough to fall for Jesse.

"There couldn't have been more than sex involved, Jesse, because you went out of here more hangdog than I've ever seen you aside from when your team lost the pennant race that second season you played baseball." She opened a drawer near the sink, fished out a towel and threw it at him. "Obviously you hated the whole idea of a relationship from the get-go. I don't know why you ever brought it up."

He mopped off his face with the towel and then scrubbed his too-long hair to dry it out. Kyra's gaze tracked his muscles in action as he stretched his arms above his head, twisted his shoulders.

"You've got it all wrong." Jesse folded the towel over the back of a barstool that sat at her kitchen counter. "I would have been overjoyed if this had been all about sex. It's precisely because there's more at stake here that I'm scared as hell to mess it up. Sorry if I acted like an ass about the whole thing, but I don't have a clue what I'm doing when it comes to dating."

His honesty deflated her anger. She'd never thought of him as a sort of dating-virgin. Maybe they were on more even ground, after all.

She had wanted Jesse so badly, but this morning she'd realized that sleeping with him had made things more complicated than she'd ever dreamed. Her irrational behavior over the whole Greta incident only proved she couldn't keep an emotional distance from the man.

She definitely needed to drag this conversation back

on firmer terrain before she fell as head-over-heels for him as every other woman he'd ever met.

Kyra leveled a finger at his chest. "Well for starters, you can't kiss women outside the main relationship. That's a standard taboo."

"No kissing other women. Duly noted." Jesse edged closer, his every muscle defined and highlighted by his wet clothes. "As long as you present plenty of kissing opportunities for me, I don't think I'll find that a problem."

JESSE WATCHED THE swirl of emotions parade across Kyra's face—the unguarded sensual response to his words, the confusion and finally the lip-pursing resistance that told him he was getting nowhere with that approach tonight.

Damn.

He hated that he caused so much uncertainty for her. She deserved a hell of a lot better than what he could ever offer her. Yet for the first time in his life he found himself genuinely wishing he was capable of giving a woman more.

Much more.

But he didn't trust himself not to hurt her. And that was no way to start a relationship.

Kyra slid out of her seat to move back toward the microwave and her very practical dinner. "Sorry, Jesse. I think we both know better than to offer each other any further sensual opportunities. Maybe you were right all along when you said we'd only screw up our friendship."

Panic chugged through him. It would hurt enough just knowing he'd never see Kyra naked again. He couldn't stand the thought of not being able to hang out at the ranch and sneak out one of her horses or try to make her blush. "You don't think we've really messed that up, too, do you?"

"I think we're pretty damn close." She pressed the buttons that would start the oven all over again. "Honestly, I'm having a hard time figuring out how to relate to you in the wake of last night. Guess I sort of underestimated how sex could screw with things—pardon the pun—but chalk it up to a first-timer miscalculation. I'm sorry I didn't listen to you that day at Gasparilla when you said this wouldn't work."

She blinked too fast. A definite indication she was upset and refusing to let it show.

But ruining their friendship?

His brain refused to hear this message. He'd jumped from one woman to another without even blinking his whole life and Kyra had remained his one constant. The Crooked Branch had been his home base when he'd been on the road with his baseball team—the one place where no one expected him to be charming or successful or to pretend he had the world by the tail.

Here, with Kyra, he'd always been able to just *be*.

"But you believe me that I never intended anything to happen with Greta, at least." How could that pushy woman's one impulsive act cost him his best friend?

Of course, as soon as he thought as much, he knew. If he lost Kyra's friendship, it wouldn't be Greta's fault. It would be his own damn doing because he'd approached the commitment thing all wrong.

"This doesn't have anything to do with her. Or the kiss." She tucked a blond strand of hair behind one ear, her quiet, unassuming air so totally at odds with every other woman he'd ever dated. He'd probably never noticed she was beautiful because she never flaunted herself in front of him.

At least not until that eye-opening day at Gasparilla.

"It doesn't?" He found it hard to believe she wasn't pissed about the kiss. Greta had put a squeeze-hold on him like an anaconda. If he'd ever seen Kyra in another man's grasp like that, he would have lost his damn mind.

"No. It has more to do with you acting like you've sentenced yourself to a prison term by going out with me. I'll admit I've always had a little bit of a thing for you, Jesse."

He nearly hit the floor with the shock of that particular news. She'd had a *thing* for him?

The automatic warmth he'd felt in reaction to the statement quickly turned to panic as he realized the fallout from this could be worse than he'd expected.

Shit.

He never wanted to hurt her.

Perhaps sensing his shock, Kyra rushed to reassure him. "But I'm over it now. You don't need to sacrifice yourself to me just because we're friends." She shrugged her shoulder in a gesture that seemed too precise to be totally careless.

Or was that wishful thinking on his part?

"I don't think I ever tried to sound like I was making a sacrifice."

"But you didn't exactly behave like a man overjoyed to ask me out."

Maybe she had a point there. "But that wasn't because of *you.*"

"That was just because you're a commitment-phobe." As the microwave timer began to beep, Kyra tugged an

Aztec-printed potholder from a drawer near the sink. "I realize that. That doesn't make your resistance any more flattering."

Jesse made a mental note never to ask a woman out before he had fully resolved any internal conflict on the subject. Obviously he sucked at masking his emotions. "What can I do to make you give me a second chance?"

She bit her lip. Furrowed her brow. Obviously wrestled with the whole notion of second chances. It scared him to realize just how important that second chance had become for him.

"I don't think I can. I'm over you, remember?"

How could she be over him when he hadn't even applied himself to the task of winning her in the first place? "Come on, Kyra. Have you ever considered getting involved with someone just because? Just for the fun of it? Just because you felt like it? Couldn't I ever potentially warrant a date like that again?"

She sighed. "I'm not saying yes."

Then again, she wasn't saying no. Jesse counted that as progress. "Understood."

"First of all, if we ever decided to date again, you couldn't bullshit me." She juggled the steaming cardboard tray on the potholder and dumped them both on a lone placemat at the kitchen counter.

"Done."

"Second, if you ever want to ask me out again make sure you do it with some sincerity." She rummaged through another drawer and came out with a fork. Waving it at him like a weapon, she expounded her point. "No woman wants to think she's being courted out of some misguided sense of responsibility. I'd like to think a man asks me out because he really wants to be with me and *only me*."

He could do that. Because damn it, he really did want to be with Kyra. He'd been thinking about her nonstop for two weeks running.

It was just the *only Kyra* part that caused him to think twice. He'd never been a one-woman man in his life. Could he pull it off now?

Just as he was thinking *hell yes* he could, Kyra sighed and stabbed at her Chicken Kiev. The woman who'd been so intent on cooking dinner now seemed to do little more than mangle her meal.

Tired of waiting for him, no doubt.

"You'd better go, Jesse. I need to get on the phone tonight to see if it's too late to offer up Sam's Pride at the horse auction in Tampa this weekend." She shoved some broccoli around her cardboard plate. "I'm thinking with all the action going on at an event like that, I might be able to trick him into loading onto another horse trailer and closing a sale on him."

"Wait a minute." He didn't want to talk about that damn horse or how badly Kyra wanted to boot him out of the business altogether. Not yet anyway. "I can do this, Kyra. You and me."

She looked up from her dinner to meet his gaze, and a tear perched on the outer corner of one blue eye. "This isn't the same as you talking me into riding with you at night while my father was sleeping, or convincing me to compete in the jumper class instead of the show ring. There's a lot more at stake here for me."

Shit.

He'd already screwed this up and he hadn't even managed to get to the date part yet. The lone tear Kyra blinked away wrenched his insides more than the practiced pouts of a whole legion of femmes fatales.

Still, he backed away, knowing he'd been at fault for putting that tear there, if only for a moment. And instead of defending his actions or getting upset about what he and Kyra might have had together, Jesse found himself pleading on behalf of her horse.

"Don't sell Sam's Pride tomorrow. He deserves another chance." His wet socks trailed footprints across the ceramic tiles as he made his way toward the door. "Don't force us both out of your life yet."

Kyra scrubbed her wrist over her eyes and stabbed another bite of chicken with her fork. "He's just a horse, Jesse. Half our business has been built on raising them and selling them. I need that extra money."

Yeah, so she could wall him out of every area of her life.

"I'm starting work on the houses full-time on Monday. I don't stand a chance of being in your way here." Already the thought of spending that much time away from the ranch didn't set well with him. Who would he regale with stories about his first day as an honest-to-goodness working stiff?

"I have to put the business first, Jesse."

I have to be practical, Jesse. She didn't voice the sentiment, but Jesse heard it between the lines.

Why the hell didn't he have the right words to convince her otherwise?

Then again, she'd probably made up her mind already and Jesse had never been able to compete with her tough-as-nails resolve once she decided what she wanted.

Her voice scratched just a little, however, as she tossed out one final "Goodbye."

"IT WAS A HELL of a performance." Clicking on the overhead light in his truck cab, Clint finally broke the silence that had fallen thick and heavy in the course of the last twenty miles.

He hadn't known what exactly to say in the wake of Greta's last desperate play for Jesse Chandler, but seeing how much passion she'd thrown into the effort had humbled him just a little. Obviously, she liked the guy more than he'd given her credit for.

Not that he was one bit sorry how the evening had turned out.

Jesse didn't deserve a spitfire like Greta. Hell, that guy could barely keep pace with Kyra Stafford, who—from Clint's observation—seemed to be the sanest woman on earth. No way could Jesse ever wade through the complex tangle of over-the-top behavior that characterized Greta Ingram.

Now, she sat in her corner of his truck, her wet purple scarf clinging to totally outrageous curves while she stared out the window at the gray blur of rain.

"What was a great performance?" She swiveled in her seat to face him. With the help of the overhead light, Clint could see her green eyes were all the more bright for the tears she hadn't shed. "You riding in to the rescue on a damn white horse? Excuse me if I don't applaud, I'm just a little choked up over that really warm reception I received from the so-called man of my dreams."

Clint had to admire her spunk in the wake of disaster. "I wasn't referring to me. You're the one who put your heart on the line and had the nerve to go for what you wanted. And when Chandler was too blind to see what was right before his eyes, you bucked up and shipped out of there just as cool as you please."

She shoved a wet hank of hair off her forehead. The small stretch combined with her transparent outfit made him recall exactly why she'd graced two *Sports Illustrated* covers in a row. Greta Ingram might be a little down on her luck, but she was a feast for the male eye.

Not that he was interested in her because of that.

Pretty women were a dime a dozen in Alabama, but none of them had ever affected Clint the way Greta did. Despite her perfect exterior, Greta had the guts of a prizefighter and a wilder spirit than any horse Clint had ever tried to tame.

She met his gaze with a level look of her own. "Sometimes we don't have any choice but to walk away."

Clint heard the message. Knew Jesse Chandler wasn't the first person Greta had needed to leave behind. One day soon he'd find out who else had been foolish enough to let this woman go.

"Damn straight. No sense sticking around someone who doesn't recognize your worth." Clint thought he noticed her shiver out of the corner of his eye. "You cold?"

She rolled her eyes.

"Hell yes, you're freezing." He reached a hand back behind the bench seat and pulled out a blue cotton blanket that had seen better days. "It's clean, I swear. You want me to pick you up something to eat?"

Greta spread the blanket over herself and shot him a surly look that was halfhearted at best. "Why are you being so nice to me today? You've been borderline hideous every other time we've ever spoken."

He steered the truck over the back roads toward

the suburbs of Tampa. The roads were peppered with palm trees and a few houses, but for the most part, they passed little traffic. The rain had slowed to a mist. "Didn't I tell you I was going to break out the refined manners tonight if you let me take you out? I'm not some hick from a Mississippi backwater town, you know. We Alabama guys have class."

"Mississippi. Alabama. There's a difference?"

"I'm going to let that slide because you're not a U.S. native." Even though he was pretty sure she was trying to yank his chain. "And yes, there's a huge difference."

He saw her gaze stop on a McDonald's sign and stay there. He wouldn't have pegged Miss Supermodel for fast food, but he had to at least offer.

"You want me to stop—"

"Bacon double cheeseburger, please. And a strawberry shake."

He slowed down but didn't put on his signal light. What woman wanted carryout burgers on a date? "I could take you somewhere—"

"No! This is perfect."

Clint turned into the drive-thru lane. "You like burgers that much?"

"I've been waiting half my life to finally eat them again. I lived on coffee and cigarettes the whole time I was modeling. I feel as if I've been given a new lease on life." She poked him in the side as he was calling his order into the drive-thru speaker. "Can you get fries with that?"

He ordered enough food for a small army and then edged the truck out onto the main road. "You mind eating while we're on the road?"

"Actually, this is perfect because I can watch you drive."

Or at least that's what Clint assumed she said. It was damn hard to tell when the woman's mouth was full.

"Did you just say you wanted to watch me?" Because he was going to be very turned on if that was really the case.

"I want to learn how to drive and buy a car. It's good for me to pick up the shifting rhythm, so I'll just observe while I eat." She popped another fry in her mouth and furrowed her brow as he hit fourth gear. "Where are we going?"

Personally, he was really hoping for third base.

"I thought I'd show you a great American tradition."

She licked the sauce oozing out one side of her burger with a sensualist's delight. "I've lived in the States on and off for years. I'll bet I've already seen it."

He rather hoped not. "I don't know. You might not have since you don't drive." He couldn't help but smile. "Are you familiar with the age-old pastime called parking?"

12

GRETA SMOTHERED A laugh. Clint Bowman was nothing if not entertaining, but she wasn't entirely certain she should allow herself to relax with him yet. Behind tonight's affable manner lurked a man with lots of dark corners and hidden depths.

Translation—Clint could still prove dangerous to a woman wary of men she couldn't control or, at very least, understand.

Jesse had been every bit as dark and enticing as Clint with his bad-boy ways, but at least Greta had the peace of mind that he channeled them into games of seduction. While she'd never stood a chance at controlling him, she'd understood him. And she'd never been fearful of sex and all the erotic delights that went along with it.

But after the tense atmosphere of her childhood, Greta refused to get tangled up with any man who possessed a scary temper or who liked to power trip. And while Greta hadn't pegged Clint for that type, she still hadn't managed to peg him for any type. Period.

Deeper emotions frightened her far more than a guy sporting a set of handcuffs or a wicked grin.

"I know exactly what parking refers to, Clint Bowman. And I may be a cheap date, but I've given you no indication that I'd be easy."

"Amen to that." He turned off the main road onto a quiet stretch of highway lined with towering Georgia pines and banyan trees. "You're talking to the guy who kicked off our first date by watching you tangle tongues with another man. I didn't think for a second you'd be easy."

Clint *had* stayed awfully calm in the wake of her throwing herself at Jesse. Some guys might have been jealous or picked a fight. Or worse. But Clint hadn't been ruffled in the least.

A man like that must surely possess great stores of patience. Which, if Greta decided she might be interested in him, would definitely be a good thing.

Now, she watched the play of his muscles beneath his white polo shirt as he shifted gears. She'd totally forgotten to look for pointers on driving in her quest to simply watch Clint. He might not have the sculpted perfection of Jesse, but his rough-hewn features and solid, muscular build had definite appeal.

Her body was warming up beneath the blue cotton throw blanket Clint had given her. And it wasn't just because her dress was drying out.

"I guess I needed to see if things were really dead between Jesse and me," she said finally, crumpling up the remains of her dinner and stuffing them in the paper bag on Clint's truck floor.

"And?"

"You saw with your own eyes how he turned me down cold. Obviously, he's not carrying a torch."

"But what about on your end? Still some sparks there?"

"Surprisingly, no." Ever since she'd stumbled over Clint at the Crooked Branch, she'd had a hard time finding much enthusiasm for her pursuit of Jesse Chandler. "I think my feelings for him died a while back, but he's just so damn perfect for the vision I have of my life that I couldn't let go of the dream. Is that totally ridiculous or what?"

"I think you're smart as hell for moving on once you figured out he wasn't right for you. Too many people settle for relationships that don't really work or that died a long time ago." Something in his voice made Greta think his thoughts had jumped far beyond the confines of the truck cab.

"Speaking from experience?"

Clint stared out the window, but she could tell his expression changed. Hardened. "Put it this way—I'd sure as hell never want anyone to feel like they were settling with me."

Again.

He didn't say the word, but Greta heard it just the same. She studied the hard angles of his face as he slowed the truck and pulled into a paved turnoff on one side of the road.

"That begs the question what on earth are you doing asking me out when you knew I was chasing Jesse?" She thought they were turning around until Clint parked the truck and clicked off the ignition. The rain had stopped completely and they stared out at a clump of trees still dripping from the downpour.

Turning to face her, Clint stared at her with intent gray eyes. "Call it gut instinct, but I couldn't see you with a guy who doesn't recognize what's in his own backyard." Rolling his window down, he tossed the crumpled up fast-food sack into a trash can some ten feet away. They sat at some roadside pull-off with zero scenery in sight. A few trees loomed in the shadowed distance. No houses lined the road. "Besides, a girl as pretty as you ought to hook up with a less-than-perfect guy. Sort of even out the gene pool a little."

She had a mind to quiz him on who he might deem appropriately less-than-perfect, but she was too curious about what they were doing out in the middle of nowhere.

"Not that I'm suspicious or anything, Clint, but I couldn't help but notice your truck is now parked." She squinted out her window, but there were no streetlights here to illuminate their surroundings. In the distance, through a scant line of fat trees, she spied little blue lights on the ground.

"So it is." He smiled, unconcerned.

"We wouldn't be parking by any chance, would we?" Okay, maybe the idea intrigued her just a little bit. All that gear shifting and flexing of male muscle had revved her engines a bit.

And for reasons she still couldn't fully fathom, she and Clint had some major chemistry going.

His mouth hung open as if he couldn't be more offended. "You wound me, Greta. Didn't you specifically nix the parking idea? I just thought an international jet-setter like you would appreciate the slow pace of Saturday night entertainment where I come from."

She waited for the other shoe to drop. "Watching the windshield fog up?"

"Watching planes take off. We're on the outskirts of

Tampa International Airport. See the runway lights over there?" He pointed to the strip of blue she'd seen before. "Although if you decide you want to work on fogging up that windshield, I'll be more than happy to help."

"Because you're such a gentleman?"

"Exactly."

Too bad the fire in his gray eyes didn't look the least bit gentlemanly. Greta was experiencing hot flashes over the idea of wrestling around the truck with Clint Bowman and all those unrefined muscles of his.

She'd picked Jesse as a potential husband candidate because he seemed so perfect for her on the outside and what a total disaster that had been. What if this time, she ignored her damned preconceived notions of what kind of man she ought to be with and dated a guy who just plain made her feel good?

And Clint had only been armed with a bacon double cheeseburger and his wit. Imagine how he could make her feel if she allowed him to use those big, broad hands of his?

The mere thought sent shivers through her that didn't have a thing to do with her limited attire.

Greta stared out the truck window for at least twenty seconds. "If this is your idea of fun, Clint Bowman, it's no damn wonder you're still single."

Making up her mind to follow her instincts instead of her old, immature notions of perfection, Greta levered open the passenger-side door and tossed off the blanket she'd been hiding under.

"What are you doing?" He reached for his hat, shoulders tense. "This is *not* a good place to hitch-hike, Greta."

The flash of concern in his eyes sent a little thrill

through her. When was the last time anyone had expended energy worrying about *her?*

She was definitely making the right decision tonight. Even if it was just a little over-the-top.

"No?" She slid out of the truck and down to the pavement. Glancing back toward the main road, she didn't see a car anywhere so she hooked one finger in the lone knot that held her dress together. "Is it a good area to get naked?"

SHE WOULDN'T.

Clint stared at Greta's right index finger curved into the loop of purple fabric at her navel. He'd been the freaking epitome of control and restraint all night long.

Even when Greta had wrapped herself around another man for a kiss that *he* wanted to taste.

Even when she'd wriggled her way into his truck with a wet scarf plastered to her body and highlighting every sinfully sweet nuance.

But he couldn't handle seeing her whipping off that scarf for his eyes only. Not when anybody could happen by their deserted stretch of runway.

He found his voice. Barely. "Outside the truck is probably *not* a great place to get naked." His vocal cords hit a new depth of bass. The rest of his body seemed to be striving to reach new heights. "Inside the truck is perfectly safe, however." He stretched across the front seat to offer her his hand. "So why don't you climb in and we'll pitch off all the clothes you want?"

Preferably starting with that fluttering piece of silk she was trying to pass off as a dress.

But dress or no, Clint just couldn't wait to put his hands on her. Any part of her. Surely even a PC kind of guy could interpret the suggestion of getting naked as a bit of an invitation?

An airplane screamed down the runway while she stood out in the Florida night air, making up her fickle woman's mind. Greta turned to watch it.

Faster.

Faster.

Before it shot like a bullet straight into the inky sky.

She laughed with the heady delight of a woman heeding the call of the wild. And with a snap of her wrist, she unleashed the scarf and banished it to the cool night wind.

That was *definitely* an invitation.

Clint didn't see nearly enough skin in his scramble to get out of the truck. He followed her out the passenger-side door, unwilling to lose track of her for even an instant.

She was already sprinting—barefoot and laughing—toward the shelter of the banyan trees at the edge of the fenced runway. Her luscious pale body caught the hints of moonbeam even in the dark, making her an easy target for a man on a mission.

He'd never been so motivated in his life.

Less than ten steps and he caught her around the waist from behind. Drew the back of her to the front of him and nearly lost his mind at the onslaught of sensual impressions.

The creamy smooth skin of her belly beneath his palm. The exotic scent at her neck that didn't originate in any dime-store perfume bottle. The perfect dip at the small of her back that gave way to hips other men could only dream about.

But mostly he felt the soft curve of her rump snuggled tightly to an erection that wouldn't quit.

At least not any time tonight.

He might have tried carrying her back to his truck. That would have been the safest, most sensible thing to do with a naked woman.

But then Greta turned in his arms to pin him with hungry eyes and a wordless sigh, and robbed him of that option.

Her breasts pressed into his chest, making him very much aware of her arousal even through his polo shirt. The tight peaks teased and tormented him, called to his mouth.

He was already bending to kiss them when she ground her hips against his and caused a white flash through his head that could only be sensory explosion. Never had any man been inundated with so much delectable woman at one time.

The dull hum of a car engine flitted through his consciousness, but Clint couldn't seem to make his feet move back toward the truck. Not now, when his lips were closing over Greta's tight pink nipple.

He nudged her back into the protective cover of the scant trees and ignored everything else but the sweet taste of her rain-washed skin. She moaned and the sound vibrated right through him. Vaguely, he wondered if he'd drawn her too far into his mouth, but he couldn't seem to let go of her enough to ask, and she kept squeezing him harder and harder.

God, she was incredible.

The car sped by the parking area, the flash of headlights behind them barely a blip on Clint's mental radar.

He normally played things so safe. He was normally a gentleman, damn it. But this woman got under his skin.

And right now, she'd gotten into his khakis in record time.

Her soft hands curved around him through his boxers and he knew he was so done for. A stone-encrusted bangle of some sort scraped against his abs, a welcome momentary sting to balance the pleasure that was robbing him of logic and reason.

"Greta, you deserve better." He wanted to worship this woman. Lick every inch of her and stir her senses all the way to multiple orgasms.

Instead, he was halfway to taking her naked in the woods. Against a banyan tree of all the freaking things.

She bit his shoulder. Kissed his neck. "I don't want better. I want more. Now."

Running her hand up and down the length of him to prove her point, Greta presented arguments too persuasive to ignore. This time.

Clint promised himself next time would be different. Next time he'd be the one taking off her clothes. And she wouldn't have a prayer of rushing him.

But for now, he was more than willing to get caught up in her wild ways.

She was in the middle of freeing him when she pulled back with a start. "Do you have anything with you? Um. Protection-wise?"

He reached for his wallet and pulled out a plastic packet. "Good thing one of us kept our clothes on."

She stared at him accusingly even as she tore open the condom. "You *did* think I'd be easy."

"Are you kidding? Hope springs eternal for every

man. I carry one when I go to church, too, if it makes you feel any better."

"Really?" She flashed him a conspiratorial smile, her blue eyes glowing with a feral light as she nudged his boxers down and rolled the prophylactic over him. "That sounds very wicked of you."

He forgot how to breathe. She stroked him with urgent fingers while she wrapped one calf around his thigh.

When he found his voice again, he steadied her hips, not ready for her to fast-forward through this. "I prefer to think of it as optimistic."

Staring down at her bared body in the moonlight, so perfect and totally uncivilized, Clint had to admit he would have never been this optimistic, however.

To have *her*.

Tonight.

The more he thought about it, the less capable he was of slowing things down. Her peeling her scarf off had been his personal breaking point—a total explosion that left them both burning out of control. And if this time was fast and furious, he could tell himself he'd only been looking out for her best interests.

He couldn't allow a world-famous cover model to be discovered running around the outskirts of Tampa International while buck naked, could he?

Yeah, right. Just call him Mr. Unselfish.

"Please, Clint." She whispered it over and over like a seductive mantra while she rubbed herself against him.

The sultry night air whispered across his senses, but mostly he could only see, feel or hear Greta. Her little moans worked him to a fever pitch while her hands

smoothed their way under his shirt and her short nails
scraped lightly against his back.

She was too fast for him, but he didn't stand a chance
of slowing her down. He settled for sliding one hand
around the back of her neck and tilting her head to re-
ceive his kiss. She tasted like sex—hot, wet and mind-
blowingly sweet.

So he indulged himself. Thoroughly.

And all the while he kissed her he sought the other
source of her heat. The silky wet essence of her that
had brushed ever so lightly against his cock and made
him insane to be inside her.

His fingers brushed over the damp curls that sheltered her from him, tunneled through the soft blond
fuzz she'd shaved into some precise pattern or another.
He'd look later.

In detail.

Right now, he bypassed that pleasure for later, needing to feel the pulsing—

Ah, yes.

She was slick and ready for him. Swollen and every
bit as eager as he was. He would have slid his finger
inside her, but she was lifting herself into his arms and
wrapping those long, perfect legs around his waist before he had the chance.

Her position placed her snugly against him, opened
her to him with an invitation he couldn't hold off any
longer. He had to be inside her.

He hoped like hell she didn't regret this later. In his
gentleman mode tonight, he'd planned to come clean
about his work and his special interest in psychology.
For some reason, he had the feeling Greta, and all her
intriguing depths, was going to have a problem with his

fascination with neurosis—human and equine alike. But bottom line, he was a horse breeder. She couldn't take issue with that.

And if she was a little incensed about his other work, he'd deal with that later.

When he wasn't on the verge of the best sex of his life.

Forgetting all about anything but claiming the woman in his arms, Clint hoisted her a few inches higher. Slowly, he resettled her, positioning her above him.

And then he was inside her and she was squeezing him all around. Greta's ankles clamped together behind his back as if she'd keep him right there forever. Her breasts brushed his cheek, filled his nostrils with her soft woman's scent.

Another motor rumbled in the distance and Clint made sure they were hidden from view of the road. But as the growl of an engine grew louder, headlights hit them—not from the street behind them, but from the runway dead ahead.

For a moment, they were caught in the bright light and Clint saw every facet of Greta with piercing clarity. Head thrown back, teeth sunk into her full lower lip, cheeks flushed with the night air and the sex.

And right there, in the middle of that white hot spotlight, she unraveled.

Her cry all but lost in the whine of the airplane engine, Greta went taut against him, her back arching with her pleasure. Clint might have gone over the edge just looking at her like that. But her body pulsing around his in quick little throbs stole all his control within seconds.

He flew right up there with her for a long, breath-stealing moment while the plane turned to accelerate up the runway. They clung together, damp with sweat and sex and Clint had never felt so fulfilled.

They were so damn right together in the big scheme of things. So balanced.

Cast in darkness once again, the image of Greta in the bright light burned itself on the backs of his eyelids.

And he knew from that one blinding moment he wouldn't be letting this woman go anytime soon.

If ever.

He'd find a way to reach past that haughty attitude she wore like armor. And once he did that, convincing a sophisticated globe-trotter to trade in her frequent-flyer miles for a life on an Alabama horse ranch would seem like a walk in the park.

13

THE AUCTIONEER'S HYPER-SPEED monologue rang out over the county fairgrounds on the outskirts of Tampa Sunday morning. Kyra scanned the crowds for Clint as she led Sam's Pride away from the unloading zone and toward his assigned stall for the day.

The glossy black three-year-old snorted and stayed close to her in the unfamiliar terrain, but after hearing Clint's thoughts on why the horse acted the way he did, Kyra suspected that was more for her protection than out of any fear of his own.

Patting the horse's broad neck, she ignored the twinge of guilt that had been niggling at her all morning. She could almost see Jesse frowning his disapproval at her in her mind's eye.

Jesse.

The pang she felt when she thought about him hurt even more than her guilt over the horse. She'd purposely found errands to do away from the ranch over the past few days just in case he dropped by.

Of course, her long absences were the reason she'd never been able to make connections with Clint about meeting her at the auction today. She'd called his cell phone several times since Thursday night but never got an answer. She'd finally left a voice-mail message for him last night with the details about the auction on the off chance he could help her out this one last time.

Technically, his work with Sam's Pride was complete and Kyra knew he had his own breeding farm to attend to in Alabama. From what she'd gathered about him from other trainers, Kyra understood Clint's first priority was his own ranch. He simply had a fascination with unusual horse behavior and enjoyed the diversion of working with those cases.

But she really would have liked the extra hands today to help her with the nine-hundred-pound Tennessee walking horse in case Sam's Pride turned nervous when she sold him. The fairgrounds were already brimming with noise and activity as the auctioneer's energetic delivery blasted over an old public address system and horses changed hands in every direction.

In the past, Jesse had always helped her with things like this. The last auction they'd attended together, Jesse had bought a few ponies despite Kyra's adamant objections. Providing pony rides and training for children wasn't their focus.

But he and his controlling percentage had won the argument. Much to her surprise, the ponies had established a veritable gold mine for the Crooked Branch, as tourists and locals alike turned out in droves to indulge their kids.

Jesse's whim was actually the business coup of the year. And now that she remembered how much she had protested that day at the auction, Kyra wondered if she'd

ever remembered to tell Jesse how right he had been
about the ponies.

Another pang of guilt pinched her as she tried to discern one Stetson from another in the crowd, still hoping for a glimpse of Clint.

But not half as much as she hoped in vain for a
glimpse of Jesse. Sure she'd told him she wanted to
take Sam's Pride to auction today. That didn't mean
he'd show up at the last minute the way he sometimes
had in the past. She hadn't realized how much having
his support had meant to her over the years. How much
his roguish smile would bolster her.

The sound of footsteps running across the gravel behind her made her heart leap nevertheless. She turned,
cursing the hopeful jump of her heart.

Clint skidded to a stop next to her, Stetson nowhere
to be found as he huffed out a greeting sporting running
shorts and a T-shirt that was…inside out? "I just got
your message this morning while I was making coffee."

"Good morning to you, too. Long night?" She nodded at his T-shirt, curious what sort of woman caught
this practical man's eye. And even more curious what
sort of woman caught it so thoroughly he hadn't even
noticed his own shirt was wrong side out.

He frowned down at the seams on his shoulder. "A
pleasantly long night. But I hauled ass over here this
morning as soon as I heard your voice mail. You can't
sell him, Kyra. Not after the way he acted the other
night."

"You think it will upset him too much?" She didn't
want to traumatize her horse, but damn it, this was business. She'd really counted on the income from his sale
this year. Not just to win a controlling percentage of

the business, but to uphold her end of the partnership and show real progress toward buying Jesse out. She'd agreed to going into business together five years ago because she couldn't have afforded to do it by herself. But damn it, she'd always intended to pay him back.

"Maybe." He stroked the horse's nose and shook his head. "Honestly, I don't know. But I do think he has something unique to offer with his protective instincts. We ought to give him a chance to show us what he can do with those skills before you sell him off as your everyday average three-year-old."

Hadn't Jesse told her the same thing three days ago? *He deserves another chance.*

She'd ignored him then, just like she would have ignored him about the ponies if he hadn't forced her to listen. Was she dead wrong about this, too?

Still, Kyra had trusted her own instincts all her life. Unable to count on her father's guidance between his medications and his battle with manic depression, she had learned to rely solely upon herself. And old habits died hard.

"Do you really think there's something rational behind this behavior, Clint? I wouldn't want to spoil a horse who's just demonstrating routine negative behavior."

Clint shoved his fingers through his hair, making it stand up even straighter. "Call me crazy, but I would swear that horse thinks he's on a mission to look out for you."

His words resonated through her, struck a nerve and a long-ago memory. Her father had visited the stables shortly after Sam's Pride was born. He'd been having one of his lucid days and he'd been fond of the horse at first sight, going so far as to christen the animal after himself—the original Sam. Her dad boasted he gave Sam's Pride a mission that day—to watch over Kyra, his other pride and joy.

She'd been touched, but she'd also been worried that her father's sensitivity would morph to sadness and she proceeded to drive him back home for the night. She'd forgotten all about the remark until Clint's words revived the memory. "You think he's on a mission?"

"It's the damnedest thing. I make no claim to horse telepathy, believe you me. But that's the sense I get from this animal every time I'm near him. He's on a mission."

Kyra wouldn't, *couldn't* give any credence to that line of thinking. Still, a part of her longed for Jesse's input. What would he think of her crazy memory of her dad giving Sam's Pride a mission, let alone Clint assuring her the horse was acting it out?

Would he howl with laughter? Or would he actually consider the possibility?

His advice seemed all the more important to her now that she knew she couldn't seek it. Although bottom-line she'd always made her own decisions, Kyra had been counting on her partner's advice more than she ever realized.

Either way, she was certain Jesse didn't think she should sell the horse.

Clint had bent to tie his running shoes while she was thinking. Now, he stood, his gaze connecting with hers again. "Don't sell him, Kyra. Or if you're really hell-bent to get rid of him, sell him to me."

Taken aback, she peered up at him. "Why would you ever want to buy Sam's Pride with all his…emotional baggage?" In the back of her mind she could hear a bid-

ding war break out on the auction floor and the auctioneer's frenzy to up the bids. Sam's Pride wasn't listed to
go up on the block until almost noon, however, so Kyra
didn't need to rush to get him to his stall.

Either that, or she was procrastinating.

"I think Sam's Pride has a lot of potential if he can
ever transfer his protective streak from you to…some-
one else." Clint folded the pamphlet with all the horses'
names listed on the day's auction roster and shoved the
paper in his pocket.

Kyra frowned. Was he just offering to buy the horse
to be nice? "You seem pretty self-sufficient to me,
Clint. I can't picture you needing this guy following
you around like a shadow." She patted Sam's Pride's
neck. "And he'd probably get upset when you went out
of town to visit other troubled horses—"

"He wouldn't be for me. I'd buy him to keep an eye
on Greta." Clint exchanged a quick hello with one of
the auction attendees shouldering their way past them.
The equine world was small enough that events like
this were guaranteed to bring together at least a few
familiar faces.

"Not Greta Ingram?" Kyra would have fallen over
if she hadn't had a hand on Sam's Pride to keep her up.
She couldn't picture the Marlboro Man and his boots
with the German Wonder-bod and her stilettos.

"One and the same. If she'll have me, that is."

Kyra immediately regretted her obvious surprise. His
inside-out shirt took on a whole new level of meaning.
"I take it the two of you hit it off the other night after
the incident in my driveway?"

"You could say that. I don't know how she'll take to
life in Alabama, though. And I wouldn't mind having

some help looking out for her while she makes the transition." He made a soft sound to Sam's Pride and the horse whickered back at him. "I wish I could convince Sam's Pride to watch over Greta the way he watches over you."

An interesting proposition. And it certainly revealed how much Greta meant to Clint if he was so concerned about her. How would it feel to have a man watch your back that way?

Dismissing the thought before she wandered down wishful paths she had no business traveling, Kyra turned her attention to Clint's idea. She'd already been questioning her decision to sell her horse today. Maybe Clint's offer would give her a few more days to weigh the consequences. "If you're going to stick around Citrus County a little longer, maybe you could bring Greta over to the Crooked Branch and introduce her to Sam's Pride. See how they get along to sort of test the waters."

"I'll get my checkbook out of the truck. How much were you hoping to get for him?"

Tempting as the offer sounded, now that she was faced with the do-or-die moment to commit to the sale, Kyra couldn't follow through. She couldn't sell Clint a horse until she was certain the animal would behave for him. Which meant she also wouldn't be selling the horse to anyone else today, either.

Especially not after what she'd learned about Sam's Pride this morning. She shook her head. "Wait to see how he does with Greta. I'll gladly sell him to you if the two of them hit it off."

Smiling, Clint stuck out his hand to seal the bargain. "You've got yourself a deal."

After making arrangements to drop by during the

week, Clint and his running shoes made tracks for the parking lot, leaving Kyra to wonder what had happened to her ability to make a decision, let alone to be practical.

Her sound business sense seemed to have waltzed out the door when Jesse had left her kitchen Thursday.

Was she being stubborn where he was concerned for no good reason? From the outside looking in, Clint Bowman and Greta Ingram probably had even less in common than her and Jesse. Yet Clint obviously had every intention of making things work between them.

If a grounded, intelligent guy like Clint could set his sights on someone as over-the-top as Greta, why couldn't she at least try a relationship with Jesse? In all fairness, she'd given up before they'd even gotten started.

Maybe, with a few practical ground rules in place, she could at least give it—give *them*—a chance.

JESSE JOGGED THROUGH the fairgrounds with his auction placard in hand, searching for any sign of horse #54, Sam's Pride, who wasn't in his temporary stall for public viewing. He'd arrived first thing in the morning to glance over the day's lineup, and when he'd assured himself Kyra wouldn't be auctioning off her horse for another few hours, he'd headed back to his workshop to put the finishing touches on the crown molding for his first home—the house that *had* to be a showplace.

It had taken him this long in life to figure out what he would enjoy doing outside the ranch, but now that he had a focus on building custom homes, he planned to do it right. First and foremost, he wanted Chandler Homes to succeed for himself. But maybe—just a little—he wanted to be able to show Kyra his success, too.

He hadn't bothered to force his ideas on her at the Crooked Branch, his need to give her something that was just for *her* outweighing any selfish need to be right. But now that she'd made it clear she wanted complete independence from him—professionally *and* personally—Jesse couldn't help the desire to prove she'd overlooked his contributions.

He might like to work on the books while watching the Devil Rays on TV. And he might look like he was having a good time doing it, but that didn't make his efforts any less important, damn it.

Kyra just didn't seem to realize work and fun could go hand in hand.

Finally, he spotted her. A blond waif in blue jeans crooning to her horse amid a crowd of cowboys in boots and cigar-smoking businessmen. And he cracked a smile to see her among the rest of the horse-crazy auction-goers. Maybe she'd developed some of her all-business attitude from hanging out with the good old boy network for too many years.

She *had* to be tough or she would have been steamrolled right out of business five years ago.

Jesse approached her slowly, waiting for her to notice him but she was too wrapped up in silent communication with the ornery three-year-old gelding who only listened to her. As he neared them, Jesse waved his red auction placard under her nose.

She snapped out of it then, her gaze connecting with his in a moment of electric awareness.

A vivid picture of her underneath him on his office sectional invaded his brain, scattered his thoughts.

"Jesse." Her voice held a tiny note of relief. Or so he chose to think. "What are you doing here today?"

I came to claim you for my own.

He would have said it in another day and age. And he would have scooped her right off her feet and walked out of there with her. Cursed modern sensibilities.

"I came to see a woman about a horse." He allowed his gaze to linger on her. To wander over her. He wanted her to know what he *meant* to say, even if he hadn't really spoken the words.

Kyra stared back at him for a moment, and damned if the slightest hint of pink didn't color her cheeks.

Obviously, she'd gotten the message.

For the first time in fourteen years, he'd succeeded in making her blush.

Before he could revel in that bit of news, Kyra plowed forward. Perhaps in an effort to distract him. "I'm not selling him. Not yet anyway."

"You're not?" Relief sighed through him.

She shook her head, her blond hair brushing the tops of her shoulders. "Clint convinced me to wait a little longer. He thinks the horse is on a mission. And you know what?"

Jesse fought past the jealousy that Kyra was listening to Clint Bowman's advice in a way she never seemed to listen to his. "What?"

He took Sam's Pride's bridle out of her hands and led the horse toward the parking lot where he'd seen Kyra's truck earlier this morning.

"You'll think I'm insane, but I swear to you I had a crazy memory when he said that. The moment he mentioned it, I remembered my dad telling me he gave Sam's Pride a mission a few days after he was born."

Jesse stopped in the center of the unused midway area, right in front of the merry-go-round. "I remember that day. I was on the road in Houston and I didn't go out that night because you were worried about Sam. You thought he was getting a little morose or something, and you drove him home so he could take his meds."

"You remember all that?" She looked like she didn't believe him.

"Geez, Kyra, you've allowed yourself to be upset in front of me something like two other times in your whole life." How could she not know she was freaking important to him? He'd always thought at least their friendship had been rock solid, and now he wasn't even so sure if she'd ever fully trusted in that. "Yeah, I can remember them."

She looked toward the parking lot, ever eager to move forward. Jesse dug his boots in the gravel a little deeper. She could take five minutes to talk to him face-to-face.

She folded her arms and pivoted toward him. "It just gave me the heebie-jeebies listening to Clint say he thought my horse was on a mission and me remembering that day with my dad telling me he gave Sam's Pride a mission to watch over me. I don't believe in any kind of supernatural stuff, but it spooked me."

Jesse let the horse's bridle fall, trusting him not to stray far from Kyra. He put his hands on her shoulders and assured himself he only wanted to comfort her.

Not to feel her incredibly silky skin. Her warmth of spirit and natural vibrancy that had pulled him to her from the first day they'd met.

"It shouldn't spook you. It should lift you up to think that even in his later years, Sam had such moments of clarity he could commune with an animal as clearly as Clint Bowman does. Hell, maybe your old man should have been the Citrus County horse whisperer."

The shadow of a smile passed across her lips. "Somehow I doubt my dad would have been able to take his animal act on the road."

Jesse tilted her chin up with one hand, drawing her gaze to his to let her know he was completely serious. "Maybe not, but it might be a sign that he'd reached a peace of sorts with his disease and where he was at in life. He might not have been able to be the father to you he would have liked, but maybe he made sure you had a stalwart guardian in the form of a four-legged protector. It's a lot more than some totally healthy parents manage to give their kids."

Kyra's blue eyes widened. Flickered with just a little spark of hope. "You really believe what Clint says about the horse, don't you?"

He rubbed his hands over her arms, needing to reassure her that she wasn't the only one looking out for her in the world. Didn't she know how much he wanted to be there for her? Even when they were just friends, he would have sprinted to her side if she ever gave him the least indication she might need him.

"I definitely believe it. Clint's theory explains every weird action that horse has ever taken. And I think it makes total sense that your old man would try to find a way to watch out for you even when he couldn't be there for you himself." He paused, letting her absorb his words. Giving her time to get used to the idea that her dad had wanted so much more for her than she ever realized. "If you want, I could take you by his grave this week. Give you time to talk to him or—"

She was already shaking her head, her hardheaded practicality back in full force. "I can't ask you to do that."

His hands fell away from her.

Frustration fired through him, an emotion that—along with jealousy—he wasn't accustomed to feeling. At least he hadn't been until he'd gotten all tied up in knots about Kyra. "Since when did you ask? Damn it, Kyra, you can't shut out anyone and everyone who wants to be there for you. I'm not going away just because you don't *need* me."

Her brow furrowed. Confused.

Didn't she realize it would be okay to need him sometimes? And why couldn't she understand that it was okay just to want him—need be damned.

"For that matter, I'm not going away until you agree to see me again. Talk to me. Hell, we never even had our date. I felt too guilty to press the issue the other night, but I don't have a damn reason to back down. You know I never asked Greta to—"

"Okay."

"—ever kiss me like that and—" He couldn't have heard what he thought she'd said. "What?"

"Okay. We'll do the date. I was upset the other night, but I know there's nothing going on between you and Greta."

Jesse felt a burden sliding right off his shoulders. "Damn straight there's not." He reached for Kyra, his hand curving around the delicate face that hid such a strong, proud woman. "I was upset, too, in the wake of the whole kiss thing and I was distracted when you asked me if I could handle just seeing *you*." He stroked a strand of hair behind her ear, then followed the silky lock all the way to the end as it curved about the top of her shoulder. "But I can handle it. And I want it more than anything."

Her lips parted in surprise. Beckoned him to assure her of his words with the persuasive power of his mouth.

But he wouldn't. Not until he'd sewed up the matter of the date in the most businesslike fashion for Kyra's benefit. He couldn't afford to leave any loopholes this time.

Somehow, one freaking date had become more important to him than a whole baseball season had been. More important than anything he could think of.

She licked her lips as if she missed tasting their kisses almost as much as he did. "Maybe we should set a few ground rules before we—"

"Not a chance. I'm not going to let you ground rule yourself into some sort of safe zone where I can't touch you. This time, I want to handle things my way."

He braced himself for an argument.

But maybe Kyra read his commitment to his own plan in his eyes because she huffed out a breath and nodded. "Name the place, Jesse. I'll try it your way. At least for one night."

One night.

The words were music to his ears. She had given him one night and he planned to make sure one night would never be enough for her.

14

GRETA PADDED her way into the kitchenette area of Clint's hotel suite, bleary-eyed and in desperate need of caffeine. For the last two mornings, Clint had served her coffee in bed, but he'd needed to run an errand this morning, forcing her to fend for herself.

Funny that in the course of a mere three days she already craved Clint more than her morning java.

She was addicted to the man.

Mindlessly, she tore open the single-serving packet of grounds wrapped in a filter and jammed the bag into the coffeepot. After spending eight years on the road with her modeling career, she had the art of hotel coffeemakers down to a science.

As she went through the motions, she thought about how much Clint Bowman had come to mean to her in just a few days' time. And even though she knew Clint was an amazing man worthy of total feminine adoration, it scared her just a little to think she had gone from sighing over Jesse Chandler to swooning over Clint in such a short amount of time.

What if she was wrong about Clint, too?

Her relationship with Jesse had started off with a bang—she snorted at that choice of images—as well. And she'd ended up being dead wrong about his affection for her. What if she had no better judgment now when it came to Clint?

Dumping the water into the machine, Greta closed the lid and flicked on the switch to wait for her brew.

Of course, with Clint this time, everything had felt more real. They'd talked in a way she and Jesse had never bothered to. She'd learned that Clint ran a horse-breeding farm in Alabama and that he took extended trips related to his business. She knew he had two hell-raising brothers whose goal in life was to never settle down.

But mostly, Clint had asked about *her.* Not her life in front of the spotlight, but her life behind it. If she was lonely on the road. What she did in strange cities to entertain herself. What her favorite airport snacks were.

Things no one ever thought to ask her before.

But she hadn't managed to share any stories about her family—her father who'd always used his strength and his temper to intimidate her. She was totally over her old man.

She just didn't happen to like to talk about him.

Other than that, she and Clint had shared just about everything. Surely all those conversations they'd had proved they were connecting on more levels than just the physical plane. And as an added bonus, she hadn't smoked a single cigarette in the three days they'd been together.

A wicked smile curled her lips as she thought about all the ways she'd traded one oral fixation for another infinitely more fulfilling one.

While Greta assured herself she couldn't be wrong about what she felt for Clint, she slid into the chair at the tiny kitchenette table while the coffeepot steamed and burbled.

The peach-and-blue silk flower arrangement had been cleared off to one side of the table to make way for a massive tome with tiny print open to a page about narcissism. Curious, Greta kept her finger on the open page and flipped the book closed to check out the title. *Advanced Studies in Clinical Psychology.*

A warning bell went off in her head in time with the beeping coffeepot letting her know her coffee was ready. Too engrossed in her new find, Greta ignored it and flipped the book back to the passage on narcissism.

A passage circled with a hand-scrawled note in the margin that read—*check her for signs of this.*

Her?

Greta's eyes cruised over the page to glean that the neurosis was a manifestation of self-obsession. A sickness that placed too much emphasis on outward appearances. And which often resulted from deep-seated loneliness.

Does it get lonely out on the road?

Okay, Clint had asked her that, but that didn't mean he thought she was narcissistic. Then again, why the hell did a horse breeder from Alabama need to lug around advanced psych texts?

Unless he thought he was dating a woman who was totally crazy.

Greta fumed, unwilling to wait around for Clint's explanation. No doubt he would only think she was narcissistic for thinking the damn book related to her.

Fine. Let him tack on paranoid, too. She wasn't sticking around to hear about it. Slamming the book closed on the table, Greta started hunting for her clothes.

She was so busy muttering to herself, she didn't even hear the door to the suite open. But all of a sudden, Clint was standing there in his T-shirt and running shoes looking utterly mouthwatering.

And like a total dead man.

He grinned. Stalked closer as if he would drag her into bed again only to psychoanalyze her while she was sleeping. "Hey, honey. I'm home."

A TEN-POUND MISSILE sailed past Clint's head, narrowly missing his temple and landing with a thud in the open closet behind him. Before he could turn to see what Greta had just thrown at him, his Stetson was winging his way like a Frisbee turned deadly boomerang.

She couldn't mess with his hat, damn it.

"Now wait just a minute." He caught the Stetson in midair and slammed it on his head for safekeeping. Storming across the room, he caught her in a bear hug from behind just as she was picking up a vase of silk flowers. "That's stainless steel, woman. Are you out of your mind?"

Prying the vase from her fingers, he set it back down on the kitchen table, the peach-and-blue flowers dangling sadly from one side.

"Obviously *you* think so, Mr. Junior Psychologist." She glared back at him over one shoulder. "Or are you going to try and pretend that you were thinking *another* woman in your life was narcissistic and not the internationally known model you're dating? Or rather the model you *were* dating."

As she spoke, Clint realized what the ten-pound missile had been that she'd sent winging past his ear. Evidently, she hadn't enjoyed the notes he'd been making in his psych book.

"Greta, you're so damn far off base you're going to laugh when I explain this to you." He had wrestled cranky horses that were less determined to get away from him than Greta. She was all elbows and knees.

"Ha! You're so damn screwed you'd probably make up anything to explain this away." Unable to break her way free, she settled for pinching him in the forearm.

Clint stifled a curse and vise-locked her hands with his own. If she flipped out over his psych background, how would he ever get her to agree to throw away her sophisticated lifestyle for an Alabama ranch? "I probably *would* make up just about anything if I had been truly trying to psychoanalyze you and I got caught in the act. But no matter how far-fetched of a story I might come up with under pressure, do you think I could ever dream up something as crazy as that I read the book to psychoanalyze horses?"

She stilled in his arms.

Obviously, he'd caught her attention.

But since he had no idea how long he'd be able to retain it, he forced out his story in a condensed version. "I should have told you earlier that I treat troubled horses on the side. Sort of a special interest job that I fell into after I worked with some abused animals confiscated from a foreclosed farm near where I grew up."

Greta hadn't moved as he spoke, so he released her. When she didn't reach for the steel vase again, he figured it was safe to continue.

"I had so much success with those horses that I developed a local reputation and a couple of ranchers came to me with questions about different behavioral problems they were seeing among their stock. Soon, word of my sideline spread all over the country and now I find myself getting all sorts of bizarre calls about troubled animals." He paused, tried to gauge Greta's expression. He knew he should have told her about this before, but he'd been afraid of her reaction. Being a shrink of any kind—even to horses—had a way of scaring people off.

"So you're the Dr. Doolittle of the equine world. Great. What does that have to do with narcissism and the note in your textbook to check somebody—a female somebody—for signs of it? Don't tell me you're dealing with vain four-legged creatures." She folded her arms across her chest, wrinkling the shirt she'd worn to sleep in last night.

His shirt.

God, he wanted to work things out with this woman. Wanted to find more than just amazing sex with her.

She was so smart. So full of contradictions with her high-profile strut and her down-home love of cheeseburgers. Greta Ingram would keep him on his toes forever.

If only he could convince her she wasn't a guinea pig for his psychoanalytic work.

"Actually, I keep the book around to jog my memory about different symptoms. You'd be surprised how many parallels there are between how horses behave and how we behave. They have as much potential to succumb to fears as we do."

She lifted a speculative brow as if trying to decide whether or not to believe him.

He forged ahead. "I make a lot of notes in the book while I work. That particular comment is over a decade old from my college days. We did a practicum each month to try our diagnosing skills on students who would fake a disorder. Must be I thought somebody was playing narcissist."

Greta sniffed. "You didn't think I was?"

Sensing a chink in the armor, he smiled. "Narcissists are totally self-absorbed. And look at you. You're wolfing down more cheeseburgers in a month than the Hamburgler because you're so happy to break out of an industry that required you to be just a little self-absorbed."

Called by the scent of brewed coffee, Clint gave Greta some breathing room and a moment to think about that while he poured two steaming mugs. Spending the last few nights with her—and consequently, a few mornings—he'd learned she was infinitely happier postjava in the a.m.

He made a mental note to purchase himself a coffeemaker with a timer feature. She'd be able to go straight from horizontal to sipping position.

Greta accepted the cup and drank gratefully. "But now that I launched into a tirade over the narcissism thing, doesn't that just prove I think the world revolves around me in a sort of 'the lady doth protest too much' logic?"

Clint shrugged. "Doesn't prove a damn thing to me. Besides, I'm the one running around playing Dr. Doolittle to horses with my college psych book in hand. I'm the last person to cast stones in the mental health department."

She tipped her head back and laughed. The warm, rich sound flowed over him, soothed and excited him at the same time. He could get lost for days in that throaty laughter of hers.

But he was running out of time to linger with her. He'd already extended his trip to Florida, first because Sam's Pride had made for such an intriguing case, and second because of Greta. He didn't regret a moment of their time together, but he knew it couldn't last.

At least, not here.

"Come to Alabama with me, Greta." He found himself saying the words before he'd given himself a chance to think about them.

And judging by Greta's semihorrified expression, he knew the moment he said them he damn well should have thought about them.

A lot.

"Go where?" She twisted a finger through her breezy blond hair, a gesture smacking of nervousness that he'd never seen in her before.

Damn.

"Alabama. Home of the Crimson Tide. Home of—" Bear Bryant, football coach with the most Division I victories in history. Like she'd give a rat's ass about that. "Home of some great state parks."

She didn't look swayed.

"Rich Southern history?" he prodded.

In fact, she looked downright ill.

"Come on, Greta. Take a week and at least check it out. We've got the best damn barbecue sandwiches in the U.S. of A. You'll never go back to hamburgers. Besides, you international women like to travel, right?"

"Preferably to places with more than one cosmetic counter in town. And preferably to cities with international flight connections so that we can haul our butts out of there if necessary."

"Birmingham International is just a hop, skip and a jump away. Atlanta's only a few hours. But if you need to come back here, I'll loan you my pickup." Hell, he'd buy her a damn pickup of her own. "And I'll teach you how to drive it, to boot."

"Clint, I'm sorry." She was shaking her head, that silky blond hair of hers sweeping the tops of her shoulders. "But I don't think—"

"Don't say it." God, he didn't want to hear it. Couldn't stand to think he'd found the only woman who would ever be right for him only to lose her over something as superficial as where they were in the world. "Not yet."

"It's not just Alabama."

His heart damn near dropped to his ankles. "It's not?"

"It's the horses, too. And all the animals in general. And just the whole—farm thing." She wrinkled her nose as if to underscore her words, but it was obvious there was more to her reluctance than that. Shadows of insecurity clouded her eyes, and Clint didn't have a clue how to interpret them.

Something was holding her back. Something bigger than her desire for a more cosmopolitan lifestyle. But if she wasn't ready to share it with him, there wasn't a damn thing he could do about it.

Yet.

Until he could figure out what worries she hid from him, he would give her some space, respect her boundaries. In his work with troubled animals, he'd learned the value of patience.

"I think we could work around your issues with rural

life, Greta. If you're not ready, I understand. But I've got to go back this week." His brothers were good about taking over for a few days. A week, maybe. By now he was really stretching it. "I don't have a choice."

She fluffed her hair. Shrugged her shoulders as if him leaving wasn't a big deal. But her hands trembled just a little.

"I want you to go with me. Stay with me. Move right in and never leave." He stared into her eyes until he was certain she knew he meant it. "If you're not ready for Alabama—or for me—I can come back here next weekend. And the one after that. However long it takes to convince you to come with me, or until you tell me not to bother anymore. But it's my home, Greta. Eventually, I'll always have to go back."

"Home is where your heart is, cowboy." She set her coffee mug on the table and stared up at him, eyes flashing a challenge. "Maybe you're just not enticed enough to try living somewhere different."

She didn't understand. Couldn't understand if she'd never been close to her family.

"It's not that. You could entice me to do just about anything, woman. And you have." After the experience near the airport runway, there'd been the time on his hotel balcony. Then the hotel elevator. "I just can't walk away from what's so much a part of who I am."

The tiny frown that crossed her face was almost imperceptible, but Clint had studied every nuance of her expression for the past three days and he saw it. Knew the idea of being apart hurt her almost as much as it hurt him.

But she wasn't ready, didn't have the advantage of

knowing with every fiber of her being that they were right together the way he did.

"I don't know if I can do a relationship of half-measures, Clint. I wasted too much time and emotional energy on Jesse when that didn't have a chance in hell of working out. I can't commit myself to a man who won't even live in the same state with me now."

There was more to it than that. And Clint intended to figure out exactly what was holding her back.

"Give me at least next weekend. Let me think about how to change your mind this week, and if you want to, you can go ahead and think about how to change mine, too. But at least give it until next weekend before you make that decision."

She stared into the bottom of her empty coffee cup for a long moment while Clint held his breath.

Finally, she met his gaze. "One more weekend. But I have to be honest with you, Clint. I can't picture me ever wanting to spend any time with one horse, let alone a whole ranch full of them." She blinked fast, as if to keep her emotions at bay. As if to make sure Clint didn't realize she was scared of a whole lot more than the horses. "And you'll have to show me a hell of a lot more than great state parks to get me to set foot in Alabama."

"I'M NOT SETTING FOOT on that yacht without you," Kyra warned Jesse as she stared up at the boat where tonight's date was to take place.

When she'd agreed to go out with him last weekend, she hadn't realized he already had a very specific event in mind—his brother Seth's engagement party.

Now, she leaned against Jesse's Jeep beside pier eleven in the sleepy beach town of Twin Palms and tried not to panic. "Why don't I go to the liquor store with you?"

"I'll only be a minute. I just forgot to pick up the champagne for the party." He slid his hands around her waist to ease her away from the Jeep. "I was too busy thinking about other aspects of tonight."

A shivery sensation shot through her at his touch, his words. The sun winked on the waves as it dipped low over the horizon, illuminating a string of surfside shops and restaurants culminating in a cedar-sided gift store called the Beachcomber, and finally, a small marina where the yacht was docked.

Twin Palms should have been the perfect date destination. Their cruise on the water tonight was a romantic's dream. But Kyra couldn't help the nagging fear that she wouldn't be able to live up to Jesse's expectations.

She'd wanted this kind of night with him forever, but now that it had arrived she only wanted to run back to the Crooked Branch and return to their friendship—an association that seemed so much safer than the edgy, scary new feelings this relationship inspired.

Her mouth went dry in response to his touch, his suggestive words. But only one response came to her nervous brain. "You'd better go search for the champagne. Your family will be arriving any minute."

Jesse's hands lingered on her waist, his warm fingers brushing the bare skin at her back that her dress exposed. He smiled even as he shook his head. "Ever the practical one. When am I going to get you to take a few chances, Kyra Stafford?"

Taking chances gave her heart palpitations, thank you very much. Of course, Jesse's touch might have contributed to that racing pulse a little bit, too. "The date is my risk for today." A pretty big one.

"You're wrong there. I'm watching over you better than Sam's Pride. You couldn't be any safer than when you're with me." Jesse picked up her hand and kissed the palm.

Slowly. Languidly.

He kissed his way up her wrist, up the inside of her arm the way Gomez had done to Morticia a thousand times. Only Jesse's technique left her breathless and weak in the knees.

"You'd better get the champagne." Before she did something crazy, like jump him in the middle of the marina parking lot. The scent of the sea had an aphrodisiac effect along with the warm breeze and lazy beachside town. Something about visiting a strange place made her feel adventurous.

Or maybe that was just because she was with Jesse.

"We have time." His kisses trailed across her shoulder to her neck. He drew her closer, broad calloused palms catching on the silky thin fabric of her navy dress. "And we still have that little matter of getting you to take some risks to address."

She might have protested, but he chose that moment to steer her hips to his. The feel of his hard length against her made her voice catch, sputter and die out in her throat.

"Are you ready to take a risk tonight, Kyra?" His words were rough, tinged with the same desire that churned through her. His hands smoothed their way up her waist to her ribs, his thumbs just barely grazing her aching breasts.

She didn't have to ask what kind of risk he had in

mind. He was proposing a clandestine encounter, some-thing hot and fierce and totally out of control.

And she wanted to share that experience with him so badly she could hardly see straight.

"This is an awfully public place." She glanced over her shoulder and noted the scant pedestrians peopling the sidewalks.

"I'll find us someplace more private." He skimmed his thumbs discreetly across the undersides of her breasts.

Her eyes fluttered closed for a long moment as the provocative ripple effect of one small touch vibrated through her. The man had probably forgotten more about seduction than she would ever learn in two life-times. "Are you trying to get even with me for abducting you and making you my sexual prisoner at Gasparilla?"

"Revenge is best when it's sweet." He kept his words a soft whisper in deference to an elderly couple walk-ing by in matching running suits holding hands. After shooting conspiratorial winks in their direction, the couple passed and Jesse cupped her chin. Ran his fin-ger over her lower lip. "And it *will* be sweet."

Oh.

A melting sensation started at that combustible point where his finger touched her and then dripped all the way through her.

"Yes." The word jumped out before she consciously decided it.

But if she was going to have this last date with Jesse, she didn't have any intention of playing games about what she wanted. She wanted *him*.

Tonight.

Now.

Even if that meant taking a few chances.

"YES WHAT?" His eyes pinned her down, wouldn't let her go until he'd wrested all the words from her. Or maybe until he made sure she knew exactly what he had in mind for them.

Their window of time before the party was narrow, but it existed. He knew Seth's boat was back in the harbor because he'd driven it to Twin Palms again just yesterday. And it just so happened the keys were still in his pocket.

But no matter how eager he was to get Kyra alone in the intimacy of a boat's cabin, he had all the time in the world to hear her say that she wanted this as much as him.

Then again, given how hot he was to have her beneath him right now, he'd probably settle for having her want this *half* as badly as he did. "Are you sure you know what you're agreeing to?"

"Does it involve a sexual encounter in the next five minutes?" She tilted her head to one side and eyed him with a smoky stare.

Gulping for air, he sought a response.

And found his throat dried up to desert standards.

He settled for nodding.

Kyra leaned just close enough to brush her breasts against his chest. And practically brought him to his knees in the process. "Then consider me well informed of what I'm agreeing to. I still say yes."

If he opened his mouth to tell her how great he thought that was, he'd only end up devouring her then and there in the middle of the Twin Palms marina parking lot. He had no choice but to let his actions do the talking.

Pulling her forward across the tarmac, he made double time to get them to the pier where Seth's boat was docked. Jesse might have lingered to hear her say that she wanted to be with him, but now that he knew where they were headed, he wasn't wasting a single second.

Never in his life had he felt this kind of urgency to have a woman. Hell, had there ever been any urgency about sex before? He'd developed a legendary reputation among women because he'd always been able to take his time. Play games. Enjoy the seduction.

But right now when he should be applying every skill he'd ever learned to wooing and winning Kyra, finesse eluded him.

He held her hand to try and help her onto the 32-foot cabin cruiser, but one look at her long leg stretched forward through a slit in her conservative navy dress had him hauling her into the boat and into his arms.

She stumbled against him, propelling them backward toward the stairs leading to the cabin door. He drew her down the steps with him, praying he could hold out another thirty seconds while he found them some privacy. He kissed her while he fished for the key in his pocket, devouring her now the way he'd wanted to onshore.

And she kissed him right back. No holds barred. Like she meant it.

He forgot about the key. Had to touch her.

But some hint of her practicality must have surfaced just enough to make her reach in his pocket. As she did so, her fingers grazed his thigh—and a hell of a lot more—an act which sent him beyond urgent and straight into desperate terrain.

Control was nowhere to be found.

He couldn't wait. Ate up the silky fabric of her dress with his hands, sought for a way to get beneath it to touch more.

When he reached for her hem, she smiled triumphantly and dangled the key in front of his nose with one hand. In her other hand, she waved another prize—a condom.

With a growl, he yanked the key back, jammed it into the lock and pulled her down into the cabin with him.

Maybe Jesse closed the door behind them. Maybe he didn't. It scared the hell out of him to think he wasn't paying attention to the details, or that maybe he wasn't taking care of Kyra the way she really deserved to be taken care of.

But her hands were all over him, her one palm still clutching the condom wrapper. And the need to have her consumed him. Drove him out of his freaking mind. Turned him into someone else completely, someone who…

Unable to finish a train of thought, Jesse focused on the only thing he could finish. This. Incredible. Freaking. Encounter.

The bedroom was too far away. But Jesse's calf bumped into a cushion for the built-in couch. The living area.

Close enough.

Sultry heat melded them together. The scent of the sea breeze permeated the cabin area, mingled with the light floral note of Kyra's skin. Her skin was hot and silky beneath his hands and somehow—thank you, God—a fraction of his bedroom prowess from another time, another life, must have helped him to unzip her dress and make the navy fabric vanish.

She stood before him in navy high heels and black lace panties.

Totally impractical.

And the thought that Kyra had indulged in something so frivolous and so decadent—possibly with him in mind—turned him on even more than the black lace.

He wanted to linger over every inch of her, taste the way her skin felt through black lace, but he couldn't wait. Not this time.

His hands found her hips and tugged her to him as he drew them down to the couch cushions. Kyra's weight on top of him a delicious restraint, he let her undo his shirt buttons, unfasten his belt.

Her hair slithered down across his shoulder and over his chest. He wound the length around his hand, allowed the silky strands to tease his palms.

Then he made the mistake of looking down. Caught a glimpse of her black lace panties up against his open fly.

And promptly lost his mind.

Releasing her hair, he rolled their bodies to swap positions. He shed his clothes faster than a virgin on his honeymoon. Two seconds later he had Kyra beneath him and her panties in his hand.

Kyra blinked up at him in the semidarkness, her eyes soft with desire and little amazement as she offered him the condom she'd been holding. "How did you do that?"

He slapped the condom on the coffee table and flung her panties away, concerned only with what they'd concealed. Reaching between their bodies, he trailed a hand over her hip to her belly, to the soft heat between her legs. "I had excellent motivation."

Eyes fluttering closed she leaned into the pillows. A sensual acquiescence. Her back arched, and with the movement, her breasts seemed to command attention.

Bending to kiss a peaked nipple, Jesse nudged a finger deep inside her to the place she liked to be touched best of all.

The heat of her closed around him as her soft sighs turned to breathy moans. When her breath caught, held, told him she was on the verge of release, he let go.

Her eyes opened wide until he settled himself between her thighs and rolled the condom on. Her short fingernails dug into his shoulders as she urged him inside.

As if he needed urging.

The boat rocked beneath them, and Jesse wasn't sure if it was from the waves in the marina or the waves they were making. But he knew for damn sure he'd never felt this good, this right, this complete in his life.

No wonder being with Kyra made him feel a sense of urgency today. There was something about *this* that was pretty damn important.

Before he could think through all the ramifications of what *this* meant, however, another wave crashed over him—a tide of sizzling sensation that drew him right back into a purely physical realm.

Kyra's body clenched around him, under him, as she hit the pinnacle high note. She yelled his name, locked her ankles around his hips.

And he was done for.

He found his release a scant few seconds behind her, drowning in a flood of sensations that were familiar and yet new all over again.

Maybe because there were a hell of a lot of unidentified emotions attached to those sensations.

But for now, he simply closed his eyes and pulled Kyra more tightly to him. He savored the rightness of being together and knew he'd finally hit on something good. Something essential.

And he had no intention of letting her go.

"THAT WAS AMAZING." Kyra finally spoke the words aloud that had been circling in her head nonstop for the last five minutes.

"Incredible." Jesse's voice held the same note of wonder she imagined must be in her own.

Was it possible he'd been as blown away by the sex as she had been?

Jesse ran warm fingers over the cool skin of her arm. "Incredible enough to make me skip Seth's engagement party if you want to hang out here."

"Oh my God." How could she have forgotten? She shoved him off her and started a frantic search for her panties. "You'll never have time to get the champagne."

He levered himself up to a sitting position. Gorgeous and naked. "Are you sure you want to go?"

She tugged her dress over her head and prepared to write off the black lace underwear until she spied them dangling from a lampshade. "Of course we are going. Seth is your *brother*."

Tossing clothes at him, she shoved her toes into her shoes.

"They might already be on the yacht. Will you mind going on board without me?" He pulled his clothes on with almost as much quick efficiency as he'd taken them off.

Almost.

"I don't want to face everyone without you." Not when she had no clue what her relationship was to Jesse anymore. Not when she didn't even know what she wanted that relationship to be. Hadn't she always been too independent to feel this attached to someone?

Especially someone with so much power to hurt her.

It was just as well their date would play out around an audience tonight. After a close encounter of the most intimate kind, Kyra sensed a need to rebuild boundaries and reinforce defenses, thank you very much.

They bolted out of the cabin and down the gangplank, still tucking and fastening. And even though she knew she needed to scavenge some distance from Jesse tonight, Kyra couldn't help but smile that she'd done all her risk-taking in life with him at her side, urging her on.

"I'll run down to the boardwalk and see if I can scrounge up some champagne." Jesse skidded to a stop at the end of the pier and straightened the shoulders of her dress, carefully tucking in an errant strap. "Hell, I'd settle for wine coolers if I can find some. If Seth goes by, just let him know we're here."

Kyra nodded, watching him until he disappeared on the Twin Palms boardwalk among a small throng of tourists arriving by bus.

If she wanted to track his progress, all she would have had to do was watch for the trail of turning feminine heads. But in the shadow of the big yacht docked along the pier for Seth's engagement party, Kyra was suddenly too busy warding off last-minute doubts to enjoy the stir Jesse always managed to create.

Funny how the man had so much presence, so much

vitality, that watching him walk away invariably filled her with a sense of loss. And made the air seem too still, too quiet all around her.

Why couldn't she just enjoy what they'd shared and leave it at that? Why worry it to death the moment he left her side?

She trusted him. Had realized he would never look at another woman as long as they were together. But strangely, instead of comforting her, the notion had only made her all the more wary. If she believed Jesse could commit himself to her—and by now, she did—then it was only another short leap to think that maybe their relationship could be bigger, more important than she'd ever dared to dream.

And frankly, that terrified her.

It was one thing to trust in Jesse. But it would take a lot more effort to believe in herself. Would she be able to commit herself to him for more than just a friendship, more than just a weekend of great sex?

Assuming, that is, he wanted something more?

She'd been so busy giving him a hard time about the whole commitment factor that she hadn't really stopped to consider if *she* was ready to take such a big step. Ever since her father's illness, Kyra had grown accustomed to being independent, to making her own decisions and running things her way. How could she ever share that role with someone else?

Tonight's date took on all the more importance in light of those fears. She had no idea if she could live up to Jesse's expectations, and now she'd have to find out in the public setting of the engagement party—in front of Jesse's family.

She'd always liked Jesse's older brother, Seth, but

how would Seth react now that she and Jesse had taken their relationship to the next level? And Kyra had never met their uncle, who would also be in attendance tonight. Would they sense in five minutes that she and Jesse had no business together?

She didn't exactly have experience with healthy family dynamics.

Not that she cared, she assured herself. It just seemed like tonight's family setting and joyous occasion upped the stakes for what should have been a simple date for her and Jesse.

Kyra smoothed the skirt of her navy dress and willed her nerves to settle, distracting herself with thoughts of what Seth Chandler's new fiancée might be like. Jesse had told her on their drive over tonight that the couple met for the first time at Gasparilla after Seth carried off Mia pirate-style. And after that, they just *knew*.

The story made Kyra question her relationship with Jesse all the more. How could Seth be head over heels and ready to tie the knot after a couple of weeks, whereas she and Jesse had known each other half their lives and still had no clue if they were right for one another?

The sound of feminine laughter caught her ear before she could worry about it anymore. As Kyra turned toward the sound, she spied two women walking out of the Beachcomber store several yards away. One of them flipped the sign on the door to read Closed before they headed in her direction juggling loaded straw platters full of food covered in plastic wrap.

She tried not to stare, but there wasn't exactly a lot of action in Twin Palms on a late Saturday afternoon. And besides, they were definitely the kind of women who caught your eye. Not in an overtly gorgeous Greta way, but simply because of the carefree, happy air about them, an easy manner that seemed inherent to people who lived by the water.

The women could have been twins—except for the maybe fifteen years between them. Long dark hair spilled over their shoulders while they balanced the jumbo trays. Still laughing, they nudged each other with an occasional shoulder on their way toward the marina in halfhearted attempts to dislodge the other's burden.

Kyra's interest in them evaporated, however, when she saw them turn down pier eleven toward the biggest yacht docked in the tiny marina. If these women were part of the crowd attending Seth Chandler's engagement party, she needed to make herself scarce before she was—

Noticed.

No sooner had she thought as much than the younger woman glanced back over her shoulder and paused.

Stared.

It was too late to hide in Jesse's Jeep so Kyra smiled and willed the woman to move along.

Kyra didn't consider herself socially inept or anything, but she did spend far more of her time with horses than people. Small talk and charm were Jesse's strengths, not hers.

And he was so dead for leaving her here to fend for herself while he searched for champagne.

Damn.

The younger brunette shouted over her platter, the breeze fluttering the petals of a red flower tucked behind her right ear. "Kyra Stafford?"

"That's me. Are you going to the engagement party,

too?" Kyra managed a smile and tucked her purse under one arm. Apparently she wouldn't be able to hide any longer. She just hoped she could remain in the background of this shindig before Jesse arrived.

"I'm Mia Quentin and I'm the lucky bride-to-be." Grinning, she nodded toward the pier, her hands full. "Come on aboard. I've been dying to meet the lady pirate who had the nerve to kidnap Tampa's most notorious bad boy."

15

GRETA SNAKED AN ARM behind Clint's neck while he drove the pickup truck across long, dusty acres of dirt road behind the Crooked Branch. She hadn't been able to pry her hands off him since he rolled into her driveway late the night before after their week apart.

Just for fun, she rested her other hand on his thigh.

"If you don't watch what you're doing there, I'll never get to show you the surprise," he growled, downshifting as he navigated a dried-out irrigation ditch.

"There's only one surprise I want you to give me right now," she whispered back, licking a path alongside his ear.

The week without him had been hell. She still didn't want to go to Alabama. And although she seemed to have him partially convinced it was because she didn't want to live next to a barn full of horses, deep down Greta knew her fears had more to do with giving a powerful man so much say in her life.

She hadn't consciously thought about growing up in her father's house in years. No, she stayed as removed from those scary memories as possible. Yet the fears of being emotionally betrayed by a man she loved still lingered.

But she'd definitely gotten a taste of how much it would hurt to walk away from Clint over the past few long, lonely nights.

As she sidled closer to sit hip to hip with him, Greta fully recognized that she was probably trying to tie him to her with the promise of awesome sex. On some level she felt like if he would come to her, take up residence in Florida to be by her side, then she still had some control in their relationship.

If she went there, on his terms, she was giving him everything. Her heart, her soul—and an even bigger potential to hurt her.

Clint peeled her hand away and kissed each of her knuckles with slow precision. The patience— endurance—of this man had proven a continual source of delight. "Trust me, you're going to like this surprise."

She could think of one other present she would really like. "You've bought a house in Florida?"

Slowing the truck just before the dirt road took a sharp turn, Clint stopped and swiveled in his seat to face her. "No. But this definitely has to do with getting us closer together."

She fought the pang in her chest. Of course he wasn't moving here. He'd as good as told her he would be trying to come up with ways to get her to move there, not the other way around. "On your terms."

"On mutual terms." He brushed his hands up her arms to her shoulders, his fingers brushing over her collarbones. "I want you to be happy, too. So answer this for me. If I can get you to like horses, would you at least give Alabama a try?"

Again with the damn horses. Of course, what could she expect when she hadn't been able to share with him her deepest fears. "I can't see me liking anything with four legs. They're too—"

Big. Powerful. Frightening.

Greta would always be intimidated by animals—or people—she couldn't control.

Clint was staring at her oddly and Greta realized she'd never finished her thought. "They're too hairy. Too messy. Too much work."

"But that doesn't answer my question. If you *did* like horses, would you come to Alabama?"

Greta had to smile. The man was incredibly focused. Would he be as determined to ease her real fears if she were ever brave enough to share them with him? "On the off chance I was ever able to get within five feet of a nine-hundred-pound animal, I might be swayed to cross the state line."

"Excellent." Clint slipped a hand around the back of her neck and tugged her forward for a kiss. A slow, deep, full-of-approval kiss. When he finally pulled away, he put the truck in Drive while her eyelids pried themselves open.

Rounding the turn, Greta grew suspicious about the whole horse conversation. "Just where exactly are we going?"

Even as she asked, the scent of the surf filtered in through the truck window. The air had turned damp somewhere along the way and the breeze carried the sound of seagulls.

"I'm taking you to the favorite place of every Florida sunseeker. The beach."

Sure enough, as they rounded the last curve, the dirt

road ended in front of a tiny patch of ungroomed sand
and gently rolling waves from the Gulf.

But the beach wasn't what snagged Greta's eye.

It was the big black horse standing in the middle of
the shore.

"Oh, no." Had she mentioned she wasn't a horse
lover? The beast on the beach could probably trample
her five different ways without even trying. "Clint?"

He was already out of the truck and coming around
to the passenger side to help her out. "You can't knock
it until you've at least said hello."

Actually, Greta was pretty certain she could do a ter-
rific job of knocking it without getting anywhere near
the huge horse, but she took Clint's hand and stepped
out of the truck. She'd always been able to count on her
sense of adventure to pull her through almost anything,
but her usual pluck seemed a bit sapped where Clint and
his horses were concerned.

She'd taken a risk just by allowing herself to be
with him—a guy so different from any man she'd ever
known. But Clint was settling for a superficial relationship from her and she knew that on a deep, instinctive
level without him having to spell it out for her in so
many words.

Maybe she'd chosen Jesse first because he'd appeared
as outwardly superficial as Greta liked to be. She could
appreciate a man who just wanted to have fun for fun's
sake. But Clint wanted—expected—so much more from
her. Jesse hadn't ever made her question what was really important to her in life the way Clint did.

As if sensing her thoughts, Clint turned toward her
as they neared the animal. "You nervous?"

Greta eyed the horse as it stomped the ground and

shuffled its feet, swinging its head around to shake off a fly. She squeezed Clint's hand. "Not at all," she lied. "I'm just hoping you've got a Plan B in mind once we leave here and I don't like this…creature any better."

Her heart hammered in her throat where it had lodged the moment she'd realized she needed to face her fear. Perhaps even from the moment she'd considered saying goodbye to Clint.

He reached out to the horse and patted its nose. Snout? Greta had no clue.

"Greta, meet Sam's Pride." Clint lifted her hand to touch the side of the horse's face.

Her fingers barely grazed its fur—hair?—when the thing bucked his head and made a snickering sound halfway between laughing and snoring.

She jumped back. "You see?"

Clint arched an eyebrow, and by the sympathetic look in his eye, Greta had the feeling he did see. All too well, and right through her.

He knew there was more to this than a fear of horses. But patient, gentle Clint seemed willing to let her work through it her own way.

"I see a tentative streak I never expected to find in gutsy Greta Ingram. How can a woman who's traveled the world alone and hitchhiked on deserted stretches of rural highway be so intimidated by a lone horse?"

Greta felt her feathers start to ruffle in spite of her fear. "I am not intimidated. And it doesn't exactly indicate bravery to hitchhike on a deserted road. I think most people would take it as a sign of sheer stupidity, but since I never learned how to drive, I get around as best as I can."

Clint moved around her and patted the horse's side.

"I'm going to help you fix that today." He pulled himself up onto the animal's back. No easy feat considering this horse didn't come with any convenient running boards or other step-stool device. "Ready to learn how to drive?"

"You've got to be kidding." She didn't know much about horses, but she was pretty sure they were supposed to have a little more equipment than this one, who looked naked, as far as she was concerned.

"Come on up here." He reached a hand down to her. As if she would take it and suddenly be transported on top of the humungous animal beneath him. "Those mile-long legs of yours surely have a few more uses than making men drool."

Okay, call her shallow, but flattery did have a way of distracting her from her fears just a little. Frowning, she stared down at her bare legs and short skirt. "I'm wearing a dress."

His voice lowered a few notches. "Then that'll just make your first time all the more fun."

Before she could follow that line of thinking, Clint slid his hands beneath her arms and lifted her through the air. She squealed, but she didn't flail, unwilling to risk his balance on the horse. A little thrill shot through her as it occurred to her how strong his thighs had to be to stay on that horse while pulling her aboard.

Settling her before him, Clint seated her with her back to his front, her bottom settled neatly against his hips. The backs of her bare thighs molded to the jean-clad fronts of his.

Having her legs spread across the back of the horse was a naughty thrill sort of like riding a motorcycle. Only her thighs were forced apart a bit more widely.

Just as Greta started to fully appreciate the provocative power of the position, Clint's hand clamped to her rib cage, the rough texture of his broad palm apparent through the thin cotton of her insubstantial little sundress. The top of his thumb grazed the bottom of her breast and rubbed the soft flesh in a slow arc.

Clint's voice rumbled behind her, through her. "Good thing you remembered to wear panties."

"Is it?" She heated up beneath those panties. Longed for him to move his hand lower. And lower still.

He chuckled. "Didn't you tell me animals were too messy? Too hairy? Too much work?" His hand slid lower over her belly. To the top of her thigh. "I figure it's a good thing you have a little something between you and him."

His fingers brushed up the hem of her dress to slip between her and the horse. She was already damp with arousal. And overwhelmed that Clint would take so much time and care to make her feel at ease when she was scared.

Clint's voice was thick with the same hunger she felt. "Are you ready?"

Leaning her head back on his shoulder, she looked up into his eyes. And in that moment, she saw something in his horse whisperer eyes that calmed her fears even as he stirred her heart and her body. A subtle communication that told her she could trust him to love her no matter how over-the-top her antics. No matter how many times she dragged him to Paris during the spring show season.

Yet, just then, Greta had the feeling she would grow deep roots in Alabama beside this man who seemed to understand her better than she understood herself.

She leaned forward to press against his palm all the more deeply. Thrusting her hips into his touch and giving herself into his care. She knew, now more than ever, that a man like Clint would never try to control her. Even now he was finding new ways to make her feel in command of her own fears, her reservations. "I think you know I'm ready."

But instead of reaching inside her panties and teasing her to the climax she wanted, Clint moved his hand back to her waist and nudged the horse forward with his heels.

Greta tried to voice her protest, but then the horse's shoulders moved underneath her as the animal walked, and then kicked up the speed even faster to run along the beach. Her protest came out as a moan, the rhythm between her thighs too obvious to ignore.

Clint held her to him, his hand locking around her breast to tease and caress even as he kept her steady. The nudge of his arousal against her bottom was made all the more erotic by the bump and grind effect of the horse beneath them.

And then the heated center of her gyrated in slow motion, keeping time with the horse's gallop. Dizzy with need, she couldn't help but throw her head back to the wind and the water the horse kicked up as it pounded through the surf. Faster.

Faster.

Until she soared right into the horizon on a wave of pure fulfillment.

Laughing and happy, there was no way Greta could ever pretend she hadn't liked this. Hadn't liked the horse. Hadn't appreciated Clint's efforts to let her face her fears.

Turning in Clint's lap to face him, she locked her legs around his hips and pressed herself to what she really wanted.

Him.

Not just now, but forever.

"I think I just got my first glimpse of the Crimson Tide," she whispered, her blood still surging through her veins in a flood of heated fulfillment. She allowed her forehead to fall against his, ready to give herself over to this man in every way possible. "When do we leave for Alabama?"

JESSE SQUINTED TO see the shoreline in the last purple rays of the setting sun. Half an hour into the engagement party cruise he had commandeered Kyra to stand at the rail with him and watch for the small patch of beach that belonged to the Crooked Branch.

He'd ridden that narrow stretch of coastline enough times over the past few years that he ought to recognize it from the water.

"There it is." He pointed over the water and used the opportunity to drape an arm around Kyra's shoulders. She was nervous and edgy about tonight. He could feel it in her every gesture and movement. More than anything, he wanted to reassure her. Distract her. Help her to have fun for a change. "Who's on our beach?"

Kyra squinted right along with him. Leaning forward over the rail just a little.

She smiled. "It's Clint and Greta."

Jesse could barely make out the couple in the last rays of daylight, but he definitely caught a glimpse of feminine bare thigh wrapped around a man's waist.

And he was probably just imagining it, but he could

swear he saw the guy in the Stetson grinning like a son of a gun.

Clint Bowman had obviously figured out how to make a relationship work. Would Jesse be so lucky?

Pulling Kyra closer, he hoped like hell he could offer her the kind of relationship she deserved. But if his vision served him and that horse Clint and Greta had been riding was the same three-year-old Jesse had asked Kyra not to sell, he had the feeling they were in for a long haul toward understanding one another. "I think it's great they found each other. But I can't help but think that was Sam's Pride they were riding. You didn't—"

"I didn't. I just loaned the horse to Clint so he could help Greta with him and see how they do." She didn't pull out of his embrace. Hadn't ignored his input to do what she wanted with her horse.

Damn but that felt good for a change.

He'd always tread carefully with her because she was so independent. But if she was willing to bend occasionally…the possibilities for a future together seemed a little more within reach.

Jesse definitely liked that. Liked holding her. They could rejoin his family in a minute. Right now, he just wanted to savor a few more minutes with Kyra. "Good. I'm betting Sam's Pride will go to Clint without so much as a whicker once that horse knows you're happy."

Kyra laughed, a soft musical sound that carried on the Gulf breeze and wrapped right around him. "So I spent all that money on a horse whisperer to figure out Sam's Pride's problems when all I had to do was ask you? I'm already happy. Why don't you just tell Sam's Pride as much for me, and that will solve a lot of problems?"

Jesse considered the matter and how to explain the esoterics of horse intuition to a woman who was as practical as she was beautiful. "I think you need to show Sam's Pride you're happy for good. That you're—"

All mine.

The thought was as plain as day. But where the hell had it come from?

Jesse blinked. He hadn't had a thought like that about any woman. Ever. His father had walked out on his mother and three kids at a vulnerable time in all their lives. Seth had pulled man-of-the-house duty for most of his life and had done a damn good job of it, but Jesse had always resented how much his old man had hurt his mother. While Seth worked his butt off to help support them, Jesse had been at home enough to see a lot of his mother's tears.

He knew how much it hurt when someone was unfaithful.

And he'd always had so much fun playing the field that he told himself it was okay as long as he didn't ever hurt anyone in the process. As long as any woman he dated understood what to expect—and not to expect—from him.

"Jesse?" Kyra stared up at him, waiting for him to finish.

But he had no idea what he'd been talking about.

He could only wonder why he thought he'd never be able to make a commitment to a woman when Kyra had been showing him by example what commitment was all about for fourteen years running.

She'd taken over her father's ranching business at an early age when he'd succumbed to bouts of depression. And she'd made the ranch work by sheer force of will, eventually taking all that she'd learned and funneling it into a business of her very own. Her single-minded determination had inspired Jesse in more ways than he could count.

He'd ignored a college scholarship to play professional baseball because she told him it was okay to follow a dream. For nearly eight years he'd lived a fantasy and paid his bills to boot, earning him a place in the minor league record books.

And when he'd achieved all he wanted to there, he'd built his own business. Slapped his name on a shingle, for crying out loud.

He was all about freaking commitment.

"Jesse?" Kyra tugged his arm, calling him from his thoughts.

Focusing on her big blue eyes, Jesse nearly drowned in them. So wise and innocent at the same time. So driven and determined to achieve her dreams. Even if she had to wear a corset in public.

He loved this woman. No question.

And he could commit himself to her forever without a single fear.

"They're getting ready to toast the happy couple." She dragged him toward the center of the main deck. "And you might want to come up with a speech. I think Seth wants you to say a little something."

Jesse smiled. He'd gladly allow this practical woman to keep him on task his whole life.

Assuming he could distract her from those damn tasks every now and then.

He brushed a kiss along the top of her head and slowed her brusque pace across the deck. "Don't worry, Kyra. I've got plenty of things to say tonight."

16

KYRA TOOK A DEEP BREATH. Exhaled. Absorbed the
warmth of Jesse's hands on her shoulders, the heat of
his chest at her back.

Sometimes being with him excited her to a feverish
pitch, but other times he grounded her in a way no else
could. She'd always been so driven. Determined nothing
would slip past her or be overlooked in her quest to build
a profitable business she would enjoy all of her life.

No question, her relentless approach had served her
well in many ways. But something about spending time
with Jesse made her relax. Catch her breath.

She couldn't stand the thought of losing that connection. Of tonight being her last chance with Jesse.

They approached the throng of Jesse's family in the
middle of the main deck. Since his sister was in Cali-
fornia working on her internship in landscape design,
the party consisted of his older brother Seth and his fiancée, Mia Quentin. Jesse's Uncle Brock and his lady
love—Noelle Quentin, who also happened to be Mia's
mother—rounded out the small group.

The four of them sprawled on blankets while the

hired captain of the yacht took care of navigation in his secluded cabin above them. Three torches positioned around the deck made the party bright and festive even in the twilight. The breeze was starting to cool down now that the sun had dipped below the horizon, but that only gave Kyra an excuse to indulge a slight shiver at Jesse's warm touch.

Noelle thumped the empty space on the deck next to her. "Have a seat, Kyra. We can enjoy the speech together."

Jesse's Uncle Brock reached behind him into the cooler, then handed her a longneck from the case of beer Jesse had brought aboard when his last-minute search for champagne had been a bust. There wasn't a liquor store on the Twin Palms boardwalk, but at least there had been a convenience store.

Complete with cold beer.

"A little something for the toast." Brock eyed the label critically. "Nice vintage, Jess. Malt hops at its best."

"Hey, at least I got the imported stuff in deference to Seth's expensive taste." He snagged a bottle of his own while Kyra settled next to Noelle.

Jesse sat down beside her, exchanging verbal guy jabs with his brother and their uncle while Kyra soaked up the atmosphere of the night.

The happiness in the air.

At least, for two of the couples on board.

Seth and Mia were obviously head over heels about one another. Even while Seth good-naturedly raked his brother over the coals for his plebian beverage choice, he kept one hand draped over Mia's shoulder, his hand tracing tiny circles on her upper arm with his thumb.

Mia glowed beside her fiancé, and not just because of the torchlight reflected on her face. She smiled with the warm contentment of a woman who knows she'll be waking up beside the man of her dreams for the rest of her life.

Brock and Noelle radiated every bit as much bliss as the engaged couple. While Brock leaned back against the cooler, Noelle sat between his thighs to rest against his chest.

And of course, the image of Greta and Clint on the horse had remained in Kyra's mind to taunt her with the kind of love that meant happily ever after.

She couldn't pretend that she didn't want that for herself.

And, if she were honest with herself, she wanted it for her and Jesse.

As she stared up at him in the flickering light, Kyra knew she would never be content to simply return to their old relationship. Neither their business partnership nor their friendship would be enough for her anymore.

Now that she'd had a taste of what they could be like together, she didn't want to go back. She wanted to sleep by his side. She wanted to go to baseball games with him and listen to his one-of-a-kind color commentary on the sport he'd always loved. She wanted to drive by the houses he was building to see his progress in his new business.

But most of all, she wanted her happily ever after with him—the only man she'd ever fantasized about.

If only he felt the same way.

Her heart ached with wishing for impossible things as Jesse whistled for attention. He settled on his knees—

a fitting height to toast a party sprawled on a yacht deck—and raised his beer bottle.

Clearing his throat with ceremony, he gave her one last wink before addressing the group. "I may have committed a small faux pas with the beer masquerading as champagne tonight, but trust me, Seth, I put more time into the sentiment than the beverage."

Brock and Noelle clapped and cheered.

Kyra smiled to watch Jesse's innate charm in action. In their partnership at the Crooked Branch she didn't usually get to see him in his "work the crowd" mode, but she'd missed seeing that charisma of his flex its muscle. She had always loved going to the press conferences after his baseball games and seeing him send all the reporters home laughing.

Jesse pitched a crumpled-up cocktail napkin at his uncle. "So without further ado, please join me in toasting Seth and Mia."

Kyra gladly lifted her bottle. She might envy the kind of love the new couple had found, but she didn't begrudge them a minute of their happiness together.

"I wish you a lifetime full of shared joys. And in between all those good times, I wish you the comfort of being able to share your sorrows. I wish you the kind of partnership that comes with knowing one another year after year." As he looked around the members of his audience, his gaze stalled on Kyra, his sentiment meant for her as much as the words were directed toward his brother and Mia.

Kyra's heart caught in her throat.

"May you appreciate one another's strengths while bolstering each other's weaknesses. But most of all, may you remember to celebrate your love and the gift you have in one another every day."

Kyra blinked away a tear. She noticed Mia didn't bother to hold hers back. Two tiny rivulets trickled down her cheeks as everyone clinked bottles and shouted agreement to Jesse's words.

Malt and hops never tasted so good.

Kyra wanted to tell Jesse how much she liked his speech. For a guy who had never believed in commitments, he sure knew how to make "forever" sound pretty appealing. Did he harbor just a little longing in his soul for the same things Kyra did?

She didn't know what the future might hold for her and Jesse or if she'd ever have another chance to find out after tonight.

But Brock was too quick to snag Jesse's attention in the wake of the toast, asking him a few building questions about converting an old storefront into a new moped rental shop Noelle hoped to open within the year.

Noelle scooted across their little circle to hug her daughter and shed a few happy tears of her own. Kyra moved closer to the women to extend her congratulations. Much as she wanted to talk to Jesse alone, ask him how he'd grown so well versed in the rewards of marriage, she wanted to congratulate Mia, too.

Now more than ever, Kyra appreciated that good committed relationships didn't just happen. They required effort, compromise. Friendships were easy. Great sex was simple—at least for her and Jesse.

But love?

She hadn't figured that one out yet. And for the first time, she wanted to crack the mystery for herself.

THE MOON was high by the time Kyra found a few moments to slip away from the party and gaze out at the night sky. Her evening with Seth and Mia, Brock and Noelle had been the closest thing to a family gathering she'd been to in more years than she could count. What would it be like to belong to a family reminiscent of this one? To share your hopes and dreams, to share the workload in making those dreams happen?

Jesse had already signed on to help Brock and Noelle update the old storefront for Noelle's moped rentals. Seth had given Jesse a few tips about managing escrow accounts for his home-building clients.

Mia and Noelle had made a deal with Kyra to trade horseback riding hours at the Crooked Branch for moped riding hours at Noelle's new shop. Kyra enjoyed every minute with the Chandler men and the Quentin women, but she couldn't help but wonder if she'd have a chance to follow through on the bargain they'd made today.

Would she and Jesse have anything left to their relationship besides a few great memories after tonight?

The idea that tonight might be her last chance sent a swell of panic through her.

Footsteps sounded on the deck behind her, upping the ante on her panic level. She recognized the pace, would know that laid-back, all-the-time-in-the-world step anywhere.

But instead of greeting Jesse at the rail of the yacht, Kyra jumped as she felt something sheer and silky slide over her eyes from behind.

A familiar pink scarf.

The warmth of Jesse's body hovered a few inches from her back. One of his hands slid down the bare expanse of her spine revealed by her navy, backless dress, while his other hand held her thin blindfold in place.

"I've got you now, Kyra." Jesse's voice wafted over her shoulder, a warm rumble across her skin. "What would you do if I kidnapped you tonight the same way you abducted me at Gasparilla?"

She swayed against his skillful touch, longed for more of those expert hands on her bare skin. Even more, she yearned for a deeper relationship with the man who had been captivating her for over a decade. "For starters, I don't think I'd give you any lectures like you gave me."

"You wouldn't?" He leaned closer, his grip on the scarf relaxing just a little. "What if I wanted a whole lot more from you than just one night of fantastic sex? Then would you break out the lecture?"

She smiled beneath the silk. Propping up the fabric with one hand over her eyebrow, she peered back at him. "I'd probably settle for telling you that you're a whole lot smarter than me."

Jesse let go of her scarf, allowing the gauzy material to settle around her shoulders as she turned to face him dead-on. The torches still flickered in the distance on deck, perfectly outlining his incredible body. No wonder one of the world's most renowned beauties had fawned all over him.

Yet Kyra saw the rest of him. She appreciated the sensitivity that made him as smart about animals as he was about people. Recognized the business savvy he'd always possessed but never smothered her with.

Now he skimmed a fingertip over her cheekbone and then down her jaw. "I do want more, Kyra. More than tonight. More than next week."

Her heart skipped. Still, she owed it to him to be honest about her fears. "I want that, too. But Jesse, I don't know that I would make a very good girlfriend. I know I've sucked as a business partner. Anyone else would have pulled their hair out trying to deal with me because I can be so independent. I don't know how you've put up with me. And I'm just afraid I wouldn't live up to your expectations if we became…more than partners."

He opened his mouth as if to speak, but as Kyra reviewed her words to him in her mind she wondered if she'd blown it by reminding him of all her bad qualities. She couldn't stop herself from blurting a last little caveat. "That being said, I would try very hard to be more open-minded if we did try to be together. Have I told you lately that you were so right about the ponies and that it was a great idea to buy them? And have I admitted that I was being really stubborn about selling Sam's Pride?"

Jesse laughed. Brushing a strand of hair behind her ear, he shielded her from the night breeze with the breadth of his body.

"You are independent, I'll grant you that. Maybe a little bossy." His brow furrowed as if starting to remember how much of a slave driver she'd been when he'd been building her barns, stringing her fences or working on their accounting reports. "And I'll be the first to admit you're stubborn as hell."

She felt the overwhelming need to toss a few of her good points out there, too, before he talked himself out of a second date with her. "But—"

"But you're also level-headed. Which is a good thing when I'm wound up because I grounded out to second base or I botched a strip of crown molding." He brushed his fingertips across her chin to tilt her face up to his. "You give me perspective."

She wanted to remind him that perspective was a very good, useful thing, but he covered her lips with the pad of his thumb, clearly ready to talk now.

"Being with you gives me a sense of peace I've never found anywhere else. For years I told myself that I always liked going back to the Crooked Branch because of the ranch environment or the horses, but it's not either of those things. I like to be there because of you." His dark eyes glittered with the reflection of the torches. Or maybe their fierce heat came from within.

Kyra couldn't help the smile that slipped across her face any more than she could staunch the hope growing inside her. Her heart skipped.

But Jesse wasn't through. He slid his hands down her shoulders, to her back. Pulled her closer and molded her body to his, hip to hip. "And all these years that I've been dating—extensively—I think I was just marking time, waiting for the right woman. The same woman I've already been committed to in a lot of ways for half my life."

Oh.

Kyra's heart quit the sissy skipping and hammered her chest with a vengeance. She felt the same happy tears tickle her eyes that Mia had shed only a few hours ago. Kyra plucked at the pink silk scarf that still dangled around her shoulders. "Then I guess I'm all yours to carry off."

"I don't think so." Jesse shook his head. "I haven't even said 'I love you' yet."

Ooooohh. Something melted inside her. "Really?"

"Not unless I missed it." He wrapped the ends of the

scarf around his finger and started winding the fabric around his skin, effectively reeling her closer.

"No. You didn't miss it. I definitely would have noticed if you'd put that out there." Warmth filled her along with a resounding sense of rightness. Her and Jesse together—it made so much crazy, beautiful, perfect sense.

"Then let me fix that right now. I love you, Kyra. In a way, I think I always have. I've just been in serious denial. And maybe I was just too scared of messing up what we had to ever take a risk on us." He trailed his lips across her forehead, to her temple. "I'm so glad your practical self took that one calculated, daring chance for both of us."

She vowed to retrieve her black leather corset from the cleaners with all due haste. The costume deserved a special place in her closet for helping her open Jesse's eyes to new possibilities.

As the moist Gulf air wrapped around them, Kyra thanked the sky full of her lucky stars for putting her in this man's path that day fourteen years ago.

For putting him in her arms tonight.

"I love you, too, Jesse. Not just today, and not just tomorrow. Always. No matter what." She arched up on her toes to kiss his mouth, to squeeze him to her in a way she'd never dared before.

In a way she would every day from now on.

Kyra had no choice about controlling her happy tears anymore. They poured freely from her eyes to his shoulders and hers, a watery baptism for her very own happily ever after.

* * * * *

Available May 21, 2013

#751 I CROSS MY HEART • *Sons of Chance*
by Vicki Lewis Thompson

When Last Chance cowhand Nash Bledsoe goes to investigate smoke at a neighboring ranch, the last thing he expects to find is a super sexy woman. But he hasn't got time for a relationship, especially with *this* female. Still, where there's smoke, there's fire....

#752 ALL THE RIGHT MOVES • *Uniformly Hot!*
by Jo Leigh

Whether it's behind the wheel of a sports car or in the cockpit of a fighter jet—or in bed!—John "Devil" Devlin has never faced a challenge like gorgeous spitfire Cassie O'Brien. Challenge accepted!

#753 FROM THIS MOMENT ON
Made in Montana • by Debbi Rawlins

Every time gorgeous cowboy Trace McAllister flashes his signature smile, the ladies come running. But street-smart Nikki Flores won't let another handsome charmer derail her future...which is definitely not in Blackfoot Falls.

#754 NO STRINGS...
by Janelle Denison

Chloe Reiss wants Aiden Landry, badly! But because of a no-fraternization rule at work, the only way they can indulge their passions is to do it in secret. Unfortunately, even the best-kept secrets don't always stay that way....

REQUEST YOUR FREE BOOKS!
2 FREE NOVELS PLUS 2 FREE GIFTS!

red-hot reads!

YES! Please send me 2 FREE Harlequin® Blaze™ novels and my 2 FREE gifts (gifts are worth about $10). After receiving them, if I don't wish to receive any more books, I can return the shipping statement marked "cancel." If I don't cancel, I will receive 4 brand-new novels every month and be billed just $4.74 per book in the U.S. or $4.96 per book in Canada. That's a savings of at least 14% off the cover price. It's quite a bargain. Shipping and handling is just 50¢ per book in the U.S. and 75¢ per book in Canada.* I understand that accepting the 2 free books and gifts places me under no obligation to buy anything. I can always return a shipment and cancel at any time. Even if I never buy another book, the two free books and gifts are mine to keep forever.

150/350 HDN F4WC

Name _____ (PLEASE PRINT) _____

Address _____ Apt. # _____

City _____ State/Prov. _____ Zip/Postal Code _____

Signature (if under 18, a parent or guardian must sign)

Mail to the **Harlequin® Reader Service:**
IN U.S.A.: P.O. Box 1867, Buffalo, NY 14240-1867
IN CANADA: P.O. Box 609, Fort Erie, Ontario L2A 5X3

Want to try two free books from another line?
Call 1-800-873-8635 or visit www.ReaderService.com.

* Terms and prices subject to change without notice. Prices do not include applicable taxes. Sales tax applicable in N.Y. Canadian residents will be charged applicable taxes. Offer not valid in Quebec. This offer is limited to one order per household. Not valid for current subscribers to Harlequin Blaze books. All orders subject to credit approval. Credit or debit balances in a customer's account(s) may be offset by any other outstanding balance owed by or to the customer. Please allow 4 to 6 weeks for delivery. Offer available while quantities last.

Your Privacy—The Harlequin® Reader Service is committed to protecting your privacy. Our Privacy Policy is available online at www.ReaderService.com or upon request from the Harlequin Reader Service.

We make a portion of our mailing list available to reputable third parties that offer products we believe may interest you. If you prefer that we not exchange your name with third parties, or if you wish to clarify or modify your communication preferences, please visit us at www.ReaderService.com/consumerchoice or write to us at Harlequin Reader Service Preference Service, P.O. Box 9062, Buffalo, NY 14269. Include your complete name and address.

HB13R2

New York Times bestselling author
Vicki Lewis Thompson is back with three new,
steamy titles from her bestselling miniseries
Sons of Chance

I Cross My Heart

"Do *you* like an audience?" Bethany asked.

If he did, that would help cool her off. She wasn't into that. Of course, she wasn't supposed to be feeling hot in the first place.

"I prefer privacy when I'm making love to a woman." Nash's voice had lowered to a sexy drawl and his blue gaze held hers. "I don't like the idea of being interrupted."

Oh, Lordy. She could hardly breathe from wanting him. "Me, either."

She took another hefty swallow of wine, for courage. "I have a confession to make. You know when I claimed that this nice dinner wasn't supposed to be romantic?"

"Yeah."

"I lied."

"Oh, really?" His blue eyes darkened to navy. "Care to elaborate?"

"See, back when we were in high school, you were this out-of-reach senior and I was a nerdy freshman. So when you showed up today, I thought about flirting with you because now I actually have the confidence to do that. But when you offered to help repair the place, flirting with you didn't seem like such a good idea. But I still thought you were really hot." She took another sip of wine. "We shouldn't have sex, though. At least, I didn't think so this morning, but then I fixed up the dining room, and I admit I thought about you while I did that. So I think, secretly, I wanted it to be romantic. But I—"

"Do you always talk this much after two glasses of wine?" He'd moved even closer, barely inches away.

She could smell his shaving lotion. Then she realized what that meant. He'd shaved before coming over here. That was significant. "I didn't have two full glasses."

"I think you did."

She glanced at her wineglass, which was now empty. Apparently she'd been babbling and drinking at the same time. "You poured me a second glass." When he started to respond, she stopped him. "But that's okay, because if I hadn't had a second glass, I wouldn't be admitting to you that I want you so much that I almost can't stand it, and you wouldn't be looking at me as if you actually might be considering the idea of…"

"Of what?" He was within kissing distance.

"This." She grabbed his face in both hands and planted one on that smiling mouth of his. And oh, it was glorious. Nash Bledsoe had the best mouth of any man she'd kissed so far. Once she'd made the initial contact, he took over, and before she quite realized it, he'd pulled her out of her chair and was drawing her away from the table.

Ah, he was good, this guy. And she had a feeling she was about to find out just *how* good….

Pick up I CROSS MY HEART by
Vicki Lewis Thompson, on sale May 21,
wherever Blaze books are sold.

The Chloe Reiss Guide
to success, money and wickedly hot men!

1. *No* relationships. Guys are just for playing with!
2. Self-sufficiency will get you everywhere.
3. Work hard. Make your own money.
4. Don't sleep with your work colleagues (like übersexy Aiden Landry). They're *competition!*
5. Well. Okay, maybe just a *little* flirting...
6. Business trips with a sexy colleague to exotic locations can be dangerous. And tempting. Resist him!
7. Okay, at least restrict your trysts to nighttime naughtiness.
8. Maintain professionalism at all times (e.g., no drooling on the hot man you're getting dirty with).
9. And whatever you do...*don't get caught!*

Pick up

No Strings...

by *Janelle Denison,*

on sale May 21 wherever you buy Harlequin Blaze books.